The Valley of Unfinished Songs

Umair Ahmed Khan is a content specialist and seasoned radio jockey at All India Radio's FM Rainbow in Mumbai. A screenwriter for television, OTT, theatre and brand ads, his expertise spans website and corporate content, along with content research for fiction, non-fiction and cultural formats in visual media. A travel researcher and tourism entrepreneur, Umair also promotes Hindi, Urdu and Persian literature through radio, theatre and lit fests. He teaches media subjects at media schools in Mumbai and holds an MBA in Human Resources from University of Mumbai.

He can be reached on:
Instagram: https://www.instagram.com/rj_umairofficial/
Facebook: https://www.facebook.com/rjumairrr

'*The Valley of Unfinished Songs* is a tender yet unflinching exploration of loss, longing and the fragile threads that connect memory to identity. The novel moves between generations and geographies with a voice that is both intimate and cinematic. Umair's storytelling is deeply humane and refreshingly empathetic. He neither simplifies nor sensationalizes—he listens. And as he listens, he gives Kashmir a chance to sing its unfinished songs.'

—Shabir Ahmad Mir

Author of *The Plague Upon Us* and *The Last Knot*

'In *The Valley of Unfinished Songs*, Umair takes us back to that long-lost melody—one that has become our only home.'

—Siddhartha Gigoo

Commonwealth prize-winning author

'Umair exhibits a remarkable command of storytelling, marked by his deep engagement with the interior lives of his characters. His narratives transcend individual grief and sorrow, opening into the broader anguish of historical and temporal consciousness. Through this layered exploration, Umair evokes a subtle, almost transcendental healing—one that seeks to reconcile the fractures of the human heart with the wounded continuum of time.'

—Rahman Abbas

Winner of the Sahitya Akademi Award for *Rohzin*

'Umair Ahmed Khan has written a novel with exceptional skill and sensitivity, depicting the tragedy of a bleeding Kashmir of the 1990s that shattered the lives of Hindu Pandits as well as Muslims at the hands of fanatical forces hell-bent on imposing an ideology of exclusion on a people proverbially famous for living in peace and amity. The author's work is a great achievement in realistic fiction.'

—Prof. Dr Ishtiaq Ahmed

Political scientist, Partition Studies

The Valley of Unfinished Songs

Umair Ahmed Khan

RUPA

Published by
Rupa Publications India Pvt. Ltd 2026
161-B/4, Gulmohar House,
Yusuf Sarai Community Centre,
New Delhi 110049

Sales centres
Bengaluru Chennai
Hyderabad Kolkata Mumbai

This is a work of fiction. Names, characters, places and incidents are either the product of the author's imagination or are used fictitiously and any resemblance to any actual person, living or dead, events or locales is entirely coincidental.

P-ISBN: 978-93-5352-636-8
E-ISBN: 978-93-5352-862-1

First impression 2026

10 9 8 7 6 5 4 3 2 1

Printed in India

For my grandparents,
who gave me books, blessings and wisdom
For my family
For the beautiful people of Kashmir
For Talha

Aaj woh Kashmir hai
Mahkoom o Majboor o Faqeer
Kal jisay Ahl e Nazar kehte the
Iraan e Sageer

Today that land of Kashmir
is ruled over, helpless and enslaved
which once the people of wisdom
knew as little Iran

—Allama Iqbal

Contents

Author's Note

There is a winter period of forty days in Kashmir known as Chillai Kalaan—a season of freezing waters and frozen breaths, where even silence feels cold. It arrives each year like a compulsory guest, one that must be honoured despite its long and testing stay. The cold settles deep into the bones of the valley, and life slows to the rhythm of survival.

Families gather in the kitchen, the warmest room in the house. The bukhari glows at the centre, the kangdi rests in every lap, kehva steams in small cups, and the pheran wraps the body like an old friend.

People sit with their heads leaning against the wall, eyes half-closed—a faint, serene peace reflecting in them, as if stillness itself has found a home there. The wall becomes a silent boundary between the frozen world outside and the living warmth within.

Every Kashmiri, whether in the valley or away from it, carries that same peace within—a calm that surfaces even in testing times, reminding them that warmth does not come only from sunlight, but from endurance, memory and faith in the return of spring.

BOOK I

Chillai Kalaan or The Great Cold

Forty days of harsh winter in Kashmir

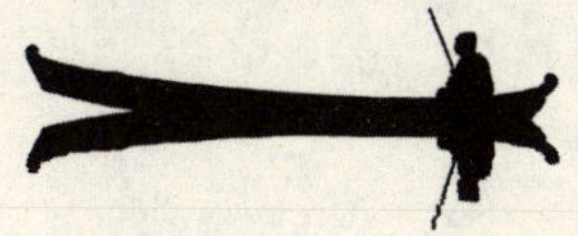

Chapter 1

19 January 1990
Gawkadal, Srinagar

She couldn't believe what she was hearing. The slogans outside were deafening, but she couldn't bear to look out the window. The constant sounds of chaos filled the surroundings, but she resisted the urge to witness the tumultuous scene. It was the period of Chillai Kalaan, the harshest forty days of winter in Kashmir. The frigid air of winter caused the chinar leaves to fall relentlessly, as if they were being stripped from their branches. Everything seemed rushed that night, as if nature itself was forewarning of a disaster approaching.

Little Kanval slept beside Iravati, but Purushottam's anxiety was palpable. Standing on the balcony, clutching their son Kabir, Purushottam trembled with worry. Their traditional grand Kashmiri wooden house, passed down through generations of musicians, quivered as chaos raged outside. The mansion, a three-story structure, boasted Zoon Dub balconies on each floor, perfect for moon-gazing, a feature favoured among the Kashmiri elite. However, the moon remained hidden, veiled by the thick smoke that filled the sky.

Desperate for news, Purushottam switched on the radio, hoping to hear from his father, the director of Radio Kashmir. But instead of his father's voice, all they could hear were the relentless slogans of the men on the bridge below.

AZAADI, AZAADI

Iravati felt a chill run down her spine. She shivered with a mixture of fear and anger as she noticed thick smoke rising from the other side of the Jhelum River. *What is burning in Lal Chowk?* Her mind raced with possibilities, realizing that they were all in danger. She was avoiding Purushottam's gaze; she knew he too was struggling to conceal his fear. This realization haunted her, and she tried to maintain her composure.

In an attempt to warm herself from the penetrating cold, Iravati clutched her Dejhoar and headed to the kitchen. She stood there watching the lined copper utensils, Kaab, Kyenz, Syin Toor, Bat Toor, Lyej, Deeche, and all the traditional Kashmiri crockery. Perplexed, she sat down near the furnace, uncertain of what to make. 'Noon Chai? Na kahvai rozie theek.' Considering kahva a better option, she removed the samovar and filled it with water. Placing the coal in the central hole, she closed the vessel and waited for the water to heat up. The heat surrounded her, in the air, in the city and within her mind.

Outside, the sloganeering intensified, echoing with greater clarity.

HUM KYA CHAHTE? AZAADI!
LEKE RAHENGE AZAADI!

Iravati couldn't help but wonder how many people had gathered outside, hundreds or perhaps thousands. The thought was terrifying, and she struggled to focus. In a hurry, she rushed to the drawing room where Kabir was playing; she noticed that he wasn't wearing his Pheran, the traditional Kashmiri garment designed to provide warmth. *Teer chi zyadi cxe kyazi looguth ni pheran*, she murmured to herself, *it's very cold, you should wear the pheran*, as she searched for the garment in the almirah to divert her attention. With a gentle gesture, she adorned Kabir with the Pheran, ensuring he stayed warm while attempting to distract herself from the chaos outside. However, conflicting emotions overwhelmed her.

Curiosity got the better of her, and she moved towards the balcony. Peering down from the balcony, she witnessed the bridge teeming with men of all ages. Purushottam couldn't contain his concern. 'I don't think these are our people, can I check with Sarfaraz?' But Iravati held him back. 'You're not going anywhere. If Bhailal or Tarannum cared, they would have already come.'

The scene challenged the long-standing Kashmiriyat prevailing in the valley, where mob culture had never been a norm. Iravati tried to ignore the chants. A figure caught her eye. 'Kyah govi? What happened?' Purushottam asked, perplexed by her sudden shift in demeanour. Numbly, she gestured in the direction of her gaze. 'Aariz,' she whispered. Purushottam froze, his eyes locked on the figure in the crowd who had captured Iravati's attention. 'Che chui winti timan peath baroas karun! You still want to trust them?' 'Who do we trust now?' she exclaimed, her embarrassment evident. Tears welled up in her eyes as she turned away from the balcony, retreating to the kitchen.

Regret flooded her thoughts as she realized she should have listened to Tarannum's repeated warnings and left for Jammu. Determined to maintain her composure, she resumed her seat in the kitchen, continuing the preparation of the kahva. Grinding cinnamon, cardamom, cloves and other ingredients, she stirred the mixture, aware that this could be the last time they would savour the taste of kahva.

Suddenly, Iravati was jolted by a thud on the door. Fear surged through her veins as she jumped up from her seat in the drawing room. Purushottam's anxiety mirrored her own, heightening her sense of panic. When the thud came again, she knew this was no ordinary visitor. 'I don't think you should open the door,' she stammered, her voice trembling with fear. Kabir, peering down from the gallery, watched the unfolding drama with innocent, wide eyes. Iravati and Purushottam exchanged worried glances.

'Sarfaraz?' Purushottam suggested, his voice shaking. Iravati's face hardened. 'I hope not,' she responded. 'Stay back, I'll go and check,' Purushottam offered, trying to summon his courage. 'Please switch off the lights.' As he descended the stairs, his heart pounding in his chest, Purushottam couldn't help but wonder if this was to be their fateful end.

Was it a mob at their door, ready to strike? 'Kus chu? Who is it?' he asked. There was no response. The desperate banging continued. 'Jinaab, aap ko humse kya chahiye, humne kya bigaada hai aapka?' Purushottam pleaded with the stranger outside. 'Sir, what do you want from us? What have we done to you?' 'Raina Sahab, ba chus Sarfaraz, jaldi kholo darwaz, Sarfaraz here, quickly open the door,' Sarfaraz whispered. Purushottam heaved a sigh of relief. As he opened the door, Sarfaraz, Tarannum and Noman hurried inside.

'Khudaya khair, cha chuk thik? Bhabhi thik? Are you good? Is Bhabhi fine?' Tarannum asked, concerned for their well-being. But Iravati was not ready to trust them now despite their years of friendship. Tarannum hugged her, but Iravati remained silent, her mind racing with fear and suspicion.

Iravati couldn't hold back any longer. 'Which rebel organization has Aariz teamed up with?' she asked, her voice dripping with sarcasm?

Sarfaraz and Tarannum looked embarrassed, but Iravati didn't care. She was angry, scared, and had had enough. Aariz had betrayed them all, and she couldn't trust anyone anymore. 'Trust me, I have made arrangements for you people. Let's quickly leave for Dal and hide in one of our houseboats. Noman will escort you from here in the boat, and that is the safest route for now.

Otherwise, there's danger everywhere. As soon as Kakalal comes from Radio, I will bring him there.'

But Iravati stood her ground. 'I can't trust Noman to escort us. He couldn't handle his son. Who knows if he's truly on our side?' Noman's face contorted with anguish. 'Don't bring my son into this. He made his own choices. But I swear on lord, I'll get you to safety.'

An angry Iravati protested. 'Trust a man whose son is on the street shouting slogans against me with my security? I am not putting my life in his hands.' Iravati blurted, her voice laced with anger and frustration. 'How do I know he won't betray us? I saw him in the crowd sloganeering. How do I know his son won't come after us with militants?'

'Excuse me,' Noman responded. 'My son is not a militant, you have a wrong impression about him.' His voice quivered as he continued, 'He was a good boy. He wanted to do something for his people, for his land, and I failed him. I failed to guide him, educate him, and now he's lost forever.'

Noman then added, 'We were here to help, but you sound ungrateful.'

'Shut up,' Sarfaraz yelled at him. 'Ye waqt hai bahes ka, Noman? Is this really the time to argue?'

'Thank you so much for your wonderful help, Bhailal, but we don't need it, at least not from this man.'

Noman quickly objected. 'I hope you are aware of why this is happening. The Governor has been sending trucks to Pandit localities to vacate them, and once you guys are out, the administration will have a free hand to shoot and kill us, that's exactly their plan.'

Sarfaraz was embarrassed by Noman's outburst. 'Khuda ka waasta hai, chup karo, Noman. For the sake of God, stop arguing.'

Iravati fumed and requested them with folded hands, 'May I

request you to please leave? I respect the fact that you have come to help. However, we are not leaving until Papa ji comes from Radio.'

Sarfaraz urged Purushottam to explain the gravity of the situation to Iravati and promised to escort Kakalal with a safe passage if the situation permitted. Noman looked distraught. 'I am not very happy that my son is out on the streets. But I want to make one thing very clear, all that has happened is a result of years of injustice to our land, and you guys have in no way supported us and the result of which is—'

Tarannum's patience finally exhausted, she cut him off. 'Stop it! Freeze your mouth! Your child is your responsibility, not theirs!' Tarannum took a deep breath and spoke with a hint of sarcasm, 'My forefathers were Kashmiri Hindu pandits, not the progeny of Sikandar-e-Azam who live in Gilgit and Hunza, so shut up. I have been listening to you very patiently.' In the same moment they were interrupted by a familiar voice coming from the radio broadcast. It was Purushottam's father narrating a poem and urging everyone in the city to calm down. They assembled around the radio.

Ye fiza ye gulshan ye bahaar
Ye Jhelum ye Nishaat ye Chinaar
Ye darakht ye darya ye aabshaar
Ye Jannat ye Firdaus ye Shehjaar
Ye adab ye Nagar ye bazaar
Ye Kehwa ye Kesar ye miqdaar
Ye Rubab ye Chenab ye ashaar
Ye Zoon ye Dub ye diyaar
Ye tera hai ye mera hai
Ye hamara hai
Aao milkar—

—Jinaab, aap kya kar rahe ho? Sir, what are you doing?

The last line was very unusual, the room fell silent as a loud gunshot rang out, interrupting the live radio broadcast. As the sound of the gunshot echoed in the room, Iravati's heart skipped a beat. Her mind raced with thoughts of what could have happened. Expressions of shock and fear reflected on everyone's faces. Even Sarfaraz, who had been calm and collected until now, looked shaken. He tried adjusting the transistor but failed.

Tarannum's heart raced as she looked around at everyone's shocked and confused faces. It was then that she realized the worst. Raina Sahab, or Kakalal as they respectfully called him, had been shot dead during the live broadcast. The air was thick with tension and fear as everyone in the room struggled to come to terms with the reality of the situation.

Noman remained silent, not expressing any sympathy towards the incident. He had always felt that their community lacked the solidarity needed to support the cause of Kashmir. His thoughts were interrupted when Purushottam collapsed onto the ground, trembling with shock and grief.

Purushottam struggled to breathe, his asthma worsened by the season. He was placed on the bed, gasping for air. Iravati rushed to the kitchen to fetch the kahva. Everybody huddled around him, trying to offer comfort as he trembled in distress. Iravati wept, while Tarannum did her best to console her. 'Sabar, Ira jani, sabar,' she whispered, 'patience, Ira dear, patience.'

Meanwhile, little Kabir was fascinated by the chaos outside. To him, it was like a cricket match, with the crowd cheering on. He had heard similar noises during live cricket broadcasts on the radio. But the reality was far from a game. Truckloads of Pandits were making their way to Jammu, with those who could help their neighbours doing what they could. The local Kashmiris, while disliking what was happening, were powerless to intervene, caught in between the two guns.

It took an hour for Purushottam to calm down. As the chaos subsided, it still wasn't safe. Sarfaraz urged them to leave, temporarily, and come back later. Iravati was way too lost to make a decision and Purushottam was too weak to speak.

As they got up, Sarfaraz instructed Noman to take them to their houseboat at the Dal Lake and keep them in the last room. The boat was ready. The Rainas made their way to it. Tarannum hugged Iravati and cried inconsolably. Noman picked up the children, while Sarfaraz helped Purushottam downstairs. 'Keep the boat on the left corner instead of the centre,' Sarfaraz instructed, his voice laced with urgency. 'Little before the Bund Road, Jhelum will cut leftwards into a small stream flowing directly to the Dal Lake—should take you an hour,' he added.

The Rainas' departure from their home was cloaked in an eerie silence. The chill in the air seemed to seep into Purushottam's bones, his body trembling with cold and his breathing ragged. As they made their way to the ghat, chaotic sloganeering erupted from different directions, adding to the tension in the air. Sarfaraz wanted them to avoid the main road filled with uncertainty of the time. Two small shikaras were parked in the Jhelum across their house. Iravati couldn't help but steal one last glance at their home, her dear home.

As they settled in the boat, Iravati sat at the rear end, holding Kanval tightly in her lap. Kabir sat across from her, a worried look etched on his face. Purushottam's condition had worsened, and he was now gasping and shivering in the cold, a sign that another asthma attack was imminent.

Noman had one leg on the floor and the other in the boat deftly controlling it, while Sarfaraz quickly untied the boat. Tarannum handed the kangdi to Noman, cautioning him to hold it carefully. However, the kangdi slipped from his hands and dropped to the floor with a loud clatter, and a gunshot was heard as he looked over the ghat.

Just then, the sound of another gunshot pierced the air, hitting Noman's temple. Sarfaraz and Tarannum froze in horror, their eyes meeting in disbelief. Purushottam was too weak to lift his head, but he heard the gunshot sensing something terrible had happened.

Iravati's heart lurched with fear as she clung to Kanval, her eyes wide with terror. Noman lay dead on the steps, blood oozing from his wound. Sarfaraz was beside himself with grief, trying desperately to revive him.

Iravati's eyes scanned the scene, and in that moment, she saw a figure holding a gun. As the figure dropped to the floor in horror, Iravati realized that the shot was intended for them, but Noman had been hit instead.

By now, the boat had already started to float in the water, but a crowd had gathered on the ghat. Iravati knew that they had to flee the scene before it was too late, sensing the danger that lurked around them. There was no time for sympathy, even though she longed to comfort Tarannum and Sarfaraz.

The scene was horrific, with Sarfaraz wiping away his brother's blood while Tarannum wailed loudly. The boat floated a hundred metres away, leaving behind a scene of chaos and despair. Iravati's hands trembled as she grabbed the oars. She had seen the shikara men row countless times, but now, with her family's life at stake, her hands were shaking uncontrollably. A strange strength stirred inside her, the strength to protect her loved ones and her future. She pulled the oars with all her might, determined to reach safety, until the ghat disappeared from view, disappearing in the smoke, fog, and bitter memory of a once-peaceful heaven. As she rowed, her heart pounded at an alarming pace, and fear gripped her. On both sides of the Jhelum stood tall mansions, the typical

Kashmiri architecture looming over her like ominous sentinels. She was lost, scared, and didn't know where to go.

She vaguely remembered Sarfaraz had told Noman about the stream cutting inwards before the Bund Road. On her right, she saw the Gadadhar ji temple as she passed across. It was during this hour that the aarti was performed, but the temple was silent, and there were no sounds of bells. By now, she could hear the sound of gushing water as it started flowing on her left. She was confused, unsure of what to do. If she went ahead, she would be floating in the endless Jhelum, but if she took the left, it would leave her in Dal. Her only hope was to go to Sarfaraz's houseboat, Ghat Number 9, 10th houseboat. She had been there many times before, but this was an unusual route.

She pulled the oars in and out, taking care not to exert too much pressure on her stomach. Purushottam's health was worsening by the minute and he lifted his head up, gasping for breath. The bone-chilling cold of Chillai Kalaan, the harshest season of winter, was entering his limbs. *The kangdi would have kept him warm*, Iravati thought.

As she rowed through the small stream and entered the vast expanse of Dal Lake, the moon's reflection on the tranquil waters, and the surrounding mountains, all seemed to add to the sense of helplessness she felt as a lone woman on the lake. Her gaze then drifted towards the distant boulevard road, where she could see some figures running away in large groups. *Pandits! Yem kot gachan? Where are they going?* she wondered, her voice barely above a whisper.

However, the sudden ringing of bells from the Shankaracharya temple over the hill caught her attention, filling her with a sense of divine presence. She felt drawn towards the temple, as if it was calling out to her for salvation. With a newfound purpose, she set her sights on the temple and rowed towards it instead of going to the houseboat, her instincts fuelling her determination. Despite being tired and exhausted, she kept rowing, knowing that her family's safety depended on it. But Purushottam's condition worsened, and he was struggling to breathe.

The boat was tilting and Iravati found it difficult to maintain her balance. 'Raina Sahab, Raina Sahab, please lie down, the boat is shaking.' She lost grip of an oar, and as she tried to pull it back, she heard a splashing sound, causing her to look back in horror. Purushottam was missing. It took a moment for Iravati to realize what had happened, but when she did, shock and disbelief washed over her. The bubbles on the surface of the water reflected Iravati's life sinking with Purushottam's drowning. The sight of those bubbles sinking into the depths of the lake filled her with a profound sense of loss, as if she were drowning with them, sinking deeper and deeper into the abyss.

2018
Mumbai

Dr Keerti pressed the transducer on Umika's belly, her eyes fixated on the screen showing images of the foetus. Kabir stood beside her, his heart racing. 'Three devastating losses and a recent molar pregnancy, I pleaded with both of you to exercise patience and allow a year to pass,' Dr Keerti expressed her concern. Kabir felt embarrassed and helpless, unable to comfort his wife.

Kabir's heart sank at the sight of the tiny Armaan growing inside Umika. It was the name they had chosen for every pregnancy, and the thought of losing him too was unbearable. Umika felt the tension in the room. She had already experienced bleeding, adding to her anxiety.

Umika was nineteen weeks pregnant, and it was clear that the foetus wasn't healthy. The couple faced a challenging biological struggle. As Umika left for the changing room, Kabir interrupted, 'If I had known, I could have taken timely action.'

Umika and Kabir drove out of the hospital, enveloped in a heavy silence. A red signal made them halt. However, Umika's life itself seemed to have turned into a yellow signal, urging her to wait. Trying to ease the tension, Kabir connected his phone to the car's aux, playing a new song. 'There's a new Kashmiri singer with his amazing single,' Kabir said as the song played. 'Dupte nuenum Dal ki waavno.'

Umika recognized Kabir's effort to cheer her up but remained unconvinced. 'Every breath I take is a reminder of the empty cradle that haunts my dreams,' she said, breaking the silence. Awkward, Kabir didn't know what to say. 'Dupte nuenum means the lover took away the stroll,' she explained wistfully, still reeling from the grief that had consumed her. 'You will have to purify the car now,' Umika added, noting the restrictions of Kashmiri culture in her home.

'Sometimes, I crave the melodies of Kashmiri words, torn between the missed teachings of Mummy and the steadfast cultural heritage upheld by your mother, which you inherited,' Kabir said, knowing Kashmir was a sensitive topic at home. It always triggered Iravati's anger. Married for eight years, Umika longed to visit her birthplace, but even the slightest mention of Kashmir would anger Iravati.

Kabir felt guilty for not providing Umika with a connection to her roots. She had revisited Kashmir before her marriage when her mother decided to sell her property. They had travelled across Kashmir and the beauty of Pahalgam was fresh in her mind. Awed by her culture and traditions, she had embraced singing Kashmiri folk songs. However, she had stopped singing them, fearing Iravati's temperament.

The only connection to Kashmir that remained with them was

the renaming of Kabir's production house to Chinar Productions, which took years for Iravati's approval.

As they arrived home, a delightful surprise awaited them. The sofa set was missing, replaced by a beautiful silk carpet and cushions neatly arranged along the walls, transforming their drawing room into a Kashmiri paradise. Umika's face lit up with joy as she observed the intricate details.

'Ye kem kor?' Umika exclaimed in disbelief. 'Who did this?'

'Ye kor mea,' Kanval replied, struggling to speak in Kashmiri. 'I did this.' Her efforts were met with a warm smile from Umika. Kabir, on the other hand, was nervous.

'Crazy, Kanval? Mummy will throw us out! You're instigating her.' 'Through all these years, I have been the one to question her, my dear brother. Now, since you couldn't, I will be the voice of courage for your beloved wife,' Kanval affirmed with a resolute tone.

'Looks like my daughter has finally found a way to rebel against me,' Iravati said with a hint of sarcasm, appearing from the bedroom and noticing the changes to the house. 'Well, I see we have turned our home into a tourist spot,' she said dryly. 'Maybe I should just walk out and let you all enjoy the scenery,' Iravati said as she surveyed the room with a poker face.

Kabir took a deep breath, his heart beating fast with anxiety. He knew how sensitive his mother was about their Kashmiri roots, and this sudden transformation of their home meant trouble.

Iravati stood there silently, her eyes scanning the room, taking note of every little detail. She turned to Kanval.

'I see you have turned our home into a museum despite my disapproval, Kanval. Maybe next time you can put up a sign saying "tourists welcome",' Iravati remarked, her tone laced with sarcasm as she looked around the renovated living room.

'I'll take care of it right away, Mummy,' Kabir said, his tone apologetic. 'Please don't be angry with us.'

Iravati just gave a dismissive nod before turning and heading towards her room. Kabir followed, feeling a mix of embarrassment and frustration. He wished his mother could be more open-minded, but he knew that changing her views would take a lot more than just a few cushions and a carpet.

'Mummy, I know you're very angry, but there's a bigger concern at the moment,' Kabir said with a heavy heart, avoiding Iravati's gaze.

'What is it?' Iravati asked sharply, her voice laced with anger.

'Mummy,' Kabir's voice trembled, urgency lacing his words. 'Something important demands your attention. Umika's pregnancy...it's complicated. I fear we may face the loss of the baby again.' He turned away, unable to meet her eyes.

As Kabir revealed the news of Umika's complicated pregnancy, Iravati's heart sank. Her eyes filled with tears, and she sat down, shocked. It was a rare sight for Kabir to see Iravati in such a vulnerable state. For so long she had been strong and resilient, unaffected by life's hardships. But the news of Umika's pregnancy hit her hard. 'Why wasn't I informed?' she asked. 'I just found out today,' Kabir replied softly. 'I'm scared, Mummy. I can't bear losing another child.' Kabir had always tried to uplift Iravati, but her haunting past weighed her down. Memories of carefree days in Srinagar with Tarannum brought both joy and bitterness.

One night had forever changed her life. Iravati had the same dream each night: of rowing the boat, hearing chilling chants, fleeing her home and her father-in-law's last words on the radio. She often wondered about his final resting place. Did his body lie near the Jhelum's banks, decayed, or was he cremated? Her past had scarred her deeply, making her reticent. Kabir's breakdown stirred long-suppressed emotions in Iravati. She struggled to console him, her heart having hardened long ago. Knowing Umika's history of difficult pregnancies deepened the void they felt, Kabir remaining childless. The sudden silence unsettled Kabir.

He had rarely seen her cry or smile. He believed her happiness was lost forever, but the pain etched on her face contradicted that. 'Mummy, please say something,' he pleaded, his voice trembling. Iravati's teary eyes met his. 'Take good care of her,' she whispered. Kabir understood the unspoken apology in her words. Iravati had endured so much that expressing her emotions seemed impossible. 'Mummy, Kanval knew how much Umika missed Kashmir, so she made our home a little Kashmir for her, to bring her joy,' Kabir said with wistful contemplation before leaving the room. Iravati sat alone, wanting to comfort Kabir but restrained by her past, afraid to let anyone get too close.

She closed her eyes, hoping to find the courage to confront her demons and make peace with her haunting past. Alone with her thoughts, Iravati wondered if Tarannum still lived, the person with whom she had shared camaraderie, discussing Gawkadal as they sat on the Jhelum ghat. She longed to escape her thoughts, just as she had fled that night twenty-eight years ago. Kanval had returned from Delhi after her post-graduation, no longer the same person. She had become rebellious, progressive and argumentative. Iravati felt she was losing her daughter to the modern world. Kanval was determined to change her mother's outlook. She had prepared a Kashmiri feast, exploring recipes online and even ordering brass utensils online to create the typical ambience of the region. Kanval understood that keeping Umika happy wasn't enough; her mother needed to confront the past instead of ignoring it. She believed that acceptance was the path to liberation, while ignoring it was akin to hiding in the closet, which would be detrimental to Iravati's well-being.

The dining table was shifted and a floor seating arrangement was made using the brass utensils Kanval had ordered. Both

Kabir and Umika were nervous, fearing Iravati's reaction. They sat, hoping for the best. Among the utensils was Tasht Nerr, a round concave vessel used for handwashing. 'How beautiful,' Umika exclaimed, running her fingers over the intricate designs. *How disastrous*, Kabir thought.

When Iravati entered the drawing room, disappointment and anger filled her. Her eyes scanned the dining table and utensils, evoking memories of their old kitchen where they dined in a similar fashion. The flood of Kashmiri food memories brought both joy and pain to her mind. 'What is this?' she remarked, but nobody responded. Kabir looked at Kanval, hoping she would answer, while Umika sat nervously.

'A little change won't bring a revolution, Mummy. Will you please join us?' Kanval replied, hoping to pre-empt her mother's anger with her logic. Iravati looked at her with fuming rage. Before she could burst out, Kanval quickly glanced at Umika, signalling at Iravati to contain her anger.

As Iravati sat, suppressing her rage, Kanval opened the lid of a dish. 'Here's something special today,' she said, revealing the nadru. 'Nadru!' Umika exclaimed, while Kabir watched his mother's expression closely. 'How did you make this?' Umika asked. *Lotus stems*, Iravati thought. She used to ask Sarfaraz to bring them from the Dal Lake floating market, as they were fresh and tasty.

'With some effort,' Kanval replied, glancing at her mother, hinting at her to make some as well. She opened another lid, revealing the rogan josh. Iravati couldn't help but think about Tarannum's rogan josh, which she used to make every Sunday and share with her. She glanced at the dish in front of her, floating in artificial red colour and oil. *Yuck*, she thought. It wasn't even made with lamb's meat, which they all used to enjoy back then.

As Kanval served each of them, Iravati couldn't bring herself to eat. 'Do we have some daal?' she asked. Kabir hurriedly got up, his anxiety evident. 'Yes, Mummy, there's some in the fridge. I'll bring it right away.'

As Kabir left, Iravati closed her eyes and took a deep breath, attempting to calm the conflicting emotions within her. She knew she had to contain her rage and reflect on her situation. While Kanval and Umika continued their conversation, Iravati remained silent, lost in her thoughts and memories.

As Kanval continued to talk about the history and significance of Kashmiri cuisine, Iravati's silence grew more and more pronounced. Oblivious to her mother's discomfort, Kanval shared her knowledge about the dishes. 'Did you know that Kashmiri saffron is considered the best in the world? It's so valuable that it's known as red gold!' Kanval, aware of the brewing storm, kept on talking. 'And the way Kashmiris use spices in their food is just amazing. The balance of flavours is perfect.' Kanval continued to share her knowledge about Kashmiri cuisine and its rich history, aware of the tension building up in the room.

Kabir and Kanval were both anxious, noticing Iravati's silence and the way she gripped her spoon tightly. 'Lotus stem made with spinach is a special Kashmiri dish, and to add to your knowledge, Kashmir's spinach is very different from those found in other regions. If you observe the edges, they look like the chinar leaf; it's very thin and very soft and it softens quickly while cooking. One important thing to note is that if it is overcooked, then it doesn't taste good. It should be a little crisp, I believe.'

Kanval mixed the nadru with rice, relishing the taste. 'Did you know that rogan josh arrived in Kashmir along with the Mughals, almost four hundred years ago?' Iravati silently fumed, clutching her spoon tightly. 'Emperor Jahangir used to come to Kashmir and was very, very fond of our food habits.'

Kabir could feel the tension building in the room like a pressure cooker about to explode. 'The great Silk Route in India crossed Kashmir, so you get to see a lot of Persian, Central Asian and even Tibetan influence in our food. Overall, if you see the local food, it reminds you of the cuisines of Uzbekistan, Samarkand and Iran.'

Iravati, who had been listening quietly until now, couldn't hold back anymore. 'Excuse me!' she abruptly left the dining area. Umika and Kabir exchanged anxious glances. Kabir tried to chase after his mother, but Kanval held him back. 'Let her go,' she said softly. 'She needs time to process this change. We can continue our dinner.' Kabir nodded reluctantly, still worried about his mother.

Kanval could sense the tension in the air and tried to lighten the mood. 'Well, I hope at least the food is to your liking,' she said with a smile. Umika held on to her belly, feeling a strange discomfort, but tried to focus on the conversation. Kabir was angry; he disapproved of the intentional provocation. He thought the least they could do was to enjoy the food without bringing up provocative history with their mother, who had come to eat with them.

'What are you up to, Kanval? What intrigues me even more is why many of you, who study in esteemed universities in Delhi, become agents of change, challenging prevailing norms and beliefs that our upbringing has ingrained in us,' Kabir's voice carried a mix of curiosity and annoyance. She met his gaze with a calm smile. 'I entered that world as a naive student, holding the beliefs we were raised with. But within those university walls, I found a sanctuary that allowed me to explore, understand, and question our nation's socio-economic fabric on a personal level. It opened my eyes to rational thinking and heightened my senses, even when society at large discourages such introspection,' Kanval's voice carried a mix of reflection, empowerment and defiance as she responded to Kabir's enquiry.

Umika felt a sudden poke from inside her belly as Kanval explained her views. 'There, I met minds enlightened by the workings of neo-liberalism and capitalism. These individuals were not confined to theoretical debates; they sought practical solutions and actively aspired to bring about meaningful change in society.' 'But haven't our own sufferings shaped Mummy's behaviour as well?' Kabir interjected. 'I understand the pain we've been through and I empathize with Mummy's perspective. Although I was too small and hardly have a memory of things that Mummy has been witness to, I refuse to let our experiences paint a broad brushstroke on an entire community. I choose to believe in compassion, individuality and breaking free from the cycle of prejudice.' As Kanval spoke, Umika felt a discomfort that intensified with each passing moment. 'Seven years in that university studying law and humanities, I have done enough research to have a mindset of my own. My professors, my colleagues, my mentors have never ever forced me to have a belief. Nobody can impose a belief on anyone; you can only form one in the course of time,' Kanval continued to engage in the serious conversation, not realizing Umika's increasing discomfort. However, Umika remained silent, not wanting to interrupt the conversation.

'I buy that, somehow. But why is your university always embroiled in controversies these days? What happened to its once-esteemed reputation?' Kabir questioned, his tone filled with genuine curiosity and a touch of worry.

Kanval responded with confidence, defending her university. 'Our university has achieved various awards for being the best in the country for its academic excellence and research. It ranks as the third best university in India and eighteenth globally. Our notable alumni list is extensive, and we have students enrolling not just from India, but from foreign countries as well.'

She continued, 'Some people have been misled into believing

that students and professors of this particular university are "anti" this or that. But anyone seeking higher education knows how difficult it is to get admission there. The mobile forwards that you speak of are doing nothing but creating a nuisance and propagating false information.'

Umika was visibly uncomfortable, still experiencing pain in her belly. Kanval glanced at her, noting her distress. Suddenly, Umika collapsed onto Kabir's shoulder, her eyes rolling upwards, causing panic among them.

Dr Keerti rushed to examine Umika. Kabir, Kanval and Iravati anxiously waited for her analysis. After the examination, Dr Keerti's face grew serious as she explained the situation. 'Umika is almost five centimetres dilated,' her voice filled with concern. Kanval, restless with worry, asked, 'And what does that mean?' Dr Keerti's face grew serious as she explained the situation. 'Well, the foetus isn't healthy. This is a case of placental abruption, where the foetus is deprived of oxygen and nutrients, causing heavy bleeding in the mother.' Kabir's heart sank as he tried to process the information. 'What kind of issues? Is she ok?' he asked, with a shaky voice.

Kabir was eager for a solution and expressed his frustration. Dr Keerti clarified that they needed to closely monitor the situation and decide on a vaginal delivery or C-section after thirty-four weeks, depending on the severity of the abruption.

Kabir felt a lump form in his throat as he thought about the possibility of something going wrong with Umika or the baby. 'What can we do? Is there anything we can do?' he asked, his voice filled with desperation. Dr Keerti nodded reassuringly. 'There are some things we can do to manage the risk, such as monitoring her blood sugar levels and blood pressure regularly. We'll also be doing some additional testing to make sure everything is progressing as it should be.'

Kabir nodded, feeling a mix of relief and worry, thinking

about the child they always wanted, and how much he wanted everything to be okay. He turned to Dr Keerti and asked, 'What can I do to help? What do I need to do?' Doctor Keerti smiled kindly. 'Right now, the best thing you can do is be there for Umika. Support her emotionally and physically. Help her follow the guidelines we give her.'

Umika lay in the hospital bed, her energy drained and dark circles under her eyes, a clear sign of the struggle she was going through. Kabir sat next to her, holding her hand and trying his best to hide his own fear and anxiety. The doctor's words echoed in Kabir's mind: the baby was in danger and there was no easy solution.

Umika's eyes pleaded for answers, but Kabir knew the truth would bring more pain. He struggled to find the right words to comfort her, to give her hope, but the weight of the situation was crushing him. The room was silent except for the sound of Umika's laboured breathing, each breath a reminder of the fragile life inside her.

Kabir's heart ached with fear. As he sat by Umika's side in the hospital ward, holding her hand, she was curious to know the problem. Kabir tried his best to explain in simple terms, 'The doctor wants you to keep happy. If you keep happy, the baby will be happy, followed by your medication. That's enough.'

Umika was not satisfied with this vague explanation. 'But why am I bleeding, Kabir?' she asked, feeling drained of energy. Kabir hesitated for a moment before finally replying, 'The baby is violently kicking because you think too much. You overthink about your earlier pregnancy and your miscarriages. What you're not doing to trust this baby. Keep yourself positive and, above all, happy.'

Kabir knew the real answer, but he couldn't bear to tell her about the complication. Umika suffered from OCD and overthinking. Any uncertainty or vague communication only added to her anxiety. Kabir could sense the confusion in Umika's eyes. 'What's bothering you, Kabir?' she asked. Kabir wanted to uplift her spirit. 'Hospitals need to be more humanizing. I mean, instead of calling the unborn a foetus, they could call it a baby,' he explained. 'Instead of referring to you as a patient, they could call you a mother. I just think it would be more comforting and humanizing to use these words instead of the cold medical terms. This environment isn't very constructive, so you must recover quickly and we must go home.'

Umika smiled at Kabir's suggestion. She was touched by his thoughtfulness and how he was always thinking of ways to make her feel better. 'You're right,' she said. 'It does sound more comforting and personal to use those words.'

Kabir smiled back at her, relieved that she had liked his idea. He felt a sense of joy and hope that they would have a beautiful, healthy baby soon. He leaned over to give her a kiss and held her hand tightly, feeling a sense of peace and comfort knowing that they were in this together.

That night, as they lay in bed, Umika was restless with her thoughts. She looked at Kabir. 'What if something goes wrong? What if I lose the baby again?' Kabir was startled but alert and had already planned to distract Umika from bad thoughts. He reached over and took her hand. 'We'll get through it together,' he said. 'I'll be there for you every step of the way.'

Umika smiled weakly, but Kabir could still see the worry in her eyes. He knew he needed to do something to lift her spirits. 'Hey, do you remember that Kashmiri lullaby you used to hum to the baby?' he asked. Umika nodded. 'Of course I do. It always calmed him down, "Hukus Bukus".'

'Well, I've got an idea,' Kabir said. 'I want to turn that lullaby into a song and record it with some of the best musicians in the country.' Umika's eyes widened in surprise. 'Really?' Kabir nodded.

'And I want you to be the singer again.' Umika looked sceptical. 'I don't know if I can do that.' Kabir squeezed her hand. 'Of course you can. You have an amazing voice, and I know you can do this. Plus, it'll be something positive to focus on during the pregnancy.' Umika smiled, feeling a sudden surge of empowerment. 'Ok, let's do it,' Kabir grinned, feeling relieved that he was able to bring a smile to her face. 'And do you know where we should shoot the video?' he asked. 'Pahalgam, my favourite place in the world!' she said, her eyes sparkling with excitement. Kabir nodded. 'I know, that's why I suggested it. It'll be a beautiful setting for the video and it'll be a great way for us to spend some time together as a family.'

Umika leaned over and kissed him on the cheek. 'You always know how to make me feel better,' she said. Kabir smiled, feeling grateful for the bond they shared and for their love that had only grown stronger with each passing day. With a baby on the way, he knew their future was brighter than ever before. She knew it was a boy; she could feel Kabir's masculinity in her belly.

Kabir could sense Umika's concern as she expressed her worry about drawing Iravati's ire. 'Don't worry, my love. Kanval has already spoken to Mummy, and she didn't refuse.' 'But did she agree? Did she say go ahead?' Umika asked curiously. 'Well, she understands our passion for music. She may not have replied yet, but she will come around. Trust me, everything will be all right.'

Umika wanted that enthusiasm for Kabir's sake. She knew he already carried a heavy burden. Kabir had set up a studio in his house, a relief that allowed him to work on audio projects and indulge in his musical pursuits from home. His dedication and love for music, ingrained in his genes, drove him to continue his family's musical legacy. Iravati, however, tried to dissuade him from pursuing music due to the painful memories it evoked from her past.

Kabir's father, Purushottam, was a creative director at Radio Kashmir, specializing in musical programmes with a PhD in Hindustani Music. Kabir's inclination towards music was difficult to suppress. At 20, he earned good money performing with his college band locally. Iravati monitored his finances, saving every penny he made from performances across the country. At 22, Kabir felt the need for growth. Dissatisfied with the music around him, he believed he could create something better with his keen sense of musicality.

He established a small music label focused on producing background scores and original soundtracks for short films and television dramas, with moderate success. As he expanded his team and focused on business development, his unique fusion of Rubab and guitar in his songs gained recognition. New filmmakers, constrained by limited budgets, sought him out. His business grew over time, and his love for Umika deepened.

At the age of 23, Kabir married Umika, who possessed a melodious voice herself. Kabir encouraged her to sing, but her discontinuation was influenced by Iravati's disapproval. Fortunately, love had blossomed between Umika and Kabir since their childhood days.

After years of not singing, Umika prepared to perform at Kabir's insistence. As she visualized hitting the high notes in the song, she felt it would have the same calming effect on their baby when he cried. Kabir had brought out her maternal instincts, and singing intensified her emotions. She practised diligently, making modern adjustments to the original lyrics.

With the scratch music ready, Umika and Kabir spent hours perfecting the flow of the song. Kanval, thrilled to witness their collaboration, found solace in their creative endeavour amidst her own pregnancy complications. Kabir's love for Umika radiated in every action he took.

As Umika practised, Kanval requested that she sing 'Mujhse Pehli Si Mohabbat', a poem written by the poet Faiz Ahmed Faiz. 'Faiz is my favourite Urdu poet, and the revolution in his poetry is very poignant,' Kanval mentioned, purposefully making sure Iravati heard. 'Faiz wrote it for his wife when he was jailed in connection with the Rawalpindi conspiracy case.'

Iravati overheard the conversation and gave Kanval a death stare. She walked inside, not wanting to be part of the conversation. Kabir noticed and asked Kanval why she was sounding so leftist. Kanval replied that she was not leftist, but she believed in doing what was right. She continued speaking about Faiz and his life, but Kabir was clueless, not being much of a history or social-political person.

Kanval tried to provoke her mother by speaking about freedom, liberty and acceptance through Faiz's literature. 'I am requesting you because our association of female lawyers is facing some compensation inequality at the hands of their respective bosses, and I am leading their cause. We shall sing it and put it on social media,' Kanval said. Kabir knew that this was not the truth; she was smiling the moment Iravati left, only trying to tease her. Kanval wanted to share the history of Faiz's anthem 'Hum Dekhenge', but Kabir stopped her, knowing that Kanval could talk for hours about her favourite topics.

The music was ready. The recording took place at Kabir's music studio. Umika received a warm welcome from the staff. The label was beautifully decorated. She was nervous but excited too; it had been many years since she last sang. Kabir reassured her that everything was going to be wonderful, expressing his confidence in her singing and her ability to bring out the best.

Umika entered the studio with Kabir, and he adjusted her

mic. Sitting on the chair, she contained her excitement. As the recording began, Kabir walked out, giving her a flying kiss gesture. Pouring her heart and soul into the song, she sang the mukhda flawlessly, evoking emotions from everyone present. The studio erupted in applause as Kabir entered, kissing her forehead and complimenting her pitch-perfect performance. He instructed her to maintain the same tune for the other verses.

Kabir noticed something strange from the console room. He rushed back into the recording studio to find Umika in distress, clutching the mic and gasping for breath. The same pattern of collapses she had experienced before was happening again. Horrified, Kabir quickly carried her to the hospital, with Kanval and Iravati by their side. Despite their efforts, it was too late. Umika was in her 28th week of pregnancy, and the doctor expressed concern. Sudden respiratory depression occurred and her oxygen pressure dropped to a dangerously low level.

Despite the medical team's best efforts, the foetal heart activity ceased and their baby was declared nonviable. Kabir's world shattered as he cried, supported by Kanval and Iravati. He had done everything he could, but fate had different plans. In his grief, Kabir realized that the lullaby they had been recording would never be heard by their child.

~

Exhausted and broken, Kabir waited for Umika to regain consciousness, dreading the devastating news he had to deliver. Sitting beside her, he gazed at her pale face, which was turning blue. He called for the nurse, and despite seven agonizing hours passing, her condition continued to worsen. Dr Keerti attempted to use the defibrillator, but it failed to revive her. The flat lines on the QRS monitor marked the end of Umika's life. Kabir's heart shattered as he mourned the loss of his wife and child.

The enormity of the tragedy struck heavily at everyone's hearts. In the silence of the room, everybody mourned the loss of a life that had once been filled with promise and joy.

Chapter 2

2017
Lahore, Pakistan

Androon Lahore, the old city, buzzed with excitement and celebration. Its narrow streets, vibrant bazaars and ancient brick buildings exuded the city's rich history. The walled city of Lahore, with its renowned thirteen gates, stood grand and majestic, enhancing the city's allure.

In the midst of the historical splendour, the Bhati Gate area brimmed with festivity. It marked the 973rd Urs Mubarak of the revered Sufi Saint Data Ganj Baksh, and the air was infused with the aroma of food, the flickering of candles and the enchanting melodies of qawwali. The shrine gleamed with illumination, and a large crowd had gathered to partake in the festivities, enjoying the langar being served.

The Sufis mesmerized the audience with their soulful raqs performances, captivating the onlookers. The malangs, who had spent their lives in isolation, swayed in a trance-like state to the music. The qawwals' voices resonated through the shrine, invoking a sense of the divine. As the raqs performance concluded, the Sufi blew the horn, signalling its end. The crowd applauded and the atmosphere crackled with electrifying energy.

The celebrations continued throughout the night, and the spirit of the Urs Mubarak lingered in the air, leaving a lasting impression on the visitors.

In the midst of the chaotic streets of Anarkali Market, a sleek black SUV manoeuvred through the crowd. Shabbir, a loyal servant who had been in Daarji's service for twenty-eight years, was behind the wheel. Daarji appeared anxious, as waiting was not his strong suit. Ajju's disappearance had deeply affected Daarji, as Ajju was like a son to him. The thought of Ajju occupied Daarji's mind, causing him anxiety, diabetes and withdrawal symptoms.

Daarji held a prominent position as the head of Tanzeem, wielding significant influence in Pakistan's social and political affairs. Shabbir empathized with Daarji, who had always treated him like a son. He knew how much Ajju meant to Daarji and understood the devastation caused by his disappearance. As the car navigated the bustling streets, Shabbir couldn't shake off the feeling of unease gnawing at his gut.

The car moved forward with Shabbir at the wheel, his heart pounding. Daarji's foul mood was evident. Shabbir had witnessed his anger before, but this time it was different. It stemmed from disappointment and betrayal caused by Ajju's sudden disappearance. Ajju had been Daarji's protege, someone he had hoped would carry on the legacy of Tanzeem. Yet, Ajju had vanished without a trace. Daarji, a powerful and respected figure, found himself powerless in the face of this loss.

Arriving at the shrine, Daarji entered with his loyal men. Shabbir stayed back, observing as Daarji openly wept at the saint's tomb. The sight was both awe-inspiring and unsettling, a stark reminder that even the mightiest of men could be brought low by the whims of fate. It was evident that Daarji had not yet overcome the pain of Ajju's disappearance. Ajju had fled with his future.

After offering his prayers, Daarji made his way back to the car amidst the vibrant atmosphere. The Sufi who had blown the horn watched his every move, as if there was a spiritual connection to Ajju, as if he possessed some knowledge. Daarji passed by the Sufi, pausing briefly and exchanging a look. Then he walked away. The Sufi held on to his staff, observing Daarji's departure, as if he knew the moral of the story that would unfold in due course.

Daarji took his seat in the car, the others quickly joining him, and they set off towards Anarkali once again. Daarji instructed Shabbir, 'Dharti ambar ek karde, par ohnu lab ke leke aa, do whatever it takes but bring him back.' The weight of Daarji's words sent a shiver down Shabbir's spine.

2018
Kashmir

Kabir looked out of the aeroplane window, mesmerized by the beauty of the mountains below and the flowing rivers. Wondering if it might be Jhelum or Chenab. The lush green vegetation and pine trees adorned the Himalayan terrain and serpentine roads. Memories flooded his mind, wondering if his mother had taken him and his sister along this route to Jammu in their younger days. The serenity and purity of the place from this height stood in stark contrast to the pain he felt after Umika's demise.

Beside him, Kanval was reading an article about the half-widows of Kashmir, women whose husbands had disappeared without a trace. She had hoped to meet them during their trip but it seemed a task. Convincing Iravati to bring Kabir all the way to Kashmir for Umika's final rites had been a daunting task. Six months since Umika's passing, Kabir remained paralyzed by grief, spending hours in a state of inertia. The loss had shattered him terribly. Umika had been his best friend, his unwavering support and the one who loved him unconditionally. Her absence made his living space feel empty and suffocating. He yearned for her presence, her messiness, her breathing and her singing. The half-empty bed and the silence of the mornings signified the void in his life, leaving him trapped in his sorrow.

Unable to bear the weight of Kabir's pain any longer, Kanval took matters into her own hands. With her maid, she entered Kabir's room under the pretence of cleaning. The asthi kalash in the corner, containing Umika's ashes, caught Kanval's attention. Instructing her maid, Kanval said, 'Sudha, clean this room thoroughly. Dust the almirah, change the curtains, and when you're done, put the asthi kalash in a polythene bag. There's a nullah between Mahim and Bandra; dispose of them there.' Kabir was overcome with shock and anger at Kanval's audacious suggestion. How could she even consider discarding Umika's ashes in such a callous manner? The idea seemed disrespectful and heartless, as Umika held immense sacred significance in his life.

Kabir grasped the asthi kalash from the maid's hands. He clutched it, refusing to let go. 'No, I won't allow this,' he said with a trembling voice, his resolve unyielding.

'Bhaiyya, please snap out of it,' Kanval pleaded, her voice a mix of concern and frustration. 'Six months have passed, and yet you remain lost in the depths of grief. While your wife and child may be gone, we, the two remaining souls in this house, still yearn for your presence and strength. It's time for you to step up and be the responsible man we know you can be. There is someone else still sitting outside! Someone who hasn't left since the cremation, still pleading with Mummy to let her daughter rest in peace.'

Her voice dropped. 'You are doing injustice not just to us but also to the woman who gave birth to Umika. She's been asking Mummy with folded hands for six months now, just to let her daughter rest in eternity.'

The door opened quietly. Iravati stepped in, gently holding Umika's mother by the arm. She looked like someone who had been waiting too long, carrying more silence than strength. Their eyes met. Kabir's were just beginning to fill and Sulakshana's looked like they had run dry long ago.

Kanval was determined to bring life back to her brother's eyes, to witness even a glimmer of emotion in his otherwise dormant stare. It pained her to see her brother suffer, burdened by his grief and haunted by his past. The idea of going to Kashmir for Umika's asthi visarjan seemed like a distant hope, but Kanval refused to give up on her brother. She knew he needed closure, a way to bid farewell to his beloved wife in a place that held cherished memories for her.

However, like earlier, Iravati's response was swift and harsh. She wanted the last rites to be performed nearby instead of in Kashmir; Kanval felt the sting of her mother's words as she rejected the idea. Nevertheless, Kanval stood her ground, fully aware that Kabir needed this closure. 'Mummy, with Umika, dad and grandpa gone, our family tree is withering. Do you want to lose Bhaiyya too?'

Kanval's words carried a mix of urgency and exasperation. 'He's slipping into a lifeless existence.' Iravati was reluctant, but Kanval continued, 'Mummy, imagine if it was me instead of Umika. Would you want my ashes to be tucked away in a corner? Or would you want me to be set free, to be part of something greater? Think about it, Mummy. Umika deserves a good farewell, she loved Kashmir, and in doing so, we may help Bhaiyya find his way back to life.'

The reality of Umika's death was too hard to bear, and Kabir needed to face it head-on. Kanval's words were strong, and they stung, but they were necessary. Kanval noticed the look of nostalgia on his face and hoped that this trip would help bring back some of the life that had been missing from Kabir's eyes since Umika's passing.

Kanval felt a sudden urge for a beverage on the flight to Srinagar. She asked the airhostess, 'Do you guys serve kahva?'

The airhostess replied politely, 'I'm sorry, ma'am, we only serve masala chai and coffee.'

all of us. It's a part of our history, our culture, our identity. It's up to us to preserve it.'

It was 4 o'clock in the evening, and the car was winding up a small uphill road with the glistening river Lidder flowing on the right. The sound of the rushing water created a sense of tranquillity, yet Kabir's mind and heart were filled with chaos. He couldn't accept the idea of letting go of what remained of his beloved wife and child. Upon reaching the resort-cum-cottage, the chill in the air started to bite. Kabir and Kanval checked in to their room on the upper floor, overlooking the river. The view was breathtaking, and the peaceful sound of the water created a sense of calm. There was a knock on the door.

An elderly man, Ramzan Chacha, entered the room. His pinkish complexion and traditional attire, including a Nehru cap and draped pheran, evoked wisdom and experience. Ramzan Chacha had been the caretaker of the cottage for many years.

'Biti, kuch chahiye? Do you want something?' he asked. 'Are you feeling cold?'

Kabir shivered, but the warmth in Ramzan Chacha's voice was comforting. 'Craving tea, Uncle.'

'I'll bring, you must also try the Girda bread,' Ramzan Chacha said, sensing Kabir's need for comfort.

As Kabir unpacked his suitcase, he carefully removed the ashes, the urn containing the remains of his wife and child. Ramzan Chacha watched with sadness and respect.

'Tum chai piyega, beta ji? Would you like some tea?' Ramzan Chacha interrupted, noticing Kabir's tears.

Kabir nodded, his voice choked with emotion. 'Han, kya? Han piyunga na chai. Yes, I'd like to have some.'

Kanval quickly wore her gloves and sat opposite Kabir. She could hardly say anything, as Kabir's state of mind was overwhelming. Iravati had been calling her every hour to check on her children, and it irritated her. Reluctantly, she picked the call.

'Why aren't you answering my calls? Are you guys all right?' Iravati's voice was filled with concern and worry.

'Mummy, calm down? We have reached safely, everything is ok here,' Kanval said, trying to hide her irritation.

'How is Kabir?' Iravati asked.

'He's fine, Mummy,' Kanval responded with an unpleasant tone.

'I wish to talk to him,' Iravati requested.

Kanval looked at Kabir, but he was lost in his thoughts and emotions. 'Bhaiyya is resting at the moment. I'll ask him to call you once he freshens up.'

'Biti, can I come in?' Ramzan Chacha was at the door, interrupting their conversation.

'Please come,' Kanval replied, excusing herself from the call.

'Hey, wait, wait. Who's there in your room? Whom are you talking to?' Iravati's suspicious tone filled the phone.

'Mummy, can I speak to you later?' Kanval disconnected the call.

Ramzan Chacha entered the room and kept the tea on the table. Kanval and Kabir sat next to each other, and Ramzan Chacha poured the tea into the cup. He glanced at the ashes in the urn—a reminder of the fragility of life. Kabir's desolate state of mind was evident, compelling Ramzan Chacha to ease his pain.

'Acche se piyo,' he said, 'drink well,' before turning to leave. But a moment of hesitation made him turn back to the siblings.

'Can I tell you something?' he asked in a gentle tone. Kabir looked at him dimly, 'Yes, please Chacha,' she said. Kanval put her teacup back on the table, giving Ramzan Chacha her full attention.

'I am 80 years old now. Not sure how much longer I will be alive. My hair has turned grey and I have limited physical abilities. Although I have lived in this heaven, I have also had my bitter experiences of life,' Ramzan Chacha said.

'Surrender brings a peculiar peace, as we let go of what we can't control. It's not just losing someone we thought would always be there, but also the dreams and plans we crafted together. It's finding peace in accepting the simple truth and letting go of the complexities we once held on to,' he continued.

Despite Ramzan Chacha being a stranger, his presence and personality were enough to draw respect from both Kabir and Kanval and they kept quiet as he spoke with conviction.

'Look at this chinar tree,' he pointed out of the window. 'It sheds its leaves every year, only to grow new ones in the next season. It doesn't cling on to the old leaves, does it? It surrenders to the natural cycle of life.'

Kabir looked at the tree, as if for the first time. He started to understand what Ramzan Chacha was trying to convey and a strange peace washed over him. He nodded slowly in agreement, affirming the wisdom with his heart.

As Ramzan Chacha spoke, Kabir felt like he could open up, let his heart a little loose and cry He had been locking himself in a jar of conflicted emotions back at home, with no one able to break through his walls, not even Kanval or Iravati, despite their best efforts. But there was something about Ramzan Chacha's presence that made him feel like he could confront his grief, even if just a little bit. Kabir felt tears welling up in his eyes.

'Letting go of people you love, your desires and relationships is very hard, especially the ones that you have loved, nurtured and invested in. It is like letting go of the self one had created to hide behind to let your true self develop and grow.' Ramzan Chacha put his hand over Kabir's head. 'Khudaye barakat karan,' he prayed with a gentle smile. 'May God bless us.' Ramzan Chacha's words were like a balm to Kabir's wounded heart.

Kanval was in awe of the people of Kashmir from the moment she landed, impressed by the deep wisdom they seemed to have gained from their natural surroundings. The mountains, the valleys and the lakes all seemed to have imparted a sense of calm and serenity to the people who lived there and it was evident in everything they did. A 20-seater van arrived at the resort's gate honking. 'I think the kids have arrived,' Ramzan Chacha said. 'Should you require anything, please call me. I'll attend to the newcomers here.' Both Kabir and Kanval were moved by Ramzan Chacha's philosophy and empowering words. From the window above, they could see him opening the main door as the lady who seemed to be the head of the group got down. One by one, the boys started to come out of the tempo. They were of all ages—6, 8, 10, 12, 14, 15. Their clothes were ordinary, and they all seemed very excited, Kanval observed. One by one they entered the entrance on the left. An 11-year-old boy was escorted by Ramzan Chacha to the main entrance, as the lady held the boy's hand. 'Blind, I believe,' Kabir said, his voice laced with pity.

Later in the evening, after finishing dinner, Kabir went back to his room. Kanval was looking for Ramzan Chacha. Suddenly, the resort became very lively. Children who had arrived were chattering and running around. The lady who had come with them was instructing the children to be disciplined. The buffet was ready, and the children lined up. The lady was feeding the blind boy she had escorted and Kanval watched in admiration from a distance where the boy's face not fully visible. Kanval left the dining hall and came out searching for Ramzan Chacha. It was chilly, and she held herself tightly. Ramzan Chacha appeared holding water bottles and heading towards the dining room. 'Biti, do you need anything?'

Kanval quickly rushed towards him. 'Can I ask for a favour? I need two pherans tomorrow morning. We need to perform a ritual, and since this is a little off-location, the market would be too far away to buy one. Moreover, buying one would be a waste as we will not need it back in Mumbai.'

'Every little thing holds meaning, my dear, especially here in Kashmir. Every purchase or souvenir becomes a cherished memory, and even the smallest contribution helps sustain the lives of those less fortunate, who rely on the support of visitors. Par koi parvaah nahi, biti, it's okay, you can take mine,' Ramzan Chacha said.

'Aur kuch chahiye, biti?' he asked. 'Do you need anything else?'

'Nothing much, just a cup of tea after an hour,' Kanval replied before going back to her room.

Meanwhile, Kabir lay on his left, observing the Kalash with moist eyes. Kanval hoped their arrival in Kashmir had fostered some acceptance and understanding within Kabir.

As night fell, the resort became deserted, and Ramzan Chacha lit a bonfire to keep himself warm.

It was a cold and gloomy morning with a light drizzle and distant thunder. The fog settled on the mountains and low-hanging clouds cast a grey pall over the valley.

After finishing their breakfast, Kanval and Kabir dressed in traditional pherans and made their way downstairs. The resort was quiet as they walked through it in silence.

The siblings made their way towards a nearby bridge, the one that connected the two sides of the river. The Lidder flowed rapidly, its waters deepened by the recent rains.

Kabir walked to the centre of the bridge, feeling lonely. He choked up. Kanval placed a comforting hand on his shoulder, but he couldn't hold back his tears. The pain of losing Umika overwhelmed him.

Kabir's voice quivered, tears streaming down his face. 'Kanval, it's...it's just... I can't...' His voice faltered and he struggled to speak. 'She...she meant everything to me, and now...' He paused, searching for solace, but his words remained incomplete.

The pain overwhelmed him and his voice fragmented into whispers. 'I... I can't...she's...gone and...' Kabir's voice trailed off and he cried uncontrollably. Kanval held him tightly, providing solace.

'It's ok to feel the pain, Bhaiyya,' she whispered softly. 'It's ok to let it out. But remember, sometimes letting go is the only way to move forward. Umika may be gone, but she will always be a part of you. Her memory, her love, will never leave your heart.'

Standing in the heavy rain, Kabir took a deep breath, unwrapped the kalash and poured the ashes into the river, watching them disappear into the currents.

Kanval embraced him tightly. 'You did everything you could, Bhaiyya. You loved her wholeheartedly and that's what truly matters.' Kabir looked up at her, his eyes brimming with tears. 'Is this the culmination of all we had? Dispersed in the wind, lost and gone?'

Kanval offered solace with a tender reply, 'Just like a drop of water merges with the vast ocean, her essence becomes one with the universe. She may be physically dispersed, but her love permeates everything around us, like the fragrance of a blooming flower that lingers long after it has withered.' Kabir took a deep breath, trying to make sense of Kanval's wisdom.

The rain gradually subsided and the clouds started to disperse, revealing a faint glimmer of sunshine. The universe seemed to have stopped crying with him, signalling that it was time to carry on. 'Thank you, Kanval,' he whispered, holding her tightly.

In the silence that enveloped them, the sound of rushing water beneath the bridge grew louder and more urgent, as if the river itself was trying to capture their attention. A piercing cry shattered the air, jolting both of them out of their grief. It was the sound of someone in distress.

Kabir's heart raced as he shed his pheran and dove into the freezing water. He swam towards the struggling figure, reaching the small boy and swimming to a nearby rock. With every muscle burning, Kabir kicked his way back to the edge of the bridge, where Kanval helped him pull the boy out of the water. They laid him on the ground, both shivering from the cold.

The boy's eyes opened, bright blue and resembling a terrified ocean. As they revived him, Kabir and Kanval realized that it was the same blind boy they had seen at the cottage. He was shivering with cold and gasping for air, but Kabir quickly began pressing the water out of his mouth again.

'Oh my God!' A lady called out as she rushed towards them with other boys. She looked Anglo-American and was the one who had accompanied the blind boy into the resort. 'Oh my God! What happened to you?' she cried, looking out for him with others. Ramzan Chacha had also accompanied them. The boy opened his eyes but was too agitated to respond. 'He almost drowned,' Kabir said.

'I think he needs something warm, let's quickly take him back to the resort,' Kabir suggested. Kanval immediately wrapped him in the pheran she was holding. The lady was worried and slapped his cheeks to revive him. Kabir lifted him, and they made their way back to the resort. They laid him down on the bed. Ramzan Chacha came in, lighting the kangdis. 'Don't worry, the water is out of his body. He is only freezing due to the cold. Let the kangdi do its work.'

'All of you go out,' the lady commanded the other boys who had accompanied them into the room. Ramzan Chacha started to rub the boy's palm while Kabir and Kanval watched.

'Thank you so much for saving his life, Sir. My name is Shamrita. I am the boarding warden for these kids,'

'Kabir here, she is Kanval, my sister.'

'I cannot thank you enough. Had something happened to him, I would not have forgiven myself.'

'Please don't be sorry. It was my duty to save his life.'

Kabir came closer to him and wiped the boy's temple.

'He's blind, right?'

'Unfortunately yes.' Kabir closely looked at him with sympathy.

'What's his name?' Kabir enquired.

'Armaan. His name is Armaan,' Shamrita responded.

'Armaan?' Kabir's face lit up. He briefly looked at Kanval before turning back to Shamrita.

'Yes, his name is Armaan.'

'Oh!' Kabir looked at her shocked. He then turned towards Armaan, gazing. That name was too personal to him. It was what both Umika and Kabir had named their child. Armaan was someone whom they wanted so dearly since their wedlock. Something in his name had just returned. He looked at Armaan, his fair skin that had turned red due to the cold, the light brown hair, the sharp jawline and the slim, straight nose. There was something different about Armaan, something that set him apart from the other Kashmiri children.

Kabir felt a spark within him, as if something that had been lost had just been returned to him. 'I had been looking out for him in the garden. I don't know how he reached the river's edge,' Shamrita said.

To Kabir, the irony of Armaan's name hit him hard. It was a spiritual comeback of sorts. He had named his child Armaan, which meant 'desire' or 'wish'. That desire had been crushed, and here there was another Armaan. The contrasting situation was too much for Kabir, so he quickly excused himself.

'Excuse me, I think I need to rest,' he said, turning to leave the room.

Kanval watched Kabir leave the room, feeling a sense of worry. The sight of Armaan had stirred something deep inside him. She followed him out of the resort and found him standing by the bridge looking lost. Thinking of the asthi kalash that had slipped out of his hand. It was gone, lost to the river. Kabir had no idea where it might have ended up. Kabir dropped to the ground and began to cry, overwhelmed by his emotions. Kanval silently took his hand and helped him up. Together, they made their way back to the resort.

Later in the evening, Kabir looked out of the window, sipping his tea observing the relaxed Lidder River. Kanval was packing their bags as they had to leave the next morning. Iravati's call flashed on her mobile and Kanval reassured her mother, 'Mummy, we are leaving tomorrow as planned. Bhaiyya is doing fine and we will have dinner soon. We haven't interacted with anyone here, so please stop worrying.' Iravati's anxiety seemed to only increase with every passing moment. She was a mother after all and the safety of her children was her top priority.

Kanval hung up the phone and turned to Kabir, asking, 'Have you done the web check-in?' Kabir looked at her with tired eyes and said, 'Can we stay here for one more day, if you don't mind?' Kanval was taken aback by his request and asked, 'I wouldn't mind, but what's the reason?' Kabir took a moment to gather his thoughts and said, 'There is a strange peace here that I feel. Despite the unsettling memories from our past, there is something in the air that's calming. I want to stay here for a little while longer.'

Kanval raised her eyebrows and expressed her concern, 'But what about Mummy? She will be here on the next flight if we don't return on schedule.' Kabir looked at her, contemplating a way out, and replied, 'Convince her or make some excuse about the weather or landslides. You please take care of this; I don't have enough energy to deal with this.'

Kanval couldn't help but smile at his cleverness, 'Sure, let's go join the kids.' Kabir nodded, feeling his tired mind finally starting to relax. He had grown strangely attached to this place wanting to linger just a little while longer.

Shamrita sat on a chair with Armaan wrapped in a blanket next to her, captivated by the warmth of the bonfire. The children around them sang qawwalis and clapped, showcasing their artistic talents. Ramzan Chacha and a few other guests were also enjoying the entertainment.

Kabir and Kanval approached them, and Kabir sat next to Armaan while Shamrita sat next to Kanval. Shamrita apologized, 'I'm so sorry I didn't introduce myself amidst the chaos.' Kanval replied, 'How is he doing now?' referring to Armaan. Kabir's eyes were fixed on Armaan, showing a mixture of affection and relatability. Kabir asked the boy, 'How are you doing?' Armaan turned to him, patting his hand to figure out who was calling him.

He grabbed Kabir's wrist and held it. 'Just encountered a superhero today, thank you for saving my life, Sir,' he responded, feeling drawn towards Kabir. 'He's fine,' Shamrita added.

Kanval turned her attention towards the children, who were having fun among themselves. 'Who are these children, Shamrita?' she asked.

'These children are underprivileged and orphans. I work as a hostel warden in Srinagar and take care of them,' Shamrita explained.

Kabir looked at the other children and their faces, before turning to Armaan with empathy. 'The name of our trust is Hafiz Welfare. Founded by an ex-IPS officer and his wife, they have been doing a lot of social work in the valleys for widows, orphans and the homeless. These are selected children who live with us. We fund their education and nurture their skills.'

Shamrita looked at the children engaged in their respective activities. 'They were selected via a scholarship and we are very proud to have them. Armaan was one of them. Although he can't see, he has great singing skills.'

'Really?' Kanval was surprised. Kabir looked at Armaan with fascination. 'That's wonderful.'

Armaan was listening to the conversation, hoping he wouldn't be asked to sing. 'Of course he can. He has a voice that no one has. Sadly, in Srinagar, we don't have enough music schools, otherwise I would have had him trained,' Shamrita explained, looking at him with pity. 'Although he has no vision, he is much more of a visionary than you and I.'

To Kabir, the idea of Armaan having a singing ability was very soothing, and something about him had already made him enthusiastic. Kabir drew closer to Armaan and whispered, 'Can you sing something for us?'

Armaan got a little nervous. 'Me?' he asked.

'Of course he will,' Shamrita responded. 'Hey bacchas, all of you quickly come here.'

Armaan's heart was beating faster. 'No, I can't sing,' he said.

'Well, every good singer says that,' Kanval laughed. 'Let's cheer him up.'

'Why don't you sing the new song you learned last week, Armaan?' Shamrita suggested.

'But I feel very cold, ma'am. My voice may not be so good,' Armaan said hesitantly.

'Relax, my boy, and show them your talent. Come on,' Shamrita encouraged him.

The surrounding silence made Armaan more nervous. Kabir held a subtle smile, waiting for him to start. Armaan cleared his throat and started to sing:

Tse kus be kus teli wan su kus,
Tse kus be kus teli wan su kus,
Moh batuk loguum Deg,
shwas khich khich wang mayam,
bhruman daras poyun chokum,
tekis takyabane tyuk.

Kabir stood there, lost in the haunting melody of the song. Memories flooded his mind, memories of Umika, memories of a past he had tried to forget. As he watched Armaan sing, disbelief washed over him.

How could this be happening? Kabir wondered.

Kanval also felt a peculiar sense of familiarity as she listened to the song. As the last note faded, Kabir struggled to contain his emotions. The past crashed into the present, unearthing long-buried memories. Looking at Armaan, Kabir's eyes widened with shock, awe and confusion. The lullaby's words unleashed a torrent of emotions within Kabir.

He leaned in closer to Armaan, kissing his forehead. Kanval couldn't help but wonder at the strange coincidence that had brought them all together. The song Armaan had sung was one of Umika's final recordings.

⁂

Kabir lay awake, unable to sleep. Kabir's mind buzzed with questions. What was the lullaby's significance? Why did it feel so familiar? How did Armaan know Umika's recorded song?

Restless, Kabir's thoughts drifted back to Umika, to their final moments together. The pain of her loss resurfaced, evading his sleep. He peered outside, yearning for a glimpse of Armaan, but he found no trace of him.

The next morning, Kanval abruptly awakened Kabir, informing

him of the children's departure. Startled, Kabir asked, 'Leaving? Where are they going?'

'The weekend is over and the children have school tomorrow,' Shamrita replied, as Kabir struggled to process the news.

Kabir's heart raced with the suddenness of it all. He wanted to know where Armaan was. But before he could ask, Kanval pointed and said, 'There he is,' as Ramzan Chacha led Armaan out of the cottage building.

Kabir's breath caught in his throat as he saw the boy looking fresh and angelic, and he couldn't help but smile at him. 'So, we are leaving, and I can't thank you enough again for saving his life,' Shamrita said. Kabir didn't want Armaan to leave. He could tell that Kanval felt the same way. He wanted to spend more time with the boy, but he knew that he had to let him go.

'Goodbye, guys. It was a wonderful time with you,' Shamrita said as she boarded the bus. Kabir was walking behind Armaan, feeling a heavy heart. Armaan stopped and gazed back. Armaan looked up, trying to sense Kabir's presence. 'Can you come and see me in the hostel?' Armaan asked, his voice filled with hopeful anticipation. Kabir hesitated for a moment, his mind wondering at the unexpected request. In that fleeting pause, Kabir felt a magnetic pull, a curiosity sparked by the young boy's earnestness. With a soft smile, Kabir replied, 'Sure, Rockstar. I'll come to see you. Kabir moved forward with him.

Armaan put his foot on the bus step, halting again. 'Thank you for saving my life, Sir. I shall wait for you. I hope you will come,' Armaan said, his voice filled with a mix of gratitude and longing.

Kabir felt a pang of sadness as he watched Armaan, a genuine desire to be there for him tugging at his heart. 'I will do my best to come and meet you.'

Kabir felt his heart swell with emotions. He hugged the boy, his words choked him up. 'Take good care and we shall meet someday, my dear,' Kabir said as Armaan boarded the bus. As the bus drove away, Kabir, Kanval and Ramzan Chacha stood there until it was out of sight.

Kabir wiped away his tears, feeling a mix of emotions. *I hope you will come.* Armaan's words echoed in his ears and he felt a deep sense of confusion and goodness. Kabir couldn't help but think about Armaan's blindness as he watched the bus disappear into the distance. He felt a deep sense of sympathy for the boy, who had faced such hardship at such a young age.

Kanval's gentle voice broke the silence. 'Are you ok?' she asked, concern evident in her eyes. Kabir nodded silently, unable to find the words to express the storm of emotions raging within him. As they walked back to the cottage, Kabir felt a sense of emptiness, as if a part of him had been left behind on that departing bus. The suddenness of the children's departure had caught him off guard. He struggled to process the conflicting emotions that overwhelmed him.

The coincidence of Armaan's name and Umika's lullaby lingered in Kabir's mind, intensifying the already overwhelming emotions. It made him reflect on the mysterious workings of life, how it brings people together and separates them with equal swiftness.

The decision to stay behind didn't sit well with Iravati; it infuriated her. However, the siblings remained unfazed and gave her a plausible excuse. The resort felt empty without the laughter and joy of the children. To ease the tension, Ramzan Chacha suggested they go on an outing to Betaab Valley, known for its natural beauty. The valley enchanted them with its lush green mountains, chinar and pine trees and the tranquil Lidder River, adorned in shades of greenish blue.

During their excursion, a tribal man approached them, offering to take a photograph with his lamb for a small fee. Kanval found delight in the encounter, while Kabir climbed up a nearby Tree House, capturing a moment in time. They also visited the scenic Aru Valley, with its picturesque meadows, misty valleys and enchanting Pine trees. The sparkling river under the sunlight creates a stress-free ambience far removed from the chaos of Mumbai.

As rain began to pour, Kabir and Kanval sought refuge in a tent, inadvertently overhearing a conversation.

One man said, 'This place is wonderful, not like the ones they show in the media. The people here are actually so wonderful in hospitality.' The other man replied, 'Well, what else can they do if they don't treat us well? This place is tourist-dependent. They depend on us for their livelihood. Considering the crimes these people have done in the past, they better behave.'

Kanval's frustration grew and she couldn't contain her response, 'Why bother coming here if you despise everything and everyone? Funny how you have all the answers while my own family, who has lived through it all, doesn't seem to share your complaints!' Kabir felt embarrassed by the confrontation but understood Kanval's deep affection for the place and her genuine care for its people. Leaving the tent, Kanval's anger simmered as she whispered to Kabir, a touch of amusement in her voice, 'He's spent his youth God knows where, harbouring all that hatred. Can't let go of negativity even with one foot in the grave.' Kabir tried to soothe her, saying, 'Calm down, young girl.' However, Kanval remained unyielding. 'Blind or simply clueless? How can he miss the mesmerizing beauty and positive vibes here? He's like a walking negativity bomb, threatening the peace and happiness of this place. Maybe he should take a crash course in appreciating life before spreading his misery around!'

Kabir chuckled at Kanval's words. Trying to calm Kanval down, Kabir spoke with a composed demeanour, 'Kanval, the world is filled with diverse opinions and perspectives. Instead of trying to change others, let us embrace our own inner peace and rise above the negativity.' Kanval shook her head in disbelief, but couldn't help expressing her incredulity, 'But wait, here's the icing on the cake—Mr Wisdom knows it all, convinced he's an expert on Kashmir just by watching those sensational news channels! It's like relying on a comedy show for accurate information. Those channels thrive on spreading misconceptions and stereotypes, completely missing the vibrant reality of Kashmir. It's laughable, really!' Kabir nodded in agreement, understanding her frustration. 'Well, Kanval, some people find their entertainment in ignorance. Let them be entertained in absurdity.' Their conversation reflected a shared understanding, and they returned to the resort to pack their bags for the next day. Kanval, curious about Kabir's state of mind, asked with a touch of concern, 'How are you feeling now?'

Kanval curiously asked as if performing Umika's last rites in the way she had insisted had made any impact on Kabir. 'Kanval, it's like I'm caught between two worlds. One pulling me towards the serenity of spirituality, while the other tugs me back to the complexities of everyday life. It's a beautiful confusion, a dance of seeking and surrendering.'

Iravati called again, and Kanval decided to answer the call. 'Mummy, can't you just—' Iravati interrupted, 'I want you to check your message box on your phone.' With that, she disconnected the call instantly. 'Hello, what?' Kabir approached Kanval, curious. Kanval opened her message inbox.

Chapter 3

Chinar Kuth, next to the bridge, Gawkadal, Srinagar

Address of our old house. You will go there and bring an old photograph of me and Purushottam hanging in the drawing room. House may or may not exist. Do not talk to anyone there, do not ask me anything else.

Kabir and Kanval sat in silence, lost in their own thoughts about their mother's strange message. 'Isn't it strange, Kanval?' he asked. Kanval confirmed. 'Certainly'

'Don't know what she is up to,' Kabir said. 'It's certain that she's torn between two worlds.' Kanval responded. 'It's like she's carrying the load of her past on her shoulders at the same time as she's trying to move forward.'

'You should have been a philosopher,' Kabir said. Kanval rolled her eyes. 'I'm just stating the obvious, maybe it's Papa or the only materialistic memory of him.'

'Mummy and her surprises,' Kanval said, shaking her head in disbelief. Kabir nodded in agreement, his mind still preoccupied with the strange message. 'I just hope we can find the house and the photograph,' he said.

Thrilled at the prospect of visiting their old house, they couldn't contain their excitement.

The next morning, they prepared to leave for Srinagar. After breakfast, Ramzan Chacha became emotional. 'Phir kab aaoge, beta?' he asked, his voice cracking. 'When will you come next?' Kabir hugged him and replied, 'We will come back soon, Chacha. Thank you for everything. You have been a great help to us.'

'Allah ke hawale, beta, may God protect you, take care,' Chacha bid them farewell.

As they departed, Kabir and Kanval experienced mixed emotions. The anticipation of visiting their childhood home filled Kabir with subtle excitement. He couldn't wait to see if the house had withstood the test of time. Guided by his mother's wish, they drove through the bustling and chaotic streets of Srinagar, a stark contrast to the tranquillity of Pahalgam.

Their journey took them past the iconic Lal Chowk, heavily guarded, and deeper into the heart of the city. Crossing the Zero Bridge, Kabir caught a glimpse of the majestic River Jhelum flowing through the city, symbolizing life itself. The temples, khanqaahs, mosques and mansions along its banks reflected the city's rich history and culture.

Kabir's heart skipped a beat at the sight of the familiar architecture of old bridges and roads, reminiscent of his childhood in Gawkadal. Amidst the passing tourist buses, the world seemed to pause as they navigated the narrow lanes of the old city, finally reaching the road leading to their ancestral house.

'There it is, our house,' Kabir exclaimed, pointing to a grand wooden mansion amidst the city's chaos. Though the house had aged, it stood tall, embodying cherished memories and stories within its walls.

As the car stopped on the opposite end of the bridge, Kabir and Kanval stepped out and walked towards the L-shaped lanes that led to their childhood home. Kanval was overwhelmed with emotions despite lacking personal memories.

Observing the scene from a distance, Bashar had grown accustomed to witnessing Pandits revisiting their homes in Habba Kadal, once a Pandit stronghold. Hand in hand, Kabir and Kanval approached their childhood residence, filled with longing and uncertainty. The dead-end street led them to a small alley that opened up to the house's main entrance. As they neared the door, Kabir noticed a large iron lock obstructing their path. Puzzled, he held the lock in his hand, contemplating their next move.

Just then, Tarannum emerged from the house, adjusting her dupatta. Initially unable to recognize them, she gradually realized who stood before her. A sense of familiarity and an undeniable connection washed over her as she quickened her steps, eventually coming face to face with them.

Tarannum's excitement and disbelief mingled in her expression. Her gaze shifted between Kabir and Kanval, trying to capture every detail of their faces. Overwhelmed, she could no longer contain her emotions.

'Kabiraaa,' she exclaimed, tightly gripping his arm. 'Sarfaraz Sahab, Sarfaraz Sahab, jaldi wala, wala yowir, come here quickly!' she called out excitedly. Her heart raced, tears welling in her eyes. Kabir was taken aback by Tarannum's sudden outpouring of emotions but soon recognized her.

'Aunty,' he said, a smile spreading across his bewildered face, recollecting her younger face embedded in his memory. 'You remember me after all these years.' 'Myoun nechu chu gomut yootah boad, my son has grown up.' Tarannum couldn't believe it. Kabir still remembered her after all these years.

She was overwhelmed with emotion as she looked at both Kabir and Kanval. 'I knew it was you,' she said, her voice choked with tears. 'I could feel it in my heart. Who else could it be?'

Kanval looked at her in confusion, trying to make sense. 'Itni badi ho gayee Kanval?' she asked, smiling. Kanval had no idea who Tarannum was. Their mother never spoke about her. It was an easy guess that Kanval was the younger version of Iravati, with similar looks.

Sarfaraz finally appeared, smiling at the sight of Kanval and Kabir. Tarannum quickly introduced them and he was overjoyed to meet them. 'Where is Iravati?' Tarannum asked, her voice trembling slightly.

Kanval held on to her arms, 'Mummy is doing fine. She's at home in Mumbai.' Although she had no idea who Tarannum was, her presence was enough to make her realize she was someone close to her mother and their family. 'Purushottam kati chu?' Sarfaraz enquired. Kabir and Kanval looked at each other again. They had no answer. Their silence was an indication enough to both Tarannum and Sarfaraz.

Kabir looked out of the window at the sparkling green water of the Jhelum. The interior was cozy, with plush sofas and armchairs inviting them to relax. The curtains were drawn, letting in a soft, filtered light that illuminated the space. The Iranian carpets on the floor were finely woven, and the cushions evenly placed at each corner added to the homely atmosphere.

Tarannum's hospitality was warm and welcoming, as if she was their mother's real sister. She had prepared a delicious wazwaan with yakhni and kebabs, served in copper vessels with intricate designs. The rice was almost like pearls, with a unique taste. There was rista curry, lehabi kabab, roghan josh and lamb yakhni. The meat was a bit hard to chew but appetizing.

'Your parents and Dadaji had a fixed appointment for lunch with us every Sunday,' Tarannum said. 'They loved the rogan josh I made.' Kabir started to feel how difficult it must have been for Iravati to contain all her emotions for so many years and not speak a word about her past.

'As much as we tried saving your family, we couldn't do so properly,' Tarannum cried. 'Iravati, she is so upset that she hasn't looked back at us once.' Sarfaraz was seemingly upset too. 'It was a fateful night for all of us. Kakalal died, Purushottam died, my younger brother, Noman, died, and within no time, we lost Aariz too.' Noman and Aariz were two new names to the siblings, but this was not the proper time to ask or enquire about them. After lunch Sarfaraz took them to their old house.

Entering their old house, nostalgia overtook Kabir. However, the deteriorating condition shattered that feeling. The once-grand house was in desperate need of renovation, with peeling paint, weakened wood, significant moisture and cobwebs. The desolate corridors and tattered furnishings spoke of the house's abandonment.

Sarfaraz explained that they used to clean and maintain the house regularly until the Municipal Corporation asked them to stop. Tarannum would secretly tend to the kitchen, knowing Iravati valued cleanliness. In the bedroom, they discovered the portrait requested by Iravati. It was an emotional moment for Kabir, as he saw his father's face after years. The partially open bedroom door indicated that someone had been residing there. The portrait hanging on the wall served as their sole reminder of their father, prompting Kabir to remove it from its place and hold it close, tears streaming down his face.

Leaving the house, Kabir felt the spirit of the home had been taken away. The memories within those walls felt coming back. The journey back to Tarannum's house was filled with silence, heavy with emotions. Kanval tried to contact Iravati but received no response. The Zargaras also lacked the strength and courage to confront Iravati. The loss they had suffered went beyond ordinary grief. Devastating tragedy that night had shattered their lives too. Kanval understood that bringing her mother back to reality and facing the past wouldn't be easy. However, with Tarannum and Sarfaraz's support, she was determined to do so. She recognized it as the only way to heal the lingering wounds that had remained open for far too long. It was time to depart. Grateful for the hospitality and kindness they had received, they prepared to return home. Tarannum and Sarfaraz pleaded with them to stay a little longer, as there was much to discuss, share and grieve. Just then, the weather took a turn for the worse. Heavy rain poured down accompanied by thunderstorms, severely limiting visibility. Kabir gazed out the window and shook his head. 'Looks like we won't be able to leave anytime soon,' Kabir remarked. They realized they would have to stay back until the weather cleared. Within an hour, they received a notification informing them that their flight had been cancelled and rescheduled due to adverse weather conditions. It appeared as though nature was determined to keep them within the confines of this house for the night.

Sarfaraz and Tarannum were delighted that they wouldn't be leaving. 'Yahan mosam aur mahol kab kharab ho jaye iska koi pata nahi, beta, you never know when the weather or the situation here might turn bad,' Tarannum said. Kanval excused herself to inform Iravati about the development. She sent a text, only to receive an immediate call. 'Leave that house immediately, do you hear me?' Iravati snapped. 'Who gave you permission to stay there? Do you realize the danger you're putting yourselves in? I specifically instructed you to collect a single item from the house, not to turn the neighbour's residence into your permanent abode. But of course, Kanval, you always have to go against my every word.'

Kanval took a deep breath and tried to keep her voice steady. 'Mummy, we're safe and sound here. Tarannum and Sarfaraz have been nothing but hospitable to us. In fact, Bhaiyya and I have been able to reconnect with each other and with our past. This place has been therapy to us and..?' 'So you are determined to disobey me?' Iravati remarked. 'Mummy, the weather is really bad right now. It's not safe for us to go anywhere. We're stuck here, whether we like it or not, and honestly, I don't want to leave just yet. We're finally finding some peace here and I don't want to let that go.'

Iravati scoffed. 'Peace? Seek peace in a nearby luxury hotel. Those people there are not to be trusted.' Kanval felt her anger rising again. 'Mummy, why do you always have to be so negative? Aunty and Uncle have been nothing but kind to us. They've welcomed us into their home, fed us and taken care of us. How can you say that they're not to be trusted?' Iravati let out a bitter laugh. 'Trust? What do you know about trust, Kanval? All right!' Agitated, she hung up.

'That was very rude of you, Kanval,' Kabir said sternly as he walked towards her. Kanval immediately felt guilty. She needed to be more respectful, especially since they were guests in someone else's house. 'I… I don't understand her, Bhaiyya. I'm trying to explain the situation, but she is heedless, not ready to listen, and…'

'Behave, Kanval,' Kabir warned her. 'Next time, you will talk to her very respectfully.' Kabir's words hit her like a reprimand from an elder.

Meanwhile, Tarannum and Sarfaraz had made Kanval and Kabir feel at home. Kabir had developed a newfound respect for them. He couldn't help but feel grateful for their kindness and hospitality.

Kabir woke up from his nap and gazed outside the window, only to find that the heavy rainfall was showing no signs of stopping. He noticed a message from the airlines, notifying him that their flight was rescheduled until further instructions. Realizing that the weather would only make it harder to leave, he decided to stay back. After dinner, they all gathered in the drawing room. For Kabir, it was a chance to learn more about their family's past and the events that Iravati had concealed. Amazed by the kindness and hospitality of his former neighbours, he couldn't fathom what could have driven his mother to distance herself from them for so long.

Sarfaraz began to recount the tragic events that unfolded on that fateful night. 'Your Dadaji was a remarkable man. He was respected by everyone in the city for his intelligence, discipline and love for others. He was a great patron of the arts and culture and contributed immensely to Radio Kashmir.' Kabir listened intently, absorbing every detail.

'What happened to my Dadaji that night?' Kabir asked, his curiosity piqued. 'It's a question that still haunts all of us. I have an idea he was killed, but it would be fair to learn it from you.' Sarfaraz took a deep breath and began, 'That night was the darkest night of our lives. The radio incident had confused us, but I wanted to confirm, so I went there the next day with much risk.'

'Did you find him?' Kabir asked, his curiosity piqued. Sarfaraz nodded slowly, 'Yes, I found him in the studio, motionless. I performed his last rites. But after that, Tarannum and I went to the camps in Jammu to search for your family, but we couldn't find you all. It was a traumatic experience, but we didn't give up. We kept searching for days.'

Kabir's heart sank at the news while Kanval wept. Sarfaraz and Tarannum both put a comforting hand on Kabir's shoulder. Kanval sat silently, her eyes filled with sadness. Tarannum reached over and patted her hand reassuringly. 'We did what we could, my dear. We couldn't bear to see our dear neighbours suffer.'

Kabir was surprised to learn that Tarannum and Sarfaraz had tried to find his family in the camps after they left Kashmir. He felt a deep sense of gratitude for Tarannum and Sarfaraz, and for their kindness and compassion towards his family. He wished Iravati knew about their efforts. Kabir was on the edge of his seat, eagerly waiting to hear more about the past.

'You said you lost your younger brother the very same night. How did he die? Also, I remember you mentioned something about Aariz. Who is Aariz?' he asked with curiosity. Tarannum and Sarfaraz exchanged a glance, a deep sadness reflected in their eyes. Kabir looked over to Kanval, noticing the worry lines on her forehead. They remained silent, causing Kabir to grow uneasy.

After a brief pause, Sarfaraz finally spoke up, his voice low and hesitant. 'Don't you remember Aariz bhaya, who took you for rides in the boat down in the river?' he said, his tone solemn. Kabir tried to remember, but his memory was hazy. 'Noman was shot dead while he was trying to help your fleeing family.'

Kabir's mouth fell open in shock, his eyes widening in disbelief. 'What?' he exclaimed, shocked to the core of his heart. 'What about Aariz? Where has he been all this time?' Tarannum and Sarfaraz exchanged glances, their eyes filled with a mix of shock and confusion. 'Didn't Iravati tell you anything?' Tarannum enquired. 'She hardly speaks about her past, let alone that fateful night,' Kabir replied.

Surprised and confused, Tarannum wanted to convey something, but hesitated. 'He was associated with the liberation movement. We lost him, Kabir. We lost him to fate,' Sarfaraz said. The revelation hit the siblings like a thunderbolt, leaving them speechless, and their minds grappling to process the discovery. Kanval was unable to contain her curiosity, she asked. 'Are you telling me that he joined the militants?'

The room fell into a silence. Sarfaraz, wearing an expression of inconclusiveness, conveyed through his face that he had no definitive answers to offer. 'Well, that was a time when militancy was at its peak. There was a revolution going on here, people of all ages, especially the youth, were gripped in what was supposed to be a freedom movement. We don't really know how and when Aariz joined them at such a young age. To us, it was very shocking. He was only a kid,' Sarfaraz explained, with a heavy voice.

Kabir finally understood why his mother had such deep-seated hatred towards their former neighbours. 'What, what happened to him?' Kanval asked, her voice laced with eagerness. 'After two days of this incident, we had gone to Jammu to look for you people, leaving him here. When we returned home he was missing, never to be found till date.' Sarfaraz revealed, his eyes filling with tears.

'Oh God!' Kanval exclaimed, her hands flying up to cover her mouth. 'We searched and made numerous police complaints but did not find him,' Tarannum added. 'We searched for him everywhere but could not find him. Some people say he must have met with an accident, some say he must have been encountered and some are of the opinion that he must have gone…' Sarfaraz trailed off, his words laced with unspeakable dread.

Kabir leaned forward, eager to hear the final possibility. 'Where?' Sarfaraz hesitated, his face contorted with pain. 'Nowhere! May God bless him wherever he is.'

Kabir and Kanval exchanged a look, sensing that there was more to the story than they were being told. But Kabir didn't want to push their former neighbours any further, knowing that the revelations were already too much for them to bear. Kanval's curiosity was piqued as she listened to Tarannum and Sarfaraz's story about their lost family members. She wanted to know more, especially about the mysterious disappearances of young men and half-widows of Kashmir. Kabir, on the other hand, felt a mix of confusion and embarrassment as he tried to process the shocking revelations.

As Kanval prepared to ask another question, Kabir swiftly raised a stern eyebrow, signalling her to remain silent. The revelation about Sarfaraz's family history left Kabir in shock. He struggled to comprehend how someone so kind and hospitable could have such a tragic past. However, he tried to maintain a calm demeanour, not wanting to cause further discomfort to their hosts. Tarannum paused, lost in her thoughts. 'Life is unpredictable, isn't it?' she mused. 'We often believe we have control over our destinies, only to be confronted with unexpected events and their consequences.' Kabir nodded in agreement, recognizing the truth of her words. After a moment of silence, Tarannum continued, revealing more about their relationship with Noman and Aariz.

'We had no children of our own, Noman's wife passed away from cancer when Aariz was just two years old. I raised Aariz as my own, showering him with maternal love and care. Iravati tutored him, providing not only academic education but also instilling discipline. Noman was unemployed and lacked direction in life. After his wife's death, he became negligent and sought quick money through unlawful means, involving himself in arms trading with grave consequences. He took Aariz along with him wherever he went so as to avoid suspicion, portraying himself as a family man.' Kabir interjected, his voice filled with disbelief. 'You were aware of his activities? You let him continue?' Tarannum lowered her gaze. 'I eventually discovered Noman's secret and expelled him from our home, keeping Aariz under my care. But by then, it was too late. This was not the Aariz we had raised. His language, behaviour and choice of company had changed drastically. We were simple people trying to build our tourism business, and had Noman been responsible, it could have flourished.'

Kanval leaned forward. 'What happened later? How did you handle the situation?' Tarannum took a deep breath, gathering her thoughts. 'After a few days, Noman returned home, deeply missing his child. Aariz missed him badly too. I allowed him back on the condition that he completely abandon his illicit activities and he promised to do so. However, Aariz became uncontrollable. We attempted to send him back to school, only to discover that he hardly attended any classes. We had no idea where he spent his time or who he associated with.'

Kabir's frustration grew. 'Why didn't you intervene? You knew he was in trouble!' Tarannum's voice quivered as she replied, 'The impact on his mind was profound. He outsmarted even his own father. Noman felt immense guilt for what he had done to his child. No amount of punishment or reprimand could change Aariz. It was as if his youthful innocence had been stripped away. We consulted Kakalal, who was deeply saddened by the reality we faced. He suggested sending Aariz abroad to a reputable school and enrolling him in a hostel without delay. We had connections with foreign tourists; a gentleman from South Africa who frequently visited our houseboat promised to assist us. However, none of us had passports at the time. We began the process of obtaining Aariz's passport, but within days, Kashmir erupted into a battlefield, throwing our lives into chaos. That night, most of us lost something or someone.' The image of a young boy becoming embroiled in a world of rebellion was haunting. Kanval's heart ached as she imagined the innocent Aariz being robbed of his childhood and manipulated by his own father. She could feel Tarannum's anguish as she spoke of their desperate attempts to save Aariz, sending him away to foreign lands in the hopes of giving him a chance at a better life.

Tarannum continued, 'Aariz was our hope for the future. But no matter how much we loved him, no matter how hard we tried to control him, we couldn't shield him from the chaos of the world. It's like trying to catch the wind in your hand.'

Kabir and Kanval sat in silence, lost in their own thoughts, realizing that the truth was never simple, that the lines between right and wrong were often blurred. He was both angry and confused, unable to conclude anything with the Zargars, and felt a pinch of truthfulness in his mother's behaviour in asking them to stay away from this family.

Kanval, on the other hand, was lost in deep contemplation. She sympathized with the Zargars, understanding the impact of the social and political turmoil that had engulfed the region. In her mind, the struggles of the family were a reflection of the larger issues that plagued Kashmir.

Tarannum explained, 'Please don't judge Aariz too harshly. He was only twelve years old, the aura that was running in the air during those times was beyond comprehension.'

Kabir retired to bed that night. He kept thinking about the conversation that happened. He was in two minds about this family. *Are they good people? Have we done the right thing by coming here? How safe are we here? Are we going to be troubled or questioned by the authorities? Are we being watched? Should we leave tomorrow and go to a hotel?* There were so many questions in his mind. He felt the best thing to do would be to sleep. He turned to his side facing the window. The thunderstorm did not cease; it continued to rain relentlessly and the flow of Jhelum had intensified.

The philosophy of the river was not lost on him. It was a powerful force that could take life or give life. *Across the same river again, with a different voyage. Rivers of Kashmir are treacherous. If you enter, you are either drowned or rescued. Its waters may lead us to safety with the aid of a boat, or they may require the strength of bare hands to save us from drowning*, he thought.

It reminded him of their voyage up to Dal Lake on that fateful night. It also reminded him of Armaan's drowning. The contrast between the two drownings was striking. In one there was isolation and tragedy, while in the other, there was heroism and a sense of purpose.

Suddenly, his thoughts shifted to Armaan, the blind boy he had saved from drowning in the river. He wished Umika was there beside him in this moment of confusion. Her presence always gave him a sense of clarity. He wondered why Armaan's memories suddenly flooded his mind. He wondered if Umika had anything to do with him being here in Kashmir, where he had met Armaan. Had her love for the place and her desire to visit it brought him there, to the very spot where he had saved the blind boy's life? Or was it just a coincidence, a mere twist of fate that led him to this moment, meeting another Armaan, who, even if not their own son, had the same name?

The next morning, Kabir woke up to clear skies after a night of rain. He immediately looked for Kanval, wanting to discuss something with her. Kanval was assisting Tarannum to prepare breakfast in the kitchen. Kabir called Kanval upstairs and began to speak. 'We should leave,' he said. Kanval looked surprised. 'Why?' Kanval could sense Kabir's confusion evident on his face. 'Uncle and Aunty are honest and kind people.' 'I know, but I was thinking about Mummy,' Kabir replied. 'We should trust her decisions.'

'Planning to leave?' Tarannum asked, as she entered the room unexpectedly. Tarannum looked at Kabir and Kanval with a gentle smile, looking at a visibly embarrassed Kabir. 'I know it's been difficult for you both, especially with Iravati's anger looming over you. But trust me, she's not angry at you. She's angry at the situation, at life for throwing her such a curveball. Sometimes, we all need time to process our emotions and come to terms with things.'

'Iravati and I have walked a path that transcends time and space. Our bond was forged long before you were even born, Kabir. I have witnessed her laughter, her tears and her deepest secrets.'

Hearing Tarannum's perspective made him realize that maybe it wasn't all about them. 'Just like the moon behind the clouds, it's there, always shining, waiting for the right moment to reveal itself. One day, my dear, she will return to her house, where her heart truly belongs.'

'I understand that, Aunty,' Kabir said, a small smile forming on his face. 'I guess we were just worried that we might be causing trouble for you and Uncle.'

Tarannum chuckled softly. 'You really think so? You and Kanval are my extended family navigating life's adventures together, so relax.' Kanval nodded in agreement, feeling a sense of gratitude towards Tarannum. Tarannum smiled warmly at them both. 'Now, let's go have some breakfast and enjoy the sunshine. Mausam thik ho gaya hai, the weather has cleared up, and you should make the most of it.'

During breakfast, Tarannum spoke up. 'Sarfaraz Sahab, I think it's best if Kabir and Kanval leave today,' she said, leaving everyone feeling awkward. 'What? Where will they go?' Sarfaraz asked. Kabir and Kanval exchanged embarrassed looks. *She must have really felt bad*, Kabir thought, feeling the need to apologize. 'Tarannum?' Sarfaraz whispered. Kabir quickly interrupted, 'No Uncle, it's ok. We'll leave...' 'Leave where?' Tarannum asked. 'I meant, you guys should leave for the houseboat today, our houseboat.' She clarified. 'You anyway have your flight scheduled tomorrow. The real hospitality and the essence of Kashmiriyat, you will feel it there somewhat. We have houseboats in the Dal Lake, which is our old tourism business. Don't you remember anything?' She complained. Tarannum hoped the experience would move Iravati to visit.

Sarfaraz accompanied them for a city tour. Bashar drove them to Dal Lake in no time. As they arrived at the boulevard and set foot on the Ghat, the sight of Dal Lake left them spellbound.

The water changed colours with the sun's gentle touch, reflecting a myriad of shades that transcended earthly beauty. The houseboats floated on the water, like blissful islands of happiness, surrounded by a flock of ducks and fluttering butterflies. Against the backdrop of the snow-capped Zabarwan mountains, the lake looked like a majestic gem guarded by the mountains' grandeur.

As they sat in the shikara, the tranquillity of the lake touched Kabir and Kanval's souls, making them feel as though they had been transported to another world. The shikara was made of deodar wood, with fine curtains and soft cotton sofas to relax on. As they journeyed towards the houseboat, they were surrounded by beauty. Lotus flowers floated on the surface of the water, ducks swam gracefully by and beautiful butterflies flew around.

The houseboat's interior was opulent and luxurious, with Mughal- and Persian-inspired wooden carvings and local artefacts adorning the walls. It featured a large drawing room with modern sofa sets, a dining room and three bedrooms with luxurious amenities. The decor was exquisite, with embroidered details and a royal feel throughout. Despite being on the water, the houseboat had all the amenities of a modern hotel, including electricity, clean water, washrooms, a heater, and a fully-equipped kitchen.

Kabir was struck by memories of his father's death in the same lake as it was his final resting place. He tried to escape the painful memories by taking deep breaths and focusing on the beauty around him. The beauty of the Dal Lake was not just in its colours but in the feeling it evoked in Kabir and Kanval's hearts.

The outer end of the houseboat was a vast wooden platform to walk, with narrow steps leading to the water. Kabir and Kanval came out on the platform to look at the beauty of the Dal Lake. It was peaceful and serene. From a certain distance, one could see a fort towering over the city on the top of a mountain. Kanval inquired about it, only to know that it was Hari Parbat.

'Well, I thought that fort was Pari Mahal. My favourite poet Faiz Ahmed Faiz was married here,' Kanval said.

'Really? Here in Srinagar?' Kabir asked.

'Yes, of course, and you know what? He had a British wife. Their marriage was much ahead of their time when interfaith marriages were almost considered a taboo. Not to forget, their nikaah was performed by Sheikh Abdullah, the then PM of Kashmir. His nikaah contract was designed by the legendary

Allama Iqbal, and it gave lots of special rights to Alys, Faiz's wife,' Kanval said.

'Did you just say the Prime Minister of the first Jammu and Kashmir?' Kabir asked in astonishment.

'Don't be very surprised, dear. With Kashmir's autonomy also came its Prime Minister, but I really, really want to visit Pari Mahal, where his marriage took place,' Kanval expressed.

Kabir was awestruck with the history and knowledge Kanval carried with her. Kanval and Kabir quickly boarded a shikara, and as they glided across the Dal Lake, Kabir was captivated by its ethereal beauty. The shades and hues of the lake were so mesmerizing that all of Kabir's doubts and hesitations about the place and its people vanished into the lake's stunning landscape. They passed by the Nehru Park Island, where a movie was being shot, and the fragrant and colourful flowers in the garden delighted their senses.

As they floated along, they encountered a floating market of vegetables and Kashmiri handicrafts, which reminded Kabir of the city of Venice. They passed by Char Chinar, an isolated yet beautiful small island with four chinar trees, and then saw the Hazrat Bal Mosque in the distance. It had a pearl-shaped white dome with minarets, appearing like a pearl in the lake from a distance. Sarfaraz asked, 'Beta, dekhna chaahoge udhar? Would you like to see?' Kabir had never visited a mosque or dargah in his life. Iravati had kept her children away from Muslim places of worship. Kabir was not sure, but Kanval instantly replied, 'Who wouldn't want to visit such a fine monumental masterpiece, Uncle ji? Please take us there.'

The mosque was located on the banks of the Dal Lake. They passed through the fountains erected before the entrance steps. Upon entering the mosque, they felt a divine silence. Kanval instantly covered her head with a dupatta. Kabir tied his handkerchief on his head as a mark of respect upon seeing Sarfaraz putting on a skull cap.

Kabir experienced a sense of peace and quiet that he had never felt before. The mosque's interior had beautiful red carpets, arch-shaped windows with fine glasses, and a special section for ladies. Sarfaraz explained that the mosque held a special significance as a strand of Prophet Muhammad's hair was stored there. Kabir was left to contemplate as Sarfaraz went to make his prayers. He watched Kanval interacting with burqa-clad ladies near the banks of the lake who were giving away traditional sweets called niyaz to people who were coming to pay respects at the mausoleum.

An old man and a lady with a blind son approached Kabir for alms and Kabir reached into his pocket instantly. Something was very divine about the place, or probably Kabir felt it was so because it was his first-ever visit to a different place of worship that made him feel different. As Kabir's gaze lingered on the blind boy, memories of Armaan flooded his mind once again. He couldn't help but recall the last time he had seen the little boy, who had looked up at him with those big, innocent eyes and asked, *Bhaiyya, will you come and visit me?* The words echoed in his mind, reminding him of the connection he had formed with Armaan during their brief time together. Kabir felt a sense of longing. He wondered where exactly the child was and what he might be doing. The fact that they were in the same city made it all the more difficult for Kabir to shake off the feeling of wanting to see him.

In that moment, the urge to see him grew stronger. He turned to Kanval with a suggestion that they visit the hostel where Armaan stayed. Kabir's emotions, which he had been holding back, began to surface. Kanval sensed the sincerity in his voice and empathetically replied, 'I am missing that little boy as much as you are.' The bond between the siblings had always been strong, but in that moment, it was as if they both shared a common purpose, which was to meet Armaan once again.

Without hesitation, Kanval suggested reaching out to Ramzan Chacha at the hotel back in Pahalgam, since he could help them get in touch with Shamrita. Soon enough, they obtained Shamrita's contact information and were on the phone with her. 'Well, it would be wonderful to have you guys here. I am so sorry that amidst the hustle and bustle, I forgot to share my contact information. You guys come quickly, we are waiting for you,' Shamrita said, her warm voice putting Kabir's mind at ease. Kanval enquired about bringing blankets or clothes for the children, but Shamrita declined, suggesting they bring fruits instead.

Kabir felt a sense of relief knowing that they would finally have the opportunity to meet Armaan. As soon as Sarfaraz arrived to meet them, he took them to the nearby Mughal garden called Nishat Bagh, located on the eastern bank of the Dal Lake. The garden spanned twelve terraces, each representing one of the twelve zodiac signs, with pools and multiple water fountains adorning the centre of each terrace. Majestic chinar trees lined the gardens and walkways ran alongside the pools, creating a picturesque scene.

As they strolled through the garden, the captivating architecture couldn't be ignored. The garden's water was sourced from the Shahe Nahar Canal that connected to the Dal Lake, adding to its charm. When they reached the final terrace, the view of the Dal Lake took their breath away. Sarfaraz explained that the chinar trees had been brought from Persia by the Mughals and it was Emperor Jahangir himself who had the garden built. Kabir and Kanval were left speechless by the sheer beauty and grandeur surrounding them. The intricate architecture, meticulously manicured lawns and sparkling water fountains blended harmoniously, creating a mesmerizing view.

As they strolled along leisurely, Kabir found himself

daydreaming about Umika. He imagined her walking beside him, her hair gently swaying in the breeze and her laughter filling the air. The mere thought of her evoked a sense of longing within him.

Suddenly, something caught Kabir's eye. He saw Umika walking in the garden, holding a child's hand. Intrigued, he followed her, and as the child turned around and smiled at him, Kabir was astonished to realize it was Armaan! Armaan was holding Umika's hand, and the sight left Kabir utterly stunned, unable to comprehend what he was witnessing. A mix of emotions overwhelmed him with confusion, disbelief and a sense of joy. Seeing Umika and Armaan together made Kabir feel strange and confused. It took Kanval's voice to snap him out of this state. Their next destination, Pari Mahal. Driving up over the hill, they reached a fortified gardened terrace that offered a panoramic view of the city. From the hilltop, they could see the Dal Lake, the old city, and the surrounding forests. Sarfaraz shared some historical information, stating that Pari Mahal was originally constructed by Dara Shikoh as a small library but later transformed into a teaching centre for Astronomy and Astrology students.

Kanval chuckled and commented on the name, thinking it would be a den of fairies. Kabir smiled at the light-hearted exchange. Sarfaraz joked, 'I'm not sure about fairies, but I'm certain that a Djinn will show up if we delay any longer.' Their laughter echoed in the air as they continued exploring the enchanting location. Kanval insisted that Kabir take a few photos of himself, as he seemed captivated by the beauty and rarely took photographs.

As mid-afternoon approached, they left for the boarding house situated atop the hill. The car manoeuvred along the rocky road, winding through twists and turns until it finally reached the main gate of the hostel. There, Shamrita stood with Armaan, visibly excited. Shamrita warmly embraced Kanval, welcoming them all. Kabir bent down, holding Armaan's arms, 'How are you,

Mr Rockstar?' Armaan turned his head towards Kabir, his dark-blue eyes scanning left and right. Kabir hugged him tightly, feeling a profound sense of joy and warmth. With a smile, Armaan replied, 'Thank you for keeping your promise to meet me, Sir'.

Shamrita led them inside the hostel, a two-storey L-shaped building surrounded by a spacious garden compound. Kabir held Armaan's hand as they walked towards the main hall upstairs, guiding him along the way. The other children had already gathered in the hall, eagerly awaiting the arrival of their visitors. Kanval handed the fruits to Shamrita, who swiftly arranged for some snacks. Settled down, Shamrita began speaking, her tone filled with mixed emotions. 'I have been managing the children here. Initially, it housed blind people, elderly couples and these orphans together. However, I don't have good news to share with you.'

Kabir's heart raced as he anxiously asked, 'What is it?' Shamrita continued, 'The management has already closed down two wings due to a lack of funds and now they want to shut down the orphanage as well.' Kanval expressed her shock and exchanged a worried glance with Kabir while Armaan sat between them. Sensing the tension, Kabir held Armaan even closer. Shamrita explained, 'I have been fighting to keep the children here, but I don't think I can convince the management for much longer.'

Shamrita's voice was emotionally charged. 'I came all the way from South Africa to take care of these children, and I have done everything within my means. I have organized skill-set workshops, focused on human resource development and tutored these children for school. I put in all my efforts to bring in some novelty in them. These children are brilliant and talented in their own ways, but sadly there's no future for them over here.' 'But in case the hostel shuts down, where will the children go?' Kabir asked anxiously. As they discussed the future of the children, Kabir couldn't help but notice Armaan's anxious fidgeting with his fingers, a sign of his anxiety. He reached out and held Armaan's hand, offering comfort and support. Kanval saw the worry on Kabir's face. Armaan, in turn, felt the warmth of the siblings as he sat between them. Armaan could feel the kindness and compassion emanating from Kabir and Kanval, and he felt a sense of safety and security in their presence. To Kanval, it was evident that Armaan had taken a special place in Kabir's heart, and the recent events had stirred up his long-buried desire for fatherhood. Kanval couldn't help but feel anxious as she thought about how this might affect Kabir's future, especially given the fact that Armaan was at an orphanage and in need of parental support, anticipating things quickly as she saw the evident scenario shaping up.

Kanval knew that Kabir had been through a lot of mental trauma after Umika's death, and his recent behaviour seemed to indicate that he was finally starting to ease out of that pain. She also knew that psychological factors related to completing his family may have been playing around in his mind and Armaan's presence had added to his incomplete joy of fatherhood. However, Kanval also knew that they had to tread carefully. Iravati's reservations and prejudices against the valley's people and the Muslim community were well-known. She didn't want Kabir's newfound happiness to be shattered because of her prejudices.

Kanval's concern stemmed from the fact that if their relationship kindled, Iravati's stance on Kabir and his relationship with the child would be a major obstacle. As she watched Kabir with Armaan, she couldn't help but think about the implications of his growing attachment to the boy. She saw the raw emotion in his eyes, the confusion and vulnerability that he was experiencing. She knew that he was in a delicate state, one that required careful handling. Kanval leaned forward and spoke in a soft tone, 'Shamrita, can I ask you something about Armaan?'

Shamrita's eyes flickered for a moment before she nodded. 'Of course, what do you want to know?' Kanval hesitated for a moment, choosing her words carefully. 'I was just wondering about Armaan's parents. Do you know anything about them?' Shamrita's expression clouded over for a moment, and she looked over towards Armaan, sitting quietly between Kabir and Kanval. 'Armaan has not seen his parents in the past five years,' she said quietly. 'He was brought to this boarding two days after I came here and I have been taking care of him ever since.'

Kabir's hand reached out to gently pat Armaan's head and he shot a sympathetic glance at Shamrita. Kanval couldn't help but notice a flicker of suspicion in the back of her mind, but she quickly pushed it away. It was best not to jump to conclusions without more information, and it was best to avoid details in front of the little boy. Sarfaraz was observing the entire scene, his heart filled with emotions. There was something about the child that caught his attention, but he couldn't quite put his finger on it. Meanwhile, Shamrita led them on a tour of the hostel.

'I can see that this place means a lot to you perhaps; you're doing a wonderful job here. It's not easy to take care of so many children, especially when they come from difficult backgrounds,' Kabir said.

Shamrita felt grateful. 'It's not just about taking care of them, it's about giving them hope for the future, that's what we're trying to do here.'

Kanval, who had finished taking selfies with the children, joined in the conversation. 'It's amazing to see how these children are learning new things and exploring their talents,' she said. 'All thanks to your efforts, Shamrita.'

'Occasionally, we have been inviting artists to conduct workshops for theatre and singing and the children have a lot to benefit from them. We have also successfully conducted

Taekwondo workshops and training and many of these children have been a pro in learning them,' Shamrita said. Looking at Armaan, Kabir asked, 'What about you, Armaan? Do you have any interest in music?'

Armaan shook his head. 'I am learning to play the guitar.'

'That's great to hear,' Kabir said, smiling. 'Had I lived here, I would have taught you myself.' But it was about time they left, as it was almost the sunset hour. Shamrita expressed her gratitude for their visit but also shared her uncertainty about the hostel's future. As Kabir knelt before Armaan, his heart was filled with emotions. He had grown fond of the little boy and was now feeling a strong sense of attachment towards him.

Armaan, on the other hand, had mixed emotions. He was happy to have met Kabir and pained to have a comforting hand leaving.

'When do I visit you next time, Rockstar?' Kabir asked, trying to keep his voice steady. Armaan remained silent for a moment, lost in thought. 'How do I connect to you again, my dear?' Armaan paused for a moment, then replied softly, 'If you share your number with me, I'll keep it safe in my memory. That way, I can reach out to you whenever I want.' A smile spread across Kabir's face at the suggestion. 'Tell me your digits.'

For Armaan, remembering numbers was an art that he had mastered over the years. As Kabir recited his mobile number, Armaan's mind started to paint a vivid picture of it. He imagined the numbers forming shapes and colours, and his fingers traced them in the air as if he could see them.

For him, remembering the number was not just a matter of practicality but also a way of holding on to the memory of their meeting and the warmth and compassion that Kabir had shown him.

Taking a last group photograph, they walked towards the car. Kanval hugged Armaan tightly. She could feel the love and warmth emanating from the child, and it was a bittersweet feeling knowing that they would have to leave him behind. The other children had also assembled to bid them farewell. Armaan had a heavy heart as Kabir was leaving. Kabir's concern and compassion had made Armaan feel important and loved.

'When will you come again?' Armaan asked as Kabir was getting into the car. 'Soon, my dear,' Kabir replied, kissing his forehead before leaving. Kanval, on the other hand, turned back and waved a final goodbye to Armaan and the other children. She was emotional too and knew that this visit to Kashmir had meant a lot to both her and Kabir.

As they drove, Kabir couldn't bring himself to turn and wave goodbye, but he saw Armaan in the rearview mirror and quickly looked away.

As they started to move, Sarfaraz asked him to stop. 'Ruk, ruk,' he said, his eyes fixed on Armaan. 'What happened, Uncle?' Kabir asked, feeling a shiver run down his spine at the strange look on Sarfaraz's face.

'Nothing, I'll just come,' Sarfaraz replied, his voice barely audible. He got down from the car and ran towards the main gate, leaving everyone else puzzled. As the others went inside, Armaan walked slowly with Shamrita.

Suddenly, Sarfaraz appeared out of nowhere, gasping for breath. He caught hold of Armaan's hand and looked at him with a strange mix of pity and fascination. 'You are ok?' Shamrita asked, trying to make sense of the situation.

Without saying a word, Sarfaraz took out his wallet and gave a five hundred rupee note to Armaan. 'Iski kya zaroorat hai, Sir? What's the need for this?' Shamrita protested, but Sarfaraz simply put his hand on Armaan's head and said, 'Baccha pyaara hai bibi, rakh lo. The child is beautiful, please keep it.'

A sudden wave of emotion had overtaken Sarfaraz the moment

he saw Armaan. 'Thank you,' Shamrita said, looking at him strangely as Sarfaraz went back to the car. 'Everything is okay, Uncle? Where did you go?' Kanval asked, sensing his emotion.

Sarfaraz shrugged away her concern. 'All good all good, let's go,' Bashar said quickly and revved up the car. The sudden silence that followed was eerie, as if each one of them was lost in their own thoughts.

As they made their way back to the ghat, Kabir couldn't help but notice how different the Dal Lake was after sunset. The chaos of the afternoon had faded away, replaced by a sense of calm and tranquillity that permeated the air.

The houseboats were lit up with colourful lights that reflected in the water. Kabir sat on the balcony sofa, taking in the moment as a vendor on a shikara prepared fresh chicken tikka and paneer. The aroma of barbequed spices filled the air, and Kabir was tempted to indulge, but politely declined. Suddenly, a musical commotion from a distance caught their attention. Kanval and the others rushed out to see what was happening. They witnessed a live musical orchestra being performed on a big houseboat that had open windows and a large hall with no bedrooms.

A wedding ceremony was taking place, with the bride and groom seated at the rear end while the baratis sat down in opposite rows. The orchestra men sang a beautiful Kashmiri song, and colourful lights illuminated the houseboat, with green, blue and yellow hues reflecting in the water.

'That is so wow, I wish to get married that way someday,' Kanval said dreamily.

'Really? Mummy's fierce gaze could make the structure sink. We better make sure your future husband knows how to swim!' Kabir responded, humour in his eyes. Kanval burst into laughter, thoroughly enjoying Kabir's playful remark.

After a delightful dinner, Kabir wrapped himself in a blanket on the balcony sofa. The fresh cool air induced a sense of perpetuity as he looked at the illuminated mountain where Armaan's boarding was located. Memories of the recent evening flooded his mind, and he stood there, filled with the desire to uphold those cherished memories.

The next morning, Kabir stepped onto the platform to witness the scenic sunrise. Kanval was already in the boat, trying to row it herself. It was a funny sight as she struggled to hold the boat in one direction, and Kabir chuckled at her antics.

After breakfast, as they made their way to the Shankaracharya Temple, Kabir felt a sense of reverence. The temple, located at an altitude of eleven hundred feet above sea level on the Gopadari hills, was the oldest shrine in the Kashmir valley.

As the car slowly climbed the winding road towards the temple, Kabir felt a knot in his stomach. The memories of his father's death flooded back to him. He tried to push them away, but they were too strong. After the security check they got clearance to proceed, and they were told to continue on foot.

As they walked towards the temple, Sarfaraz shared intriguing details about the place.

'This temple has witnessed many repairs throughout its life. King Zainul Abideen renovated it after a major earthquake, Sheikh Mohiduddin carried out repairs, and Raja Gulab Singh added a major pathway. In 1925, the premises were electrified,' Sarfaraz informed them of these historical details with reverence.

Kabir listened attentively, but his mind wandered to the spot where his father had tragically drowned, just a few metres away from the ghat. The memory deeply affected him, evoking a mixture of emotions.

'There's something more to this place that I know about,' Kabir interrupted. 'Papa had drowned exactly there, at that point.' He pointed at the water, tears welling up in his eyes.

Sarfaraz looked at him in shock, his voice breaking. 'Khudaya, Purushottam died by drowning? I thought he passed away in Mumbai.'

Kabir nodded, unable to speak, overwhelmed by the pain. It felt as if he was reliving the night of his father's death all over again.

Sarfaraz, overcome with emotion, started to cry, and Kabir quickly took him aside to the car. Kanval watched in silence, sensing the weight of their grief.

As they arrived at Sarfaraz's house, Tarannum quickly served them lunch. Looking at Kabir, she felt a deep sense of sympathy. The thought of him becoming a widower at such a young age was too much to bear.

It wasn't until they left with Sarfaraz for the trip that Tarannum began to reflect on it more deeply. The thought of another death in Iravati's family brought tears to her eyes. Tarannum knew that Iravati had only one son and witnessing his loss at such a young age was a tragedy beyond words. She felt the weight of that loss in her heart, as if it were her own family member who had passed away.

The pain in her eyes was all too real for Kabir. Tarannum couldn't fathom the depth of his grief, but she knew that the loss of his wife would stay with him forever.

'Kabira, take care of yourself and your family. You are just like Iravati, strong and determined,' Tarannum said, her voice choked with tears. 'I can't imagine your pain at such a young age. If only Iravati were here, she would know what to say.'

Kabir tried to hold back his tears as he listened to Tarannum's words. 'Thank you, Aunty,' he said, his voice trembling with emotion. 'I feel like I'm falling apart. I miss Umika every day. It's hard to imagine what else I could lose.' He took a deep breath before continuing.

'Being here with you and Uncle has reminded me of the good

times we shared. It's given me hope that things can get better.' Kabir wiped away his tears and managed a weak smile. 'I'll do my best to take care of my family.'

'For 28 years we haven't smiled, we've stared at these walls, hoping to find the echoes of our laughter. The river flows silently, mirroring the emptiness in our hearts. Iravati, Noman and Aariz are memories now, leaving us with empty smiles and the solitude of these walls and the flowing river.' Kanval placed a comforting hand on Tarannum's shoulder. 'I understand how you feel, losing loved ones is never easy, and it's even harder when you feel like you're all alone. But you have us, and we'll always be here for you.' Kanval gave her a reassuring squeeze.

'Your family has been more than just neighbours to us,' Sarfaraz said, his voice filled with emotion. 'Kakalal taught us the true meaning of parenthood, Purushottam was like a brother to me, and Iravati made us feel like we were part of their family, despite being from different religions.'

Tarannum surprised Kabir and Kanval by bringing out an old box that contained Iravati's precious jewellery that she had left behind. She had safeguarded them all these years, knowing the value it held for her children. Tarannum then presented her children with the jewellery and a new frame for the portrait of Iravati and Purushottam, which had been in poor condition. The gesture left Kabir and Kanval deeply moved and grateful for the responsibility and care that Tarannum had shown towards their family's belongings.

Kabir's voice trembled as he spoke, 'I pray that my mother sees the kindness in your heart, Aunty. Please don't mind her silence, for healing takes time. I know this because I am still healing from my own loss.'

'Thank you, Aunty, for everything that words fail to capture but is etched in the depth of my being. Kanval and I possess different spirits; while she exudes warmth and empathy, I have reserved those qualities solely for music and Umika. Although I may have forgotten the melodies, I am determined to transform myself from this moment onward. Your kindness will forever resonate within me.'

As they passed through Kabir's old mansion, Kabir stopped for a moment looking at the structure. 'Uncle, will you please do me a favour?' he asked. 'I shall give you written permission to carry out some renovation of this house so that no one objects. Please let me help with the bills, but get the house renovated moderately so that someday when Mummy comes, she does not go in a state of shock at seeing the state of her house.'

'Bill?' Sarfaraz asked with a smile. 'Renovating this house will never be a bill for me, my dear. It will be an investment for you people to return. I will make sure it is restored to its former glory,' Sarfaraz said with a smile.

Kabir's eyes welled up with tears, 'Your kindness will never be forgotten.' Sarfaraz put his hand on Kabir's shoulder.'

Kanval looked at the two men and felt a lump in her throat. She terribly wished Iravati were present. Kabir and Kanval exchanged hugs with Sarfaraz and Tarannum before leaving for the airport. As they watched them leave, Tarannum couldn't hold back her tears. Within no time, they were at the airport. Bashar had learned almost everything about Kabir's visit by now. He dropped them off and refused any tips they offered. 'I am one call away the next time you come to Kashmir, Bhaya,' he said. They bid him goodbye and entered the airport. Kanval's thoughts raced as she dialled Iravati's number, but it went unanswered. 'Experiencing the best moments prepares us for the worst,' she mused to herself, bracing for the storm that awaited them. Kabir, sensing her concern, spoke softly, 'Brace yourself, Kanval. Another storm awaits us back home.' The aircraft left the skies of Kashmir and its experience continued to leave the siblings speechless.

BOOK II

Chillai Khurd
or
The Small Chill

Twenty days of slightly milder cold
after Chillai Kalaan

Chapter 4

Lahore

Daarji's health had worsened over time. The power struggle for the next president had consumed everyone in various ranks. With declining health, the only person he trusted was Shabbir, who took meticulous care of him, providing nurture and motivation. Shabbir reminded Daarji of Ajju's imminent return, the dear boy whom Daarji had raised as his own. Lying on his deathbed, Daarji expressed his doubt, 'Do I deserve such a disfavour?' Shabbir held Daarji's hand and reassured him, 'A selfless person like you need not resort to questionable assurances, Daarji. For many of us who had no parents, no direction and no future, you were the beacon of hope. Your decision to bring us here for a better life was undeniably virtuous and honest. Please do not doubt your undertaking even for a moment.'

Daarji's curiosity tinged with pain, 'Then why did he leave?' Shabbir advised against passing judgement, 'Let's not judge him, Daarji. When I arrived here with Ajju, he remained obedient, never rebelled or misbehaved. He submitted himself to your will. So why do you think he…' Daarji interrupted, expressing his deepest desires, 'I wished he'd rebelled. I wished he'd displayed anger. I wished he'd desired something. But it seems his submission lacked his soul.' The weight of emotions overwhelmed Daarji, and he struggled to catch his breath. Shabbir hurriedly offered water and comforted him. 'Enough, Daarji. Rest for now,' he insisted.

'I am about to rest forever, puttar. But what I fear are the vultures waiting for my demise to take over. This place is meant for Ajju, and I need you to make a promise.' Curious, Shabbir enquired, 'What promise, Daarji?' Daarji replied, 'I hope you see it in my eyes.' Although Shabbir understood Daarji's request, he found it difficult to fulfil at the moment. 'Daarji, we will discuss it later,' Shabbir said before leaving the room hastily. He couldn't make any promises to Daarji.

Despite their extensive search, Ajju remained elusive. Shabbir feared that ambitious rebels within the tanzeem, aiming to replace Daarji, had already eliminated Ajju. Ajju, while a natural heir to the throne, lacked the qualities necessary for the position. To many, he was weak, dull and unfit, and Daarji's proclamation had ignited jealousy and bitterness among the ambitious rank holders. Shabbir had already marked many rebels for elimination. Daarji's words hinted at a truth that sent a chill down Shabbir's spine. There was a prevailing truth that Shabbir had an idea where Ajju must be but to imagine him being there sent a chill to his soul.

Mumbai

Kanval was glued to the television set as the news anchor read out news concerning Kashmir.

> Ghalib Guru, son of Mohammed Afzal Guru, executed following the conviction of the parliament attack in 2013, passed the Matriculate Examination with distinction, scoring 88 per cent. The younger brother of slain Hizbul Mujahideen militant Burhan Wani, Naveed Alam, secured 77 per cent marks in the science stream.

Iravati's fingers trembled with anger as she sliced the bhindis, her mind consumed by thoughts of betrayal and Kanval's provocation. Kanval raised the volume of the television, trying to draw her attention.

> Congratulatory messages poured in from friends and relatives of both boys, but overall, girls performed better than boys in the examinations. The results, declared on Sunday, showed an overall pass percentage of 67.22 per cent. The recent lockdowns had affected the studies and this percentage could have been much higher. The board has introduced various new educational policies aimed at enhancing the competency-based skill set of students.

Kanval watched her mother's reaction, hoping for a response. 'Listen, Mummy, this is positive news. You need to hear this.' Iravati ran out of patience, her eyes fixed on the bhindis she was cutting. 'My life thrives on endless positivity with every drop of negativity you graciously add.'

Kanval sensed her mother's anger but couldn't help provoking her further. 'It wasn't just any trip, Mummy. We learned so much about ourselves and the world. Bhaiyya is a different person now. He's happier, more open.'

Iravati snorted, 'Is it? You went there, had a little picnic instead of the last rites, and now my son is a changed man.' Kanval retorted, 'I understand your reservations, Mummy, but that "picnic" was a solemn occasion, your daughter-in-law's last rites, not a leisurely outing.'

Kanval was infuriated. 'You know what? You're right. It was a mistake. We should have stayed home, never attempted to better ourselves or learn anything new, or even try to bring your dear son back to life. Is that what you want?' Iravati glared at her. 'Don't talk back to me, young lady. Stop putting words in my mouth. I just think you should have obeyed me before gallivanting in the meadows, rivers, mountains, and of course with those people.'

Kanval paused, allowing the tension in the room to settle. 'Bhaiyya needed to experience the warmth of Kashmir and its people, to help him heal from his trauma and rediscover love. If your so-called "wonderful people" had truly made an impact on Kabir, he wouldn't have been holed up in his room for the past three months since his arrival. The power of the magical people and their warm hugs didn't cure all his trauma.' Iravati seethed with anger as she thought of Kabir reconnecting with those people from Kashmir, momentarily feeling rejuvenated and happy there. She had always believed that the place and its people were nothing but trouble.

Kanval's behaviour had only made things worse and now, there was this little blind boy, Armaan, whose story had struck a chord with Kabir. It was all too much for Iravati to bear and she couldn't help but feel deep concern about the impact this would have on Kabir. Iravati clenched her fists, feeling her anger bubbling up inside her. She had spent years building a wall around her family, protecting them from the wonders of Kashmir and its people but now, everything was falling apart.

Kabir stood there, silently watching them argue. He missed the peaceful and welcoming nature of Kashmir, where people were compassionate and empathetic towards each other. In Mumbai, everything was fast-paced and emotionless, with concrete structures all around him. He decided to speak up.

'Mummy, I truly understand the distress our visit has caused you and I deeply apologize. From now on, we won't discuss anything you dislike. However, Kanval's argument may hold some truth. We've encountered some untold truths that you haven't shared, and I respect that. Let's avoid further conflicts within our family.' Kabir tried to apologize but he actually surprised Iravati. She couldn't believe Kabir was reasoning with the Zargars. Before Kabir could say something, she interrupted, 'While we try to teach children all about life, our children teach us what life is all about.'

Kabir felt guilty and asked Kanval not to discuss the topic

again. Kanval entered her mother's room and before she could say anything, Iravati cut her off with a mocking tone, 'Well, well, if you're here to offer your apologies, spare me the theatrics.' Kanval's eyes rolled with irritation, 'Sorry, Mummy, but brace yourself for disappointment. I didn't show up to apologize. Instead, I had the audacity to beg for a tiny ounce of mercy for your dear son.' Iravati raised an eyebrow, 'What?' 'I am concerned about his emotional state. You don't seem to understand him at all,' Kanval said. Iravati scoffed, 'And what makes you think that?' 'You don't pay attention to his feelings. You're too focused on practicality.' Iravati rolled her eyes, 'Oh, I see. And you think you know better?' 'Yes, I do. I know Bhaiyya better than you do. I have been there for him all his life.' Iravati fumed instantly, 'Behave! You think you're the better mother?'

'I'm sorry, I'm not saying that, but I do think you need to be more understanding.' Iravati leaned forward, 'Let me tell you something, Kanval. I may not be the perfect mother, but I know what's best for my son. What he needs right now is a wife.' 'A wife? Seriously?' Kanval asked incredulously. 'Yes, I am. Kabir needs someone to settle him down and give him a sense of purpose. He needs to start a family,' Iravati said. 'But he's not ready for marriage! He's still not over Umika,' Kanval protested. Iravati waved her hand dismissively, 'That's just an excuse. He needs to move on. I've already found a suitable girl for him.' Kanval was outraged, 'You've already found someone? Without even talking to him?'

Iravati stood up, 'I don't need his permission. I'm his mother and I know what's best for him. And if he can't see that, then that's his problem.' Kanval shook her head in frustration, 'I can't believe you're so insensitive. Bhaiyya is still struggling with his emotions and you're more worried about getting him married.' Iravati glared at her, 'I'm being practical, Kanval. That's how life works. If you can't understand that, then maybe you're not as smart as you think you are.' The two women stared at each other in silence, the tension between them thick and real.

A few months later, Kabir was fixing the enlarged portrait of his parents that they had brought. 'Hey, when did you get the portrait enlarged?' Kanval asked. Kabir looked at the portrait deeply but chose not to answer. He walked straight to his room, leaving Kanval behind. Iravati came in immediately to see what Kabir was up to. She smiled when she saw the portrait hung up on the wall. It gave her hope that he might be open to the changes she wanted to bring about in him. She went to Kabir's room and found him lying on the bed, staring at the ceiling. 'Well, I was thinking of making some paneer for dinner, my dear, I'm sure you'd love to eat,' she said. Kabir glanced at her, his eyes lingering for a moment before reluctantly nodding in agreement.

Iravati emerged from the room, her face adorned with a forced smile. Kanval observed her mother's suspicious behaviour and couldn't help but question, 'What's on your mind, Mummy?' Iravati paused, then approached Kanval, her annoyance evident in her tone. 'I need to speak with you,' she replied curtly. 'I need your help.'

Kanval raised an eyebrow, her scepticism growing. 'My help? Well, this should be interesting.' Iravati's voice turned serious as she explained, 'I need to find a way to heal Kabir. I believe he needs a new partner, someone who can help him move on from his past and start a new life.' Kanval couldn't believe her ears. 'You want to force him into a marriage?' she exclaimed, her disbelief apparent. 'That's not the solution, he needs to find his own path, in his own time.'

Iravati retorted with a hint of superiority, 'You always think you know better. Sometimes you need to listen to your elders. I've lived longer than you and I know what's best for my son.'

Kanval's eyes rolled in response. 'Just because you've lived longer doesn't mean you always make the right decisions,' she countered firmly. 'What makes you think getting married will solve all of his problems? That's just a temporary fix.'

Defensive, Iravati fired back, 'I didn't say it would solve all his problems. But it will give him something, something positive to work towards.' Disagreeing, Kanval shook her head. 'That's not how it works. Happiness can't be forced. He needs to find his own way, and it's our duty to support him in that.' Frustrated, Iravati huffed, 'Well, I don't see you offering any solutions.' 'Maybe that's because I don't believe in forcing someone into marriage just to fix their problems,' she stated firmly.

'You always have to be right, don't you?' Kanval remained composed as she replied, 'It's not about being right or wrong but doing what's genuinely best for him. I don't think getting married, just because you think it's the answer, is what's truly best for him.' The two women locked eyes, neither willing to yield.

Iravati walked into Kabir's room, holding a mug of coffee, but hesitated upon seeing the cigarette in his hand. Deciding to give him some space, she quietly left the room and headed to the drawing-room where Kanval was engrossed in watching the news on television. Iravati glanced at the screen briefly but found no interest in the current affairs. She made her way to the kitchen, preparing a cup of tea for herself, lost in her own thoughts.

Meanwhile, Kabir's phone continued to ring persistently. Feeling a hint of annoyance, he finally answered on the eighth ring. 'Sir, I urgently need the lyrics for the scratch we've been waiting for seven months,' pleaded his assistant.

Iravati returned to Kabir's room, observing his focused demeanour as he worked on his laptop. Trying to strike up a conversation, she asked, 'Working on a new song, beta?' Kabir nodded, not breaking his concentration. Sensing an opportunity to connect with her son, Iravati decided to open up.

'Kabir, when your father passed away, I was the same age as you, with two young children. I understand the feeling of being alone and uncertain about the future,' Iravati said, her voice filled with empathy. Kabir glanced up from his laptop as he worked on the lyrics, intrigued by his mother's words.

'I know the pain of losing a spouse and the mix of emotions that come with it. There are no rules on how you should feel,' Iravati continued, her voice gentle and understanding. Kabir closed his laptop, expressionless as he listened intently to his mother's words.

'Kabir, I know someone who can help you through this difficult time,' Iravati suggested, hoping to offer her son a source of guidance. Before she could elaborate, Kabir interrupted with a question that had been lingering in his mind. 'Then why didn't you remarry, Mummy?' Kabir asked, his voice filled with curiosity. Iravati smiled wistfully, reminiscing about her past.

'Being a parent and fulfilling my responsibilities to you and Kanval took precedence over seeking personal pleasures. Marriage entails a package of roles and responsibilities that later provide their own rewards,' Iravati explained, reflecting on her choices.

Just then, Kanval's voice resonated from the drawing room, calling them over urgently. Iravati and Kabir hurriedly joined Kanval, who appeared bewildered as she stared at the screen. The newscaster's voice filled the room.

> With the scrapping of Article 370 and 35 A, Kashmir will no longer have a separate constitution and will have to abide by the Indian Constitution like any other state. All laws will be automatically applicable to Kashmir and people from outside the state will be allowed to buy property there. The government is of the opinion that it will bring development

> to the region. A major pilgrimage has been cancelled and thousands of troops have been deployed. Tourists had already been asked to leave the valley last week. Telephones lines, internet connectivity and any mode of communication has been cut off with regional political leaders and separatists being placed under house arrest. The Government of India feels that it is within its rights to bring the changes and that flexible decisions have been taken by previous Government along similar lines in the past. There is an ambiguity over the protest, backlash and violence being reported because of the media backlash. Several opposition leaders who flew to Srinagar for expressing their solidarity have been disallowed to leave the airport. A small portion of opposition parties have dared to oppose the move but the leading opposition has chosen to remain quiet as Kashmir's autonomy is an emotive issue with many Indians and most parties would find it difficult to oppose the move with the fear of being branded as 'anti-India'.

'What on earth is this?' Kanval exclaimed in disbelief, her eyes glued to the TV screen. Iravati, adopting her usual apathetic tone, responded with a sarcastic remark. 'You've managed to surprise me, Kanval! I thought there was some groundbreaking news worth paying attention to!' Kanval's disappointment turned into frustration as she gazed at her mother. 'Mummy, don't you grasp the gravity of the situation? Are you completely oblivious to the fact that 13.6 million people are being cut off from the rest of the world?' Kabir joined them, his expression mirroring Kanval's concern. Iravati, displaying her indifference, simply shrugged. It was evident that Iravati couldn't care less as it was a place she intentionally refused to venture into. Kanval let out an exasperated sigh and turned back to the television. Conflicting perspectives continued to unfold, fuelling her frustration even further.

> 'Finally, the government has taken a step towards dismantling the so-called "autonomy" in Kashmir. This decision is a victory for all those who have been fighting against the separatist forces in the valley. It's time for the people of Kashmir to fully integrate with the rest of India.'
>
> 'It's about time!' We've been waiting for this for years. This will bring stability and development to the region. For too long, the people of Jammu and Kashmir have been given special treatment, as if they were different from other Indians. It's a historic day for us.'
>
> 'Our sentiments were attached with the Article and we have been shocked by the decision. We are trying to connect to our loved ones at home but cannot do so. Revoking the Article does not mean we cannot express our resentment, today we feel we have lost our identity and it is very unfortunate that the Government has taken a decision that will create more resentment among the people rather than peace.'

'I hope that there won't be any violence, I am very worried,' Kanval expressed her concern to Kabir. 'But is this supposed to be good news or bad, Kanval?' Kanval looked at him with a straight face. Kabir was very confused. 'I am going to answer you but first quickly call up Tarannum Aunty and Sarfaraz Uncle, and please check on them.' Kabir hesitated before ringing them. 'Bhaiyya please!' But Kabir dialled Sarfaraz's number repeatedly with no luck. Kanval was distressed.

'Can we check with Ramzan Chacha?' Kabir had special respect for him in his heart. 'Poor Uncle must not have a number; he does not even know how to operate a mobile phone, I believe.'

The interviews with Kashmiris continued on the television set.

> 'My sister's wedding is scheduled for next week, and we've already made all the necessary preparations. However, considering the unexpected turn of events, I'm uncertain whether the wedding will actually take place.' Another woman expressed her concerns, saying, 'Once the curfew is lifted, we have no idea how the situation will unfold. It feels like we're heading towards the worst of times.' A man from Jammu voiced his discontent, stating, 'My children are studying outside the state, and I have no contact with them. I'm sure they're extremely worried about the situation here and I can only imagine what they must be going through.'

'That's your answer, Bhaiyya? This is what troubles me,' Kanval exclaimed, shutting off the TV and immersing herself in her mobile phone, seeking solace in conversations with her friends. Kabir shared her perplexity and couldn't fathom the abrupt severing of communication in Kashmir. 'I can't believe they can just cut off all contact like that. What about the people there?' Kanval expressed her disappointment to one of her friends, her voice tinged with concern.

Meanwhile, Kabir sat in silence, his gaze fixed on the television screen, as conflicting reports and debates played out before him. Politics was not his forte, unlike Kanval. However, deep within him, an empathetic ache began to stir. His heart went out to the people affected. Lost in contemplation, a sudden surge of worry washed over him. 'I hope Armaan is safe,' he whispered softly, his fingers nervously tapping on the armrest of his chair.

Seven months had passed since the scrapping of the Article and normalcy in the state remained a subject of intense debate. With a media blackout in effect, reports of protests, disagreements, violence and resentment remained elusive. Fragmented news of encounters, arrests and detentions trickled in through unverified sources. Kabir, grappling with creative blockage, had succumbed to the habit of chain smoking. On one such day, Iravati entered the studio with a cup of coffee, hoping to engage Kabir in conversation.

'Are you still working on the music for Mr Kriplani's film?' she enquired. Kabir sighed wearily, 'Yes, Mummy. Just trying to create a scratch.' Iravati, pouring him a cup of coffee, quipped, 'Well, if smoking doesn't provide the inspiration, perhaps this coffee will.' Kabir expressed his remorse, saying, 'Sorry, Mummy. I just couldn't resist the urge to smoke.' Observing his appearance, Iravati remarked, 'Have you looked at yourself in the mirror? You need a trim and your hair has grown long and curly. I'll take you to the salon tomorrow.'

'Take me out of this world, Mummy,' Kabir said tiredly, his eyes fixed on the laptop. 'Well, we are all destined to go out of this world someday. What matters is the quality of life that we spend here. Quality depends on the choices we make,' Iravati said thoughtfully. 'Mummy, let me be clear. You can flatly refuse the girl's family,' Kabir retorted, his frustration visible. 'Vidhi is a good girl, Kabir. She has all the qualities that Umika had,' Iravati persisted, attempting to persuade him. Annoyed, Kabir snapped back, 'But she's not Umika, right? Why do I have to keep repeating something so simple?' Iravati, undeterred, insisted, 'Beta, she would be a wonderful wife for you.' Kabir's irritation grew and he firmly stated, 'Let me tell you something straight, Mummy. It's about how I feel. I can't control my feelings. It would be unfair to any other woman who tries to be with me. Umika's presence would always loom large, making it impossible for anyone else to fill her shoes. We have been through so much together, finding solace in each other's company in times of joy and sorrow. I will live my life with the memories I have of her. There is so much to a marriage, Mummy. I have had my piece of experience with it, and since life is all about experience, this was enough to be a long-lasting memory.'

Iravati tried her best to convince Kabir, but her efforts were in vain. She turned to Kanval, hoping she could lend a hand, but with her any conversation turned into an argument.

Iravati persisted, attempting to initiate a conversation, but Kanval always debated Kabir's marriage. To her, it was a forced union, but Iravati saw it as an escape. She believed that women possessed a magical ability to captivate men, to make them feel responsible and fulfil their paternal desires.

The seventh month of lockdown weighed heavily on Kanval, especially during dinner time when she couldn't resist the temptation to check her social media. 'I'd like you to know the story of someone which has remained untold so far.' Kabir, eager for a diversion, urged her, 'Tell me.'

Kanval had come across a post written by a fellow Kashmiri colleague:

> Dialled her number after seven months, feeling a mix of eagerness, strangeness, energy and above all, love. The clock struck 7, and a different voice answered on the other end. 'Is Beenish there?' I enquired, but there was only silence. Assuming a weak phone network, I repeated the question, only to be met with the heartbreaking sound. 'Today is her fortieth day! She is dead,' her mother replied.

Kanval's heart ached, feeling the weight of the tragedy that had befallen the Kashmiri people. 'Poor Akram,' she uttered. 'That is terrible, extremely terrible.'

Kabir looked at Kanval, sadness reflected in his eyes as he shared in her pain. However, Iravati remained disturbingly quiet, showing so little empathy that it alarmed Kanval. 'Did you call up Sarfaraz Uncle or Shamrita?' Kanval asked. Kabir's silence revealed that he had never made an attempt to reach out to them.

Expressing her frustration, Kanval voiced her concerns about the people of Kashmir, questioning how they were meeting their basic needs during such uncertain times. 'The groceries, food, medical emergencies, pregnant women...we have no idea what is going on there,' she lamented, her heart breaking for her homeland. Growing increasingly frustrated with Kanval's continued focus on the situation in Kashmir, Iravati felt her concerns were baseless and her constant chatter grated on her nerves. Unable to bear it any longer, Iravati abruptly stood up from the table and left without uttering a single word. Kanval and Kabir exchanged bewildered glances as they watched her departure.

'This is what I dislike about her, can't we even discuss something?' Kanval expressed, her voice tinged with disappointment. 'This is also the problem at large, the moment you try to speak something human about Kashmiris and show a sense of concern, people start looking at you as if you represent Pakistani Embassy or they immediately want to know your stance on Balochistan or sometimes they question your nationalism.'

'This will get you into trouble someday, Kanval, you must really avoid conflicted conversations,' Kabir pointed out. 'The other day, I was watching a news debate. Sometimes I feel these news channels have created more havoc in the country than the situation itself. Splitting the screen in ten boxes with stupid panellists barking like mad dogs and cats and nothing fruitful comes out of it!' 'I second that,' Kanval replied.

'Surprising, how not being able to communicate can tear us apart. I can only try to fathom the mental health of everyone there. Such a strict lockdown with no internet, no communication, and sitting home 24/7 can cause severe depression, stress and mental health issues.'

Kabir interrupted, 'Well, Mummy has proposed another girl

to me, Vidhi is her name, please take care of it?' Kabir informed her. 'Again? Alright!! Maybe it is about time I ask her to look for a groom for me.' Kabir smiled and went back to his room. He stood aimless at the window. Recalling Kanval's words made him worry in his heart for Armaan. Seven months and no idea about his well-being. *Let me ring Shamrita, just in case the call gets connected*, he thought. *No, it's too late to ring someone at this hour!!! But hey, wait, let me...let me...take a chance.* The operator's automated response informed him, 'The number you are trying to reach is unavailable.'

The moment he disconnected the call, he received a message from his Music Assistant.

```
Sir, please send me the pending scratch
you were to make today. Client deadline
tomorrow.
```

Kabir was irritated. He couldn't focus on music. Umika often used to hum a basic scratch for anything he worked on and it worked wonders. He was frustrated. *Do it yourself*, he wrote and sent him.

Iravati was sure Kanval would never help her with her plan to settle Kabir down. Kanval had a rebellious streak that she wore like a badge of honour. She had a strong opinion about everything and no one could control her. They had a fundamental disagreement about Kabir.

Iravati believed that a husband and wife's relationship had the power to change lives for the better. Kanval, on the other hand, was always on edge, eagerly waiting for news about Kashmir and its people.

'Kanval, if we could just find a way to collaborate, perhaps we could help Kabir find a suitable partner. It would significantly contribute to his well-being and help him regain control over his life,' Iravati said.

Kanval scoffed. 'Because, you know, it's a piece of cake to find the perfect match for a grieving widower, isn't it?' she retorted.

Iravati raised an eyebrow. 'Kanval, it's not about finding a perfect match. It's about helping Kabir heal and move forward from his loss,' she explained. 'Don't act like you're too busy to lend a hand. What have you been doing all day?'

Kanval shot her mother a pointed glare. 'In between fighting for justice and capturing the essence of the world through my photojournalism, I guess I can spare a few moments for the "family" too, can't I?'

'Yes, exactly! It's about focusing on our family and helping each other,' she asserted. With a smirk playing on her lips, Kanval fired back. 'Oh, so you're trying to settle me somewhere, Mummy?'

'For now, Kabir's on my list!' Iravati replied. Kanval shook her head. 'I don't agree, Mummy. I think there are other ways to help him.' Iravati felt a sudden wave of fury. 'Other ways like your magical trip. I'm sure that will solve all of Kabir's problems, can we please focus on the issue at hand? Kabir needs our help.'

Kanval turned towards her. 'You think I don't want him to heal? You think I'm just sitting here twiddling my thumbs?' Iravati interrupted. 'I know you care about Kabir. But we need to find a way to help him. And a marriage could be the catalyst he needs.'

Kanval shook her head. 'You're oversimplifying things, Mummy. Bhaiyya is not ready for marriage yet. He needs time to heal. He needs time, healing and confidence, which will evolve only with a right approach and I know what that approach is! Why do you think I am focused on normalcy in Kashmir? It's because if Bhaiyya revisits the place, he would find peace and healing, let him do some projects there, let him evolve—' Iravati interrupted sharply, 'Hold up, there's no timc for your make-believe stories.'

'How long do you wish run away from reality, Mummy? You are not even ready to listen to me, how do you think this will work?' 'Why do you wish to keep going back to things that are not healthy? Unrealistic? To things I have drawn a line, I have done that with the lessons I have learnt and the experiences I have so the least you can do is trust my grey hair!' Iravati left even before Kanval could respond. Kabir was witnessing the dialogue from his room. Witnessing his mother and sister fight for him to bring him back to life in their own ways, he felt useless.

Both of them were making efforts in their own ways to revive him but he was stuck somewhere he couldn't identify. *I am the cause of the rift in between them, he thought. They do not even talk properly, damn it!* An unknown number flashed on his mobile phone for the second time which he ignored. He pulled the keys of his car and drove all the way to the beach leaving his cell phone behind. Almost no one on the endless sand, Kabir sat down, watching the waves as they crashed on the shore. He lit his cigarette, watching the illuminated shore with fine yellow bulbs. Looking at the pattern of the waves, he drew a conclusion—*life is similar to these waves, as much as you want to touch the best part of life, you will always be pulled down to the limits.* Puffing on his third cigarette within 30 minutes of his solace at the beach, a jeep arrived with police at patrol, parking in front of him. 'Do you know this is not the time you should be here?' the police informed. Kabir looked at him, not giving a damn who was talking to him. 'Is it? Where do you think I should be?' 'As per the rules, in the lockup for smoking at a public place and trespassing during a prohibited hour. The jeep drove away with Kabir.

Lahore

Daarji found it difficult to breath. Shabbir was vigilantly with him in the ICU.

The hospital resembled a fortress, guarded by armed gunmen who stood watch in the lobby. Tanzeem's men, their faces marked by sorrow, knew all too well that time was running out for Daarji. The presence of VIPs, politicians and bureaucrats, along with a swarm of media personnel, added to the gravity of the situation.

Shabbir knelt on the carpet, his forehead pressed against the ground in prayer. The rhythmic sound of his whispered invocations filled the air. Daarji's fragile state was interrupted by a fit of coughing, causing Shabbir to swiftly complete his prayers. He rushed to Daarji's side, motioning for the nurse to leave and cradled his frail body, helping him sip some water.

'Take it slow, Daarji,' Shabbir gently advised, placing a soft cushion behind his head.

Resting uneasily, Daarji's weakened voice trembled with suspicion. 'There is something you're keeping from me, something you hesitate to share.'

Shabbir, taken aback, responded earnestly, 'Daarji, I swear I have never contemplated hiding anything from you.'

Daarji issued a warning with laboured breaths. 'Beware of those eagerly waiting for my last breath. I am certain you have taken care of them.'

Suppressing his emotions, Shabbir implored, 'Daarji, please save your strength. You need rest.'

'No, I need nothing more. What I entrusted to you has already been conveyed. I have faith that, like a loyal son, you will fulfil the responsibilities bestowed upon you,' Daarji managed to speak between gasps for air.

Deeply affected, Shabbir's voice cracked as he assured Daarji, 'Of course, Daarji, I will do as you wish. But you must understand—'

Interrupting him, Daarji's eyes pierced through Shabbir's soul as he sought the truth. 'Tell me, where is Ajju? I can see it in your eyes. You know.'

Caught off guard, Shabbir felt a flush of embarrassment. 'No, Daarji, I genuinely do not know his whereabouts,' he responded truthfully.

Unyielding, Daarji remarked, his voice barely audible, 'A man on the brink of death sees clearly, even when the truth hides in the deepest recesses of the universe. I implore you to bring him back. He is in a dangerous place, where he shouldn't be.'

Overwhelmed by sorrow, tears streamed down Shabbir's face. 'More than inheriting my chair, it is vital for Ajju's own well-being that he returns. I beseech you, not for the sake of prestige or inheritance, but for his safety. He is in grave danger.'

Daarji's voice trailed off, his weakened state making every word a struggle. 'Daarji, once Ajju is back, we shall celebrate with an extravagant feast and mark his triumphant return. Lahore will witness a festivity like never before. But for that, I need you to regain your health. Bhabhi does not deserve to see you in this condition. I'll… I'll be held responsible for your ill health, so you better listen to me and recharge your core instinct.

'Also, you need not worry about those vultures that you fear might take over. I have taken care of them, and those few who still have the courage will be wiped off in some time. So, Daarji, I hope you-' Shabbir suddenly stopped mid-sentence and drew closer to Daarji. 'Daarji? Daarji?' he called out, but there was no response. Shabbir felt a lump form in his throat. The monitor beeped, indicating that Daarji's heart had stopped. Shabbir felt like his own heart had stopped beating. He looked at Daarji's still face, tears streaming down his own. Then he remembered Daarji's final words.

'Dharti ambar ek karde, par ohnu lab ke leke aa. Unite the earth and sky if you must, but find her and bring her back.'

Mumbai

Kanval drove home with Kabir, the sun high in the sky. 'Instead of going to the police station, why didn't you bribe him ?' she asked, glancing at her brother. Kabir stared blankly out the window. 'A little presence of mind could have gone a long way,' Kanval continued. Kabir remained silent. 'Excuse me?' she prodded. Kabir finally replied, 'Since I have no presence of mind, I had forgotten my wallet and phone at home. Do I need to tell you more?' Kanval had bailed Kabir out after he spent a night in jail for misbehaving and smoking in public. Arriving home, Kabir went straight to his room, ignoring Iravati's questions.

He took a long shower and checked his phone to find 24 missed calls, but he was too drained to respond. He went to bed and slept for thirteen hours. Fuming, Iravati made her way to Kanval's room. She knocked on the door. Kanval watched her silently, sensing the turmoil within her. Iravati's eyes were puffy, and her face looked drained of colour. Kanval knew she had been up all night, worrying.

'He was in jail!' Iravati said, her voice trembling. 'Just for one night, but still.' Kanval nodded sympathetically. 'I know, it was a difficult situation—' 'Difficult situation? Kabir's reputation is at stake.' Kanval placed a calming hand on Iravati's shoulder. 'I understand, Mummy, but we need to approach this with composure.' Kanval felt a pang of guilt. 'I'm sorry, Mummy. I was a little occupied with work and couldn't keep a watch over him.' Iravati sighed. 'It's not about apologies, Kanval. It's about putting our differences aside now, at least for Kabir.' Kanval nodded. She knew her mother was right. Kabir was not in a good place mentally. 'What do you suggest, Mummy?' Iravati's face brightened a little.

'Let's focus on the music,' she said quickly. 'That's Kabir's second love, after all. The business is suffering too. We need to work together to turn things around.' Kanval felt relieved. For once, she didn't have to argue with her mother. She could see the logic in Iravati's words. 'Okay, Mummy. Done! Leave it to me,' she said. As she hugged Iravati, a sense of peace prevailed over her mother that she hadn't felt in a long time.

The next day, Kanval and Iravati walked into the music label's studio, radiating authority. As they entered, they were immediately struck by the chaotic and undisciplined atmosphere in the studios. 'Goodness gracious! What is happening here?' exclaimed Iravati, her eyes scanning the disarray. Kabir's absence had led to a complete breakdown of the system. Sound engineers, maintenance staff, dubbing directors and other key personnel were nowhere to be found. The recording studios seemed to have transformed into a party zone.

Rishab, Kabir's assistant, approached Kanval with visible anxiety. Without wasting a moment, she issued her instructions in a firm tone. 'Provide me with a comprehensive list of pending assignments for song recordings, scratch making and dubbing projects,' she commanded. 'Also, compile a record of the assignments we have lost due to missed deadlines. Include the names of staff members and their respective tasks, clearly indicating what has been completed and what remains pending. I need accountability for every aspect. You have one week to accomplish this.'

A deafening silence hung in the air after Kanval's instructions. Even Iravati was taken aback by the assertiveness displayed by her daughter. As they prepared to leave, Rishab hesitantly approached Kanval, his voice quivering. 'Excuse me, Ma'am,' he said. 'Let me be honest, none of the work has been completed.' Kanval's eyes locked onto Rishab's as he trembled before her. 'Excuse me? That is unacceptable,' Kanval snapped, her voice cold and authoritative. 'I demand a detailed report of what has been done and what is still pending. Provide me with a list of every assignment we have lost due to missed deadlines, along with the names of the responsible staff members.'

Rishab retrieved his mobile phone and opened his mailbox. 'I have been trying to contact Kabir Sir for the past year, but he never responds to my calls. These emails are proof that he has ignored all queries. The pressure has become overwhelming and I am considering resigning. I cannot work with an unresponsive boss.' Rishab recoiled as Kanval leaned in closer, her eyes burning with intensity. 'My brother's unavailability is no excuse for neglecting your responsibilities. Do you understand?' Rishab nodded meekly, his face drained of colour. 'Rishab, tell me honestly, how many times have you or any of the staff members visited our house to check on him? Did anyone offer him motivation, enquire about his health and well-being? Did anyone make an innovative effort to bring him back to the label, engaging him with his passion for music? What steps did you take to support him during his difficult times?'

Rishab looked down, recognizing his mistake. 'I'm sorry, Ma'am. We should have done more. But we didn't know how to approach him.' Rishab's reply was unwavering. 'That's not a valid excuse, Rishab,' Kanval replied firmly.

'Bhaiyya has always treated everyone here like family, not just as a boss. In a family, we look out for each other, especially during tough times. You all let him down,' Kanval declared, her words filled with disappointment. Rishab felt a surge of shame and guilt, knowing that Kanval was right. 'I promise that we will do better from now on,' he vowed.

'Step up and take responsibility for what has been happening here.' Iravati observed the exchange from the sidelines, a sense of pride welling up inside her at the way Kanval was handling the situation.

Kabir woke up from his sleep, his mind still groggy from the events of the previous night. As he took a drag from his cigarette, Kanval and Iravati entered his room. Iravati greeted him. 'Breakfast, Kabir?' 'In a while,' he replied. Without skipping a beat, Kanval launched into a new plan. 'Both of us have decided that we will no longer accept any more excuses, and starting from tomorrow, you will go to the office.' Anxiety and resistance filled Kabir's mind as he didn't feel ready to face the world just yet. As they discussed, an unknown number kept flashing on his phone.

Kanval informed him, 'I have instructed your assistant to organize all the pending work for you so that you are aware of what is going on.' Kabir felt his head spinning, unable to focus on anything. The number continued to flash. Iravati commanded, 'Pick up the call, Kabir. It must be your assistant. Come on, pick it up.' Reluctantly, Kabir answered the call, with his mother and sister watching intently.

'Hello,' he said unenthusiastically. 'Hello, Hello, Kabir Sir,' a voice on the other end greeted. Kabir was taken aback by the voice but didn't reveal his surprise. 'Hello, Kabir Sir?' the voice repeated. Kabir's heart started racing as he struggled to place the voice. It sounded familiar, yet he couldn't quite recall who it was. 'Who is this?' he asked, his voice betraying his confusion. 'Hello, Kabir Sir?' Kabir's face lit up with a warm smile as he recognized the voice on the other end. 'Armaan? Armaan beta?' he exclaimed. Kanval's excitement ignited and Iravati's jaw dropped in astonishment.

'I'm good, how are you?' Armaan responded. 'How is Didi?' Kanval smiled, and Kabir replied, 'Didi is also doing well.' Armaan continued, 'Is this your number, Armaan? Where are you now? Are you still at the hostel?' 'No, no, I am at home with Mummy and Daddy now,' Armaan replied. Kabir's heart skipped a beat as he absorbed Armaan's words. 'Mummy and Daddy?' he repeated, his voice filled with surprise. Kanval's eyes widened in astonishment, sharing a quick glance with Kabir.

They had always assumed that Armaan was an orphan. A mix of emotions washed over her upon learning that he had a family. 'Assalamualikum Sir ji, aap tik ho? Gar pe sab tik hain?' Armaan's father greeted Kabir in the typical Kashmiri accent, asking about his well-being and that of his family. Kabir smiled and replied, 'I am good, in fact, everyone here is doing well. I must tell you, you have an amazing son. Anyone can fall in love with him.'

Filled with gratitude, Armaan's father said, 'Had it not been for you, Sir, my son would not be alive. Thank you so much for saving his life,' his voice thick with emotion. Kabir felt a lump in his throat recalling the moment. 'You are embarrassing me, Uncle. It was my duty to save him.' Armaan's father continued, 'I cannot express how happy I am to talk to you. Due to the lockdown, we could hardly leave our place. The network was restored a few days ago, in fact we have been trying to reach you constantly to express our gratitude.'

Kanval could sense the sincerity in Kabir's voice as he spoke. Knowing that he genuinely meant every word made him feel worthy, as if someone had stirred words of motivation in his soul. 'Uncle, your words mean so much to me. Armaan has always been special to me too. He has faced numerous challenges in his life, yet he never lost his smile. I am so proud of him, and I'm sure you, as his parents, are proud of him too.' Kabir nodded, his own emotions still raw. 'I can only imagine how difficult it must have been for him,' he said. 'But please know that he has touched many lives with his sweet voice, including mine. I will never forget the day he sang for us. It was one of the most beautiful moments of my life.'

Instantly, Iravati got up and abruptly left, her mood visibly shattered and tense, leaving the siblings silently watching her departure.

Armaan's father continued, 'You are courteous enough to extend your gratitude by showing respect to us. Armaan told me that you specially came to the boarding house to meet him. Who else on earth would do this? I am certain that you come from a great family, here speak to my wife.' Kabir was filled with gratitude. 'Hello Kabi—' The line went dead. 'Hello, hello?' 'I think some network issue. Damn, I had wanted to talk to him.' Kanval expressed her discontent. 'Thank God, he's alright,' Kabir exclaimed with a newfound enthusiasm. 'I always assumed he was an orphan, without any parents.'

'But isn't it a relief that he's not an orphan? Who knows what circumstances led him to the boarding school,' Kanval chimed in, her surprise evident in her voice.

'Absolutely! But you know what's even more amazing? He actually called us,' Kabir continued, a hint of wonder in his tone.

Their conversation took an unexpectedly positive turn, leaving them both pleasantly surprised by the connection they had formed with this mysterious young individual.

Kabir had a sudden stir of ecstasy. He couldn't express how happy he was. 'I feel they are unwinding the lockdown in phases. Bhaiyya, please check with Tarannum Aunty and Sarfaraz Uncle,' Kanval requested. 'Wait, let me call them. The call didn't get through. No luck, Kanval.' 'Maybe tomorrow we can try to call them.' 'Tomorrow is fine but today is not going to be an easy day.' Kanval hinted at her mother. 'Well, I agree, but as usual I am sure you will manage her.'

Iravati had no chill. All her life, she had tried to distance herself from her past in Kashmir, but it seemed like it was catching up with her. She felt a sudden tension in her chest. She couldn't shake the feeling that something was coming back to her, something that she had long tried to forget. Her children's reconnection with their Kashmiri roots only added to her unease. In her mind, Iravati knew that her fears were rational. She had no idea what lay ahead, but the unease lingered with Armaan's call. Iravati felt a sudden tension rise within her as she heard her children connect with both old and new people. All her life, she had tried to keep her past behind her, but it seemed to be catching up with her. What exactly? She had no idea but there was something for sure.

That night, Kabir's mind was consumed by the call from Armaan. He longed for more time with the kid, to hear his voice and connect with him on a deeper level. It was as though spring had arrived in his life, bringing with it a renewed sense of purpose and joy. He went to the kitchen and prepared saffron milk, with the same saffron that was a gift from Tarannum along with the dry fruits she had given them. Opening the plastic case of saffron and smelling it brought back memories of Kashmir.

The smell of pine trees, the running river and the chinar leaves, everything reminded him of the time spent there. As he sipped the warm milk and listened to Umika's incomplete song on his mobile phone, he felt a sense of peace wash over him. It wasn't just the saffron milk or the old recording of Umika's voice that made him feel this way, but the rekindling of a connection that he thought had been lost forever.

Unbeknownst to him, Iravati had been watching him from afar. She was appalled by the instant changes she saw in her son, the way he seemed to be drawn back to his past and the people he had left behind. In a fit of anger, she entered the kitchen and threw the saffron into the trash. *This couldn't be happening,* she thought. She needed to put a stop to it before it went too far. Later, she snuck into Kabir's room to check on him and found him fast asleep, a small smile on his face.

The happiness he radiated after the conversation was not lost on her. *What if these people tried to contact Kabir again? What if Bhailal or Tarannum called him up tomorrow? What if Kabir went back to Kashmir and got himself into trouble? Why is this happening to me again?* The anxiety gnawed at her, the image of the saffron container still burning in her mind.

Chapter 5

Iravati scanned the garden the next morning, searching for Kabir, but he was nowhere to be found. She woke Kanval and she answered half asleep, 'Why don't you just call him, Mummy?'

'Iravati peered out the window at the empty parking lot. She pulled out her phone and dialled Kabir's number. He answered on the first ring. 'Hello?'

'I was looking for you. Where are you?' Iravati asked.

'I'm at the music studio,' Kabir replied.

Kanval sat up in bed and asked, 'What's he doing there so early?'

'He's trying to get back to normal, apparently,' Iravati said, with a hint of scepticism in her voice.

Kanval raised an eyebrow. 'That's a good thing, right?'

'I'm not sure this is the right way to go about it,' Iravati replied as she tied her hair up in a bun.

'Why not? He's finally showing some initiative,' Kanval argued.

'He's only doing it because of that phone call,' Iravati said with a sigh. 'I just wish he could find motivation for himself, without needing someone else to push him.'

'Isn't it better that he's trying to move on? That's what we've been hoping for,' Kanval asked.

Iravati turned to face her daughter. 'Of course I want him to move on, but it has to come from the right place. This sudden burst of enthusiasm is just a reaction to that call. It's not sustainable.'

Kanval shook her head. 'I don't get it. Why can't you just be happy for him?'

'I would be happy if he were doing it for the right reasons,' Iravati said firmly. 'But this isn't the right way to go about it.'

Kanval shot back. 'Sometimes I think you just don't want him to be happy.'

'That's not true,' Iravati said, her voice rising slightly. 'I want him to be happy more than anything. But I want him to be happy in a way that's healthy and sustainable.'

Kanval nodded, knowing better than to argue with her mother when she was like this. 'I understand. But let's just give him a chance and see how it goes, ok?' She flopped back onto her pillow and muttered to herself, *Knew it.*

It was 11 o'clock in the morning, and hardly any staff were present in the office. When Rishab entered the studio, he was shocked to see Kabir there. Rishab was embarrassed as he himself was late and was not expecting Kabir to be around.

'Hello, Sir,' Rishab trembled as he spoke.

'Hi, Rishab. I thought you were already here. Where are the others?' Kabir asked.

'I think they must be on their way, Sir,' Rishab replied, still shaken.

'I see. Come, sit. I need to talk to you,' Kabir said, motioning for Rishab to take a seat. Rishab sat down, not sure what was going to be asked of him.

'Ok, so I just came across this data on the computer that you have segregated. It seems we have lost out on a lot of profit due to my negligence, isn't it?' Kabir said, getting straight to the point. Rishab heaved a sigh of relief. Kabir had acknowledged the cause of the mismanagement.

'It seems we don't really have any projects going on,' Kabir continued, his voice filled with anticipation. 'Yes, Sir,' Rishab nodded. 'Is there anything that we can still do or begin with?' Kabir asked.

'Yes, Sir,' Rishab replied, 'but I think it's not feasible to go ahead.'

'Tell me the reason? Have we also lost our reputation?' Kabir asked.

'No, Sir, that's not the case,' Rishab replied.

'Then what is it?'

'The J&K Tourism Department contacted us a few days back. They want us to conceptualize a theme song to boost tourism that can be promoted on social media,' Rishab explained.

Kabir's face lit up with interest. 'And?'

'I'm sorry to say, but I shared the last incomplete recording with Umika Ma'am because I felt it was strong enough to woo them,' Rishab said, looking slightly sheepish.

Kabir's expression turned serious. 'Then?'

'They loved it, but the song is incomplete,' Rishab said, hesitantly. Kabir's heart sank.

'That song was being made for a different purpose, Rishab. You should have at least asked me. But wait, I am sure you asked and I must not have been responsive. Is there anything else we can do?'

Kabir sighed, running a hand through his hair. 'Can we have another singer onboard and redo the complete recording?'

'That's not happening, Rishab. No one is touching that song,' Kabir said firmly.

'Can we do another song for them?'

'I'm not so sure about it, Sir. They really loved this one,' Rishab said, looking apologetic.

'Well, Rishab, it's time to get things rolling. Let's set up a call with the tourism officials and show them what we've got,' Kabir said with newfound enthusiasm.

'Absolutely, Sir. I'll get right on it,' Rishab responded.

Kabir started searching through the recordings in Umika's

voice, feeling a sense of excitement building inside him. As he scrolled through the list, a file named 'Myon Watan' caught his eye.

'What's this? I don't remember recording this,' Kabir said as he put on his headphones and hit play. The song started playing, and Kabir was immediately transported back to 2009. He felt a surge of emotions as he listened to Umika singing about his homeland.

'Rishab, stop everything! We have to include this song in the pitch to the officials. It's perfect for the theme they're looking for,' Kabir exclaimed with a hint of excitement in his voice.

'Sure thing,' Rishab replied, happy to see Kabir finally getting back into the groove.

Kabir continued to work tirelessly, eager to revive his label and take on new projects. He had a newfound energy and drive that he had not felt in years. Listening to the song, he was transported to a different world. He saw himself strolling with Umika in the beautiful valleys of Kashmir, rowing in a shikara and plucking cherries. The memories flooded back. Rishab watched him from a distance, concern evident in his eyes.

Feeling a sense of urgency, Kabir instructed Rishab to gather the entire staff within the next two hours and postpone the meeting for the next two days. He emphasized the importance of preparing the music for the song, instructing Rishab to bring in composers, a Rubab expert and two young boys for backing vocals. The completion of this song had become their sole focus and Kabir was determined not to lose this opportunity.

'Sir, don't worry. I'll make sure everything is arranged,' Rishab reassured him.

Before leaving, Rishab paused as Kabir stopped him with a question. 'Do you know the meaning of "Myon Watan"?' Kabir asked.

Rishab appeared unsure and replied, 'Sorry, Sir? What is it?'

'It's Kashmiri,' Kabir explained, reminiscing about Umika's deep understanding of Kashmiri verses. 'Umika must have recorded it. I'll provide you with more details later. Let's reconvene in an hour.'

Taking a deep breath, Kabir rose from his seat and made his way to the pantry. He brewed a cup of coffee, hoping to calm his racing thoughts. Just as he was about to savour the first sip, his phone rang, and he saw the name 'Sarfaraz Uncle' flashing on the screen. A smile spread across Kabir's face and he eagerly answered the call.

'Hello, Uncle! How are you?' Kabir greeted with delight.

'Beta, I'm doing fine. I just started making calls today. How is everyone at home?' Sarfaraz's voice came through warmly.

Relieved to hear from him, Kabir responded, 'They're all fine, Uncle. We've been trying to reach you several times, but your number was unreachable. We were getting worried.'

Sarfaraz explained the difficulties they had faced and then enquired about Kabir's family. 'Kanval te Iravati cha thik? How is it going with Kanval and Iravati?'

'They're both doing well, Uncle. How is Tarannum Aunty doing?' Kabir asked. Sarfaraz's voice filled with worry as he replied, 'She is unwell. Her diabetes has worsened.'

Offering a solution, Kabir suggested, 'Uncle, please take her to a doctor for a check-up. Now that things are opening up, it's important to prioritize her health.'

'Yes, I'll do that soon,' Sarfaraz replied.

'Let me know if you need any help,' Kabir said. 'By the way, Kabir beta, do you remember that young orphan kid we met when we visited the boarding? Armaan, right? How is he doing?' Sarfaraz asked with curiosity.

'Yes, Uncle, spoke to him yesterday. He's doing fine. We found out that he lives with his parents somewhere in Awantipora,' Kabir shared with relief.

'I'm glad to hear that, beta,' Sarfaraz expressed warmly.

'Kabir, if Iravati is willing to talk, could you please ask her to speak to Tarannum? She's not well and misses her dearly,' Sarfaraz requested, his voice filled with concern.

Kabir paused for a moment, feeling a sense of helplessness as he knew his mother's reluctance to connect. But he mustered the courage and replied, 'Uncle, I understand. I'll surely try to persuade her to talk to Tarannum Aunty. I cannot promise anything, but I will definitely make an effort.'

'Thank you, beta. It means a lot to us. We're really grateful for your support and we shall wait for your call,' Sarfaraz expressed his gratitude.

'Of course, Uncle. You and your family are always in my thoughts. Take care,' Kabir said, conveying his genuine concern.

Kabir felt a mix of emotions as he contemplated the situation in Kashmir. He couldn't guarantee that he could fulfil Sarfaraz's request for the conversation between Iravati and Tarannum, but he was relieved to hear that they were safe and doing well. The spirit of Kashmir still resonated within him, even after returning to Mumbai. The reconnections happening instantly—first Armaan's call, then the project, and now Sarfaraz's call—amazed him. He quickly sent Kanval a text.

> Just spoke to Sarfaraz Uncle; they're all safe. But Tarannum Aunty isn't well and wants to speak to Mum. Please try to arrange that. Also, could you please check the meaning of 'Myon watan'?

Kanval approached Iravati and asked, 'Mummy, what does "Myon Watan" mean?' Iravati, absentmindedly watering the plants, answered, 'My motherland.' Suddenly, she tightened her grip on the watering can, realizing what had just transpired. She turned back instantly, looking at Kanval with a blank expression. Kanval smiled and said, 'Thanks, Mummy.'

Iravati's growing anxiety reflected in her voice, 'Wait, why did you ask that?' Kanval paused and looked back at her mother. 'I sense that there is still a remnant of Kashmiriyat within your thoughts and heart. Therefore, may I kindly ask you to converse with Tarannum Aunty? She isn't keeping well and wishes to speak with you.' Kanval's words left her shocked. *The communication in Kashmir has been restored and these people are trying to contact my children.* She couldn't let that happen and decided that it had to stop—it certainly had to stop.

It was 11 p.m. and everyone felt the exhaustion of a long day. Kabir was engrossed in composing the music, the musicians in the studio were tapping away on the daffli, and the rubab sequence had just ended. 'Those who want to eat can take a ten-minute break or I can order dinner for everyone here,' Kabir offered. The staff wanted to go home but Kabir offering them the10-minute break was a clear message that they were not going anywhere.

'Bhaiyya won't be coming home tonight. There's an urgent project he is working on,' Kanval informed her mother. 'What? Did he call you?' Iravati asked. 'Nope! He left me a text,' Kanval replied casually. Iravati was worried about Kabir. 'It's too late, let me call him.' 'I have already tried doing so, Mummy. It would be much better if he keeps busy. In fact, I am loving this sudden change in his personality,' Kanval replied with a hint of tease. Iravati was caught off guard by Kanval's response. 'I see. But the reason behind this change is not something I'm fond of,' she replied with a despondent tone. Kanval then brought up Tarannum again, 'Have you received a call from her?' Iravati was surprised, 'Tarannum? I don't recall hearing that name before'. 'She's unwell. Please call her soon,' Kanval spoke with concern in her voice, ignoring her mother's oblivious tone. 'I am going to sleep now,' Iravati started to depart. 'Well, wait. I have something to tell you,' Kanval said, sensing her mother's hesitation. 'What is it, Kanval?' Iravati asked with a sudden jerk. 'Your son is working on a Kashmiri song, "Myon Watan", for the tourism department of Jammu and Kashmir very dedicatedly.' Iravati's heart skipped a beat. Her children were slipping out of her hands. She couldn't respond to Kanval and kept looking at her. She mumbled a goodnight and retreated to her room feeling helpless as everything was coming back to her in the name of Sarfaraz, Tarannum, Armaan and Myon Kashmir! Kanval wanted to reach out to her but she held back. *If she couldn't be happy for her son's professional endeavours, then what would keep her happy?*

The night had been a gruelling one, with everyone working tirelessly to complete the song. At 6 a.m., the music was finally complete and everyone collapsed wherever they could find a spot to rest. Kabir was sitting with his eyes closed, lost in the song, when Iravati walked in with breakfast. She could see the look of ecstasy on Kabir's face and couldn't help but feel a sense of confusion for her son. As he opened his eyes and saw her, Kabir asked, 'Mummy? When did you come?' 'A few minutes ago, with some breakfast. You must be hungry,' replied Iravati. 'You are a saving grace, Mummy,' said Kabir as he started to eat.

Iravati hadn't slept all night and she suddenly felt the need to get closer to her son before someone else took him away. She realized that she had to be a little more flexible with him, even if it meant sacrificing some of her principles.

'Can I tell you something, Mummy?' Kabir asked.

'You don't really have to take my permission, beta,' she responded.

'I am sorry for every nuisance I have caused you, Mummy,' Kabir said, pausing in his eating.

'What for, Kabir?' asked Iravati, surprised.

'Mummy, I've had a wake-up call. I deeply regret the mistakes I made after Umika's death, causing a rift between you and Kanval. I'm sorry. I want to rebuild our bond with a renewed perspective,' Kabir earnestly conveyed to his mother.

Iravati's motherly instincts kicked in and she realized that she had been too hard on her son, locked up in her own depression. 'Well, let me be very sorry to you, my dear. There are times when parents should apologize to their children and I am genuinely sorry. But I want you to know that I'm just trying to be protective,' she said.

'I understand, Mummy. Maybe you can give me some time. Getting back to normal isn't too normal for me,' said Kabir.

Rishab interrupted them, knocking on the door. 'Sir, may I?' he asked.

'Something urgent, Rishab?' Kabir replied.

'Sir, we have received an email from the authorities. They want to take the meeting today itself. What do I reply?' Rishab asked.

'Fix the meeting at 11 a.m. The song is almost ready. You guys quickly go home, freshen up and come back.'

'I need your blessings, Mummy. This project is very important for me. To be tagged with the government's services can be a great start,' Kabir said.

'All the very best, beta. I'm sure you have done something wonderful,' Iravati replied.

'Mom, can I request something?' Kabir asked.

'Sure, tell me,' she said.

'Well, nobody here understands Kashmiri better than you. Would you please listen to the song and tell me how it is?' Kabir requested.

Iravati hesitated for a moment but realized that being rigid wouldn't bring her son closer to her. With much self-resistance, she agreed. Kabir was happy, and he started to play the song. Iravati wanted to run away, but she held back. She couldn't help but feel uneasy as she listened to the song that Kabir played for her. Despite the unease churning inside of her, she kept her composure and did not express her discomfort to Kabir.

As the song continued to play, it served as a catalyst, intensifying the negative emotions already brewing in Iravati's mind but she remained composed, determined not to let her true feelings show. When the song finally ended, she abruptly got up from her seat, ready to leave.

'I'll leave, beta,' she announced, surprising Kabir. He looked at her with a mixture of surprise and curiosity. 'Mummy, would you not give any comments?' he asked, genuinely puzzled by her sudden departure. Iravati turned back to face him, her gaze unwavering.

'Do I need to praise Umika's voice? Or your fantastic piece of art?' she retorted tactfully. Kabir was taken aback, unsure of how to interpret her response. But before he could say anything, Iravati continued to gaze at him, her expression softening. 'It's wonderful!'

Thankful for her unexpected approval, Kabir responded, 'Thank you so much, Mummy.' Iravati's smile widened, 'I'll see you at home, do not overwork yourself; come quickly.' Kabir witnessed another shade of Iravati he hadn't seen before.

Kabir felt compelled to share his mother's newfound happiness with Kanval via a text. 'Mummy seems happy.' Kanval, aware of their mother's stubbornness, replied to herself, *rather pretending.* She understood the complexities of Iravati's emotions and the effort it took for her to show her happiness.

Iravati acknowledged the need for a fresh start with Kabir. He had already immersed himself in his work, once he found stability, she resolved to prioritize his marriage.

Kanval worried about Tarannum's health. 'Would you speak to Tarannum Aunty once?' Kanval stared at her mother, contemplating her response. 'And why do you think I would?' she replied, her scepticism apparent. Kanval wasn't surprised by her mother's words.

Later that evening, Kabir rushed home, his excitement observable. As he joined Kanval and Iravati at the dinner table, Kanval couldn't resist. With a mischievous grin, she asked, 'Your song has been approved, hasn't it?'

Kabir was taken aback by her astuteness. Suppressing a smile, he asked, 'How did you know that?' Kanval laughed in response, saying, 'Well, your enthusiasm says it all.' Iravati couldn't help but share in her son's joy, expressing her congratulations with a warm smile.

'Thanks, Mummy. But there's something more to congratulate me for,' Kabir said, his tone turning serious. He paused, carefully choosing his words. 'I will have to travel to Kashmir. We have been awarded the contract to shoot the music video.' Iravati's jaw dropped in shock. 'Why?' she exclaimed, her voice trailing off. Kanval could see her mother's disappointment and frustration, but she could hardly control her laughter and tried suppressing it. 'They were so impressed with the music that they have asked us to produce the video,' she interjected. Iravati was speechless. Kanval could see her mother's disappointment and frustration.

Iravati was quiet, still trying to process the news. 'For this, I need immense support from both of you. This will be the first-ever video production other than music,' Kabir said, looking at both of them. 'Mummy, you look lost,' he added, noticing her silence. 'Lost? No, no, no, I'm not lost. I was just thinking if you drop...' Iravati trailed off, unable to finish her sentence. Kanval interrupted, 'You have our backs, my dear brother, go ahead.'

Kabir's thoughts reassured him that Iravati wouldn't object, and even if she did, Kanval would handle the situation. Above all, this project was of the utmost importance and the aura was such that nobody could stop him. 'I'll just freshen up,' Kabir said, heading to the washroom. Once he was out of sight, Kanval snapped at her lost-in-thought mother. Iravati was overwhelmed with feelings of hurt, sadness and frustration, but she struggled to express herself.

'Hello, Mummy.' Irritated, Iravati snapped back, 'What?' Sensing her mother's anxiety, Kanval gently urged her to relax. Iravati looked away, bitterness seeping through her words as she accused, 'I'm sure you're enjoying this,' her anger apparent.

Kanval was taken aback by her mother's words. 'That's not true, Mummy,' she asserted firmly. 'I want Bhaiyya to be happy. I want him to live his life on his own terms. But you can't keep holding on to him like this. You need to let go.'

Iravati's face twisted with disgust as she spat out her words, 'So, you're telling me to just let him go? To let him walk blindly into danger?' Kanval sighed heavily, trying to maintain her composure. She firmly but calmly conveyed, 'No, Mummy. I'm saying that your son is an adult and he needs to make his own decisions. He needs your support, not your constant criticism and fear-mongering.' Iravati's eyes narrowed, her emotions trembling on her quivering lip. 'I just want him to be safe. Is that too much to ask?'

Witnessing her mother's pain, Kanval softened her tone, understanding the depths of Iravati's concerns. 'No, it's not too much to ask, Mummy. But you can't protect him from everything. You have to trust that he's capable of making his own choices.'

Iravati's hand twitched with anger, and in a sudden burst of rage, she slapped herself hard across the face. The sound reverberated through the room, causing Kanval to flinch. 'Are you happy now? You want to hurt me too? Go ahead and slap me.'

Kanval was taken aback by her mother's outburst but quickly composed herself. 'Stop this, Mummy,' she said urgently, rushing to intervene and stop Iravati.

But Iravati was consumed by her emotions. Kanval was taken aback by her mother's sudden outburst, but she refused to succumb to the anger.

'Relax, Mummy! Relax!' Kanval said firmly. 'I won't let you do this. Is this how a grown-up behaves?' Slowly, Iravati lowered her hand and sank back onto the couch. Tears were streaming down Kanval's face. She squeezed Iravati's hand tightly. 'It's going to be ok, Mummy,' she whispered. 'We'll get through this, together.'

Iravati left the room, her emotions still raw and unresolved. Kabir emerged from his own room, sensing that something had transpired between his mother and sister. With a concerned frown, he asked Kanval, 'What just happened, Kanval?' Kanval hesitated for a moment before replying, 'Nothing, everything's ok. Mummy is just really happy about your achievement.' Kabir felt a lingering doubt and pressed further, 'But is she ok with me going to Kashmir?' Kanval took a deep breath, trying to reassure him, 'I've explained everything to her, Kabir. She's calm about it.' However, Kabir remained unconvinced, insisting, 'Are you sure? Maybe I should talk to her myself.'

Kanval knew that delaying Kabir from reaching out to their mother would be the best course of action. 'Do it tomorrow morning,' she suggested. 'And don't forget to credit Pandit Dinanath Kaul for "Myon Watan" in your music video. I just found his name while surfing the internet.' Kabir's eyes widened with excitement, 'Yeah, of course! Thanks, Kanval. This is really happening!'

That night, Kabir found himself tossing and turning in bed, unable to sleep. His mind buzzed with questions and ideas about the music video project. *Who would direct it? What locations would be ideal? Who would play the lead roles?* He had so much to plan and he didn't know where to start. But the thought of going to Kashmir filled him with a sense of peace. He longed to escape the concrete jungle of the city and immerse himself in the simple beauty of nature.

The next morning, Kabir came face to face with Iravati. Gathering his courage, he broached the topic on his mind. 'Mummy, I know you might not be thrilled about this, but I've decided to go to Kashmir,' he said, bracing himself for her disapproval. Iravati listened intently, her eyes softening as she observed the passion in her son's voice. Fixing her gaze on Kabir, she spoke in a tone that surprised him, 'Trying to stop you now would be like trying to stop a bird from flying,' she said, a hint of sarcasm in her voice. 'You've always followed your heart, so do what's best for yourself.'

Iravati's words were spoken with a mix of resignation and acceptance, reflecting the conflict within her. Her response confused Kabir, as it seemed she both agreed and disagreed. However, Kabir chose to focus on the approval, ignoring the confusion for now. 'Thank you, Mummy. I promise I'll take care of myself,' he replied, his eyes still searching for her confidence. Iravati smiled, but there was a hint of sadness in her eyes that didn't quite reach her smile. She wanted to caution Kabir about reconnecting with Tarannum, Sarfaraz and Armaan's family, but she knew she couldn't say much.

'Come back to me safe and sound,' she said softly, reaching out to hug him. Kabir hugged her back, feeling grateful for her understanding. As they pulled away, he could see the reluctance in her eyes, causing him to pause. He knew this wasn't easy for her, but he was determined to make the most of this opportunity.

As Iravati was about to leave, she took a moment of pause and turned back, looking at Kabir who anxiously awaited something unspoken to come from her. Her face hardened slightly as she gazed at him. 'Don't do anything that will disappoint me, Kabir,' she stated with a pointed look. Kabir caught the intensity in Iravati's eyes as she gave him a stern look. He understood exactly what she was trying to convey. It felt as though she had said a thousand words with just one expression, and it suddenly gave him a sense of concern amidst his excitement.

As Kabir rushed around, Iravati busied herself with packing his bags. She carefully placed his newly-bought clothes in his suitcase, ensuring everything was neatly organized. But as she reached for the shopper bag, her hands trembled slightly. Her eyes widened as she saw what lay inside—a small gift wrapped in brown paper. She knew exactly who it was for. Her heart raced as she tried to calm herself down. She couldn't let Kabir know it was overwhelming her.

The next day, Kabir was full of excitement as he prepared to leave for the trip with the crew. He had barely slept, but his energy was infectious. Iravati and Kanval accompanied him to the airport. Kabir reassured his mother asking her not to worry, and promised to be back soon.

'Telling a mother not to worry about her child is like telling water not to be wet,' Iravati said with a hint of sadness in her voice. Kabir noticed her fatigue and concern. 'Mummy, it seems like you haven't slept properly. The first thing you'll do when you go home is rest,' he suggested. Iravati smiled. 'I have heard somewhere that mothers don't sleep, they just worry with their eyes closed.'

I thought she would give a list of dos and don'ts, Kabir thought. 'Sure, having known my worries, I hope you return with my expectations.' As they said their goodbyes, Iravati's mind raced with thoughts of what Kabir would be up to and who he might end up meeting. Kanval noticed the worried expression on her mother's face. 'Mummy? Thinking too much?' Kanval asked. Kanval put a hand on her mother's shoulder. 'You'll see, he'll come back with great stories and new experiences.' Iravati nodded, partly feeling assured by Kanval's words, but the unease didn't dissipate. She couldn't shake off the feeling that something was about to change.

The moment Kabir stepped out of the airport, he was greeted by a breathtaking sight of towering mountains. Memories of his previous visit flooded his mind. The familiar scents of pine trees and wildflowers filled the air, evoking a sense of nostalgia. Smiling, he gazed at the sprawling landscape before him.

Kabir scanned the crowd for Bashar, their trusted driver. Spotting him, Kabir hurried towards Bashar, eager to embrace him after such a long time. However, he couldn't help but notice the lack of enthusiasm in Bashar's eyes. The vibrant spirit that had always characterized him seemed to be missing. Kabir hugged him tightly, sensing a tinge of sadness in the air. As they pulled away, Kabir couldn't ignore the melancholic look in Bashar's eyes. Something had changed and he wondered what could have caused such a shift in Bashar's demeanour.

The crew members, already seated by the windows, were captivated by the majestic beauty of Kashmir. The lush valleys and glistening mountains added to the charm of this paradise on earth. Their first destination, as per the request of the Jammu and Kashmir Tourism Department, was Gurais Valley—an unexplored gem. The journey to Gurais was long and challenging, with eight hours of non-stop driving on partially snow-covered roads and mountains. The chinar trees stood bare, their fallen leaves casting a rustic bronze hue. The temperature was low, hovering around five degrees Celsius and the crew members were bundled up in warm jackets.

The bus made several stops due to the unpredictable climate, but each stop became an opportunity to witness the exquisite beauty of Kashmir. Their first destination was Bandipora, a town adorned with majestic mansions and hospitable locals. En route, they visited Mansabal Lake, a serene freshwater lake where shikaras peacefully floated. Unlike the bustling Dal Lake, Mansabal was a hidden gem, known for its tranquillity. Continuing their journey, they passed Wular Lake, an awe-inspiring sight impossible to overlook. The villages they encountered was equally breathtaking, untouched by artificiality and showcasing the essence of this earthly paradise. Although the road to their final destination had deteriorated, Bashar expertly manoeuvred through the twists and turns.

At the army checkpoint, they registered their presence, drawing amused glances from the locals who perceived them as urban dwellers. As the bus meandered along a narrow road, the river flowed gracefully on the left, offering a magnificent spectacle. Passing through Bagtore Village, Bashar pointed out the Indian and Pakistani checkpoints on opposing hilltops, separated by the Line of Control. Finally, after a long and exhausting journey, the bus reached Dawar at 6 p.m. The crew eagerly headed straight to the J&K Tourism Department's guest house, a modest accommodation due to the place still being developed as a tourism hub. Kabir, longing to alleviate the biting cold, indulged in a comforting hot water bath. As the sun began to set, the crew gathered in the guest house compound, their hands wrapped around cups of steaming tea, filled with a contagious excitement. The place felt like a slice of heaven within the already heavenly Kashmir.

The next morning, Kabir awoke early and embarked on a walk towards the Kishan Ganga River. The scenery that unfolded before him took his breath away. The river surged with tremendous force, its crystal-clear waters reflecting the sunlight, evoking the image of countless shimmering diamonds. Lush green hills enveloped the surroundings. Closing his eyes, Kabir surrendered himself to the symphony of nature, feeling as if the entire world had momentarily ceased to exist.

In that transcendent moment, Kabir sensed a presence beside him. Opening his eyes, he was greeted by a flock of birds gliding through the sky, their wings moving in perfect synchrony. Kabir was mesmerized by their graceful flight; they soared higher and higher before vanishing into the ethereal clouds above. Filled with awe, Kabir took a deep breath, allowing the crisp mountain air to revitalize his being

He watched as the camera crew set up their equipment and the make-up artists hurriedly applied the finishing touches to the actors' faces. The Indian Armed Forces were present, ensuring the security of the shoot. Kabir knew how important it was to show the world the beauty of Kashmir, to rebrand it as a hub of peace and prosperity rather than conflict.

The first shot began, with the group of youngsters playing and dancing to the Rubab tunes. The camera captured their joy and enthusiasm, their faces glowing with happiness. Kabir had selected young crew members to be a part of the sequence, giving them a chance to showcase their talent and be a part of something special.

After the shoot, the crew moved on to the Habba Khatoon natural water spring, where they shot a sequence of a young girl washing her wound in the medicinal waters. The spring was breathtakingly beautiful, with crystal clear water gushing out of the rocks and flowing downstream. The camera captured the healing power of the spring, the girl's relief evident on her face.

The day ended with an aerial shot of the Gurais Valley, showcasing its natural beauty and magnificence. The crew then relaxed and enjoyed their time at the river site, with camps set up for their convenience. But amidst all the fun and laughter, Kabir felt a strange calm stirring in him. The mountains seemed to whisper to him and the air seemed to carry the scent of peace.

Kabir couldn't help but miss Umika terribly. He knew that she would have loved this place. But he was also grateful to her for showing him the way, for making him see the beauty in everything around him.

That night, as he sat on a rock, observing the sound of the water, he was interrupted by a voice. 'Bhaalu aajayega, andar aajao!' someone ordered in a husky voice. 'A bear might be around, come inside.' Kabir turned around instantly. It was Bashar.

'Bashar! You scared me,' Kabir said, surprised to see him.

'I am telling you the truth,' Bashar replied, 'there are many wild animals around, including bears. Beware!'

Kabir noticed that Bashar seemed quieter and more depressed than during their previous trip but was trying to mingle forcefully. He could sense a deep alienation within him. 'Come sit here, Bashar,' Kabir called out to him.

Bashar sat with a subtle smile, looking at the river. Kabir studied him briefly, then spoke. 'I'm sure you're very angry with the Article being brought down, right?'

Bashar said nothing, gazing deeply at the campfire.

'Tell me,' Kabir insisted. There was silence again, but Kabir was determined to get Bashar to speak up.

'Our forefathers made some wrong decisions and now we are bearing the brunt of it,' Bashar finally said, looking Kabir straight in the eye.

Kabir understood what Bashar meant. 'It's true that some of us have found ways to bear the brunt of it all, with patience or tears or frozen emotions,' he said. 'But what I still struggle to accept is the way it was all brought down upon us. Sayeeda, my wife, was pregnant and went into early labour. With no way to leave or seek help, I finally mustered the courage to appeal to the CRPF for help, but it was too late. By the time we reached the hospital, she was already gone.'

As Kabir looked at Bashar, it was as if he was seeing a reflection of his own pain in the other man's eyes. The loss of a loved one was a wound that never truly healed, a constant ache that could only be understood by those who had felt it themselves.

'It's way too late, please sleep,' Bashar said, leaving for his tent.

Kabir looked at the stars. 'Someday we all become stars after we leave the earth,' he thought.

The crew started early in the morning for Gulmarg, making sure to avoid any possible traffic. They had to bid farewell to the wonderful place. After an eight-hour journey, the crew reached the Tangmarg District. The road to Gulmarg was a circular hill, surrounded by the densely forested range of Pir Panjal at every turn. It required careful driving and Bashar took it slow.

Much of the day had already passed. Kabir didn't want to waste the remaining time and started a conversation with Bashar about possible locations and the types of shots they could capture for the video. Bashar shared his ideas and together they discussed the highlights of Gulmarg, known as one of the world's finest skiing destinations.

There were speculations about snowfall, which could potentially disrupt the shoot. The shoot was supposed to cover the cable car ride with the youngsters. Cameras were fixed in the three cable cars. The cable car began to move for phase one of the ride.

As the cable car ascended, the actors gazed down with excited expressions, and as luck would have it, it started to snow. The beauty of the snowfall was captured amazingly on camera. Down the hill, some tourists had chosen to come up on horseback instead of taking the cable car, and they were visible from above. As the cable car continued its ascent, they passed by small huts. There was no room for reshoots, so Kabir had to carefully capture the passing shots as well as those with the crew.

As soon as the crew reached phase one, the snowfall turned

into rain, casting uncertainty over the shoot. 'Gulmarg is full of uncertainty,' Bashar remarked, aware of the unpredictable weather in the area. But the crew's enthusiasm couldn't be dampened. Most of them were outside, embracing the cold rain and enjoying themselves. Kabir knew he couldn't let them stay out for too long. 'Get them in or they'll fall sick, Kabir Bhai,' Bashar advised.

Watching the crew enjoying the rain, Kabir couldn't help but smile. He grabbed an umbrella and went out to gather everyone. However, as he stepped on a rock, Kabir slipped and fell to the ground, his umbrella flying a few metres away. The crew burst into laughter, encircling him. Kabir felt a hint of embarrassment, but it quickly transformed into amusement.

Drenched in the rain, Kabir felt an unexpected urge to open himself up to the universe. Without hesitation, he spread his arms wide, as if ready to embrace the world. His chest expanded, inhaling the air around him. Closing his eyes, he surrendered to the moment, allowing himself to be carried away by the rain on his face and the wind in his hair. It was as if he was shedding all his worries and fears, merging with the world around him.

A strange surge of energy ignited within him. He started running aimlessly, bewildered. Before he realized it, he found himself at the edge of a steep cliff, his heart pounding in his chest. As he stood there through the dense fog, a feeling of liberation washed over him, as if he were shedding all his fears and doubts. In those moments, he was free, truly and wholly free; until he knelt on his knees, and everything went blurry—from white to black.

Kabir awoke to the clock glaring at him, showing 12.30 a.m. Bashar, half asleep in the nearby chair, stirred at Kabir's call. 'Bashar, Bashar,' Kabir said urgently, seeking his attention. Bashar instantly woke up. 'What's wrong, Bashar? Is everything all right?'

'Not really,' Bashar replied, pulling closer. 'When the leader of the group behaves irresponsibly, things are bound to go downhill.' He quickly poured tea from the flask avoiding eye contact while Kabir tried to recollect the recent events.

'Can I ask you something, Kabir Bhaya?' Bashar enquired. Kabir remained silent as he handed him a cup of tea, taking a sip himself. 'Did you actually plan to end your life by jumping off the cliff?' There was a pause. 'No,' Kabir replied softly.

'Then why the hell did you run off like a madman?' Bashar exclaimed. Kabir had no answer. 'It took the officers four hours to track you, and if they hadn't, you would have rolled down ten thousand feet to your death.'

'Oh God!' Kabir was shocked. 'I don't know what came over me, Bashar.' Bashar continued to observe him. 'I think I was overwhelmed by something, can you please update me on the shoot and the crew? Is everything all right?' Kabir asked anxiously.

'Witnessing a tragic incident today was enough of a movie scene,' Bashar replied. 'The only person you need to answer to is the officer from the Tourism Department, and he's quite annoyed.'

Kabir was in a dilemma. The pressure prevented him from sleeping. What if the officer complained about him? What if the shoot got cancelled? What if they lost the contract? His mind raced with thoughts. He decided he would meet the officer first thing in the morning.

The morning greeted him with a beautiful view of the cable car platform from a distance. Kabir couldn't eat or drink until he had spoken to the officer. He had no answers but he desperately needed to convince him. Kabir went down to the dining area, searching for the officer. Some crew members who were already there tried to approach him to inquire about his health, but he waved them off.

Finally, he faced the officer, who was filling his plate with breakfast. 'Hello, Sir, how are you?' Kabir greeted him nervously.

The officer glanced at him and motioned for him to sit. As Kabir walked over to the dining table, the crew members watched, filled with tension.

'I won't waste your time and get straight to the point,' the officer began. 'You have nearly jeopardized this project. I already discussed it with the department yesterday. Moreover, I won't lecture you because of your health right now. If you have something to tell me, you have exactly one minute.'

Kabir trembled, feeling the anxiety building up inside him. He couldn't afford to lose this project. The officer, Mohan Kachroo, in his tourism uniform with a name badge, caught Kabir's attention, prompting him to act instantly. 'Since I have only one minute,' Kabir began, 'let me share something: my late wife, Umika Raina, used to say that she believed that we should give our children two gifts—roots and wings. Today, after twenty-nine years, I have come back to my roots, to this land that witnessed my frenzied running, my desperate quest for purpose. I think I flew a little too high with those wings and lost my balance. So like a child whose enthusiasm needs a gentle hold, I ask you to forgive me.'

The officer's expression changed upon learning Kabir's identity through his surname. He placed his tea on the table and looked to the side. 'Oh God,' the officer said, feeling a connection as a fellow member of his community. Kabir continued, 'I'm sorry, Sir, but this project means a lot to me and—'

The officer interrupted, 'All right! Be careful and take good care of yourself.' Kabir's face lit up with joy and he thanked the officer.

Despite his fever, Kabir couldn't contain his excitement. He quickly prepared, covering his head with a monkey cap, putting on gloves and wearing a thick leather jacket. Bashar ensured there was no room for carelessness. The crew boarded the cable car to reach phase two, witnessing the breathtaking vistas along the way.

Their first location was the stunning Alpather Lake, with its calm and enchanting greenish-blue waters. Kabir felt a desire to abandon the shoot and simply sit there, embracing the serene atmosphere. 'Five more kilometres of trekking upwards and you'll witness the actual Line of Control between India and Pakistan,' someone informed Kabir. As they moved forward, the altitude increased and some members of the crew struggled with the reduced oxygen. Soon, fog rolled in, indicating bad weather. 'We have to stop the trek here,' the guide announced. Within minutes, heavy rain began pouring down. The crew swiftly protected their equipment and rushed back to the cable car base.

After an hour, they returned to the hotel for the check out. However, they had one more location to cover en route to Srinagar, the Drang Waterfall. The place resembled Pahalgam, with a fast-flowing stream along the route. The last three kilometres were rocky and still under construction.

'This spot used to be a tax collection point for tourist vehicles heading to Gulmarg. Due to the hills in the backdrop and the Ferozepur stream running in full flow, it turned into a tourist destination,' the tourism officer said. Within no time they reached the waterfall.

The officer explained, 'Right now, as you see, the waterfall cascades downwards, but it freezes in winter.' The waterfall was a marvel to behold. The place was untouched by human interference, filled with pure oxygen that refreshed the senses. The crew captured stunning visuals, even shooting some impromptu scenes of them playing under the waterfall.

After the shoot, the crew returned to the vanity bus, shivering from the cold water. They were quickly served hot Maggi and coffee to warm themselves up. Kabir was in awe of the place and wished Kanval was there to witness its beauty. He requested a cup of tea at the waterfall itself, wanting to soak in the tranquillity of the location. He dipped his feet in the water, but it was too cold to bear for more than a few seconds. Kabir couldn't help but think that it was an injustice for people to spend a fortune on Switzerland, unaware of thein their own country. He was determined to capture the soul of the place.

Upon reaching Srinagar, Kabir felt nostalgic as they crossed the Jhelum River on the Zero Bridge. The river flowed with vigour, a significant stream running through the heart of the city. The crew checked into a five-star hotel situated on a hill overlooking the Dal Lake.

Kabir immediately reworked the sequence and locations for the city shoot. He decided to include religious shrines in the scenes, aiming to attract a diverse crowd that reflected Kashmir's secularity. Alongside the Shankaracharya Temple and Hazrat Bal Mosque, he added the ruins of Avantiswami Temple. Surprisingly, there were fewer tourists, making it easier to shoot with clear views.

They filmed an aerial view of the Dal Lake with enthusiastic youngsters in shikaras. Although Kabir wanted to shoot in Sarfaraz's houseboat, the network connectivity was poor, and he couldn't get in touch with him. Instead, the Tourism Department had arranged a luxury houseboat for them. The dinner sequence was shot with delight, emanating a sense of calm and contentment. The authenticity of the scene was substantial. The next day promised to be the busiest, with six locations on the agenda, including the dancing sequence. Kabir and his crew set off for the shoot at 5 a.m., fuelled by an early breakfast. They visited the Mughal gardens, Pari Mahal, Khanqaah, Hazrat Bal and Shankaracharya Temple. Each shot highlighted Kashmir's diverse cultural heritage.

Since Awantipora was a long drive away, Kabir had requested that the dancing sequence be filmed before departing for the ancient ruins. Bashar suggested that they attend a wedding in his locality and shoot the authentic dancing sequence there, while covering a traditional Kashmiri wedding.

Kabir quickly developed the idea that Bashar should escort the actors to the wedding in his locality. A wide shot of the old city's downtown area was taken, showing River Jhelum flowing through it and both banks connected through bridges. The wedding took place at an old wooden house that gave a perfect feel of the old city. The house was beautifully decorated with lights and flowers, and the womenfolk of the house were singing the traditional song 'Roshe' with dafflis. The scene was enchanting, and a large space was carved out in the house itself for the dance sequence. As the women sang songs, the artist danced on their tunes, and it was so real that it felt like they were witnessing an actual wedding. The guests at the wedding were served with appetizers and the wazwaan in the traditional dawat that concluded at midnight.

Kabir decided to shoot at Avantiswami Temple in Awantipora District. He was nervous because it was the village where Armaan lived and he had not informed his family about his arrival in Kashmir. He had no idea if they would welcome him or ask him to stay back.

The crew visited two temples known as the Avantiswami Temples, dating back to the ninth century. The Avantiswami Temple was in ruins. As the guide explained the history of the temple, Kabir was preparing the camera. The temple had a feel of Greek architecture and the columns, with carvings of apsaras and well-elaborated art, were far from ordinary,. Kabir shot a closeup of the Navgrahas, the nine planets in Hindu astrology, carved on the stone walls. As the crew wrapped up the shoot at Awantipora, Kabir couldn't help but feel a sense of melancholy. He had come to Kashmir hoping to capture the essence of the place, but the more he saw of it, the more he realized he could never do justice to its beauty even with the greatest lens.

The crew started to pack up and it was a time for leisure for them. They were headed to Pahalgam and were to leave the day after. Kabir had another plan. Kabir beckoned Bashar to a corner and asked, 'Do you remember the blind boy we visited at the Srinagar hostel?' Bashar furrowed his brow, trying to recall. 'Hafiz Welfare?' he ventured. 'Exactly,' Kabir said, nodding. 'Well, I've learned that he actually lives in this village. Would you help me find his address?' Bashar nodded, 'I don't think it will be difficult. The village is close by. But I recall he was an orphan. Who does he live with now?' 'Nah! He isn't an orphan,' Kabir explained. 'Ah, I see. Do you have their phone number?' Bashar enquired. 'Yes, I do but can't get through, and anyway I want to surprise them,' Kabir said, a mischievous glint in his eyes. 'All right then, let's go find him,' Bashar said, a smile playing on his lips.

Lahore

Shabbir was appointed acting president of the Tanzeem until Ajju's return as per Daarji's last will. He was a powerful man now, with greater control over the Tanzeem's affairs. He had designed a comfortable structure for them to ensure the new recruits wouldn't escape or leave Lahore unable to adjust, as had been the case with Ajju. Shabbir knew the underlying faults in the structure and had wanted to improve them. Shabbir had revised the entire training module with much discipline and had provided special concessions to the recruits such as medical facilities, scholarships for their children's education and monthly maintenance. He had already eliminated the rebels who wanted to take over after Daarji's death. Those who wanted to enjoy the wealth by becoming a Sardar and had little to do with the Tanzeem's mission were finished the moment he became the president.

After offering Zohar prayer at the Badshahi Masjid, Shabbir and his men left for the Miani Sahib graveyard to pay their respects to Daarji, who was laid to rest there. Shabbir offered supplications and duas at Daarji's simple flat grave with a rose sapling planted over it. One of Shabbir's men asked him if he thought Daarji's grave should be customized with a mausoleum built over it. Shabbir kept quiet and did not answer.

Upon reaching their SUV, Shabbir opened the gate and stopped. 'Mitti to aaye thhe, mitti to chale gaye, they came from the earth, and to the earth they returned,' Shabbir said. 'It was his wish that his grave be flat, simple and ordinary. He was a simple man observing a greater mission and disliked the idea of being a spendthrift.'

Wearing a black Pathani with a Sindhi shawl over his shoulders and a Punjabi pagdi, Shabbir's personality was governing. He was six feet tall with an athletic body and most of his intonation was copied from Daarji. As they made their way back to the old city, Shabbir asked his men about the information they had on Ajju. 'Our men have tracked his house, but heavy security is deployed in the overall region due to—' Shabbir interrupted him. 'You must understand that we don't have much time. Ajju's life is in jeopardy and he has risked others too. Make sure we have him back here as soon as possible.'

His men knew how serious Shabbir was in his mission to bring Ajju back. Had it been possible, Shabbir himself would have gone to bring him back but the idea was next to impossible. The tension in the haveli was building up as they prepared for the next move.

BOOK III

Chillai Bacche
or
The Baby Chill

Final ten days of the cold season after Chillai Khurd

Chapter 6

The village, nestled in the countryside of Kashmir, offered breathtaking natural beauty with many mustard fields around. Taking a right turn from the main highway, Bashar stopped the car. The villagers looked at them curiously as they enquired about Armaan's family. Bashar spoke in local Kashmiri, describing Armaan's appearance and blindness.

'Aapko unse kyun milna hai? Why do you want to meet them?' A shopkeeper asked suspiciously. Kabir and Bashar exchanged a meaningful glance, unsure of how to respond.

'I'm just a well-wisher, I want to meet them,' Kabir said. The shopkeeper scrutinized them briefly before providing directions. 'Shukria Jinab,' Bashar expressed gratitude, thanking the shopkeeper. As they departed, the shopkeeper swiftly dialled a number and spoke in hushed tones, 'Assalamualikum Jinab, kuch log aaye hue hain yahan par. Some people have arrived here.'

Kabir noticed the heightened military presence in the village, with armed men patrolling the streets. 'Bashar, why are there so many military men around?'

'It's a sensitive area, Bhaya. The lockdown has just been lifted, so the military is here to maintain law and order,' Bashar explained. The atmosphere felt tense and Kabir could feel his nerves unravelling. 'Is it safe here?'

Bashar reassured him with a smile, 'Don't worry, we've witnessed worse.' However, during their conversation, Bashar detected a fleeting change in the shopkeeper's expression. Being well-acquainted with the people of Kashmir, he recognized it as a sign that something was amiss. Bashar knew the locals were often guarded, but this seemed different. Bashar's mind wandered, contemplating an excuse to leave. 'Listen, Kabir Bhaya, I think it's best if I take off now. You're a tourist here and have nothing to worry about. But things can get unpredictable around here and it's better for you to remain cautious.'

Kabir nodded, comprehending the underlying message. 'I understand, Bashar. I'll be careful and keep in touch if I need anything.'

'Good,' Bashar replied, 'and if you do need assistance, just give me a call, I'll be there to pick you up. But please try to finish your work quickly.'

Kabir smiled and nodded, 'Sure, take care of yourself too.'

With that, Bashar drove away. Kabir watched him depart before turning his attention to the surrounding shops. One shopkeeper caught his eye, conveying a hint of concern through his gaze. Kabir wondered what it could mean but dismissed it momentarily, determined to continue exploring the village. Standing outside Armaan's modest home, Kabir's heart raced with anticipation.

He couldn't help but feel nervous about what lay ahead. Would Armaan's family welcome him? He took a deep breath and knocked on the door. As he waited for someone to answer, Kabir couldn't help but notice the curious stares of passersby. He felt a pang of self-consciousness, wondering what they thought of him. But he quickly pushed those thoughts aside as the door opened and a woman peered out. Her eyes widened in surprise as she saw Kabir. Quickly covering her face, she turned sideways and greeted him with a polite 'Assalamualikum, ji kaun? Who is it?'

Kabir smiled warmly at her. 'I'm Kabir, Kabir Raina,' he replied, his voice steady despite the nerves that still churned in his stomach. 'Kabir? Kabir Sahab?' The woman's face lit up with recognition. Kabir nodded in response. 'Sahab ji, Sahab ji, atthe aao, Kabir sahab aayene. Please come here, Mr Kabir has arrived.' Armaan's father appeared at the door, his eyes wide with shock. 'Kabir?' he exclaimed, his voice thick with emotion. Without hesitation, he pulled Kabir into a warm embrace. 'Please come in,' he said, his voice choked with emotion. Kabir noticed Armaan's sharp resemblance to his father.

Kabir stepped inside, taking in the modest surroundings of the house. He felt a sense of humility wash over him, seeing the simplicity of the space, and also a deep sense of gratitude for the warm welcome he had received. As he sat down in a chair, Kabir's eyes eagerly scanned the room, hoping to catch a glimpse of Armaan. Armaan's mother quickly served him water and the family chatted excitedly with him. 'There could not have been a better surprise for us than this, Kabir Sahab,' Armaan's father exclaimed, his joy evident.

Kabir couldn't help but feel a sense of relief at their warm reception. He had been nervous about how they would react to his unexpected visit, but their kindness and hospitality put him at ease. Armaan's father beamed with joy as he welcomed Kabir into their home. 'I hope I'm not disturbing you by dropping in unannounced,' Kabir replied, feeling a little guilty for showing up without warning. 'No, no, nothing like that. Why didn't you call us?' Armaan's father asked. 'I tried calling your number, but it was out of network,' Kabir explained. 'Ah, yes. I forgot to text you my new number, the old network was really bad.'

'I was here to shoot for a song sequence, so I thought I'd just see Armaan,' Kabir said. 'Ae to changi gall hui, puttar,' Armaan's mother interjected in Punjabi. 'Well, that's a good thing.' Kabir tried to peek around the room. 'Where is Armaan, Uncle?' he asked. 'Armaan will be here in a little while. He is at the Masjid for his Arabic lessons,' his father explained. 'Oh, no worries,' Kabir said. 'Armaan would be so happy to have you here.' 'I was in Kashmir last year for the last rites of my wife when I met Armaan and his boarding mates. Let me tell you, your child is incredible.'

A heavy silence hung in the air. Kalsoom's eyes turned misty as she exchanged a glance with Armaan's father, her heart aching for Kabir's loss. There was a visible sense of shock and sadness in the two, as they shared an unspoken bond of empathy for Kabir's plight. Armaan's father let out a deep sigh, his eyes conveying the depth of his sorrow for Kabir's loss. One that spoke volumes about the human capacity for compassion and understanding.

'Khudaya, this is terrible news,' Armaan's father said, shocked to see a young man losing his spouse. He placed a comforting hand on Kabir's shoulder, 'We are always here for you, beta. You are like a son to me.' Kabir's eyes moistened at the words. Kabir admired the kindness and warmth of Armaan's parents, and he instantly felt like he had a second home with them. 'But why did you keep him in the boarding school, Uncle?' Kabir asked, his face etched with concern. The question surprised both Kalsoom and Armaan's father and they exchanged quick glances. 'There are no good schools for specially-abled children in this village, beta. Armaan may be blind, but he's brilliant in many ways. We got him enrolled in a good school in Srinagar under the specially-abled quota, but the boarding school had to close down due to insufficient funds and the lockdown. When Shamrita Madam left soon after for Dharamshala, we couldn't trust anyone else to take care of Armaan, so we did not send him back there.'

'For now, Kalsoom is tutoring him at home,' Armaan's father said.' Kabir nodded. 'I know, Uncle. Armaan has a good grasp over almost everything, from academics to art. He even surprised us with things that are beyond his limitations.'

As they spoke, a soft voice interrupted them, causing all eyes to turn towards the door. 'Papa ji,' the voice called out.

All eyes were on the main door as Armaan made his way into the house. Kabir watched in amazement as he saw how much Armaan had grown up. Wearing a loose shalwar kameez and a skull cap, Armaan looked angelic. His deep-blue eyes and delicate moustache replicated a younger version of his father. Kabir couldn't help but smile as he saw Armaan walking slowly and carefully, unaware of his presence. As Armaan made his way towards his father, Kalsoom started to tell him about Kabir.

But Kabir gestured to her to keep quiet and let him speak. 'Papa ji, I am finding it difficult to pronounce the Urdu letter Kaaf,' Armaan complained. His father replied, 'Is it? Let's practise it in the evening.' Armaan said, 'No, I want to pronounce it correctly now.'

Kabir was amazed as he watched Armaan. He noticed how he looked a little different, grown up in height, with a subtler moustache and a handsome face. It was like watching a younger version of himself. Memories of the Asthi Kalash, his drowning and the last moments at the resort flooded Kabir's mind. And here was Armaan, right in front of him, reminding him of his past.

'Try pronouncing it again, let's give it a try,' Armaan's father said. Kalsoom was smiling at him from the corner of the room. 'Kaaf,' Armaan said, irritated. 'That's not correct. Try again,' his father said. 'I must have tried saying it five hundred times,' Armaan said, frustrated.

Kabir got up and walked closer to him. He held Armaan's hands and said, 'Now try saying it from the epiglottis, Qaaf.' Armaan lost his expression all of a sudden. 'Wait, who's this?' he asked, touching Kabir's face with suddenness. 'Papaji, who's here?' he asked, becoming aware of a visitor's presence.

'Before I tell you my name, give it a try again. Try saying "Qaaf" from the epiglottis. Touch your epiglottis to your throat and then say "Qaaf".' Armaan was thrilled. He knew who it was but was unsure of his presence. 'Give it a try,' Kabir said. 'Qaaf,' Armaan attempted. 'Once more, you are closer. Don't touch the tip of your tongue to the lower central tooth, else you will make it "kaaf",' Kabir said. 'Qaaaf, Qaaaaf. Correct, Kabir Sir?' Armaan said, thrilled at his presence. He hugged him instantly.

'How did you crack the mystery, Armaan?' Kabir asked, still engulfed in a warm embrace. Armaan beamed, his joy evident. 'Sir, your voice is etched in my memory like the scent of your Aqua deodorant from our first meeting at the boarding house,' Armaan playfully revealed. Kabir chuckled, pleasantly surprised. 'Well, I guess my fragrance became my unintentional calling card. Who knew it would become my secret giveaway!'

'Come, sit here, and please stop calling me Sir, it sounds very formal! Call me Bhaiyya,' Kabir said. 'Ok, but how did you reach here, Bhaiyya? You never had the address,' Armaan asked with a surprised expression. 'Well, you don't need the address for people living in the heart,' Kabir replied with a smile. 'Didi has also come?' Armaan asked with sheer joy.

'Nope, your Didi is at home, but she definitely wants to talk to you. Come, let's take a picture and let me send it to her,' Kabir said, drawing Armaan closer to him. 'Uncle, Aunty, please join us,' he added, urging Armaan's parents to join in the picture. Armaan's parents were hesitant. They were simple and shy people.

Kabir sent the snap to Kanval, and Kalsoom graciously served lunch. The aroma of saag, rajma and rice filled the air, and Armaan's father expressed his apologies for the simplicity of the meal. 'I am very sorry, my dear. This is very simple food. Had we known that you were coming, something better would have been prepared,' he said with regret.

'No, Uncle, all I can see is love served across.' His genuine gratitude brought warmth to the room, melting away any concerns about the meal.

As Kabir took his first bite, he felt an overwhelming urge to feed Armaan with his own hands, a gesture of deep affection and connection. The lunch proceeded, and with every passing moment, Kabir found himself reluctant to leave. His hesitations about staying back were swiftly dismissed by Armaan's father, who surprised him by saying, 'If at all you are planning to leave, beta, that's not happening.'

Caught off guard, Kabir hesitated to respond. He knew he had obligations and pending work in Srinagar, but Kalsoom, speaking in Punjabi, insisted, 'Bus theek ae, Kabir sahab, tussi kal ja sakde ho, aik din aur thahro. Then it's decided that you can leave tomorrow and stay one more day.' Her words resonated within Kabir. Armaan, with a wide smile, added, 'And I am not letting you go anywhere, Kabir Bhaiyya. This is such a short visit.' Kabir felt a mix of confusion and awkwardness. How could he stay with them? He knew his mother would not approve of it.

As Kabir wrestled with his conflicting thoughts, Armaan's father, sensing his hesitation, urged him, 'Stay back for Armaan. He would be overjoyed.' The words struck a chord in Kabir, making him contemplate the idea. *Should I stay? Would it be a good decision?*

Kabir's eyes fluttered open as he awoke from his nap, greeted by the warm afternoon sun streaming through the window. The gentle sound of Armaan humming a ghazal reached his ears, captivating him with its melodic beauty. Intrigued, Kabir sat down beside Armaan, fully engrossed in listening to his enchanting voice that was maturing.

'You're still not pronouncing Qaaf properly,' Kabir gently remarked, noticing a furrow in Armaan's brows. Perplexed, Armaan responded, 'Really? But I've been practising.' Kabir smiled reassuringly, 'I know, but the word you said earlier was "ishk", when it should be "ishq". Listen closely—ishq.' Armaan repeated his instruction. At that moment, Kalsoom appeared in the doorway, her eyes crinkling with amusement. 'Kabir puttar, tussi Urdu da talafuz barey bohat kuch jaanday o?' she teased affectionately. 'Do you know Urdu that well?' As Kabir heard Kalsoom speaking in Punjabi, a quirky notion crossed his mind. He dismissed it thinking she was a Punjabi flower blooming amidst the Kashmiri landscape. 'I'm a musician, Aunty. It goes hand in hand with good pronunciation.' Kalsoom's remark brought a lightness to the room as she gracefully offered him tea.

'Umika was a Kashmiri folk singer,' he said, his voice carrying a touch of sorrow. 'She had a wonderful grasp of Kashmiri, Urdu and Hindi. Her mother, deeply connected to her roots, taught her everything about this place. And Kanval Didi, Armaan, she is an Urdu lover. She is very fond of revolutionary Urdu poets. Seven years in Delhi and she learned it perfectly. Both Umika and Kanval used to hound me for the correct pronunciation from singers.'

Kalsoom listened attentively, her heart heavy with emotion as Kabir continued. 'Umika was a grammar Nazi,' he added with a hint of nostalgia. 'She used to get very irritated when someone pronounced "jara" instead of "zara", "fool" instead of "phool", "baaki" instead of "baqi", "gham" instead of "gam". Sadly, the corrector has gone.' The room fell into a contemplative silence as the absence of Umika lingered in the air.

Armaan's father joined them, returning home with some snacks. Kabir spoke softly, his voice carrying a tinge of sadness, 'Sometimes I feel that death is peaceful, and life is harder. Harder for the one who is left behind.' Kabir turned to Armaan, placing a comforting hand on his head. 'Armaan, please excuse us for a moment, dear.' With obedience, Armaan quietly left the room, his curious gaze lingering for a moment before disappearing.

Taking a deep breath, Kabir's mind wandered back to

memories of Umika and the child they had lost. 'Had it not been for my mother and sister's efforts, I would not be here today. Not only did I lose Umika, but we lost Armaan too.' Kalsoom and Armaan's father exchanged surprised glances, curious about the revelation. 'Armaan?' Kalsoom asked tentatively.

'Our unborn baby,' Kabir explained, his voice trembling with emotion. 'We had already named him Armaan. We had great hopes for his birth, but...' His voice trailed off, the pain too raw to put into words. Kalsoom's eyes welled up with tears as she swiftly offered him solace, 'Tainu koi fikar na honi chahi di, puttar. You needn't worry. Eh Armaan vi tere bachey ne, tere chhote bhai ne. Armaan is just like your child, your little brother.' Armaan's father's eyes were filled with compassion as he acknowledged the depth of Kabir's loss.

Kabir nodded, the pain of his loss still weighing heavily in his heart. Reflecting on Kalsoom's words, he found solace in her definition of Armaan's relation to him now. It eased the emotions he had been grappling with, allowing him to feel a sense of belonging within the family. Wanting to shift the focus, Kabir asked, 'Anyway, Uncle, have you tried taking Armaan to a good doctor?'

Armaan's father sighed heavily, his face etched with worry. 'Beta ji, we have tried almost everything,' he replied. 'Doctors have different opinions, a surgery is advised once he grows up but nothing is guaranteed.' Armaan's father added, 'If the surgery doesn't work, we fear he will sink into depression. Delaying the surgery until he's eighteen will allow him to better cope with the potential disappointment at such a young age.' Kabir's heart ached for Armaan. He wanted to help him in any way he could, but he didn't know how. 'What if we take him to Mumbai for better treatment?' he suggested, trying to sound hopeful. Kalsoom and Armaan's father exchanged puzzled glances. 'We're simple people, beta ji,' Armaan's father said. 'We've never been to a city. But if you think it will help...' Kabir realized he had made a hasty overcommitment.

More than anything, Kabir knew how Iravati would react. It wasn't the right time to bring up his idea. He quickly made up with a reassuring smile. 'No worries, Uncle. Let's wait until Armaan is older and stronger. For now, I'd like to give him some music lessons. Maybe we can check his progress.'

'Armaan, quickly come here, take Kabir Bhaiyya for sightseeing to Jhelum,' Armaan's father suggested. 'That river will be a perfect place for both of you to enjoy music.' Armaan smiled and nodded. Despite being blind since birth, Armaan was familiar with his surroundings. He reached out and took Kabir's hand, gently leading him through the village. As they walked, Armaan's head tilted, capturing the sounds of rustling leaves and the soft whispers of the villagers. Occasionally, he would pause, listening intently before resuming their journey. Kabir couldn't help but notice how Armaan's fingers moved, counting the steps as they walked. It seemed as though he was mapping it out in his mind.

Kabir felt a slight unease as he noticed some curious villagers staring at them. 'Armaan, I've noticed something. People here stare at me a lot,' Kabir remarked, feeling a bit awkward. Armaan chuckled. 'Of course, won't they stare at a famous celebrity singer?' Kabir clarified, 'I don't generally sing, buddy.' Armaan furrowed his eyebrows, confused. 'But you make songs, right?'

'Yes,' Kabir replied, smiling. 'I used to sing, but not anymore. I create the lyrics, compose the music and design the overall structure of the song.' Armaan's curiosity was piqued. 'I don't get it. You don't sing, but you make songs?' Kabir took a moment to explain, 'Well, let me break it down for you. Any song consists of four parts. First, there are the lyrics, which are the lines of the song. Second, there's the background music, known as music composition. The third part is the person who sings the song in the desired tone, and the fourth part is designing the overall structure of the song, deciding which music will fit which line or antara or mukhda.'

'Oh! I never knew that.' Armaan's eyes lit up with excitement. 'So, if you do music direction, you are the boss!' he exclaimed. Kabir chuckled, saying, 'Haha! You may say so.' Armaan was eager to learn more. 'What is antara and the other thing you mentioned? Mukhda?'

'Mukhda!' Armaan repeated, trying to pronounce it correctly. 'No, say mukh-da,' Kabir corrected him gently. 'Mukhda,' Armaan pronounced it correctly. 'Well, here's a note for you: any song that starts will have a mukhda, which is the starting two welcoming lines of the song, also known as the face of the song. The rest of the stanzas in the song are known as antara,' Kabir explained. Armaan found the conversation interesting and informative. They held hands and walked across the bridge. Jhelum was almost there, flowing steadily. As they reached the bridge, Kabir could feel the excitement building inside him. 'Let's sit here, Armaan,' he suggested.

Armaan smiled and nodded, his fingers tracing the edges of the bridge as he found his way to the seat. The sound of the rushing river filled the air, drawing their attention. In the distance, Kabir noticed a flight of steps leading down to the water, and decided it would be a perfect spot to sit.

With anticipation in his eyes, Kabir requested Armaan, 'Sing a song for me, Armaan.'

Armaan instantly agreed and started singing the famous ghazal by Urdu poet Ahmad Faraz, 'Ranjish hi sahi.' Kabir was captivated by the beauty of Armaan's voice, marvelling at the newfound maturity and velvet touch that had developed since the last time he had heard him sing.

'Bhaiyya…Bhaiyya? Are you there?' Armaan's touch brought Kabir back to the present moment. He opened his eyes and looked at Armaan, still under the spell of the performance. 'That's it? Why did you stop?' he asked, longing for more.

'That's it, Bhaiyya, I knew only this much of it. How did you like my song?' Armaan asked, a glimmer of hope shining in his eyes.

Kabir, deeply moved by the performance, pulled Armaan closer and said, 'Well, the song was amazing, especially the quick jump from "Ranjish" to "hii". It was very well-synced.'

Kabir nodded, appreciating the talent before him. 'It was wonderful except for a minor pronunciation mistake in one of the words,' Kabir gently pointed out, his voice tinged with disappointment.

Armaan looked at Kabir with confusion, eager to correct his error. 'Pronunciation? Which word?' he inquired.

Kabir teased him, saying, 'Guess, guess.'

Armaan, feeling clueless, decided to sing the third line again. 'Aa fir se… Oops sorry, I recollect it's "phir", not "fir".'

Kabir acknowledged his correction.

There was a curiosity running in Kabir's mind. 'Armaan, unlike other children your age who prefer to sing pop and Bollywood songs, you always sing folk songs and other serious genres like ghazal. Why is that?'

'Because that's all I know, Bhaiyya. We don't have a television or a radio at home,' Armaan said, his voice tinged with sadness. 'Oh, all right,' Kabir said, trying to hide his surprise.

'Shamrita Didi used to arrange music sessions for us as a part of the workshop at the boarding school, and sometimes other boys used to play it on their mobile phones. That's where I used to listen to the songs,' Armaan explained. 'I see. But tell me, where did you learn this ghazal? Do you know who had mastery over it?' Kabir asked, intrigued.

'No, Bhaiyya,' Armaan said. 'Okay, so keep in mind that this ghazal was sung by the legendary Mehdi Hasan Khan Sahab,' Kabir said. 'I'll keep that in mind. However, I learned this ghazal from my mother. She used to sing it for my father,' Armaan said, a hint of sadness creeping into his voice. 'For Uncle? Is it?' Kabir asked, sensing that there was more to the story.

'Yes, she always sings the ghazal when Papa goes away and then comes back to us occasionally,' Armaan said, his voice trailing off. The sentence drew Kabir's interest. 'Comes back occasionally? I didn't get this. Where does he go, but? Tell me?' Kabir was curious to know more. In that moment someone tapped him from behind, interrupting their conversation. Kabir turned to see a CRPF personnel standing behind him, causing his heart to race.

'Can I check your ID, please?' the personnel asked, their expression stern. Kabir's mind started racing, wondering why he was being asked for his ID. He tried to keep his voice steady as he handed over his ID, which the personnel briefly glanced at before handing it back. 'Thank you,' the personnel said before walking away. Kabir's anxiety grew and his mind raced with possible scenarios.

Just then, the sky darkened and the wind started to pick up, whipping their hair into their faces. 'Bhaiyya, let's go home,' Armaan said, sensing the sudden change in weather. The two of them started running through the rain, trying to reach home as quickly as possible. They passed by the bridge and the graveyard and Kabir's attention was momentarily drawn away.

As they finally reached home, Kalsoom greeted them at the door. 'Rabba ve, tussi toh bilkul geele ho gaye ho.' Kalsoom exclaimed in a concerned tone as she saw Kabir and Armaan drenched in the rain. She quickly handed Kabir a towel and began wiping off the rainwater from Armaan's face.

She then served them evening breakfast, consisting of samosas, tea and paranthas. 'I hope you didn't face any inconvenience?' Armaan's father said, smiling warmly.

Kabir tried to keep his voice steady as he replied, 'No, Uncle ji, I am fine. But can I ask you something?' His heart was pounding in his chest, and he couldn't shake the feeling that something was off.

'Yes, dear, what is it?' Armaan's father asked, curious about Kabir's question.

Kabir took a moment, gazing at the floor deeply, deciding to keep his question to himself, not wanting to cause any panic or inconvenience to Armaan's parents, but the unease in his heart remained.

'What do you do for a living?' Kabir asked, his curiosity piqued. Kalsoom and Armaan's father were puzzled by the unexpected question and remained silent. 'Armaan told me you mostly keep away from home, so how is everything managed?'

The room fell silent as Kabir's unasked question hung in the air, adding to the tension that surrounded them. Armaan's father appeared bewildered, as if something had caught him off guard. *Did Armaan disclose something to him*? he thought. 'I hope I haven't asked a wrong question,' Kabir said, looking embarrassed by the silence of his parents. Kalsoom remained quiet, waiting for her husband to respond. Finally, he spoke, 'No, no beta ji, of course I have a profession. I am a professional gardener and people hire me on contract for gardening services wherever required.' Kabir nodded, trying to mask his suspicion. 'I keep travelling wherever I get a contract, sometimes in the Mughal Gardens at Srinagar or the homes of VVIPs, botanical gardens, hotels.' Armaan's father's tone was slightly too enthusiastic, perhaps also sensing Kabir's doubt and wanting to ease his mind. 'That's quite a creative work, Uncle.'

'Creative?' Armaan's father chuckled. 'Ha ha, I am just a poor man trying to do something in life.' Kabir felt the tension ease in his mind. He realized that his question may have caused some inconvenience, but he couldn't help his curiosity. 'If my sister was here, she would have started to sing "Gulon me rang bhare baad e nau bahaar chale,"' he said with a nervous laugh.

Armaan began to sing a song and Kabir offered him some quick tips and tricks to manage his upper notes. He was amazed by Armaan's natural talent and quick grasp of the technicalities. As they sang together, Kabir felt a sense of warmth and camaraderie with Armaan that he had not felt in a long time. Armaan's voice filled the room as he sang, his talents shining through. For the first time in a long time, Armaan felt a sense of joy and connection. Growing up in boarding school and then being stuck in lockdown, he had often felt isolated from the world and missed out on the warmth of his family's touch. Darkness had become his norm and he sometimes wondered if everyone saw the world as he did, without the gift of sight.

As the family sat down for dinner, Armaan couldn't help but feel a sense of longing. He wanted Kabir to stay back for one more day, to extend their time together. As the family sat down for dinner, Armaan couldn't help but feel a twinge of sadness. He didn't want the day to end. He wanted to continue learning from Kabir, the stranger who had suddenly become a mentor and friend.

So he gathered up the courage to ask, 'Bhaiyya, can you please stay for one more day? Please?' His desperation was palpable. 'I am already staying back, Rockstar,' Kabir replied.

'No, I meant tomorrow as well,' Armaan requested quickly, drawing his parents' attention. But Kabir's response was regretful. 'I'm sorry, my dear, I have some important work in Srinagar and then I have to leave for home. My tickets are already booked,' he explained.

Armaan's disappointment was clear, yet he refused to give up. He pleaded with Kabir again. Kabir's refusal was gentle, but it still stung. 'Next time maybe?' he offered, trying to ease Armaan's pain. Armaan didn't know how to express the overwhelming emotions he was feeling. He sat quietly in a corner, trying to hide his anxiety and sadness from the rest of the family.

Armaan had started to feel like an outsider in recent days, detached from the world around him. He was born with a sight that could not perceive the beauty of colours and the marvels of nature. He was confined within the four walls of his house. And then, Kabir walked into his life like a ray of sunshine on a cloudy day. He had a genuine interest in Armaan's passion and was more than willing to share his knowledge. For the first time in his life, Armaan had a friend who understood him, who cared for him, who made him feel enthusiastic.

'Armaan, tang na kar, sweater pura kar, chal chetti kar, stop troubling us and quickly complete the sweater,' Kalsoom stopped Armaan, as he pleaded insistently with Kabir. Kabir looked at Armaan in shock as Kalsoom handed him a set of knitting needles and an unfinished woollen sweater. 'Are you telling me Armaan is going to do that?' he asked incredulously.

Kabir looked on in disbelief as Armaan sat in the corner, weaving the woollen sweater with the dexterity of a seasoned pro. Despite being blind, Armaan was counting the loops and sticks on his fingers, weaving in a way that even those with sight would be envious of. Kabir couldn't believe his eyes.

Armaan's father noticed Kabir's surprise and explained that Armaan had learned the basics of weaving and computer operation at a workshop in the boarding school he attended. Despite the gap, Armaan remained focused, determined to complete his work.

But as Kabir watched Armaan weave effortlessly and create

something beautiful, he couldn't help but be struck by a profound realization. Armaan's blindness didn't diminish his ability to create or learn new skills; it simply forced him to approach things from a different perspective. Kabir felt humbled and inspired by Armaan's resilience and determination to thrive despite his physical limitations.

'Uncle, you said that he can play guitar too, right?' he asked. 'Yes, he learned the basics,' Armaan's father replied. 'However, we don't really have a guitar here, so he must have forgotten by now.' Armaan spoke up, a hint of sarcasm in his voice. 'Get me a guitar and let me show you how to rock Awantipora!' he said, still focused on his weaving. Kabir and Armaan's father laughed.

'Had I known that you love playing guitar, I would have brought one for you,' Kabir said with regret. As they chatted, a power failure plunged the room into darkness and outside it began to rain heavily. Kalsoom quickly lit a lamp, and they all continued their conversation in the dim light. Kabir was struck by the contrast between Armaan's ability to continue weaving in the darkness and the discomfort of those who could see but were now temporarily blinded. Kalsoom noticed Kabir's empathetic gaze and called out to Armaan.

'Armaan, chor de, let it be, saade naal aaja, come with us now,' Kalsoom insisted. Armaan left the skull cap unfinished, his forehead creased with concentration. Suddenly, he let out a scream and collapsed to the floor. Everyone in the room rushed towards him in a panic, their faces etched with horror. Armaan's father rushed to his side, 'Wallahi, it's started again.' Kabir could see the worry in his eyes as he knelt down next to Armaan. The young boy was screaming in agony, clutching his head with both hands. Kabir was frantic. *Is he doing this just to delay my departure*? he thought to himself.

Kalsoom rushed in with a vessel of chilled ice water and

napkins. Kabir looked at Armaan's contorted face, twisted in pain. He had never seen him like this before. Kalsoom quickly covered his forehead with the napkin, her own face etched with worry. She gave him a painkiller, hoping it would alleviate the pain. Armaan's father explained to Kabir that it had become a constant problem, with sudden and severe headaches.

'Armaan, try to calm down,' Kabir whispered, his heart racing with worry. 'It's going to be all right.'

But Armaan didn't seem to hear him. He was still writhing on the ground, clutching his head, screaming in agony. His father rubbed his feet, trying to ease his pain, but it was no use. Armaan's body was contorted, his breathing ragged and heavy. Finally, after what felt like an eternity, Armaan's screams subsided. He opened his eyes, swollen and wet from tears. Kabir couldn't help but feel a sense of relief, but he knew that this was far from over. The light had come by then.

'Why didn't you get him treated earlier, Uncle?' Kabir's voice trembled with worry as he raised the question. Armaan's father explained the situation, 'There's hardly any specialist here. I showed him to the local doctor, who advised us to put cold napkins on his forehead and gave him a painkiller.' Kabir noticed the grief etched on Kalsoom's face, yet she remained composed and strong in the face of Armaan's pain.

On the other hand, Armaan's father appeared petrified and at a loss for what to do. Filled with worry, he added, 'Earlier, we thought it was just a mild headache due to weather, but it has only increased over time. I'll surely take him to the doctor soon.' It dawned on Kabir that this was not just a mild headache due to weather; it was something much more serious.

During dinner that night, Armaan barely touched his food. Kabir lay next to him in bed, lost in thought. As Armaan's last day with him approached, Kabir's heart grew heavy, dreading the impending goodbye to the boy who had become so dear to him in such a short time. Breaking the silence, Kabir asked, 'Are you feeling ok?' Armaan nodded, but it was evident that he was lost in his own world. Kabir hesitated, unsure if he was crossing a line, before mustering the courage to ask, 'Armaan, can I ask you something?' Armaan, with his deep-blue eyes searching for Kabir's, responded, 'Tell me, Bhaiyya.' Kabir carefully articulated his question, 'Do you see everything as dark? Is it like a black screen in front of you?' Armaan paused for a moment, contemplating his answer.

After a brief silence, he finally spoke, 'It's like a tunnel. Sometimes I see a faint light at the end of it, but most times it's just dark and silent.' Kabir's heart sank as he tried to imagine living in a world without light. 'Do you ever feel like you're walking out of the tunnel?'

Turning towards Kabir, Armaan's eyes filled with a profound intensity. He began recounting a harrowing experience, 'Do you recall the time when I was drowning, and the raging current was dragging me further away from the shore? I was filled with terror as I realized that I couldn't even reach the surface and panic set in. I struggled with all my might to swim, but the current was too strong, relentlessly pulling me under. The water was frigid, like icy needles stabbing my flesh. The current was cutting off my air and oxygen supply. As I screamed for help, I thought of my parents and how desperately I wanted to see them. The thought that I might die without ever seeing them was crushing. I wished with all my heart to grow older so that I could witness the world, but at that moment it seemed impossible.

'As my body weakened, I began to experience flashbacks of conversations with my parents. It was as if they were right beside me, urging me to hold on and not give up. But I was helpless, and the current had its way with me. Silence enveloped me underwater, and the only sound I heard was my own laboured breathing. Everything else was muffled and distant, and I felt as if I were floating in a void. Darkness surrounded me and the silence was deafening.' Armaan paused, taking a deep breath before continuing.

'But then...the tunnel reappeared. A dark, endless tunnel. It was as if the world had turned mute and I was alone in that darkness. But then suddenly, I felt a tug, as if someone was pulling me towards the light. It was like I was being brought back to life. The transition from the water's dark depths to the brightness of the surface was like being reborn. I felt both dead and alive, grateful to be alive yet haunted by the memory of how close I'd come to death. You saved me. You brought me back to the surface, to the light. You pulled me out of the darkness, and for that, I will always love you.'

Kabir listened intently to Armaan's emotional narrative. Armaan was not merely recounting an incident; he was pouring his heart out through his telling of the tragedy. Goosebumps formed on Kabir's skin as he absorbed the depth of the boy's words. Witnessing an accident and experiencing it oneself were vastly different. The boy's honest and innocent expression resonated deeply, his words carrying profound meaning.

Questions flooded Kabir's mind, each one more pressing than the last. What was his role in this child's life? Was it fate that had brought them together or was it mere coincidence? And most importantly, was Armaan truly his godchild? Kabir glanced at him, who had already fallen asleep with his head on his shoulders. He witnessed the purest sight he had ever seen, intensifying his confusion.

Could he be the light in Armaan's life, the guiding hand on the other side of the tunnel, helping him escape the darkness that seemed to imprison him? Was it possible to get him the necessary treatment for his poor eyesight, enabling him to see the world in a new way? He knew he couldn't abandon this kid, not after the connection they had formed. But how could he return to his old life now, knowing that this child might need him?

Kabir looked out the window at the rain still pouring down, mirroring the storm of emotions raging inside him. The morning was gloomy, the rain showering softly outside.

Kabir woke up to an empty bed and realized that Armaan was missing. Concerned, he searched for him and finally found him entering the house with the Kashmiri bread, girda. They sat down for breakfast, but Armaan remained quiet, and Kabir could sense the weight of their impending separation. Kabir reached out, taking Armaan's hand gently. 'Armaan, my little rockstar,' Kabir said, trying to break the silence. 'How is your headache?' Armaan murmured, his eyes downcast, 'It's gone.'

Relieved to hear that Armaan's headache had subsided, Kabir continued, 'That's good to hear. Listen, I know you don't want me to leave, but I promise I'll be back soon.' Armaan remained silent, his mood reflecting the sombre sky outside. Trying to lighten the atmosphere, Kabir turned to Kalsoom and complimented her cooking. 'Aunty, this egg fry is so tasty. What's the secret ingredient?' Kalsoom smiled and replied, 'Zaiqa sarson de tel da hai. It's the unique flavour of mustard oil.'

Armaan's father soon returned, placing a basket of dry fruits for Kabir on the table before taking his seat next to his quiet son. He tried to lighten the mood, saying, 'You know, Kabir, you've troubled Armaan a lot with your visit.' Kabir felt a pang of embarrassment and quickly apologized, 'I'm sorry, Uncle. I didn't mean to cause any trouble. I promise to come back soon.'

As they finished breakfast, a sense of sadness enveloped Kabir. He looked at Armaan's innocent face and emotions welled up inside him. 'I hate to leave you like this, Rockstar,' Kabir said.

'I know how much you hate goodbyes.' Armaan didn't reply, but Kabir understood the pain they both felt. He embraced Armaan tightly, and they held on to each other, not wanting to let go.

After breakfast, Kalsoom and Armaan's father approached Kabir in a separate room, their expressions hesitant and filled with doubt. Kabir sensed the gravity of the situation and patiently waited for them to speak. 'There's something I need to share, but finding the right words is challenging, but I hope you don't mind.' Kabir nodded, his eyes fixed on the man's solemn face.

'With your recent trips to Kashmir, I'm sure you have an idea of the social and political situation here,' Armaan's father continued. 'Tourism may sound wonderful, but there's also a darker side to the place. Lockdowns, curfews, encounters, disappearances and much more have caused serious havoc to the social atmosphere. But above all, the education of children suffers the most due to the curfews and lockdowns. Children sit at home with empty minds, and as they say, an empty mind is Satan's dwelling. There's hardly any good internet for them to have online classes or pursue any meaningful courses. When the Article was curtailed, no one could go out, and there was an atmosphere of grief which impacted people of all ages, especially children.'

'I am most worried about my boy since his education is being impacted,' Armaan's father continued. 'I want him to become worthy in life and not depend on anyone. Already he has no eyesight, and for now, we are alive to take care of him. But God forbid if something were to happen to us, who will take care of him?' Kabir nodded, his eyes locked on Armaan's father's gaze.

'I want him to study and become successful in life, to become a role model. However, education, especially for visually impaired children, is elusive here. We had enrolled him in a boarding school that got shut down due to the situation. My child, like every other child here, is brilliant in academics and can do wonders if given proper facilities.'

Kabir's heart went out to the family. *Maybe Uncle would ask me to finance his education, ummm, not a big task*, Kabir thought to himself, knowing that he would have done that anyway.

'But when Armaan returned home, he spoke greatly about you, and we have hardly seen him so fond of someone. Please take him to Mumbai, away from this place, for better education under your supervision.'

Kabir was taken aback by the proposal, feeling both honoured and overwhelmed. 'Don't worry about the money. I will do whatever it takes to finance him, but all I want for him is your guidance, supervision and company,' Armaan's father said.

Kabir was taken aback by the proposal. *Oh God, this is difficult*, he thought to himself. 'If there's anyone I can trust besides Kalsoom, it's you. I've seen the warmth, affection and love you have for him in your eyes, and it's equally reciprocated by my son.' Kabir's face turned red with anxiety. 'Please take him with you, just in case it's possible?' Armaan's parents looked at Kabir with hopeful eyes, but he remained quiet. Armaan's father couldn't help but wonder what Kabir was thinking. *I hope I haven't caused him discomfort. Ya Khuda! What must he be thinking now?*

After a while, Kabir spoke. 'Uncle, I wish I had the power to remove everyone's pain, fear and shortcomings. But then I realized that without pain and afflictions, we wouldn't get stronger or more robust in life. When I met Armaan, I felt a divine connection with him. Maybe it was nature's way of connecting us so dramatically. I learned new things about your grown-up boy when I came here and it pained me so much to hear about his medical condition. But you need not worry, I will do anything within my power to help him.'

Armaan's parents felt hopeful. 'However, there are things you don't know about me, my background and what we've been through. Twenty-nine years ago, my family had to flee the valley like other Kashmiri Pandits. During the exodus, I lost my father and grandfather. Since then, my mother has raised me and my sister with hardships that no one can fathom. Words would fall short for describing her plight and endurance in these many years. Since then, my mother has naturally been very apprehensive about this place and its people, for the reasons that you may also understand.'

'As much as I want to parent Armaan and bring him to Mumbai, I cannot do anything that would put my mother at unease, at least for now. She is in a very delicate frame of mind concerning me and my future. Maybe after some time, if Kanval and I can convince her, I'll fly the very next day to bring Armaan home.'

'Kanval?' Armaan's father asked with a pinch of curiosity. 'Yes, Kanval, my younger sister,' Kabir replied. Armaan's father was lost in an array of curiosity, wanting to know more about his family without making what he was speculating in his mind too obvious. 'What is the name of your mother, Kabir? I can only imagine the strength and resilience she must have possessed to raise you and Kanval all on her own.' Kabir's face froze for a moment, his eyes darting away as a pang of unease gripped him recollecting the memories. 'Her name is Iravati.'

Armaan's father's eyes widened ever so slightly upon hearing the name 'Iravati', a glimmer of curiosity dancing in his gaze. It was a fleeting moment, quickly concealed behind a veil of polite detachment.

'Maafi, Kabir, tuhanu takleef vich rakhan layi, forgive me for bringing you discomfort. Allah teri ammi nu barkat deve, may Allah bless your mother.' Kalsoom said, wanting to normalize the awkward situation they created for Kabir. Armaan's father quickly brought himself back to the conversation. 'I'm sorry to learn about this, beta, and I'm also sorry to bring this proposal to you. More than a proposal, it would have been a mercy to us. However, your concern for my child is more than enough.'

'I'm so sorry, Uncle ji, to let you down. If you trust both me and Kanval, we love Armaan with all our honesty. Who wouldn't want to have such a joyous and innocent being in their lives? But don't worry. Together, we'll figure something out for Armaan, his health and his wonderful future. For now, I won't be able to take him for reasons that you understand.'

'Koi gal nahi puttar, maafi na maang. It's okay, do not apologize.'

'It's ok, Aunty, of all the happiness that I have had, a stay at your house completes it. I can't thank you enough for your kind approval of Armaan and the wonderful, homely presence you gave me here,' Kabir expressed his gratitude.

She handed him the dry fruits. 'Can I speak to you for a minute, Aunty?' Kabir insisted on talking in private. Kalsoom agreed and they walked into a different room.

Meanwhile, Kabir gave Kalsoom some cash. 'Ae ki puttar? What is this?' Kalsoom resisted. 'Aunty ji, I understand the financial condition of your home is not much promising; please take it from me if at all you consider me your son.' Kabir insisted, trying to help. Kalsoom simply refused and asked him to confront a visibly upset Armaan. Kabir, upon understanding Armaan's dilemma, felt like preparing a speech.

Soon, they were in the drawing room, and Kalsoom gave Kabir a packet full of flowery seeds to plant them at his Mumbai residence, urging him to make it a mini-Kashmir.

Kabir was all set to leave when he drew closer to Armaan. 'Hey, you little Rockstar, come here. So, I am hopeful that the tutorials we had for upper notes along with the pronunciation will be very well-revised by you.' Kabir looked for a response, but Armaan hardly said a thing, looking elsewhere.

As they stood together, Kabir was filled with anxiety and was waiting for Armaan to say something comforting to relieve his tension. But Armaan remained silent, overwhelmed by his emotions. Kabir knew that he shouldn't expect too much from him, given his age and emotional state, so he hugged him tightly, silently reassuring him that he was loved and cherished.

Armaan tried to contain his smile. 'Ok,' Armaan replied in a straight tone. Kabir found it difficult to leave him and both of them could read each other's heart. Kabir was waiting for Armaan to say something, but he didn't speak up. 'Take care, Bhaiyya, go home safely,' Armaan finally said. Kabir felt anxious, wondering why Armaan wasn't saying something comforting. *Damn, you are expecting too much out of someone his age, Kabir; he is emotionally overwhelmed. Shut up, hug and leave*, Kabir said to himself.

As Kabir held Armaan's hand and walked him to the main door, he could feel the heaviness of the moment. He hoped that Armaan would call him in his typical style once more, but Armaan remained silent. Kabir understood that Armaan was upset by his sudden departure and felt guilty for not staying back for a day. But Kabir reassured himself that Armaan's silence was due to his illness and inability to express his emotions.

He hugged Armaan's father, assuring him that everything would be all right. Kalsoom broke down, praying for both Kabir and Armaan silently. Bashar had arrived to pick him up and was waiting right outside. Kabir hesitated to sit inside the car, looking back at the three of them. Kalsoom was silently weeping, covering her face with her dupatta; Armaan's father had a forced smile containing his emotions. Kabir realized that Armaan's father was feeling hopeless about his son's condition.

'Bashar, you sit, I'll come,' Kabir said, quickly going back to them. He held Armaan's father's hand and assured him of Armaan's bright future. 'Don't you forget Qaaf, Rockstar,' Kabir tapped Armaan's cheek and he instantly smiled. As he left, Kabir felt relieved to have had that gesture coming from Armaan. Armaan could feel the warmth of his embrace slowly fading away.

As the car pulled away, Kabir stood there, feeling a deep sense of emptiness. He couldn't bear the thought of being away from his family, but he knew that he had to trust that everything would be ok. He took a deep breath and wiped away the tears that had formed in his eyes and badly wished Kanval was with him. As Kabir left and had gone a few metres, Armaan's father called out to Kabir to stop, and quickly coming to the window, said, 'Here, note down my new number, that old number isn't working.'

Kabir reached for his phone and saved the number. He turned back smiling and said, 'I just realized, I've been calling you Uncle this whole time, what name I should save it as?' Armaan's father smiled warmly and replied, 'Save it as Aa—' He hesitated for a moment. Kabir looked at him awaiting a response. 'Save it as Ajju Chacha.'

Chapter 7

Iravati eagerly anticipated Kabir's arrival, feeling a surge of excitement. With dinner preparations underway, she meticulously rearranged the drawing room to the Kashmiri sitting to his liking. *These subtle adjustments will bring Kabir closer to me.* Although she felt uncomfortable, influencing Kabir was necessary. *Once Kabir settles down with work, I'll propose Vidhi to him again.*

She firmly believed marriage would provide Kabir emotional security, a realistic future and someone to care for him. *I must get him married soon. Even a slight delay might set his mindset on permanently wasting his life behind the old and newcomers from Kashmir.* Kanval, on the other hand, understood Kabir's complex feelings and supported him in the way he desired. Kanval noticed the sudden changes in the house and expressed her suspicion. 'Mummy, what's with all these sudden changes? It doesn't feel genuine to me.' Iravati paused and looked at her daughter. 'What do you mean?' She raised an eyebrow and continued, 'I want things to be nice for Kabir's arrival. I know Kabir can be impulsive and emotional, but I just want to help him make the right choices.' 'I'm not saying there's anything wrong with it. It just seems a bit forced, that's all. Like you're trying too hard. What's on your mind, Mummy?' Kanval's suspicion lingered as she questioned Iravati.

Iravati hesitated, avoiding eye contact, and spoke while wiping the dining platform, 'I can't watch him waste his life on people who bring him down.' Kanval raised an eyebrow. 'And who are these people, Mummy?' she asked. Iravati curtly replied, 'Don't you know them?' 'Mummy, you can't keep living in the past,

Bhaiyya needs you to be there for him, not constantly try to control him.' Iravati bristled at the accusation. 'I'm not trying to control him, just doing what is the need of the hour.'

Kanval responded, 'Controlling will only cause him to drift away, Mummy.' Iravati sarcastically remarked, 'I had no idea my daughter had pursued psychology alongside LLB in Delhi.' The doorbell interrupted them. Kanval noticed Iravati hastily making changes for Kabir's arrival.

'Mummy, why are you trying so hard?' Kanval asked, her curiosity piqued. 'Kabir has arrived and I need your cooperation. I've tried everything I can to help him, but it always fails,' Iravati replied. 'Maybe you should try healing him instead of controlling him with your forceful opinions,' Kanval suggested. 'I'm not controlling him. I'm trying to build him up in a way that you don't understand,' Iravati countered. Kanval sighed, 'Mummy, just let Bhaiyya come to you and tell you if he wants to get married. Why force a decision? Maybe someday he'll feel ready,' Kanval suggested. 'Marrying at the right time is important,' Iravati insisted. The doorbell rang for a second time. Iravati declared, 'From now on, everything will happen as I say. No more discussions.' Kanval felt frustrated. Kanval firmly believed that there was a key to every closed door and sometimes you just had to be patient and look for it instead of constantly knocking and demanding access.

Iravati's heart skipped a beat as she opened the door to find Kabir standing there with a straight face. She felt a sudden rush of excitement, but before she could even utter a word, Kabir pulled out a hand from behind his back. A figure appeared, holding on to Kabir's hand, nervously gazing on his right. Iravati's jaw dropped as she realized who it was. Kanval quickly wiped her hands and rushed to the main door to greet Kabir.

'Oh my God!' she expressed her shock in silence. She quickly noticed that her mother's eyes were filled with tears of anger and hatred. Kanval could not fathom the situation. Iravati's eyes turned into fiery orbs of anger and disbelief and she began to fume with rage. Her body shook as if hit by an electric shock. Iravati remained standing there, her eyes fixed on Armaan. 'Kabir Bhaiyya, what a surprise? Like you didn't tell us? Everything's ok?' Kanval asked, trying to break the tension. She looked at Armaan and hugged him, hiding her shock. 'How are you, Armaan?' Armaan forced a smile. Kabir stood silently, watching Iravati's reaction. Kabir hesitated for a moment, struggling to find the right words to break the news to Iravati. Iravati's expression changed as she looked at Kabir's face, speculating that there was something more to the situation. 'What is it?' She enquired with a sense of curiosity. He took a deep breath and continued, 'Tarannum Aunty expired, mummy.' Kanval's hand flew to her mouth, shocked.

The news hit Iravati like a ton of bricks. Her eyes moved from Kabir to Armaan, reflecting her inner anxiety. Armaan's face was a canvas of confusion, his sightless eyes betraying no emotion but his furrowed brow reflected his inner anxiety. To Iravati, two emotions hit her at once. The shock of Armaan's arrival and Tarannum's departure. Looking at Armaan briefly, she excused herself and went to her room, her mind racing with memories. But she couldn't control them. 'Jaldi yease benia bea karey chun intezaar,' Tarannum had said. 'Come soon, dear sister, I'll be waiting for you.' Her last words echoed in Iravati's mind, asking her to come back soon, twenty-nine years ago.

Kabir's words followed. 'Tarannum Aunty expired.' Confused, weeping, she asked herself, 'Wait! Why the hell am I crying? Why should I be bothered?' But as much as she wanted to appear unaffected, she just couldn't. She tried to shoo away the emotions but failed. Kabir sat in the drawing room with Kanval and Armaan, who was already nervous. He recounted his visit to Chinar Kuth, where he had gone to check on the renovation.

'Aunty's eyes held the pain of losing Aariz, Noman Uncle and Mummy, her best friend, leaving behind an empty shell.' Kanval nodded understandingly, while Armaan continued to hold her hand, trying to understand the gravity of the situation.

'Sarfaraz Uncle was lost in her painful eyes, reflecting the sorrow of a river whose banks had eroded away, leaving him vulnerable. His longing reminded me of Umika.' Kabir leaned forward, his gaze fixed on the table. 'You know, Kanval? Sarfaraz Uncle's loss reminded me of my own. It's like...like I've grown very sensitive to deaths.' 'I didn't want to be alone with my thoughts, that's why I asked Armaan to come with me,' he said, glancing at him, who sat silently between them. I didn't tell his father much about what had happened, but he agreed instantly. Iravati, who had just opened the door and overheard their conversation, made a snarky comment. 'You should have brought Bhailal too,' she said, her tone dripping with sarcasm. 'And maybe we could have organized a prayer meet here.' Kanval and Kabir looked at her in shock, while Armaan's heart skipped a beat with the coldness of her words. He couldn't see her face, but he could sense the sharpness of her voice and the bitterness in her words. 'Mummy?' Kanval said, her voice trembling. Iravati slammed the door shut, cutting off any further conversation. Kabir took a deep breath. 'Please take Armaan inside,' he said softly. Kabir had felt drained since Tarannum's death and was hoping for empathy from Iravati.

But when he entered her room, tension filled the air. Iravati sat on the bed, anger etched on her face, refusing to make eye contact. Kabir took a deep breath and began to speak, 'Mummy, when you lose someone close to you, the world around you becomes dark and scary. It feels like the ground has been pulled from under your feet and you're left feeling helpless and vulnerable.' He hoped that his mother would listen to him, but her eyes remained fixed on the wall.

'I've been struggling with my mental and physical health since Umika's death and Tarannum Aunty's demise just stirred those emotions again,' Kabir continued. 'I've been experiencing chest pains, exhaustion and disturbed sleep.' He looked at Iravati, hoping to see some sign of understanding, but all he saw was indifference. Suddenly, Iravati interrupted him, 'Did I ask you to go to her house? How am I responsible for your vulnerability?' Kabir was taken aback by her callous response. He couldn't believe that his own mother couldn't understand his pain. 'Mummy, don't you see?' Kabir exclaimed, frustration creeping into his voice. 'I've been through so much, and all I wanted was some understanding from you. But you're acting like none of it matters.' The absence of an emotional reaction to Tarannum's passing served as a poignant reminder of his growing disappointment.

'Iravati's eyes widened as Kabir's tone grew more heated. 'You're acting like nothing bothers you, like you don't care about anything,' Kabir continued, his voice rising. 'I can't take it anymore, Mummy. Your temperament is too much for me to handle.' Kabir got up, ready to storm out of the room, but he stopped and turned back. 'Also, having a blind companion is just the icing on the cake of my chaotic life. It's like having a personal guide who can't actually see anything. But it adds a unique twist to my already eventful journey. Luckily, he'll be gone in a few days, so enjoy the 'blind leading the blind' while it lasts.' With that, Kabir slammed the door shut and left Iravati alone in her room.

Iravati couldn't believe that Kabir had started back-answering her. Her obedient son had transformed into a stranger who dared to challenge her authority. She felt frustrated and disappointed, slapping herself and weeping. *They're taking Kabir away from me*, she thought. Kabir went to the garden and started smoking, visible from the window. Kanval knew this situation required careful handling.

As Kabir listened to his mother's cold reaction, he began to question her behaviour. He couldn't understand her disrespectful attitude towards the deceased. He had always obeyed her, but now he wondered if it was too much to ask for some flexibility. *Sometimes, you have to stand up for what is right, even if it means going against those you love,* he thought.

Kanval was closely observing the situation. She was concerned about Iravati's cold treatment of Armaan and its impact on their bond. If Armaan felt mistreated, he might not want to stay. Kanval knew she had to handle the situation carefully to preserve their relationship. She realized Armaan was not just Kabir's hope but also a reflection of him. Damaging their bond would hinder Kabir's growth in other areas. It was crucial to manage the delicate situation, including Iravati. Kabir returned to his room feeling frustrated and helpless. He saw Armaan already sleeping. Kabir switched off the lights and lay down on the bed, but sleep was far from his eyes.

Kabir and Armaan assembled for breakfast the following morning. Kanval was serving breakfast, but Kabir could sense that Armaan was feeling out of place. 'This boy needs to put on some weight.' As Kanval served him a glass of milk, two boiled eggs, dates and a parantha, Armaan's expression was one of disbelief, sensing so many things served in front of him. Armaan felt anxious and overwhelmed with the variety of food that was served in front of him that he was not used to eating. Kabir noticed Armaan's discomfort and said, 'Take it slow, Armaan, let Didi feed you, you don't have to eat it all.'

His tone was straight while his mind wandered to Iravati. Iravati walked by and stopped when she saw them sitting together. Her face was tense and unfriendly. Kanval tried to include her in the conversation, however she just looked at them with a bristly rough face and walked away. Kabir felt his angst slowly developing.

We have a guest in our house and she hasn't even greeted him properly, he thought. Kabir felt a wave of anger and frustration building up inside him, but he tried to suppress it.

'I have some urgent work at the studio. Armaan, you stay here with Didi,' Kabir said, trying to calm himself. Kanval noticed his discomfort and said, 'Don't worry, I'll take care of him. Meanwhile, we will go to the beach in the evening. Since I learned that you also play the guitar, let's practise it.' The idea made Armaan smile; he had remained anxious upon learning that Kabir was leaving. 'Sure, Didi. Do you have a guitar here?' 'Only guitar? We have an inbuilt music studio at home, dear.'

Kanval entered Iravati's room with breakfast, noting her mother's firm face. 'Mummy, I'm not here to argue, but I didn't expect Bhaiyya to do this,' she said, trying to ease the tension in the room. Iravati was uninterested. 'Keep the breakfast and leave,' she replied curtly. 'I will, but there's something I need to say,' Kanval persisted as she kept the tray on the table. Iravati raised an eyebrow. 'Look, you've been patient with Bhaiyya for a long time, a little more patience could win his heart. Then you can put things in order,' Kanval suggested. Iravati shook her head. 'Not at the cost of my dignity. That boy is a hindrance,' she said aggressively.

'But Mummy, that little boy has no eyesight and he can hardly harm anyone.' Kanval took a deep breath. 'He's going to leave soon, but he'll remember how you treated him. Please bear with him until he's gone,' Kanval urged. 'Sorry, Kanval, whatever said and done, do not expect me to be hospitable to anyone of any age and any limitation.' 'You don't have to go out of your way to be hospitable, but at least don't be rude to him. I understand your reservations, but maybe the kid can leave with some good memories if you are kind to him. He's not going to forget how you treated him and it will impact his relationship with Bhaiyya.'

Iravati's silence filled the room and Kanval took it as a cue to continue, 'Bhaiyya is super stressed and maybe he can't express his ordeal properly so he…' Iravati interrupted, 'Are you trying to say that my children will not be discussing their ordeals with me? Or I am incapable of dealing with their problems? If so, then I failed you people as a mother.' 'Sorry Mummy, but you are taking this conversation elsewhere, all I am trying to say is there are lines that we all draw in our relationships; not agreeing with you does not amount to disrespecting you. Please enlighten me on what impression are you going to leave on that little boy by not talking to him and making him feel unwelcome? Displeasing a guest at home is not in our culture.' Kanval left, hoping her mother would reflect. She sensed her own frustration building up but she had to remain calm.

Armaan felt overwhelmed in the bustling Mumbai streets. Blind, he couldn't see the skyscrapers or the crowds, but he felt the heat of the city on his skin and heard the honking of the cars as he nervously sat on the front seat of the car with Kanval. He sensed the busy streets, full of people with a different way of life than he was used to back in Kashmir and noticed the towering skyscrapers offering shade from the sun.

Kanval asked, smiling at him. 'What do you think of Mumbai so far?' 'I'm trying to understand your city, Didi,' Armaan replied. 'It feels new, vast, fast and chaotic.' 'That's just how Mumbai is, my dear,' Kanval reassured him. 'But don't judge it just yet. There's so much to explore and I'm sure you'll come to love it here.' 'Didi, can I tell you something?' Armaan said, wrinkling his nose. 'Right now, it smells like salty fish in the air.' Kanval laughed as she drove past the fishermen's colony, where dry fish were being sun-dried. In no time, the smell dissipated and they arrived at the beach. Armaan felt a new sensation under his feet as he stepped on to the sandy shore.

He tightly held on to Kanval's hand as he found it a little challenging to walk on the soft, powdery sand. It was a completely different experience for him. Kanval explained to him the history of the city, how it was once known as Bombay and how the seven islands were merged to form one big vertical city of dreams.

As Armaan sat on the sand, facing the sea, he felt the infinite vastness of the salty breeze and the crashing waves. The water body was unlike anything he had experienced before, as Jhelum, the only one back home, had fluctuating currents. 'There's so much air here,' he said, taking deep breaths. Kanval brought him coconut water, a refreshment he had never tasted before. Back home, there were no coconut trees.

She herself enjoyed watching the little boy discover the beach. Soon, Kabir arrived, saying he could only stay for twenty minutes as the studio was nearby. 'Can we go closer to the water?' Armaan asked excitedly. 'Of course we can,' Kanval replied, smiling. As they reached the shore, Armaan giggled as the waves tickled his feet. When they reached the shore, Kabir, knowing he had limited time, suggested they take a photograph. Kabir handed Kanval his cell phone and asked her to take a photo of them, holding Armaan's hand as they ventured a few steps towards the water.

As they approached the shore, waves continued to tickle Armaan's feet, eliciting laughter from him. Getting his feet wet in water was a new joy for him. The sudden high tide splashed all three of them making them completely wet, causing Kabir to burst into laughter while Kanval regretted the sea's suddenness. Drenched in water, his fair skin turned red, and he listened to the constant sound of aeroplanes taking off and landing nearby. Back home, the sky was usually filled with the noise of helicopters during emergencies and lockdown patrols. The freedom he felt was different from what he was accustomed to. They embraced the liberty of getting wet in the water, speaking fast and being a bit untidy. The idea was new, but Armaan started to enjoy it.

As the sun began to set, they decided it was time to head back. Armaan couldn't help but feel exhilarated as they climbed into the car. Kabir, always seeking thrills, decided to change their plans and embark on another adventure. The engine roared to life and they sped off, the wind rushing through their hair. Armaan's heart raced at the speed, 'The army men would stop and interrogate you.' Kanval and Kabir shared a glance smiling. 'Well, unlike Kashmir, my dear, Mumbai doesn't have paramilitary patrolling,' Kabir explained. 'Here, there are traffic police to take care of speeding vehicles.'

Armaan was taken aback by the stark contrast. In his hometown, constant checking, convoys, document verification, confiscations, arrests, curfews, detentions and encounters were a part of everyday life. But here in Mumbai, none of that existed. He felt a sense of freedom and lightness. Upon returning home, they were greeted by Iravati's disapproving look as they entered drenched and dishevelled. Kabir, unfazed, confidently walked into the house, disregarding her disapproval.

The next morning, Kabir instructed the gardener to plant the seeds given to him by Kalsoom in the lawn. Iravati observed their conversation, saying to herself, *Dumbo does not even understand that the soil and topography are different, the seeds won't germinate, and that these are not seeds of blossoms but seeds of discord in this house.* As Kabir left for the studio, Kanval engaged Armaan in conversation about his experience during the lockdown in his village. She noticed the apprehension in his voice, but she convinced him that it would be their secret. Armaan quickly found a gossip partner in her.

'My boarding was closing down and we had a week to relocate. Shamrita Didi tried her best to prevent the shutdown but failed. Some students were sent to other boardings in Jammu or Badgam, while reservations hindered my placement due to lack of facilities for disabled children. The boarding felt empty, with only a few of us remaining.

'One day, news spread of thousands of paramilitary forces being sent to Kashmir. I accompanied Shamrita Didi to buy groceries, witnessing panic-stricken tourists fleeing Dal Lake as if a flood had struck Jhelum again. Traffic chaos reigned, with tourists rushing to the airport. My heart raced, sensing impending danger. Shamrita Didi tightly gripped my hand, leading us back.

'Turning on the television, we discovered a threat to the Amarnath Yatra, prompting tourists to evacuate. Shamrita Didi sensed something more significant than what was being shared. She informed us of her departure to Dharamshala, assuring she would return when everything settled. I felt a void. Her comforting words reassured me, but uncertainty clouded my mind.

'A sense of motherly loss overwhelmed me. That night, fear gripped me as Srinagar seemed abandoned by the world. Complete silence enveloped the air, broken only by the patrolling paramilitary forces, instructing everyone to stay indoors. Strict protocols were in place.

'Lockdowns, protests and gunshots were not new to us, but this situation felt different. This situation was truly frightening. Ten of us, along with two watchmen and a warden eager to return to his village in Kupwara, remained in the hostel.

'The following morning, the trust owner, an ex-IPS officer and his wife, arrived in a tempo with CRPF personnel in an armoured Bakhtarband jeep. Urgently, they instructed us to vacate the hostel. With the help of my friends, I packed my belongings and boarded the tempo, unaware of our destination or fate. I yearned for my mother, feeling wretched at having to leave the boarding that had been my home for five years.'

'As the tempo rolled onto the main road, the absence of

birdsong struck me, as if they had fled the Kashmir skies. The officer sat before us, his presence intimidating. After an hour, he called my name, stirring fear within me. Dark thoughts consumed my mind, I feared I would be abandoned on the desolate highway. Stepping down from the tempo, I joined him as two CRPF personnel accompanied us, while the others remained behind. Gathering courage, I asked where we were headed. 'Your home,' he replied, his voice tinged with anxiety. A sense of relief washed over me.

'Over my village, hung a strange stillness, with the footsteps of patrolling paramilitary forces echoing nearby. After a single knock, my mother opened the door as if awaiting my return. I stepped inside and she invited the trustee to enter, but he was in a hurry and swiftly departed. However, before leaving, he turned back, handing some money to my mother, urging her to take care of me. Among the students, I was fortunate to have a home, unlike the orphans who were taken to Jammu with special permits. My mother's tears of joy flowed as she embraced me.

Mummy had shut the door and the windows as if she were sealing a fortress. There was enough ration at home for two of us to sustain ourselves for some time. Occasionally we heard the sound of intense protest, gunshots and chaos. I used to cling to Mummy, very, very scared. No matter who banged our door for what reasons, Mummy never ever opened it. I have a slight sense of sunlight when it falls over me, however Mummy had draped the windows well with dark curtains so as to avoid any peeping in and out. There were no prayers in the Masjid Sharief even after the call to azaan was made. Our village had the best unity though. Somehow, they managed the food stock by sharing it among themselves with very, *very* silent moves. Even if one egg was brought to any house, it was shared.

'Mummy kept me busy by making me memorize the Quran. Being home and having almost nothing to do made me bored. Whenever I used to sing songs Mummy would quickly stop me. She feared my loud voice could attract anyone to peep into the house. Soon I started to get headaches. It was a mix of dizziness, boredom and migraines. Mummy used to give me Crocin, but it didn't help me. She was scared to take me out to a doctor.'

Kanval was captivated by the narrative, feeling a surge of emotion. 'What about your father, Armaan? Where was he during the lockdown?' she enquired. Suddenly, Armaan fell silent, lacking an answer. A pause enveloped him. 'He returned home four months later,' he finally revealed. 'The day I arrived, phone lines were severed, internet services halted, schools closed and even television broadcasts ceased.

'One boy, overwhelmed by stress, sneaked out of his house and never returned. His whereabouts remain unknown to this day. A pervasive silence enveloped the surroundings, and wherever one went, there were very few people. The residents had become numb, even children my age. Some children occupied themselves with mobile games, while schools and colleges remained closed. It was a challenging time for all of us and we sincerely hope it won't happen again.'

Iravati, though not actively participating in the conversation, observed them closely. She listened to Armaan's narrative, recognizing that his experiences were far from her own. Curiosity compelled Kanval to ask about militancy, whether they encountered militants during the crackdowns and if they tried to forcibly enter houses for meals or relaxation at gunpoint. However, sensing the discomfort in the room, Iravati quickly entered the drawing room, displeased with the question, raising an eyebrow to signal that the topic was unwelcome.

Iravati left the scene, her presence fading into inconsequence.

Meanwhile, Kabir had completed his Kashmir Tourism video, a result of his hard work paying off. The visuals were captivating, accompanied by the melodious voice of Umika, creating a magical touch. The Tourism Department was impressed and celebrations were in order. Kabir organized a party for his staff and friends to commemorate their success.

Kanval took Armaan to the mall to shop for new clothes, an entirely new experience for him. Kanval, being his supportive friend and guide, accompanied him on this adventure. She described the various stores and promotions, leading him through the throngs of people. The tempting aroma of spices and food wafted through the air, making Armaan's mouth water.

Approaching the escalator, and with Kanval's assistance, he stepped onto the moving stairs. The sensation of effortlessly ascending filled him with wonder, and he couldn't help but chuckle with joy. Reaching the top, Kanval directed him to a clothing store. Kanval selected new clothes for him and as he changed into them, he savoured the softness against his skin. The blend of new fabric scent and perfumes immersed him in a whole new world.

The food in Mumbai differed from what Armaan was accustomed to in Kashmir. Chicken, vada pav, masala dosa, upma, poha and local vegetables dominated the culinary landscape, unlike the regular consumption of rista and kebabs in Kashmir. For lunch, they ordered grilled pomfret fish, a salty and spicy delicacy that tasted distinct from the trout fish popular in the valley. It had likely been years since Armaan had enjoyed fish, but he was gradually adapting to Mumbai's flavours and eating habits. He relished the taste so much that he requested another serving.

As Kabir joined them, he offered Armaan an ice-cream, eliciting confusion on Armaan's face, who wondered if he'd have patches on his skin if he ate ice-cream with fish. Fear and shock washed over him. Trembling, Armaan asked, 'Bhaiyya, are you serious?' Kabir and Kanval couldn't contain their laughter at his innocent reaction. 'No, no, Armaan,' Kabir reassured him. 'It's just a silly myth. Eating ice-cream with fish won't turn you white.'

Armaan looked relieved, but still a bit sceptical. 'Are you sure?' he asked, his brow furrowed in confusion. Kanval chimed in with her own bit of humour. 'Actually, Armaan, that's called lactose intolerance,' she said, grinning mischievously. 'Not all of us here suffer from it.'

Armaan's face scrunched up in confusion. Kabir said, patting him on the back. 'It just means that some people have trouble digesting lactose, which is a sugar found in milk. But it's nothing to worry about.'

Armaan looked relieved once again, but still a bit embarrassed at his own innocent mistake. 'I guess I still have a lot to learn about Mumbai and its easy beliefs.'

After lunch, they spent some time in the gaming zone. Although Armaan had limited options, Kabir played bowling with him, holding his hands and aiming at the bottles. Armaan thoroughly enjoyed the experience. It was a day filled with new experiences, and Armaan was grateful to have such caring people in his life.

'Mummy, what are you wearing for the party tonight?' Iravati was silent. She took a moment to reply. 'I don't believe in parties; ever seen me celebrating a party in these many years, Kanval?'

'I agree, Mummy, that you have had a simple life. However, this is a success celebration for Bhaiyya. The video has been much appreciated and is the talk of the town, bringing him a lot of work. Your presence is important.'

'My contribution to his success, his work and support has been nil. Hence I see no logic in celebration. Perhaps I have been a hindrance in most of his work and decisions, so I advise you not to roll out any invitations for me.'

'You don't really need to put effort into celebrating the success of a loved one, Mummy. Your absence will upset him.'

Iravati wanted to boycott the event. She wanted Kabir to know of her lack of interest and the obvious reason that had triggered it. The who's who of the music industry had descended upon the five-star hotel in South Mumbai, all gathered to celebrate Kabir's latest success. Singers, producers and the studio staff were in attendance, mingling with one another and discussing their upcoming projects.

Armaan arrived at the party dressed in a casual blazer, with his hair neatly rolled back, accompanied by Kanval who looked stunning in a vintage red saree paired with a black blouse. Kabir, the host of the evening, looked suave in a tuxedo. For Armaan, everything in Mumbai was a first. He couldn't remember the last time he had been dressed up so well. Armaan and Kanval made their way through the crowd, receiving warm greetings and compliments along the way. Armaan was introduced to some of Kabir's colleagues and other industry professionals. Armaan felt a mix of excitement and nervousness, but Kanval's reassuring presence by his side kept him grounded.

As the night progressed, the atmosphere became livelier with music and laughter filling the air. Armaan found himself immersed in conversations about music, films and the industry. Despite his initial reservations, Armaan started to enjoy the party and felt a sense of belonging among the creative and passionate individuals around him. Throughout the evening, Kabir made sure to spend time with Armaan, appreciating his presence and talent. Armaan felt a sense of validation and encouragement, knowing that he had found a mentor and friend in Kabir. As the party continued, Kabir went over to the dais.

'A year ago, my world turned upside down when I lost my wife and baby in a tragic event. It was not just the loss of a person but also the loss of a world. Her passing left me shattered and heartbroken. But as they say, time is a great healer, and with time, I learned to cope with the pain of her loss. Although she's no longer with us, I can feel her presence around me, guiding me through every step of my life. I've come to understand that death is not the end but merely a transition from one state to another. It's like a seed that falls to the ground, and from it grows a tree that bears fruits for generations to come. My wife was the seed that gave birth to the idea of this project and her memory is the tree that has grown from it. Her love has given me the strength to keep going even in the darkest of times. I believe that even after she's gone, her love will continue to inspire me to create something meaningful, something that will touch people's hearts and souls. Every time I stumbled and fell, I picked myself up and kept moving forward, with my wife's memory as my anchor. In life, we're all like travellers, walking on a long and winding road, with no clear destination in sight. But what makes the journey worthwhile is the people we meet along the way, the experiences we have and the lessons we learn. And I'm grateful to have met so many amazing people who have helped me on my journey. I would like to take this opportunity to thank some special people who helped me along the way. Firstly, my dear mother, who unfortunately isn't here with us today; she has been my rock and support. Secondly, my lovely sister, Kanval, who constantly provoked me to live a life when I felt dead. And then there's Armaan, the little boy sitting next to my sister. He's technically not able to see the world, but his presence has given me the vision of life. He's a divine gift, a treasure to me and my family. Thank you, beta, for everything that your presence has illuminated. Last but not least, I want to acknowledge my studio staff who worked tirelessly to make this video possible, and the Department of Tourism, Jammu and Kashmir, for their support. Thank you all for being a part of my journey. Ladies and Gentlemen, presenting to you "Myon Watan".'

The audience applauded and cheered, recognizing the hard work and creativity that had gone into its making. Armaan couldn't help but feel a swell of pride for Kabir's accomplishment and the role he had played in it. Newbies in the industry circled Kabir, luring him, trying to get work.

Kanval, being the social butterfly that she was, introduced Armaan to influential personalities, opening doors for potential collaborations and opportunities. Armaan was yet to be introduced in his magical way to everyone. Kabir quickly took over the mic while people were enjoying themselves, calling over Armaan to sing a song. It made him instantly nervous and he refused, feeling overwhelmed by the crowd. Kanval encouraged him and joined him on stage. The crowd exchanged hushed whispers. *They must surely be talking about me*, Armaan thought. His heart was beating faster, and he trembled walking up to the mic. He had never ever held a mic in his hand before. Kanval helped him assemble on the stage, but he still couldn't gather the courage to sing. Kanval planted a kiss on his cheek and asked him to go ahead.

Armaan paused briefly until the silence around him made him aware that a huge crowd was now looking at him. He was the most beautiful of all the people who stood there. 'Maybe I'd like to sing if Kabir Bhaiyya plays the keyboard,' Armaan requested. It surprised everyone. The ballroom already had a keyboard. With a three, two, one countdown, Armaan started to sing 'Hukus Bukus'. Kabir's subtle keyboard made it even more mesmerizing.

The audience was in awe of Armaan's singing, and his pure raw talent made everyone feel a fresh breath of art. When the song concluded, applause filled the ballroom in appreciation. To Armaan, the claps instantly made him feel appreciated and admired. A powerful energy stimulated his body as he heard those unending claps erupting for him. Armaan felt a sense of approval from the posh crowd. It started to develop a sense of confidence in him.

A press conference followed by a photo session concluded the evening. As the night drew to a close, Kabir, Armaan and Kanval bid farewell to the guests, their hearts filled with gratitude and a newfound sense of belonging. On the way back home, Armaan had already fallen asleep in the back seat. Silence followed between the two siblings.

'I have started to understand the meaning of toxic, Kanval, this is what it means,' Kabir murmured. Kanval knew her brother was boiling from inside. 'That's not toxic, Bhaiyya, that's her tolerance.' 'You must be joking, Kanval. You call her behaviour tolerant? Care to explain?' 'Well, your surprise has really got her mind racing. She's trying to sort through her thoughts and figure out what's right and wrong, but I hope she doesn't get too frustrated. I don't think she's toxic, but I do worry that her emotions may get the better of her.'

Iravati was already asleep when they arrived home. Kanval opened her door to check on her. Iravati lay facing the wall with closed eyes, seemingly awake but closed off. Kabir found himself drawn to Armaan's quiet determination to learn music. As they progressed, Kabir witnessed Armaan's fingers gaining in confidence as they moved over the guitar strings. Strumming together, Kabir pondered the deeper meaning of music. It was more than sounds and rhythms; it expressed emotions that words alone couldn't convey. Kabir felt a profound connection with Armaan, one that extended beyond music. He saw in him a reflection of his own struggles, pain and journey towards finding hope. It reminded Kabir that amidst the darkness, there was still light in the world. The bond between Kabir and Armaan grew stronger each day. Kabir admired Armaan's unwavering determination and eagerness to explore. He believed these qualities would lead Armaan to great heights. As they practiced together, Kabir opened up to Armaan about his own struggles and life's challenges.

It was a way of connecting with him on a deeper level and sharing a part of himself with the boy who had become so important to him. Armaan's blindness, far from being a hindrance, had become an inspiration for Kabir. It had taught him the value of perseverance and the beauty of looking beyond what was visible to the eye. It had shown him that true sight came from the heart and that the most important things in life were often the ones that could not be seen.

As Kabir watched Armaan play, lost in the music that filled the room, he couldn't help but think of Umika and her unwavering support. She had been the one to connect him to Kashmir, to show him a joy that had long been dead in his life. And now, with Armaan by his side, he was experiencing that joy once again. He knew that no matter what life may bring, this bond would endure, one note at a time.

Kabir's mind started racing with an idea. He realized that Armaan's voice would be the perfect complement to Umika's unfinished song. After discussing it with Kanval, they began training sessions in the studio. For Armaan, it was a completely different world, and he was learning so much about music. There was an adrenaline rush in his body as he was exposed to a life that was free and fun.

Kabir couldn't help but feel emotional, knowing that Umika had passed away before she could finish it. But Armaan persevered, and it took him almost four takes to perfect the mood and feel of the final recording. As he listened to the playback, he felt a sense of accomplishment and pride, knowing that he had brought Umika's vision to life with his voice.

One morning, Armaan woke up early and headed to the

kitchen for a drink of water. Unfortunately, he slipped and fell, catching the attention of Iravati, who was brewing tea at the time. Despite having passed by him numerous times before, this was the first time she had ever looked at him clearly.

As she stared at him, a sense of familiarity washed over her, and she suddenly realized that she was hesitant to help him up from the ground. Just then, Kabir entered the room, alerted by the thud of Armaan's fall. He immediately rushed to help Armaan, shooting an angry glare at his mother for her heartless behaviour. Making her embarrassed by the incident, Kabir, in turn, shared his shock with Kanval. *Let them think whatever they want to*, Iravati said to herself.

Despite Iravati's cold vibes, Armaan found solace in the warmth and affection of everyone else including the studio staff. He had become their favourite and Mumbai, in turn, had quickly become Armaan's safe haven with Kabir and Kanval by his side to offer comfort and support when needed.

As Kabir listened to the finished audio track, he was struck by the perfect harmony of Armaan's voice with Umika's vocals. To him, it sounded like a mother and son singing a lullaby, a tribute to Umika's memory. Kanval agreed, and the weight of her words lingered in the air. Kabir and Kanval decided to take Armaan on a fun outing to the amusement park. For Armaan, this newfound freedom in Mumbai was a breath of fresh air compared to the strict restrictions and uncertainties of life in Kashmir. Although it was a paradise in its own way, it often felt like a cage.

As they discussed the possibilities of shooting a music video in Kashmir, the world was slowly awakening to the threat of the coronavirus, a disease that no one seemed to be taking seriously at the time. Despite the joy of his new life in Mumbai, Iravati's cold demeanour still haunted Armaan. He found himself becoming more disciplined and stopping his activities whenever she was present. Nonetheless, he continued to develop his musical talents, learning the basics of guitar and piano and developing a strong telepathic connection with Kabir.

The vibrant atmosphere in Kabir's home was suddenly shaken when Ajju called and shared the news of a nearby school willing to enrol Armaan. Kabir felt a knot tighten in his stomach as he discussed the possibility of sending Armaan back with Kanval.

'It's time to send him back, Bhaiyya. He's had a wonderful time here with us and we'll never lose him again,' Kanval reassured him, sensing the anxiety in Kabir's voice.

Armaan, on the other hand, was caught in a swirl of conflicting emotions. He longed to stay back, but at the same time, the thought of reuniting with his parents was equally appealing. As he tried to sort out his feelings, a subtle sense of grief crept up on him, realizing that his time with Kabir and the others was coming to an end.

Kanval walked into Iravati's room hesitating for a moment before deciding to break the silence. 'Mummy, would you please speak a few good words to him before his departure,' Kanval said, trying to soften his mother's demeanour. Iravati remained silent, refusing to give Kanval the satisfaction of a response. She knew that her silence was like a weapon, able to make almost any complaint from her children null and void.

Kabir was observing their conversation from the kitchen. Iravati remained silent for a few moments before finally responding. 'He is leaving tomorrow and that is that. He knew he was never going to stay here forever,' she said with a cold tone.

Kanval sighed. He knew that there was no point in arguing with his mother. 'Mummy, how wise is it to be so stubborn, especially with a differently-abled child?' she pleaded.

Iravati remained stoic. 'That's ok. He was just another person living in our house. Now he's leaving and life will go on,' she replied, her voice devoid of any emotion.

Kanval couldn't help but feel frustrated at his mother's lack of empathy. 'I don't understand you sometimes, Mummy. How can you be so cold and heartless?' he said, raising his voice a little.

Iravati's expression didn't change. 'I am not heartless. I am just practical. Life is not a bed of roses and we cannot waste our emotions on every passing guest who enters our lives,' she replied firmly.

Kanval knew that arguing with her mother was futile. She gave up and left the room, feeling a mix of sadness and anger. As she walked away, she couldn't help but wonder if Iravati would ever be capable of showing any kindness to someone outside her immediate family. Kabir's heart ached with disappointment at his mother's behaviour, yet he realized that sometimes the deepest pain comes from those we hold closest.

As Armaan slept next to Kabir, he finally spoke up. 'Bhaiyya, I think your mother despises me.' Kabir was shaken to his core by Armaan's words. He had no idea how to respond and quickly rubbed his forehead, feeling embarrassed. 'It's not hatred towards you, my dear. It's just her...' Kabir's words trailed off into a heavy silence. He looked at Armaan, who had already drifted off to sleep. In that moment, Kabir knew that Iravati's icy demeanour had left an indelible mark on Armaan's heart.

The following morning, as Kabir and Kanval prepared Armaan for his departure, there was a noticeable heaviness in the air. Kanval carefully packed Armaan's bags and even bought gifts for his family. As they made their way to the airport, Kabir couldn't help but steal glances backward, hoping to catch a glimpse of his mother, but she was nowhere in sight. Upon reaching the airport, Kanval tightly embraced Armaan, heavily emotional. Kabir also hugged him, feeling a lump form in his throat. It was hard to fathom that the boy who had brought so much radiance into their lives was now departing.

As Kabir held Armaan tightly, he whispered, 'You may not see the world, but the world will see you, my little rockstar.' Armaan could feel the warmth of Kabir's embrace and the sincerity of his words. With a lump in his throat, he whispered back, 'I may not see the world, but I can feel it. And I'll always cherish all the happiness you and Didi gave me.'

As the flight attendant escorted Armaan to the check-in at last, Kanval observed him until he disappeared from sight. As Armaan bid farewell to Kabir and Kanval, a profound sense of emptiness and loneliness overwhelmed him, despite the warmth of their hugs and the love reflected in their eyes. He couldn't shake off the feeling that he was leaving a part of himself behind. As he settled into his seat, a deep sigh escaped his lips, as he attempted to push away the ache in his heart. Closing his eyes, he whispered a silent prayer, hoping that one day he would find his way back to them.

Kabir's house, once filled with life and joy in Armaan's presence, now seemed empty and hollow. Kabir and Kanval sat in silence, burdened by the weight of Armaan's departure.

'Let's not succumb to sadness, Bhaiyya. We must focus on securing a sustainable future for Armaan, planning for his treatment and education,' Kanval spoke, breaking the silence. Although Kabir felt downcast, he couldn't help but agree. 'You're right. The least we can do is help him with his eyesight.' Kanval's regret was apparent on her face. 'Unfortunately, we couldn't arrange for a doctor's visit to address his headaches and vision problems. Perhaps next time we can do so; thankfully nothing serious occurred during his stay. Maybe we were so consumed by our own selfish joy that we neglected to have him checked.'

'He complained about mummy's silence last night,' Kabir

interjected, causing Kanval's heart to sink, looking at him in shock. 'This is what I feared the most,' she said, her voice cracking with emotion. Iravati's unyielding mood was beyond Kabir and Kanval's comprehension. Kanval had hoped that after Armaan's departure, their mother would return to normal, but it seemed that was not to be the case. Upon returning home, both siblings noticed Iravati's unchanged temperament.

'We're back home, mummy. Armaan has left and it's time to move on from this bitterness. Let's talk and find a way to heal this family.' However, all she received in response was a stony silence from Iravati. Avoiding eye contact with Kabir, she made it clear that she had no interest in communication. 'As she wishes,' Kabir muttered to himself and walked away.

It was already past 5 o'clock in the evening, two hours since Armaan's flight had landed at Srinagar airport, and yet Kabir hadn't received any update from Ajju regarding Armaan's safe arrival. Kabir had been anxiously waiting for the call, pacing back and forth with his phone in hand, hoping to receive news of Armaan's safe arrival. 'Why hasn't Uncle called yet?' he muttered to himself, worry and fear starting to creep in. Kanval, who was sitting nearby, noticed Kabir's anxiousness and asked, 'Has Uncle called to inform about Armaan's arrival?'

'I was just about to ask you the same,' Kabir replied. 'I checked the flight status, and it shows that it arrived on schedule. I tried calling Uncle several times, but there was no answer.'

'Really? Do you think it could be due to network issues or something common in the valley?' Kanval asked, trying to calm Kabir down.

'I don't know, Kanval, but I'm really worried. I hope Armaan has arrived safely,' Kabir replied, his tone heavy with anxiety.

Just then, Kanval received a message from Ajju on her phone that said, 'Armaan is home, thank you.' Both Kanval and Kabir were surprised and relieved, but Kabir's relief was short-lived as he realized something was wrong. 'Why isn't he answering my calls, Kanval? I don't understand why he's avoiding me,' Kabir said, disappointment and frustration creeping into his voice. 'Let's not jump to conclusions. We'll hear from him soon, I'm sure.' But the next day was just as frustrating. Ajju still wasn't answering Kabir's calls. Kabir was beside himself with worry and disappointment. 'How irresponsible of Uncle, this is not done,' Kabir fumed. Kanval was also tense about the latest developments. 'Let's just wait for a day. Maybe, he is just busy with something or maybe it's a bad network,' she suggested. 'I hope so,' Kabir replied, but the following day was the same story. It infuriated him. 'What could have happened?' Kanval thought anxiously.

Kabir gave it some thought and looked at Kanval deeply. 'I fear Armaan must have told his parents about Mummy's attitude. Perhaps they felt hurt,' he said, his voice tinged with disappointment. 'That could be one possibility, but I'm not certain. Armaan is a sensible boy; he wouldn't do something like this.' 'Did I suddenly become responsible for someone's discourtesy?' Iravati walked past her children, wearing a disdainful expression. She continued walking without acknowledging them. Kanval and Kabir looked at her in surprise. 'I told you, this has little to do with Mummy. Let's not mix two issues together,' Kanval said, her voice filled with logic.

Kabir took a deep breath and turned to Kanval. 'What should I do now, Kanval? It's been two days and we still haven't heard anything from Armaan. I can't just sit here and wait.' Kanval pondered for a moment and suggested, 'Maybe we can ask Uncle Sarfaraz to visit Armaan's place and check on him.' A glimmer of hope appeared on Kabir's face, but it quickly faded as he remembered something. 'No, that's not a good idea. He hasn't been well since Aunty Tarannum passed away, and I haven't even checked up on him. It would be selfish to ask him to do this.' Kanval nodded in agreement. Kabir sighed and sank back into his chair.

Kanval then suggested, 'Wait, can we ask Bashar to visit Armaan's house?' Kabir quickly called Bashar, but his excitement vanished instantly. 'Kanval, unfortunately Bashar has developed symptoms of the new disease we keep hearing about.' 'Coronavirus?' Kanval asked. 'Yes, he recently had a tourist from Italy, and now he's showing symptoms,' Kabir replied. 'Oh my God! How is he doing now?' Kanval asked, filled with concern. 'He says he has been put under quarantine for fifteen days. Poor fellow was coughing so much,' Kabir replied, feeling overwhelmed by all the information and limitations. 'I don't know, Kanval. What should we do? Do you think Ajju Uncle has contracted this disease?' Kabir asked.

'Maybe, maybe not. I don't believe there is a widespread epidemic of coronavirus in Kashmir, not to the extent that we are witnessing here. They have already been in a strict lockdown with hardly any tourists in the past year,' Kanval replied. 'There's one more way to reach out to them, but I don't think it's feasible.' 'What is it?' Kanval enquired, sensing Kabir's urgency. 'Ramzan Chacha?' 'No way, it's too far for the old man to travel, and considering the current state of affairs, I don't recommend it. Let's just wait,' Kanval advised.

'I need to escape this chaos for a while, I am going to the studio.' As Kabir got up to leave, Kanval reminded him to take necessary precautions. 'Buy yourself a mask and sanitizer, Kabir. The situation is deteriorating every day.'

Chapter 8

The Indian government's announcement of the first-ever lockdown due to COVID-19 sent shockwaves throughout the country. Flights, trains and all other modes of transportation were halted. A nationwide lockdown was imposed. It was as if the world had come to a complete standstill and time seemed to have slowed down to a crawl.

News of deaths and the rapid spread of the virus poured in from all modes of communication. Kanval, in particular, was consumed by panic and fear. She went to extreme lengths to protect her home from contamination, forbidding Iravati from stepping outside, not even into the garden.

Kabir, already distressed, faced a challenging time at home as well. He completed his pending assignments from the home studio, which kept him busy. Iravati, on the other hand, seemed unperturbed by the situation. She had lived through curfews and lockdowns in the past and did not seem to be as frightened by the present situation. She maintained communications with Kanval, but barely spoke with Kabir.

Kanval would not let anyone enter the house. Her fear of infection and obsession with maintaining hygiene had a clinical impact on her mind. She would pick up milk packets six hours after the milkman had gone away, tearing apart a part of the packet and putting it several metres away from her face. She would already have a vessel on the stove and quickly make her way to the kitchen, pour the milk and then make her way back to the lawn where the dustbin was kept. She would use her elbows to spray sanitizer on one palm, repeating the same for the other, and then move to the washbasin to wash her hands again, being careful not to touch the tap with her exposed hands.

She ordered all the household items online and repeated the same procedure for almost everything. For items that she could not purchase online, she herself went out to buy them despite Kabir's request to not go outside. But she did not trust him with following the COVID-avoidant protocols. All the stock that entered the house was kept in the lawn for one complete day, which was followed by spraying them with disinfectant.

Kanval's mysterious moves in the lawn were regularly observed by both Iravati and Kabir. All the discarded materials brought from outside were dumped into a large metal box to be burnt. She quickly lit a fire inside the dump and ran inside the house, closing the windows and doors.

'What happened, Kanval? Why did you shut everything?' Kabir asked, perplexed.

'You have no idea how mysteriously this virus can travel,' Kanval replied.

'Please, would you care to explain,' Iravati interjected, still avoiding eye contact with Kabir.

'What if the garbage was exposed to the virus, and upon burning, it starts to vaporize, entering our nostrils and causing us to contract COVID? Here, wear this mask quickly,' Kabir was stunned.

'What? Really, Kanval?' Kabir burst out laughing, and Iravati tried to control her erupting smile.

'You are laughing at yourself, Bhaiyya. Death is knocking on our doors. Let's just be a little serious,' Kanval responded.

'Kanval! This is extreme! Please relax,' Kabir pleaded, but Kanval was not ready to take any risks. She would clean the house herself, wash all the utensils and clothes. Despite the relaxation of lockdown measures, Kanval refused to let the maid come home, leaving her hands pale and white from frequent washing. Her weight loss began to worry both Kabir and Iravati, and her self-isolation had become a cause for concern. While Iravati found solace in reading magazines and watching television and Kabir engaged himself in the home studio, Kanval longed for a return to normalcy. The development of the vaccine was uncertain, and Kanval's frequent cleaning habits turned into compulsive contamination-related rituals. She developed insomnia and hyperacid reflux and any doorbell or stranger near the house triggered panic attacks.

Recognizing the severity of her condition, Kabir and Iravati decided to seek professional help. 'Mummy, I believe Kanval has developed serious psychiatric trauma due to the lockdown. We need to do something,' Kabir said, and Iravati agreed. 'Maybe we can look for an online therapist to help her. Otherwise I see this matter escalating,' she replied softly. After much persuasion, Kanval agreed to undergo an online therapeutic session with a doctor and all three of them sat together during the sessions. The therapist advised Kanval to stop consuming negative news and to stop watching TV, which Kabir promptly disconnected. She suggested that all three of them share household chores as a team to alleviate Kanval's physical exhaustion. Kabir and Iravati worked together in the kitchen and they divided the cleaning chores among themselves. Kanval began to meditate and exercise, reflecting on herself and realizing the pressure she had taken on herself. Whenever Kabir saw her lost in thoughts, he would snap her out of it.

Kabir and Iravati started communicating in a subtle and respectful tone when required. During dinner, Kanval brought up a thought that had been on her mind. 'You know, this lockdown has been tough on all of us, but it's hard to imagine what people in Kashmir must have gone through. They were under a serious lockdown for almost a year with severe limitations, including no access to basic things like the internet. I can't even fathom how that must have impacted their mental health.'

Kabir looked over at Iravati, who had a sour expression on her face.

Kabir nodded, understanding the point that Kanval was trying to make. 'I see what you're saying. It's important to remember that not everyone is experiencing lockdown in the same way.'

As Kanval looked over at her mother, she realized that Iravati had been quiet this whole time. From basic talk to important ones, Kabir and Iravati started to speak. Kanval was happy. To her, it looked like progress. They would do the chores together and go out together to buy necessities. The lockdown was eased, but schools and offices remained shut. Kanval did not step out. She wanted to leave the house only after things had returned completely to normal, which was taking longer than expected. Nearly a year after the lockdown began, news broke of a successful vaccination, to be administered first to the elderly.

To Kabir and Kanval, getting Iravati vaccinated was a priority too. Kabir had reopened the studio for a couple of hours. Flights had started to operate with limited routes. Iravati took her first dose. Kabir had taken her to the hospital and they returned home. It was a sense of responsibility that Iravati felt Kabir was taking, like an obedient son, despite the differences that had erupted between them, isolating the two. It was mid-March of 2021. The daily COVID cases had fallen and life was slowly starting to return to normal.

Kanval had taken up the task of planting an organic garden in the lawn to avoid outdoor activity. Kabir was helping her spray pesticide while Iravati plucked the veggies. Kabir's phone rang, and he excused himself to a quiet corner to answer it. Iravati's gaze followed him as he stood frozen, his body trembling. She gestured to Kanval, sensing that something was wrong. As the conversation progressed, Iravati's grief grew. Her fears were confirmed when Kabir's face contorted with anguish.

After a moment, Kabir disconnected the call and walked towards them, his face contorted with distress. 'What happened, Kabir? Who was on the line?' Iravati demanded, her voice sharp with concern. Kabir could barely speak, his sobs shaking his body. Kanval looked on in growing alarm. 'Bhaiyya, what happened?'

Kabir took a deep breath and spoke in a numb voice. His body language screamed of agony. They rushed to his side, their worried eyes fixed on him. The silence was deafening and Kanval was the first to break it. 'What happened?' she asked, her voice filled with concern. But Kabir remained silent, lost in his grief. His eyes darted back and forth, as if searching for answers. Suddenly, he burst into traumatic crying. It was a heart-wrenching sight and Iravati's underlying grief was notable.

She knew something was wrong, and her fears were confirmed when Kabir finally spoke. Kabir's voice cracked, choked with tears, as he poured out his heart. 'Armaan...he's...he's not...he's not well,' he managed to utter between sobs. His words were heavy with anguish and despair, the depth of his pain palpable. 'His condition...it's...it's gotten worse. There was a tumour...a tumour growing under his eyes all these years...and we had no idea.' The weight of the revelation pressed upon him, making it difficult to continue. 'Now...now, he's slipped into a coma...for... for four days,' he stammered, his grief pouring out uncontrollably. Kabir's eyes were swollen and bloodshot, his face contorted in a heart-wrenching display of sorrow. 'All those headaches...his... his blindness...it was all because of this slow, relentless tumour. And now...now we might lose him, Kanval,' he wept trembling with the profound fear of losing someone he deeply cared for.

Iravati's eyes flickered with a mix of grief, guilt and anxiety as she tried to console Kabir, her mind burdened with the weight of the news. Kanval's face fell as she heard the news, her own health struggles momentarily forgotten as she struggled to process the gravity of the situation. She struggled to find her voice, trying to process the information. 'Armaan? How could this happen?' she finally managed to say, her voice trembling with emotion.

Kanval broke down in tears as she pleaded with Kabir, 'We have to do something for him. My poor little soul was enduring so much without complaining to anyone.' Kabir's face darkened as he looked at Iravati. 'I am sure you are happy now?' he asked, his voice tinged with bitterness. Iravati looked visibly shaken. 'What do you mean?' she asked, her eyes wide with fear. Kabir continued to stare at her, his voice rising with anger. 'You know exactly what I mean.'

'What's going on?' Kanval's eyes darted between the two with confusion. Kabir's eyes burned with anger and hurt as he looked directly at Iravati. 'You asked Ajju Uncle to end all communication with us, didn't you? You insulted, abused and maligned him horribly. Why did you do that?' His words cut through the air like a sharp knife.

Iravati's face went pale and she stumbled backward, unable to meet Kabir's gaze. 'I...I don't know what you're talking about,' she stammered, trying to hide her guilt.

'Don't lie to me, Mummy,' Kabir spat the word out as if it was poison on his tongue. 'I have proof of your actions. How could you be so heartless?'

Iravati's heart raced as she realized the gravity of the situation. 'I...I didn't mean to hurt anyone,' she whispered, her voice trembling. 'I was just trying to protect us.'

'Protect us? From whom? A blind child who has suffered enough already? An ailing soul who is on his deathbed? Or perhaps a poor father and mother who are grieving the loss of their son? Enlighten us, who are we in danger from?' As Kabir stood there, accusing their mother of something unspeakable, Kanval looked on in confusion. She had no idea what her brother was talking about.

'Bhaiyya, what are you accusing Mummy of?' she asked, trying to make sense of the situation. Kabir turned to face his sister, his expression softening slightly as he realized she was out of the loop. He took a deep breath and began to explain, his voice laced with pain and regret.

'Kanval, our great mother asked Ajju Uncle to cut off all communication with us,' he began. ' Not only that, she insulted, abused and maligned him horribly.' Kanval's eyes widened in shock as she tried to process what her brother was saying. 'What? Mummy did that? Why would she do something like that?' she asked, feeling a rising sense of anxiety.

'When both of us returned home after dropping Armaan at the airport, I was at the studio inside making music while my phone was in the drawing room. Ajju Uncle had called on my number, precisely to inform that Armaan has reached safely. Uncle spoke to Mummy in Kashmiri, in a very apologetic tone right from the beginning. Even though I don't understand Kashmiri, the way she replied to him during her conversation was enough to sense the malice, scolding and even threats. It didn't matter that the words were foreign to me; her tone and intentions were crystal clear. She even deleted the call logs to hide the evidence.'

Kanval looked on in horror, realizing for the first time the depth of their mother's betrayal.

'After some days Rishab had sent me a music scratch; my phone has an automated recording mode. When I opened the folder to listen to the scratch, that's where I discovered the call recording.' Iravati remained silent, her eyes downcast, as Kabir's heart sank at the sight of his mother's shame.

'I knew about this, Kanval,' he said softly, turning towards her. 'But I kept it to myself for two reasons. Firstly, I didn't want to burden you with this knowledge when you were already going through so much. And secondly, I tried to step into Mummy's shoes to understand her perspective. I thought that if she wasn't happy, I was ready to sacrifice my own desires for her sake.'

Kabir's voice choked with emotion as he struggled to maintain his composure. 'But now, with Armaan on his deathbed, all that understanding and sacrifice seem so worthless. How can I forgive myself for not standing up for what was right? How could you be so cruel and heartless?' His eyes filled with tears as he gazed at Iravati.

'By the time I could do something, Uncle had already changed his number. Those poor people must have been so embarrassed that they had to resort to isolation from us,' Kanval expressed her pain. 'For you, Mummy, Uncle did not tell me a word but if something happens to Armaan, I will live like a corpse for the rest of my life.'

Kabir gazed at Iravati fiercely, his eyes burning with anger and frustration. He pointed accusingly at Iravati. 'If something happens to him, Kanval, she will be responsible for it!' His words hit Iravati like a wrecking ball, and she could hardly find the words to defend herself. But Kabir wasn't done yet.

He came down heavily on her, his words tearing through her like a knife. 'I am sure you are very happy, Mummy? Let's celebrate, yayyy, Mummy, what a memorable day for all of us!' He started banging his head against the wall, his rage boiling over. Kanval quickly intervened, pulling her brother away from the wall. 'Stop it, Bhaiyya, this is insane,' she pleaded, looking at him with concern.

Iravati trembled as she watched her son's outburst. Her secret was out, and there was nothing she could do. 'I was just trying to protect you, Kabir,' she protested weakly. 'Believe me, I am your mother and I know what's right for you. I have raised you and…' But Kabir cut her off, his voice rising with each word. 'I have lost four children, Mummy, four! And if this boy dies, this will be the fifth child I will lose. And trust me, I will know who killed him!'

Iravati's face turned red with anger as she listened to Kabir's words that hit her like a slap in the face. 'You will never understand what it feels like to lose a child. Have you ever lost a child? Did you? No, right? You have no idea how it tears you apart from the inside and leaves you feeling dead.' She couldn't believe her own son was speaking to her like this.

'What role do you have in his life? Have you ever defined your role? Come on, tell me?' she raged with equal fervour, her voice trembling with fury. 'That boy is simply not your child. He is not your blood, your lineage, and more importantly, your community. Get that straight in your brain.'

Kabir let out a bitter laugh at that. 'Community? You really think that matters in the grand scheme of things?' Kanval watched the argument unfold, feeling helpless and caught in the middle. She rushed to Kabir's side as he seethed with rage, but he pushed her away.

'Community? Is that what it's all about, Mummy?' he scoffed. 'When I jumped into the river to save him, I didn't stop to ask which community he belonged to. All I knew was that a child was drowning and I had to act. And now, after all that, you have the audacity to throw his community in my face as if it matters more than his life? Shame on you, Mummy.'

Iravati bristled at his words, her own anger boiling over.

'How dare you speak to me like that? I have always done what's best for you, even if you don't see it. I will not let you drag me down with your delusions!'

Kabir glared back at her, his own anger boiling over. 'He may not be my blood, but he's more my family than you've ever considered him!' he spat back. 'You don't get to decide who I care about or who I consider a part of my community, and you, you have no right to decide who is or isn't my family!'

'What do you know about reality, Kabir?' Iravati hit back with equal rage. 'You live in a fantasy world! You think Armaan's parents will just hand over their only son to you? Call them and ask if they will give you their child! Let's have a reality check, shall we? Quick, Kanval, get me the phone. Call Aariz. Call him!'

Kabir and Kanval gazed at each other, momentarily confused by what Iravati had just said. 'Ajju, Ajju is his name, right?' She took the phone from Kanval's hand and gave it to Kabir.

As Kabir's anger reached its peak, he couldn't hold it anymore. He took away Kanval's mobile from Iravati's hand and smashed it on the ground, shattering it into pieces on the wall. 'Only if he survives!' he screamed. His voice trembled with emotion as he spoke.

Kanval, unable to bear the intensity of the situation, quickly fled the room. Kabir continued to weep uncontrollably, like a child in pain. Iravati looked at him with a mixture of disappointment and shock. This was the same Kabir who had always been a dutiful and obedient son, but now he was a different person altogether, a person who cared for strangers more than his own family.

She tried to approach him, to console him, but he pushed her away. 'Leave me alone,' he said, his voice cracking. 'You are not the mother I thought you were.' With that, he stormed out of the room, leaving Iravati alone with her thoughts.

Have you ever lost a child? Did you? No, right?

His words echoed in her ears. The situation had escalated to a point of no return and the tension in the room was suffocating. Iravati stood there, stunned by Kabir's outburst and his sudden transformation. His words echoed in her mind, taunting her with the truth she couldn't declare to her children.

Tears welled up in Iravati's eyes as she slowly sank to the floor, her legs unable to support her trembling body. She clutched her chest, feeling the weight of guilt and regret pressing down upon her.

'I have never lost a child?' she whispered, her voice filled with sorrow. 'I have lost my children in a different way... I have lost their trust, their love and their respect.' The impact of Kabir's behaviour crushed her spirit.

Kanval took a deep breath and composed herself, as she had almost reached a state of a panic attack. She walked out to the lawn where Kabir sat quietly, staring at his phone, wondering if the bell would ring to inform him that Armaan had passed away. Kanval sat down and briefly looked at him, but he didn't acknowledge her presence.

She took his phone and excused herself, spoke to Ajju and then returned to Kabir. 'His condition remains critical, Bhaiyya. A doctor from Delhi who is an expert in dealing with tumours is going to Srinagar to check on him,' Kanval said softly. Kabir's hope intensified. 'Will he be able to save him or is it too late?'

'That cannot be guaranteed,' Kanval replied, her tone low.

Kanval took a deep breath before speaking again. 'I spoke to the family. They are struggling to afford the operation.' Kabir's expression changed and he asked, 'How much is needed?'

'It's a significant amount and they don't have the funds to cover it,' Kanval replied, her voice heavy with concern.

Kabir sighed deeply. 'I'll take care of it. Money can't stand in the way of saving a life.'

Kanval was relieved. 'But I can't meet them, Kanval. I can't face them after what my mother did,' Kabir said, his voice filled with shame.

Kanval put a hand on his shoulder. 'I understand. But your support and presence could make a world of difference to them.'

Kabir looked away, lost in thought. 'I know you're right, Kanval. But I don't know if I have the strength to face them.'

'You're not alone,' Kanval reassured him. 'He is a warrior; he will surely emerge a triumphant.'

Kanval had requested Sarfaraz to visit the family at the hospital. The cold, tense silence between Kabir and Iravati continued for next fifteen days and even Kanval could not bridge the gap between them.

On the sixteenth day, Kanval hurried towards Iravati's room, heart pounding with a sense of urgency that pulsed through her veins. She needed to share the news about Armaan. But when Kanval arrived at Iravati's room, she found it empty, an unsettling absence.

Panic welled up within Kanval as she searched every nook and cranny, desperate to find her mother, but their home was devoid of any clues or signs of Iravati's whereabouts.

10 April 2021
Gawkadal, Srinagar

Thirty years had passed, yet the bridge exuded the same atmosphere. The air was subtly cold and the Jhelum River carried the familiar scent. As she started to move, her feet hesitated and the voices echoed in her ears.

Jaldi yease benia bea karey chun intezaar. Come soon, dear sister, I'll be waiting for you.

It was 7 a.m. in the morning, and everything appeared normal. The sweeper diligently swept the bridge, eagles hovered in the sky, boats were neatly parked at the ghat, and school children passed by in their uniforms. Things looked different, but they had the same essence. The Jhelum appeared greener yet dirtier, the arrangement of homes, mosques and temples along the ghat maintained their symmetrical alignment, except for the absence of the temple bells that used to chime during the regular aarti-chanting thirty years ago. A sudden cold breeze blew, reminiscent of the dip in temperature during Chillai Kalaan. Despite her attempt to feign composure, her emotions raged within. Another slogan reverberated, causing her to turn back instantly.

AZAADI, AZAADI

An old man smoking in a corner of the bridge gave her a blank stare. As she continued walking, she saw Tarannum and herself sitting on the ghat stairs in her mind's eye.

A school bus honked, snapping her out of her thoughts. The bridge, once made of wood, now stood as a concrete structure. The sun rays illuminated her rosy face, welcoming her. Iravati stood in front of her house after thirty years. Slowly, she reached the end of the bridge and descended the stairs. The dry fruit shop at the lane's end was still there, visible to her. She peered into the small bylane that connected to the ghat and touched the brick wall of her house. As she continued walking, the temple gradually came into view, its dome rusted and dilapidated. The narrow lane stretched ahead, and she could see the barricaded wall beneath which the Jhelum flowed as if it surged upon her arrival. A glance to her right revealed a full view of her once majestic old house, which she had left behind thirty years ago.

A carpenter was working outside the main door. The name plate retained the name CHINAR KUTH with fresh paint. The carpenter simply looked at her and continued working. He looked non-Kashmiri. As she glanced around, she saw that most of the Pandit homes were crumbling and decaying. The exterior of her house had been freshly renovated. Did someone shift here? Next to her house stood Tarannum's. *Oh my God! That's Tarannum's house.* Iravati started to shiver. The main door of the house was open, so she quickly entered it. It bore the smell of apricot wood, just as it did thirty years ago. The wooden staircase leading upwards seemed to have a fresh polish and the paint on the sidewalls gave her a welcoming feel.

Moving upwards, there she was, in her own house. The curtains in the drawing room flew with a gentle breeze, while the Rubab hung over the wall just as the family had left it behind. She made her way to the kitchen, only to witness the same old setup intact. She saw the samovar in which she had made the kahva last time before departing. It was the holiest place for her in the entire household. The antique telephone was still in its place, and the radio, which gave them the terrible live broadcast of her father-in-law's death, was placed next to the sofa. She couldn't believe that she had brought herself back to the place which had so much that was left behind.

As she peeked through the window, the bridge brought back the old memory of the harrowing night. Another glance leftwards brought back the memory of Noman falling dead on the ghat while she rowed the boat with Purushottam and her kids. Several noises of the dark night echoed in her mind. She quickly made her way to the bedroom. It was painted a fine green colour. She could not contain it any longer and started to weep. She wept her heart out. All the memories came flashing to her mind and heart. It had taken her a great deal of effort to come back to this place. She cried her heart out with so much that was buried inside of it.

As she peeked out at the neighbourhood from the iconic location of her house, something inside of her felt lighter. She gazed through the window made in the Dhajji Dewani architectural style with a fine polish. 'Who must have renovated the house? The new tenants?' she said to herself as she looked at the window from a distance. 'Kabir,' a voice answered from behind. Shocked, she turned around only to see Sarfaraz standing with a numb welcoming face.

Mumbai

Kabir's hands were trembling as he stared out of the car window. The thought of his mother, Iravati, missing for two days now was suffocating him with fear and guilt. He turned to his younger sister, Kanval, who was driving them back home from the police station, hoping for some reassurance.

'Am I so terrible that my own mother would run away from me?' Kabir blurted out, his voice cracking. Kanval glanced at him briefly, then returned her eyes to the road. 'Of course not,' she said firmly. 'Mummy is just...Mummy. She does what she wants when she wants. You know that.'

'But she wouldn't just disappear without telling anyone,' Kabir protested, his mind racing with dark scenarios. 'What if she's hurt, or sick, or...or...'

'You're not helping anyone by freaking out. We've done everything we can for now. The police will find her, or she'll come back on her own. We just have to wait and see.'

Kabir sank back into his seat, feeling more helpless than ever. He knew Kanval meant well, but her calmness was starting to irritate him. Didn't she care about their mother as much as he did? 'You don't seem very worried,' he said, trying to sound casual but failing. 'Do you know something that I don't?'

Kanval sighed and shook her head. 'No, Bhaiyya. I'm just trying to stay positive. I know Mummy can be difficult sometimes, but she's also strong and smart. She wouldn't do anything stupid or dangerous and if at all you are wondering if she's jumped somewhere, she would already have done that thirty years back, so relax.'

Kabir frowned. 'How can you be so sure? And you always ended up arguing with her, so how can you claim you know her when you were not in sync with her thoughts?'

Kanval gripped the steering wheel tighter. 'That's not true and you know it. I never argued with her to prove that I was right, or that my opinions were better than hers. But all that is not important. Let me tell you something, it's your behaviour you're now regretting, because you think you drove her away.'

'That's not fair, Kanval. I love mummy, I...I just had one disagreement with her, that's it!'

Kanval nodded, her eyes softening. 'I know, Bhaiyya. I'm not blaming you. We all have opinions and sometimes we are very stubborn about them, but we have to be there for each other, especially when things get tough, like now.'

Kabir realized that Kanval was right, as always. He had to stop blaming himself and start thinking of ways to help find their mother.

He had to trust that she was safe and sound, somewhere out there, and that they would see her again soon. As they reached their house and got out of the car, Kanval put a hand on Kabir's shoulder. 'Don't worry, Bhaiyya. We'll find her. And we'll make things right, between all of us.'

Kabir knew he had a long way to go before he could forgive himself for the harsh words he had said to his mother. To him, Kanval looked more responsible and mature than she was earlier.

As they approached the door, Kanval said to Kabir, 'With all those arguments with her, you know what I have learned?' Before Kanval could complete her sentence, the door opened and they saw a figure standing in front of them. Kabir and Kanval exchanged a confused look, wondering if it was a reality. Armaan looked at them with a small smile, his eyes sparkling with newfound sight. 'Welcome home, Bhaiyya,' he said, his voice filled with joy. Kabir and Kanval were both speechless, still trying to process what they were seeing. Armaan, who they had always known as blind, was now standing in front of them, looking right at them.

Kabir broke the silence. 'Armaan, you can see?' Armaan nodded with a smile. 'Yes, but you are taller than I anticipated.' Kanval turned to Kabir, her eyes filled with surprise and joy. 'Oh my God, Bhaiyya! Look at Armaan!'

Kabir was speechless as he stared at him, who was looking at them with his bright blue eyes. Suddenly, Iravati appeared behind Armaan and held on to his back. Her presence took Kabir and Kanval by surprise. They both turned to look at her, their expressions a mix of shock and disbelief. Kanval rushed towards her and hugged her tightly, tears streaming down her face.

Kabir stood a few feet away, his expression a mix of guilt, surprise and conflict. He couldn't bring himself to move or say anything. 'I knew you would come back,' Kanval said, holding Iravati. Iravati gently patted Kanval's back before turning to face Kabir. She looked at him with a composed yet sad expression, as if she knew what was going through his mind.

After two hours of awkward silence, Iravati finally summoned Kabir and Kanval to her room. 'Kabir, Kanval, please come into my room,' Iravati commanded. Kabir's heart raced as he walked in, knowing that he was in for a scolding. 'Come sit.' Her tone was firm yet composed. Kabir and Kanval took a seat, avoiding eye contact with their mother.

'I want to talk to both of you,' Iravati began, her voice steady. 'I understand that emotions have been running high lately and we have all made mistakes. I want to make it clear that I am not without fault either. I should have communicated with you both before leaving for Kashmir, and for that, I apologize.'

Kabir looked up, his eyes filled with a mix of relief and gratitude. He had expected anger and disappointment from his mother, but her willingness to acknowledge her own mistakes gave him a glimmer of hope.

'I know we have our differences and disagreements, but as a family, it's important that we stick together,' Iravati spoke earnestly. 'There's something I need to share with you all, something you were too young to comprehend back then,' Iravati reflected, her tone tinged with nostalgia. 'But now, since you're grown up, it's time for me to reveal the untold chapter of my life, the complexities that shaped who I am.'

19 January 1990
Srinagar

Iravati called out to Purushottam several times in the deep, dark water of the Dal Lake, freezing with bone-chilling cold of the sub-zero temperature. The only gleam that reflected on the horizon was the moonlight. It was as if in the entire universe, the moon was the lone witness to the terrible plight of Iravati and her family.

'Raina Sahab, neabar near,' she yelled for him to come out. By now, even the bubbles oozing out of the water had frozen. She called out his name several times, her voice echoing across the still water, but there was no response. The bubbles that rose to the surface with each passing minute were the only indication of where he might be. It was as if the universe itself had conspired against Iravati, leaving her alone in her grief and despair.

She felt like a prisoner trapped in the icy, isolated expanse of the lake, with no hope. Even her children's presence provided little solace. The bitter cold pierced her skin, but the chill in her heart was even more unbearable. She lay in the boat, her body wracked with sobs, feeling as though her entire world had been submerged and swallowed by the frigid waters.

The only light in the distance was from the Shankaracharya Temple. Suddenly, the oar she had been holding slipped from her grasp and fell into the water. It floated towards her, brushing against her outstretched hand. In that moment, she felt a jolt of sensation, as if a divine force had intervened to awaken her from her stupor. She wiped away her tears and looked around, noticing the ghat a few meters away, with the temple looming in the background.

Her eyes fixed on the temple, she cried out, 'This happened in front of you, Shiv ji! How could you let this happen?' A sudden urge to end her own life swept over her but soon the bells of the temple began to chime, as if signalling Iravati to stop.

Iravati felt torn between the desire to end her own suffering and the obligation to care for her children. 'I am coming there, Shiv ji,' she whispered to herself. 'But I can't be selfish. I can't do this.' With renewed determination, she picked up the oar and began to row with all her might towards the ghat.

The vast expanse of the lake, with its dark, looming mountains, seemed to stretch out endlessly before her. But Iravati was determined to make it to the ghat, no matter what. When she finally reached, she pulled Kabir out of the boat, holding him close as tears streamed down her face. It was a small victory, but one that gave her the strength to keep going, to keep fighting for her family, even in the face of unspeakable tragedy.

Iravati cast one last glance at the unforgiving waters of Dal Lake, searching for any sign of Purushottam. But there was nothing, not even a ripple, to indicate his presence. Iravati, in the depths of despair, had to make a choice to leave the place where her husband had been lost, perhaps forever. It was not a choice she wanted to make, but a choice she had to make for the sake of her children and her own survival.

As she crossed to the other side of the isolated road, all the shops were shut. A jeep passed by with several masked men inside wearing pherans. Suspecting them to be militants, she quickly hid herself in a tiny bylane. They were indeed militants, carrying Kalashnikovs and parading openly as if in a military drill. It was not safe at all.

Looking back at the spot where Purushottam lay lifeless in the water, with a numb and hopeless face, Iravati turned her attention back to the main road. She made her way towards the temple through the sideways, taking a quick turn up the hill along a serpentine road. Another jeep passed by, with masked militants, and she quickly hid behind a large chinar tree. Their presence pierced her heart.

Barely a few metres away, she spotted another family, with a few men, hiding behind a tree. A woman called out to her to join them immediately. 'Yoor yi, yoor yi benia. Come here, come here, sister!' It was a family of three: Roshanlal, Sulakshana and their daughter, who was about Kabir's age. Iravati felt a sudden surge of relief. The man asked her where she was going, but she was so dazed that she had no idea what to say. 'Beni kotei drayakh? Where are you going, sister?' He pressed again. 'Hoar mandar gachav. We will go to the mandir,' she replied. But Roshanlal, unsure how safe the passage was, asked her to join them instead.

Suddenly, there was a blast on the other bank of Dal Lake and some houses were engulfed in flames. The children were scared and started to cry. 'Sopp kar, Umika, bilkul sopp,' Sulakshana said, as Umika's cries could attract attention. Slowly and steadily, they all made their way to the Dal Gate, where other Pandits had gathered.

'Let's go to the bus stand,' a young man among them insisted. 'Make sure no one is left out. No one is here to help us.' As the group approached the crowded bus stand, the scene was nothing short of chaos. Pandits huddled together, looking lost and hopeless, while Iravati's face reflected the trauma she had just endured. Sulakshana could feel the weight of her grief as she stood by her side, offering her comfort in the midst of the turmoil. The arrival of the trucks brought a glimmer of hope, but the reality of the situation was stark and appalling. The faces of men, women and children alike were etched with pain and anguish, their voices choked with sobs.

The driver sternly commanded them to keep quiet. The scene was heart-wrenching, a reminder of the fragility of life and the devastating consequences of conflict.

The truck passed through the Badami Bagh area, the gateway to Srinagar that had turned into an exit route for the Pandits. In no time, the truck found itself on the Jammu-Srinagar highway. The truck continued on the Anantnag Bijbehara road. Women in the truck wailed until they found solace in sleeping on each other's shoulders. The truck passed through the flourishing towns of Qazigund, Banihal and Ramban, with twirling ghats and a gorge with the Chenab River flowing beneath.

'Where are we going?' Iravati asked Sulakshana. 'Jammu,' came the reply. The twirling ghats caused Iravati motion sickness and she felt the urge to vomit. Sulakshana requested a halt, but it was deemed too risky. Most of the women had removed their dejhoar and bindis and covered their heads with scarves. Iravati vomited from the moving truck. She was exhausted, drained and defeated.

In the early morning, the truck reached Jammu. It was a misty morning with a very different landscape. Most of the ladies, including Iravati, had travelled to Jammu for the first time. It was the first time in her entire life that Iravati had travelled without Purushottam. A camp was set up for the Pandits on the banks of the Tawi River, a tributary of the Chenab River. It was a morning devoid of hope.

Pandits from the apple towns of Shopian to Sopore, and from the crowded downtown areas of Habba Kadal to the prosperous Rainawari, had fled the valley. Kashmir, once a land of tranquil mountains and rivers, had suddenly turned into a burning hell. Refugees from all over the valley started accumulating at the camps in Jammu, each with a fearful story of escape.

Within days, the number of Pandit refugees overflowed the camps. The conditions in the camps were appalling. Thousands of Pandits were lodged in various refugee camps in Jammu, most of which lacked basic hygiene facilities. There were only limited latrines for hundreds of people. In the name of lodging facilities, each family was allotted a tent that offered minimal privacy.

Kashmiris, who prided themselves about living in Jhelum-facing multi-storeyed homes with multiple bedrooms and finely crafted wooden interiors as well as exteriors, found themselves in shabby, torn and derelict tents. The pheran was no longer required as the heat became unbearable for most Kashmiri Pandits. Men, women and children fainted under the scorching sun. Their fate had pushed them from gardens of bliss to an arid desert of an uncertain future.

Iravati had lost herself somewhere. Her eyes were swollen and her lips spoke little. Like many others at the camp, Iravati too had no idea what life beyond Kashmir would hold. She was allocated a small tent next to Sulakshana's. The camp was laid out below the bridge on alluvial soil, with mice, snakes and insects creeping beneath. Stray dogs roamed the river plains. There was very little food supply and uncooked vegetables were distributed; even that ran out of stock within minutes and failed to fulfil the needs of the people present.

The authorities brought vegetables on a cart, and in a moment, thousands of people pounced and grabbed whatever they could, leading to fights among themselves. Sulakshana complained bitterly, 'Baati chu ka devan ke ehsaan chuk karan? How can a servant ever repay their master's kindness?' As if the authorities were doing them a great favour. She sat next to Iravati, witnessing the madness while their children cried with hunger. Sulakshana gazed at Iravati, who was running a high fever. The fever, in a way, expressed the mournful state of mind that her lips and eyes could not convey. Roshan Lal brought a handful of roasted peas for all of them.

As the night deepened, the silence at the refugee camp on the banks of the Tawi River grew more profound. The only sounds that could be heard were the distant chirping of crickets and the occasional gusts of wind rustling through the leaves of nearby trees. Suddenly, a piercing scream shattered the peace of the night. It was Sulakshana's voice, filled with terror and agony. Iravati was jolted awake at the sound. She quickly got out of her tent and saw a crowd had gathered around Sulakshana's tent. Iravati rushed inside the tent to find a shocking scene.

Roshan Lal was lying on the ground, his body convulsing violently. His face had turned blue and purple and he was frothing at the mouth. It was clear that he was in the throes of death. Iravati's heart sank as she realized what had happened.

A venomous snake had bitten Roshan Lal and there was no hope of saving him. Sulakshana was beside herself with grief, sobbing uncontrollably at the sight of her friend's untimely death. The next morning, Roshan Lal was cremated on the banks of the Tawi River. Sulakshana, still reeling from the shock of his sudden death, could not stop lamenting her fate.

'What kind of fate is this?' she cried out. 'He had no intention of dying today; after all that tedious escape, only to be killed in a place that we thought would be safe!'

Iravati could not help but agree with Sulakshana's words. 'Most of us escaped death only to meet another death, a living death,' her voice filled with sorrow and resignation. As the night wore on, another layer of misfortune was on its way. The stench emanating from the toilets was unbearable, making it impossible for anyone to relieve themselves there. Explaining to Sulakshana that she needed to go relieve herself, she asked her to look at her kids. Iravati set off into the darkness, trying to ignore the feeling that she was being followed. There was little illumination in the dark.

Iravati quietly made her way to bushes near the river. She quickly relieved herself and walked back towards the camp, but in a split second, suddenly someone grabbed her mouth and pinned her to the ground. Iravati struggled to escape, but her assailant was too powerful. He forced himself on top of her, pushing against her stomach as she fought back.

With no other options left, Iravati reached for a rock near her hand and struck her attacker on the head with all her might. He was a dark-looking man with visible obesity, smelling of alcohol and moving clumsily. Despite the blow, he managed to overpower Iravati once again, forcing himself on her.

But just as she was about to lose hope, a large rock hit his head from behind. He instantly loosened his hands and his eyes rolled back. Iravati pushed him away, only to see Sulakshana standing still there with an anguished face. Sulakshana wasted no time and hit the man another time with the same rock, delivering a fatal blow.

'Kanjar, scoundrel!' Sulakshana ridiculed him. Iravati's stomach ached terribly. Sulakshana quickly comforted her and put her scarf on her torn dress.

As they watched blood gushing out of his head, he soon lay still on his face. Stray dogs started to bark, alarming the two women. Sulakshana had come to check on Iravati as she hadn't returned for some time. 'Let's go quickly, before something else happens,' Sulakshana urged her. 'Where to?' Iravati asked, sobbing in pain. 'Anywhere, just get out of here,' Sulakshana insisted, urging her to escape the place immediately. They silently made their way back to the camp and Sulakshana turned off the lantern.

Iravati's nervousness and pain knew no bounds. She was restless with excruciating pain. Sulakshana requested her to escape, as it was a new place with no support. Moreover, they had just killed a local, which could land them in jail. Unguided, frightened and scared, both women panicked.

'Where to go?' Iravati asked. 'Anywhere far from this paradise, away from here,' Sulakshana replied urgently. The women got up, picked up their children, and made their way out of the camp, avoiding any eyes that could see them.

Away from the camp, as Iravati struggled to walk, Sulakshana noticed blood stains dripping from her ankles. Before Sulakshana could say anything, a train honked. The railway station was right in front of them. Sulakshana wanted to get away from the place as soon as possible.

With great struggle, the women, along with their children, made their way to the railway platform. The train was slowly moving, and Sulakshana pushed Iravati and their children into it, without a ticket. The train departed from Jammu and Kashmir, headed towards an unknown future.

Chapter 9

Iravati's voice trembled as she spoke, 'I've carried this pain in my heart for thirty years now. Every night when I close my eyes, those memories haunt me.' She paused, taking a deep breath before continuing, 'But I've kept it to myself all this while, until now.'

Iravati took a moment to compose herself before speaking again. 'When you accused me of not understanding the pain of losing a child, I couldn't keep silent any longer,' she said, her voice breaking. 'I was three months pregnant when we left Kashmir. And then...I suffered a miscarriage. I lost my husband, my father-in-law and our baby all at once.'

Tears streamed down Kanval's face as she reached out to hold her mother's hand. Kabir was in shock, unable to comprehend the weight of his mother's pain. Iravati continued, her eyes conveying the agony she had been holding inside for so long. 'I know what it's like to lose a child, Kabir,' she said, looking directly at him. 'I know what it's like to have your dreams shattered and your life turned upside down. I know what it's like to feel like everything you held dear has been taken away from you.'

Her voice was barely above a whisper now, but her words hung heavy in the air. 'And the worst part is not having your partner to lean on. To feel like you're facing the world alone.'

Kabir's heart ached with the realization of how wrong he had been to judge his mother's pain. 'I'm sorry, Mummy,' he said, his voice choked with tears. 'I had no idea... '

Iravati held out her hand, and Kabir took it, holding on tightly as if he never wanted to let go. 'It's ok, my son,' she said, her voice gentle. 'You couldn't have known. But now you do.'

Iravati looked at Kabir with mixed emotions. 'When you accused me of being insensitive, I had to let loose my chained senses of what I had zipped up thirty years ago,' she said, her voice trembling with emotion. 'I had suppressed my grief for so long that it had become a part of me. I had convinced myself that it was the only way to move forward, to keep living. But I was wrong.'

She paused for a moment, gathering her thoughts. 'Suppression is a dangerous thing, Kabir. It can eat away at you, bit by bit, until you are nothing but a shell of the person you used to be. And it doesn't just affect you, it affects everyone around you. That night changed everything for us, and I was so consumed by my own pain that I failed to see how it was affecting you and Kanval. I'm sorry for that.'

Kabir listened intently, his eyes fixed on his mother's face. 'I had something to look forward to because of you two,' Iravati continued. 'But you, Kabir, lost everything. It's not that I never understood your pain, your spiritual confusions, your desire for a family. I wanted the best for you, but I didn't know how to help you. If this child keeps you fulfilled, go ahead and nurture him.'

'Kanval, you had this unique way of pushing me out of my emotional constipation,' she confessed. 'It's not your blunt words or arguments that I refuted, but your honest analysis. You helped me realize the weight I carried within me for far too long.'

Her voice filled with a sense of liberation. 'That's why I finally decided to visit our house in Kashmir. It was there that I found release, a profound sense of letting go. It allowed me to forgive, forget and truly move on.'

Kanval listened intently, her eyes wide with surprise and appreciation. Iravati continued, 'Nature has a way of teaching us to let go.'

Kanval's heart swelled with pride and happiness. She never expected her mother to acknowledge her in such a way. It was a moment of realization for both of them, that despite their differences, they still had a deep connection. 'I need to tell you something, Kanval. I want you to know that I don't hate a particular community. The man who forced himself on me that night was surely from the community you feel I dislike. It was just that I wanted to close the chapter on all the good and bad related to Kashmir, to try and escape the worst traumas of my life as if they didn't exist. I thought the way out of pain was to never look at the wound.'

As Iravati spoke, her voice was raw with emotion. 'I don't hate anyone, Kanval. Not a religion, not a region, not a clan. If it weren't for Tarannum and Bhailal, I wouldn't be here right now. They risked their lives for me, looking out for me in that camp with such intensity that it moved me to tears. They were more willing to help and ease me out of my misery than my own relatives who saw me in the camp but turned away. But I couldn't let them help me any further, not with the danger they were already in due to Aariz.' Tears welled up in Iravati's eyes as she continued. 'So I hid myself away, even though all I wanted was to embrace Tarannum and cry on her shoulder. Tarannum was the only friend I had left in the world. The only one who kept searching for me, wanting me back. But her death destroyed me. So, I assumed Tarannum never existed. I kept my worries to myself, not wanting to burden anyone else with my pain and pretended as if it didn't exist.'

Iravati's voice trembled as she recounted the events of that fateful night. 'I just wanted to wipe away my terrible past. Any reminder of it would have killed me. It was too much to bear. I didn't want to go back to that night, Kanval. The night of 19 January 1990, when my husband and father-in-law didn't receive a proper funeral. I wanted to erase it all, to start afresh.

'And that's why I had to impose those restrictions on myself, so that I could live in the present and not be haunted by the past. But now, nothing haunts me anymore. My past, the loss of lives and the tale that I left behind thirty years ago have all been released. I must thank you for pushing me to face the reality that I chose to ignore. Visiting Kashmir flushed out the pain I carried within my heart for so many years. I cried, cried and cried until the pain was flushed out of my eyes.'

The three of them hugged and embraced each other, finally united as a loving family. Armaan, who had heard the whole climax, stood still in the corner of the room. Iravati called out to Armaan, and he approached them feeling deeply ashamed. 'Come here, beta,' she said, drawing him closer. 'By now, it should be clear to you that your Bhaiyya loves you like his own son. You must promise me that if you love him, you will never disappoint him.'

Kabir kept his gaze fixed on the floor. Iravati's voice quivered as she looked at him, urging him to pay attention. 'Kabir, my dear, please listen to me,' she said, her eyes holding his gaze. 'This boy, Armaan, he is your responsibility now. You must take care of him, protect him, nurture him and guide him in a way that his parents cannot. You must ensure he receives the best education, manners and opportunities to grow into a fine human being.' Iravati's eyes shone with pride and affection as she looked at Kabir. She knew that he would be an exceptional father figure to Armaan, just as her father-in-law was. Kabir understood the gravity of his new responsibility and felt a sense of awe and humility at the task before him.

'You will give him a bright future, whether you raise him here or in Kashmir. I leave it to you and his parents to decide,' Iravati continued. 'You will experience the joy of being a parent through him, Kabir. Listen to me carefully,' she said, her voice firm yet gentle.

'You must raise Armaan as your own, with all the love and care that a child deserves. But remember, you should expect nothing in return. True love and selflessness come without any expectations or conditions. You must give Armaan your best, with the hope that he will grow into a good human being so that no Aariz is reborn. That is the only reward you should seek. Do you understand? Just as my father-in-law was a true guardian to Armaan's family, now you will play that role.'

As soon as Iravati uttered those words, a sudden hush fell over the room. Kabir and Kanval exchanged confused glances, wondering what their mother could possibly mean. 'Guardian to Armaan's family? When?' Kabir asked with intense curiosity. Iravati drew a deep breath, gathering her thoughts. She drew Armaan closer to her.

'Nature has a strange way of repeating things, there's one last truth that you must know,' she said, her voice soft but firm. 'It's not an easy truth and I don't know how well it will sit with you. But I expect you both to be kind.' Kabir and Kanval looked at each other, a sense of foreboding settling over them. 'What is it, Mummy?' Kanval asked.

Iravati paused for a moment, steeling herself for what she was about to say. 'There's a truth about Armaan that came to light when his father called up to inform about his arrival. The conversation in Kashmiri that you did not understand. But it was not just a conversation, it was a revelation that his father made and perhaps the only thing you understood was my brutal reaction.' She began, but before she could continue, the doorbell rang, interrupting her. Two officers stood at the door with a police van.

'Kabir Raina?' an officer asked. Kabir instantly got up, and Iravati followed him as Kanval stood by the door. 'Kabir here,'

Kabir responded, his voice filled with surprise and apprehension. Iravati looked nervous.

'Do you know this man?' the officers showed them a photo of Aariz. 'Of course I know him. He is a dear family friend, Ajju Uncle,' Kabir replied, turning back to look at Iravati and Armaan. Iravati drew Armaan closer to her, gripping Kabir's shoulder.

'What happened, Sir?' Kanval enquired, her voice filled with concern. 'Did you help this person with a sum of five lakh rupees?' Kabir was surprised by the question, recalling that he had transferred the money to Ajju's account for Armaan's urgent treatment.

'Yes, I did so sometime back, but please tell me what happened?' Kabir asked, seeking answers. The officer immediately handcuffed him, sending a wave of shock through the room.

'We are arresting you for funding terrorist activities.' Kabir felt like he was in a nightmare. This couldn't be happening. 'What? Terrorist activity? What nonsense! Please explain?' he pleaded. Iravati's grip on his shoulder tightened as she looked at him with worry and concern. Kanval stood frozen, unable to believe what was unfolding before him.

'We are arresting you on charges of aiding and financing Aariz Zargar, a former militant who illegally entered India from Pakistan ten years ago and has now gone missing again with your monetary assistance.'

2010
Srinagar

Aariz stood in the dimly lit courtroom, his heart pounding against his chest. He had returned to Kashmir, his homeland, after a tumultuous journey through the shadows of clandestine immigration from Pakistan. Aariz, upon his return, chose to surrender himself to the authorities, seeking transparency and hoping to find a semblance of homecoming under the policy designed for former militants. Yet, little did he know that his sincerity would be fraught with challenges, far from the ease he had imagined.

As the defence presented their case, a flicker of hope still lingered within Aariz. He glanced at Kalsoom and Armaan, who sat nearby, their worried eyes conveying a mix of fear and determination. Armaan sat unaware of the impending storm that threatened to shatter their fragile existence.

The charges against Aariz were grave. The prosecution accused him of illegally leaving and entering the country, breaching immigration laws and raising suspicions of possible involvement in militant activities during his time in Pakistan. Aariz maintained his innocence, vehemently denying any wrongdoing. Yet, the evidence stacked against him seemed insurmountable.

However, there was one glimmer of mercy amidst the darkness. Armaan, their beloved child, was blind, his sight stolen at a tender age. It became clear to the court that imprisoning a blind child would be an act of cruelty, contrary to the principles of justice and the child's best interests. The judge, his brow furrowed with contemplation, recognized the unique circumstances surrounding Armaan's condition. He understood the importance of preserving family unity and safeguarding the child's well-being. The judge rendered a decision that would shape the path of Aariz's journey through the twisting halls of justice. Aariz would be detained, and his case would proceed under the watchful eyes of the court. But the child, innocent and vulnerable, would not share the same fate.

To ensure his safety and well-being, the judge imposed conditions upon Kalsoom. Regular reporting to authorities, restricted movement and supervision by the NGO became the terms that would allow Kalsoom to care for Armaan outside the confines of a prison cell. Understanding the challenging circumstances faced by Kalsoom and Armaan, the judge granted occasional furloughs to Aariz, allowing him temporary releases to support his family during the legal proceedings. These furloughs provided a brief respite from the confines of imprisonment, enabling Aariz to offer emotional and practical assistance to his loved ones. While the furloughs provided temporary relief, they also came with increased scrutiny and strict conditions to ensure Aariz's compliance with the court's orders.

The court recognized the necessity of specialized care and support for a blind child. Social services and organizations specializing in disability assistance were to be involved, providing guidance and resources for Kalsoom and Armaan's journey through the uncertain terrain that lay ahead.

With the weight of the court's decision settling upon them, Aariz, Kasloom and Armaan embarked on a new chapter, their lives intertwined in a complex dance between the pursuit of justice and the preservation of innocence. It was a journey where truth would be sought, alliances forged and the resilient human spirit tested.

However, in a tragic turn of events, during one of these granted furloughs, Aariz went missing, breaching the court's orders and unleashing serious consequences. The disappearance cast a cloud of suspicion and uncertainty over his case, complicating the already complex legal proceedings.

~

2020
Srinagar

Kalsoom, devastated by Aariz's sudden vanishing act, grappled with the consequences it brought. The hope that the furloughs had provided was shattered, replaced by a wave of uncertainty and fear. The judge's initial decision to grant furloughs, intended to maintain family ties and alleviate some of the burdens faced by Kalsoom and Armaan, now became a haunting reminder of the fragility of their situation.

As the courtroom braced itself for the repercussions of Aariz's breach, Kalsoom found herself caught in the crosscurrents of loyalty, desperation and a relentless pursuit for answers. In the realm of uncertain shadows, Kabir's noble intentions became a perilous snare. When he had selflessly offered financial aid for Armaan's treatment, little had he known that his compassion would end in a sinister twist.

The remaining funds intended for Armaan's well-being had vanished with Aariz, leaving Kabir in a state of disbelief and betrayal. Questions loomed over him like a heavy cloud: Where had Aariz fled to? What was his motive for absconding with the funds? And why did Kabir extend his assistance beyond what was required?

The answer to the last question lay in Kabir's unwavering determination to provide the best possible care for Armaan. Money was not to be an obstacle in his pursuit of ensuring Armaan's well-being, and without a second thought, he had transferred the funds to Aariz, trusting him implicitly. But little did Kabir know that his act of kindness would be repaid with betrayal, as Aariz vanished into the unknown with the surplus funds.

Now faced with the weight of consequences, Kabir found himself in the centre of a storm, a victim of his own altruism. As the authorities investigated Aariz's disappearance and the missing funds, Kabir stood under their scrutiny, his reputation tarnished and his character called into question.

Kanval's relentless pursuit of justice aimed not only to prove Aariz's innocence but also to establish a crucial link between the two cases. Clearing Aariz's name would not only secure his freedom but also provide a solid foundation for exonerating Kabir, highlighting the interconnectedness of their lives. Kanval had taken up the case and was working tirelessly to locate Aariz, but he seemed to have vanished into thin air.

When Aariz had made his courageous return, he'd chosen to keep his arrival a secret from Sarfaraz and Tarannum, understanding that his presence could jeopardize their safety. He maintained the facade of having only a distant memory of his birthplace, claiming that his escape at a tender age had left him with hazy recollections. It was only when Kanval arranged for Sarfaraz to visit Armaan in the hospital that the veil of secrecy unravelled, revealing the long-lost connection between the families and setting in motion a chain of discoveries that would forever change their lives.

Kalsoom had already gone to stay with Sarfaraz, hoping to find any clues that could help locate Aariz. Kanval visited Kalsoom at Sarfaraz's house to discuss their next move. Sarfaraz had just returned from Friday prayers and his face was grave as he joined them in the living room. The sound of Jhelum River flowing beneath their house provided a melancholic background to their conversation.

'I don't think Aariz is hiding, Kanval,' Sarfaraz said in a sombre tone. 'We need to find him before it's too late.'

'But where can he go?' Kanval desperately asked them. Kalsoom cried out. 'Keh eh Lahore wapas challa gya ae, ya kisi ne uss nu maar ditta ae, main nain pata. I don't know whether he went back to Lahore or whether someone has killed him.'

Kanval could see the despair in Kalsoom's eyes and feel the weight of the situation on her shoulders. 'We won't give up until we find him, but please enlighten me why would someone kill him?'

'Because they may be thinking of him as an Ikhvani,' they said. Kanval was puzzled. 'What's an Ikhvani, Uncle?'

'It's a term used for those who collaborate with the militants, but then switch sides to join the government,' Sarfaraz explained. 'They consider them traitors, and they are not treated kindly.'

Kanval's expression froze in disbelief as she heard the unknown term. 'What? Does this even happen, Uncle?'

As they talked, they noticed two military personnel had been deployed beneath Sarfaraz's house, a clear sign that the situation was becoming increasingly dire. They exchanged worried glances and knew that time was running out. Kanval had no time to indulge in emotions, her brother's life was at stake.

'I understand how you feel, but we can't afford to be emotional right now,' Kanval said firmly to Kalsoom. 'We need to gather more evidence and build a stronger case for Uncle's citizenship. And if he wasn't involved in any militancy, we need to prove it.'

Kabir's case was closely linked with his assistance to Aariz, who had been accused of being involved with militancy years earlier. It was crucial to prove that Aariz had no involvement in any such activities before or after his return, as it would help ease the case.

The sound of the Friday Salaams from the nearby Khanqaah echoed through the city as rain started to drizzle outside. 'I understand your worries, Aunty. I'll do everything in my power to bring justice for Aariz Uncle, but his absence is not helping our case,' Kanval reassured her.

Just then, the drizzle turned into a heavy downpour, and Sarfaraz couldn't help but worry about the rising water levels of Jhelum. 'Wallahi, I hope this rain doesn't turn into a sailaab,' he murmured, his eyes fixed on the turbulent waters below.

The rising water level of Jhelum was a reminder of the urgency of their situation, as they all prayed silently that the storm would not turn into a catastrophe. Kalsoom got up immediately, confronting him, 'Jhelum thhe wich jadon sailaab aanda hai to ode andar jinniya vi cheezan dabi chuppi hondiye ne, unna no bahar soth denda hai, haina? Whenver the Jhelum floods, it expels whatever is in it.'

As the rain continued to fall in the running stream, the trio kept staring at it. 'No human can bear the tragedy of Kashmir that Jhelum has witnessed,' Sarfaraz said. Kalsoom was petrified by Sarfaraz's words. 'Nimaz padh le, Kalsoom. Baarish me duayen qabool hoti hai, prayers are accepted when it rains.' Sarfaraz motivated a grieving Kalsoom. 'To phir to saddi yahi dua hai ke woh Jhelum ki godh vich na mile. Then I sincerely pray that he isn't lying in Jhelum's embrace.' Kalsoom immediately excused herself.

Sarfaraz terribly wanted to avoid the possibility that Aariz's dead body had been dumped in Jhelum, as Kalsoom was fearing and as was the case with many missing people who were later found floating in it.

~

To Sarfaraz, Jhelum was a haunting river. Its deep-green colour had turned dark in the course of time from everything it had absorbed. The military personnel had sheltered themselves inside the house, resting on the staircase since it was raining profusely. Sarfaraz prepared tea for them and went down to hand it over, which they politely accepted. Kanval followed him.

A very pained Sarfaraz walked out with Kanval near the ghat steps and stood beneath the shelter of the Zoon Dab window balcony of his house, protecting them from the rain. The current of the river intensified, as if it wanted to escape the terrible time in the city. Sarfaraz kept looking at it, adding another day to its troubled history.

'I was writing an article on the disappeared persons in Kashmir that remains unfinished till date, Uncle. I hope Aariz Uncle does not have to find mention in my article,' Kanval was very scared with what Kalsoom worried about. Sarfaraz kept looking at the river.

'You know the reason why this river haunts me?' A lost Sarfaraz questioned Kanval. 'As Kalsoom said, when Jhelum flows above the danger mark, it brings unidentified objects within it.' 'Which objects, Uncle?' Sarfaraz took a deep breath. 'Three decades ago, during the insurgency, Kashmir was deprived of the tourism it was flourishing on. No tourist came here and our houseboats remained shut for years. I had to do something for a livelihood. Tarannum suggested that I dig sand from the river and sell it to make ends meet. It would fetch me a nominal pay. I decided to take up the work, sailing my boat in this river once or twice a week, unlike the usual regular times I used to.'

Sarfaraz stopped and gazed deeply at the river. Kanval was expressionless and awaited his continuation. 'I was very, very afraid of what I used to come across. It was both blinding and terrifying.' Kanval continued to look at him deeply. Sarfaraz looked at her and then looked away. 'Sometimes when I used to shovel out the sand from the banks, I used to find myself staring at broken skulls, broken skeletons or cracked femurs. Most of the dead were young men. One could easily make out from their shiny teeth or from their skull that the dead must have been very, very young.'

Kanval's hand turned cold. 'One day, with great courage, I sailed again and shovelled the riverbed. I found a young man, or a boy, I must say. He had been terribly tortured. His hands and feet had been chopped off. I quickly sailed back home and decided not to go again. Some days later, after falling short of money, I decided to go again. This time I went to a different edge of the river and started to dig around and came across a small skull. He must have been a boy of about thirteen or fourteen years. His thigh had flesh over it. For a moment, his skull reminded me of Aariz. I could not control myself and what I did next was a madness of some sort. I quickly dug a marshy soil near the bank and pushed the skeleton inside it. I recited a Fatiha and rushed home, never ever to go back again.'

Kanval could not contain herself and immediately puked. The two officers quickly came to the scene. Sarfaraz gestured for them to relax. Kalsoom watched them from the balcony, silently crying. Kanval came back to Sarfaraz; to her, the narrative was a hard pill to swallow. 'Jhelum is not just a river, it is a sentinel, watching over the miseries, pain and injustice endured by all Kashmiris who have lived or are living here. It bears witness to the ocean of tears shed by Kashmiri mothers,' Sarfaraz paused, his eyes glistening with emotion. 'It is also the final resting place of my dear father.' Kanval's eyes welled up with tears as she looked at the river. 'I never realized how much pain and suffering this river has witnessed,' she said softly.

As the rain finally ceased, the sun rose above the blue-grey pines and the white snows of the Himalayas surrounding the city.

Kanval was at a loss for what to do next. Aariz's disappearance had caused bigger havoc than she could have imagined and the stakes were high. The lives of three people were hanging in the balance: Kabir, Kalsoom and Armaan. Aariz had met Kalsoom in Lahore, during quieter days spent under Daarji's care. Daarji was the man who led the outfit and kept Aariz close, yet away from its workings. Kalsoom was Daarji's daughter, and their marriage was never something he chose or questioned. Armaan was born in Lahore, part of a life that had felt like another test, handed to him without a choice. If Aariz wasn't found soon, Kalsoom and Armaan would likely be stateless for illegally entering India without any documents. Kabir's future looked bleak, with serious charges of militant funding looming over him. Everything rested on Aariz's return or, at the very least, on tracing his whereabouts.

Kanval was determined to leave no stone unturned and would not give up until she found him. With the hearing only two days away, time was running out. The following morning, Kanval approached Sarfaraz with excitement, disconnecting a call as she did so.

'Uncle, I think we've found some traces of Aariz Uncle. We have to leave quickly,' she said. Sarfaraz was suddenly filled with hope. 'What? Where?' he asked. Kanval promised to fill him in as they left, telling him to quickly get the car ready while she freshened up.

However, Kalsoom stopped her before she could leave. 'Unno leke aayen, puttar, menu na ummeed na karee'n. Bring him back, please, don't take away my hope.'

As Sarfaraz drove out of Gawkadal, he was very curious to know where exactly they were heading. 'So Uncle, one of my lawyer friends who works with the high court here told me to visit this place called Haji Bal close to LOC and…' Safaraz quickly stopped the car, giving both of them a jerk. 'What happened, uncle?' Kanval asked, noticing the car come to a sudden stop.

'What else did he tell you?' Sarfaraz asked, his voice tense and tight. 'He was in a hurry and before I could speak to him much, he moved in for a hearing,' Kanval replied, confused by Sarfaraz's reaction. 'That's it?' he asked, his tone urgent. Kanval nodded, sensing that something was wrong.

'What's going on, Uncle? You look worried,' she said. Sarfaraz wriggled in his seat before starting the car once again. 'Why don't you tell me what you know? Or let me call my friend again,' Kanval suggested, her anxiety growing. But Sarfaraz quickly put a stop to that.

'No, beta ji, do not call,' he said firmly, cutting off Kanval's call to her lawyer friend. 'Uncle, what's wrong? Why does this place seem to have upset you?' she asked, her voice filled with concern. Sarfaraz looked very anxious, so Kanval decided not to push him further. But she also knew that they had to keep going. For Aariz, for Kabir, for Kalsoom and Armaan, and for everyone else who was counting on them.

As they drove through the winding roads, the picturesque views of the mountains and the lush greenery of the meadows failed to quell the tension in the air. The sight of military personnel and the countless checkpoints only added to the unease. Kanval couldn't help but notice the melancholic expressions etched on the faces of the locals, seemingly coming to terms with their lives after the relentless lockdowns.

After hours of driving, they finally reached the village. As they stepped out of the car, they were met with the curious eyes of the children and the blank stares of the men and women.

Kanval walked up to a shopkeeper, showing him Aariz's picture and asking about him. Sarfaraz watched her from a distance, his heart pounding in his chest. He knew what this place was famous for, and it was his worst fear. When Kanval returned with an empty expression, Sarfaraz knew what she was going to say before she even uttered a word. 'Which grave?' he asked, his voice trembling. 'That the graveyard will tell us,' she replied solemnly.

Sarfaraz couldn't help but feel a deep sense of dread. Kanval's enthusiasm lay flat the moment she learned what exactly the place was famous for. They both knew what lay ahead. Sarfaraz and Kanval walked towards the graveyard with a sense of dread looming over them. The scenery around them had changed from the picturesque beauty of the mountains to a desolate landscape. The once lively villages were now silent, as if mourning the loss of life and freedom.

As they entered the graveyard, Sarfaraz and Kanval were struck by the bleakness of the place. It was a mass graveyard, with no markings or names on the graves. It was as if an entire generation had been erased from existence. An old man was reciting a prayer over a freshly dug grave. Sarfaraz's heart sank as he wondered if it might be his nephew's final resting place.

Kanval approached the old man, whose name was Majid Gul, and explained the reason for their visit. She handed over Aariz's photo and Majid studied it closely before glancing back at the grave he had been praying over. Sarfaraz held his breath, hoping for a miracle. 'I am sorry but I can't confirm his identity,' he said. 'The man buried here was brought in with a badly disfigured face, like many others buried in this graveyard.'

Sarfaraz collapsed to the ground, overcome with grief and despair. Kanval felt helpless, watching him struggle to come to terms with the reality of the situation. Majid's words had extinguished any hope they had left. As Sarfaraz stumbled away from the graveyard, Kanval and Majid watched on in silence. It was a stark reminder of the brutality and senselessness of the ongoing conflict in Kashmir, a conflict that had claimed the lives of countless civilians.

Kanval sat down on a nearby stone, her mind still reeling from the hopefulness that Aariz might be alive. She looked up at the old man in front of her, his face etched with the memories of a lifetime. As he spoke, his voice was filled with the weight of years of experience.

'Sit down, my dear.' She lowered herself onto the stone beside him, grateful for his comforting presence. 'What do I do, Uncle?' she asked, her voice trembling with emotion. 'Help me, I am helpless.'

Majid's eyes softened as he looked at her. 'Pushraav Khudayas, Tawakkal Allah, Allah par bhrosa rakh, biti, may Allah protect you, have faith in Him,' he said. Kanval closed her eyes and let his words wash over her. As she opened her eyes, she saw Majid looking at her with a sense of understanding.

'Kasheeri kahaai ghar,' he said, quoting a famous proverb. Kanval was puzzled, not understanding the meaning behind the words. 'Tske chhuke Koshur bolaan?' Majid asked her if she spoke Kashmiri, seeing her confusion. Kanval shook her head, indicating that she did not speak the language.

'It means there are only eleven households in Kashmir,' Majid explained, his voice carrying a sense of sadness. 'A limited option. We Kashmiris witness an unedited Kashmir that is not brought to the world with limitations, through newspapers or television, which paint the living and the dead as either lucky blossoms of heaven or sinful devils being tormented in the graves.'

Kanval felt a chill run down her spine as she realized the weight of the old man's words. The beauty of the landscape they had seen on their journey here had masked the deeper, darker truths that lay beneath the surface. She looked around at the graves that surrounded them, each one a silent witness to the violence and conflict that had torn this land apart. Majid fell silent, lost in his own thoughts. For a moment, there was nothing to do but bear witness to the truth of the place, to the stories that lay buried beneath the ground.

'What is your story, Uncle?' she asked. A solemn expression crossed his face. 'Perhaps without a good ending,' he replied with a pause, the pain of his past loss evident. 'I am a farmer by profession,' he continued. 'This land was once a thriving rice farm that provided me with a decent livelihood. But one cold night, everything changed. The police arrived with two hundred truckloads of bodies to be buried.'

Kanval gasped, horrified by the revelation. Majid continued, 'It was my Islamic religious obligation to bury the dead, but the task was beyond anything I could have imagined. I laid to rest chopped bodies, faceless bodies and those with nylon ropes still straining their necks. I buried tortured bodies, young boys and older men, sometimes cramming three or four into one grave.' Majid coughed and paused, lost in the memory. Kanval's hands grew cold. 'I am haunted by the defaced bodies in my dreams. It is as if I am being punished here on earth, but with the hope of being spared in the hereafter.' Kanval could sense that there was more to Majid's story than what he had revealed so far. She wanted to know what he had been keeping to himself.

'Uncle, I know there is more to your story. Please tell me,' she implored.

Majid paused for a moment, lost in thought. Finally, he turned to Kanval and said, 'You really want to know the truth? The truth is that no one wants to hear it. Politicians and journalists only present what they want us to see, not the reality we live in.'

Kanval nodded in understanding, but she persisted. 'But what about your story, Uncle? What happened to you? Did your son also go missing?' Majid's eyes had turned moist. He took a deep breath and looked away from Kanval. After a moment, he turned back to her, his eyes still glistening with tears. 'Yes,' he said, his voice heavy with emotion. 'He was my only son.'

Kanval's grief started to knock. 'My 18-year-old son, who was an electrician, went missing mysteriously. There was a power plant being set up nearby where he worked. We searched for him everywhere we could but in vain. We filed a police complaint to trace him. Days turned into weeks and weeks turned into months, but there was no news about my son. It was as if he had vanished into thin air. I felt helpless and lost, not knowing what to do.'

Kanval could sense the pain and grief in Majid's voice and she listened attentively. 'Days later, in the middle of the night, the police asked me to bury the body of some militant that had infiltrated from the LOC. He was identified as some Rashid

Malik from Sialkot. His bullet-ridden body had a face that was disfigured beyond recognition. With one glance, I could make out he was my son Khaleel. Even blind parents can feel the presence of their children; you think it was confusing for me to identify my son? My wife never smiled or laughed since that day. Since then, any body that was brought here, whether of a militant or a civilian, I don't shy away from its burial. Maybe someday when I die, someone will come up and recite a Fatiha over my grave here the way I do, Biti.'

Kanval's heart was aching. The old man put his hand over her head. Sarfaraz approached with a heavy heart, his hands filled with flowers to pay his respects to the departed souls.

He joined Majid in reciting prayers and scattered the petals over the graves with great care. It was evident that he had a deep sense of reverence towards those who had left this world. Sarfaraz recited the Fatiha over each grave, including the one he suspected to be Aariz's. As the sun started to set, Kanval and Sarfaraz quietly left the village, leaving behind the graves of those who had lost their lives to the senseless violence.

The experience had left them both shaken, with a renewed appreciation for the fragility of life and the importance of cherishing the time we have with our loved ones.

'There remains another important aspect in Aariz Uncle's identity.'

'Wansa,' Sarfaraz replied with tired eyes as he made his way into the city.

'Uncle?' Kanval said, unable to understand the word.

'Sorry, beta, tell me.'

'It's such a shame that I don't know my mother tongue,' Kanval regretted. 'I will teach you someday,' Sarfaraz replied.

'Aariz Uncle's birth identity has to be established for the sake of his citizenship. I will need all his documents.'

Sarfaraz was perplexed. 'Beta, this must have been in Tarannum's knowledge. She was the one who maintained all the documents. Let's go home and check.'

The next day, they searched the entire house, ransacking it, but no documents were found. They searched in every nook and corner, but nothing could be recovered.

'Itne saal ho gaye ne, menu lagda hai ude documents deemak ne khaa ditta, it's been so many years that I think the termites must have eaten his documents,' Kalsoom remarked.

'That is funny, Uncle, that's not happening,' Kanval wanted to laugh but could not, considering the seriousness of the situation. 'We have searched everywhere in the house. From his birth certificate to his school identity, nothing could be found.'

Kanval looked at Sarfaraz with disbelief. 'That's ok, Uncle. But where's your ration card?' she asked.

Sarfaraz seemed confused. 'Ration card?' he echoed. 'Uncle, are you telling me you have no ration card?' Kanval asked, feeling helpless.

'I believed we had one, but...' Sarfaraz trailed off.

'But what, Uncle? That's highly irresponsible! How are we supposed to produce something in court to confirm Aariz Uncle's identity and nationality, or explain his physical absence that is messing this case?' Kanval's tone was accusatory and there was a tense silence in the air.

'Ok, there's one more way out. We can surely get details from his school. Please take me to his school,' Kanval said, trying to calm herself down.

Sarfaraz looked confused again and Kanval couldn't help but remark, 'Uncle, again? I hope the school isn't missing now?'

Sarfaraz replied, 'This is Kashmir, beta, anything can disappear.'

Both Kalsoom and Kanval were blank. 'Let us go and check there.'

Sarfaraz drove them to Bandipore district. Kanval questioned, 'Why didn't you enrol him in a school in Srinagar, Uncle?'

'Kakalal, your grandfather, had suggested that Aariz be kept out of the city's growing insurgent environment, and be put into a hostel or a strictly disciplined place that is academically driven. There was this famous school here in this district that we immediately got him enrolled in, with Kakalal's persuasion and help, but...' Sarfaraz took a deep breath.

'School is not some vapour in the air that it will vanish,' Kanval retorted. Sarfaraz continued, 'The principal of the state-run school was Kakalal's Pandit friend, famously known as Mattoo Sahab. Two years after Aariz's enrolment, the Army had moved into his school, taking away a part of the building to make it their headquarters. The school was fortified with wires, thick walls, watchtowers and sandbags. The school compound had been turned into a military camp, with tanks and Bakhtarband stationed inside. The outer circumference of the school was altered, creating a rectangular-shaped mini chamber with machine guns protruding and military guards keeping watch. We used to visit him every week and could freely walk into the compound, but things quickly changed.

'All the visitors were thoroughly checked. Our identity cards, along with names, addresses and phone numbers, were recorded. During one such visit, Aariz asked us to take him back home. He smiled less, ate less and looked scared. Upon enquiry, he told us that the building next to his hostel had been turned into a detention room. Whenever there was a crackdown in the nearby village, the military men brought suspected militants in military trucks. Most of them were young boys. He complained of severe, harrowing tortured voices coming out from the adjacent building. He and his friends often discussed the kind of tortures they heard. They were so traumatized that they used to put fingers in their ears to prevent any sound from entering. Given the nature of the military camp that had taken its place in the school, it became susceptible to a guerrilla attack. The soldiers, sensing the possibility of an attack, had asked the warden to restrict activities after sunset. The soldiers continued setting up camps in nearby schools. The militants feared that more camps would be erected, so they destroyed possible schools with good open spaces.

'One night, Aariz's school-turned-military camp came under attack. Heavy firing and grenades were exchanged. Aariz told us that all the students locked themselves in the assembly hall. They were shaken by the heavy armour. One student in the room had a music cassette and he played it at top volume on the radio set to pre-empt the noise of mine blasts, grenades, gunshots and mechanical sounds.

'When the news reached us, we hurried to the school, but the area had been cordoned off and no one was allowed to go near it. There was a heavy gun battle between the militants and the military men, with grenades and bombs causing extensive damage to the school structure. The gun battle continued for three long days and we anxiously waited for the children and staff to be rescued.

'Finally, the armed forces managed to get the children and staff, including Mattoo Sahab, out of the school to safer outskirts. Aariz had collapsed due to suffocation and smoke in the locked room where they had taken shelter. Many other children in that hall and their respective dorms had wet their trousers out of fear and panic.

'Aariz was traumatized for days and had to be tranquillized with medicines due to the violence he had witnessed. Aariz had been exposed to a particular worldview through his father Noman. As a child, he accompanied Noman regularly, who moved in the circles of separatist sympathizers and men loosely affiliated with militant networks. Aariz would overhear discussions laced with anti-state sentiment, talk of azaadi, and grievances around identity, suppression and autonomy. Though young, this exposure had already begun shaping his perception of Kashmir's political landscape. The violent encounter he later witnessed, where his friends and fellow co-religionists were killed, became a personal, visceral turning point. It wasn't just a tragic event; it confirmed, in his fragile adolescent mind, the warnings and ideologies he had absorbed in those earlier years. His trauma, compounded by what he saw as an assault on his community, sealed his emotional leaning towards a desperate belief in an alternative Kashmir.'

Sarfaraz stopped the car in front of a plain ground with chinar trees and a dilapidated rock stone structure. Kanval's heart broke as she saw the site. They got out of the car. Some children were playing with sticks and rolling tires. Upon closer inspection, it appeared that the site had been turned into a memorial ground with graves and a tomb inscribed as a tribute to the lives lost.

Two guards were positioned at the broken gate, and upon enquiring, they learned that the military camp had become a regular conflict zone between the militants and the military. In 1993, an armed attack had occurred resulting in the heavy loss of lives of school children, staff, and military soldiers, completely destroying the school and leading to its conversion into a memorial site.

Feeling helpless, they drove back. Kanval's voice trembled with emotion as she spoke to Sarfaraz, 'Do you realize the impact of violence on a young, fragile mind? It's like a stone thrown into still waters, causing ripples that can extend for years.'

Kanval was filled with a profound sense of sorrow and empathy for the pain Aariz and others had endured.

'Trauma doesn't discriminate based on age.' Kanval couldn't help but ponder the domino effect of violence on young minds like Aariz's. She couldn't help but wonder how that one traumatic incident set off a chain reaction.

Sarfaraz recalled the turbulent days. 'Those days had killed the very fabric of Kashmiriyat. Kakalal was very worried about Aariz's education. Aariz was petrified that he never wanted to go back to his school. In fact, he never wanted to go to any school and hence kept the company of his father. People started sending their children to schools outside of Kashmir as a solution to the academic disruption. Those who were rich sent their children to good universities in Europe and the US. These were mainly bureaucrats, VVIPs, politicians and rich traders of shawls, carpets and handicrafts. Average and middle-class people started getting their children admitted to the University of Punjab, Aligarh Muslim University, or to universities in tier-one cities like Delhi and Bombay where their children would be safe. But Kakalal was very sure about sending Aariz out of India and spoke to someone he knew in South Africa who agreed to get Aariz enrolled in a good British school. We applied for his passport under Kakalal's guidance, but fate had something else in store for him.'

Kanval interrupted, her voice filled with anticipation. 'Wait a minute, Uncle! Did I hear you right? A passport? That could be the golden key to unlock his identity! Where is it?' Kanval's eyes widened with hope.

Sarfaraz looked at her, a hint of surprise in his eyes, and replied, 'I'm not sure if we received it, Kanval. We did apply for one, but during those tumultuous times, everything was thrown into chaos.'

'It doesn't matter if it's expired or lost, we need that passport. It's the ultimate proof of his identity that we can present in court. Uncle, please take me to the passport office,' Kanval's voice was urgent, and she was determined to get her hands on the elusive document.

The following day, Kanval made her way to the passport office in Srinagar with Sarfaraz. It was a busy place, and Kanval was doubtful if the authorities would help her. However, she knew that the time spent would be worth the wait. Initially, she tried speaking to an officer who refused to give her any information. After much intervention, the officer agreed to retrieve the records from almost thirty years ago. They were asked to wait as the officer had piles of work on his table.

Three hours passed. People came and went with small and bright faces, while Kanval and Sarfaraz anxiously waited. In Kashmir, making a passport was a tedious task due to the special laws and regulations governed by intelligence agencies and CID. Those under their scanner often found themselves making rounds of the passport office, considering it one of the most elusive tasks in the world.

At the end of the day, when the office was supposed to be closed, the officer realized that he had kept them waiting. Kanval was furious, but the officer went inside his work desk to retrieve the information. He walked out to them with a blunt expression and informed them, 'You will have to go to the Jammu Passport office and check.'

Kanval and Sarfaraz were surprised and frustrated. Kanval asked, 'Jammu? Why so?' The officer replied, 'We don't have his record here. Maybe it was done in Jammu.' With that, the officer left the office, leaving both Kanval and Sarfaraz feeling anguished. 'Travelling to Jammu by road will take us eight to nine hours, but a flight will only take forty minutes. We have only one day with us.' The next morning, Kanval and Sarfaraz took an early morning flight to Jammu and reached the passport office. The scene was visibly chaotic, and unlike Srinagar, Jammu was burning with heat.

Kanval requested the lady officer for priority assistance, but she received a blank stare in response. The officer instructed them to sit and wait. A couple of hours later, Kanval, visibly frustrated and upset, lost her cool. She exclaimed, 'Do you understand this is priority?' However, the lady officer showed no interest in entertaining her exasperation. 'I can't leave my work and do yours. I'll see you after the break.' Kanval walked away, staring at her in disbelief.

After an hour, the lady officer called them to her table. She asked, 'Aariz Noman Zargar, right?' Kanval confirmed, 'Yes, that's him.' The officer peeped into her records for a moment, creating an air of suspense.

'The passport was dispatched on 17 January 1990 to Zargar house, Gawkadal, Srinagar,' the lady officer disclosed, leaving them shocked. Kanval questioned, 'If it was already dispatched, where is his passport, Uncle?' Sarfaraz was clueless. He tried to make sense of the dates, saying, 'If it was dispatched on 17 January, then it must have been delivered probably by the next day, which was 18 January. 19 January was the day your family left, and on 22 January, Aariz went missing. Ya Allah.' Kanval looked at him with hopelessness. They had searched the entire house for the documents, but it was nowhere to be found. It brought them back to square one.

After a long and tiring day, Sarfaraz and Kanval returned home empty-handed. Kanval had nothing to present in court and the charges against her brother were serious. Iravati, their mother, was devastated. The following day would seal their fate.

Aariz's disappearance on his furlough was seen as a breach of trust and a violation of court orders, putting him on the brink of being declared a fugitive. The authorities launched a relentless search, intensifying scrutiny and tightening the legal noose and leaving him with limited options for defence.

As they sat on the balcony, avoiding each other's eyes, Kalsoom broke the silence. 'Menu te ae vi nahi pata ke woh menu jail vich band na kar lain ya phir menu kar wapas kar denge. I don't even know whether they will imprison me or send me back home,' she said, her voice trembling with fear. Her words sent a chill down Kanval's spine. 'Mai votti han ae bewa maano aavi nahi pata,' Kalsoom continued softly, 'I do not know whether I am still a wife or a widow,' her tone heavy with helplessness.

Wives of former militants who had surrendered after returning to Kashmir from Pakistan faced a similar fate. Militants who crossed the LOC for arms training often settled in various cities of Pakistan, marrying local girls. Their wives, who once had a flourishing life in Pakistan, found themselves in a deadlock after their husbands chose to come back to Kashmir, either due to their families' insistence or the lucrative policy designed by the state government for the returnees.

Their husbands either tore or destroyed their passports upon arrival in India, ensuring that their wives would stay with them forever. This limited their movement within the country, let alone travelling to Pakistan or anywhere else in the world, due to existing laws. These women were not allowed to go back and were not granted civil rights, rendering them stateless. Many of them missed funerals of their relatives. Upon their arrival, many of these women did not receive a warm welcome from their in-laws due to being non-Kashmiris. The return of former militants also meant sharing property, which did not sit well with their relatives.

To add to their misery, some husbands remarried at their families' insistence. Most of these women, having no chance to go back to their motherland, ended up in heated arguments with their husbands out of frustration.

Some of these women sought divorce, while others took the extreme step of ending their lives, overwhelmed by depression and loneliness. They had left behind everything they had in Pakistan, including their wealth, families and good times. Their associations have been demanding that they either be deported to Pakistan or be granted Indian citizenship, so that they can visit their families. Kalsoom's case was particularly complicated. She was in Kashmir without citizenship and the law prohibited her from leaving the region. She became stateless the day she entered India. Although she learned about her father's death, she could not attend his funeral. 'Badqismati vekho, pyo di mayyat vi naseeb na hui, look at my misfortune—I wasn't even destined to attend my father's funeral,' she said, tears welling up in her eyes. 'Ae Jannat nahi ae sohna qaidkhana hai, khulla qaidkhana. This isn't paradise but a beautiful prison, an open prison.'

No one slept that night. The following day would determine the fate of Kabir, Armaan, Kalsoom and Aariz, if he was still alive. With Aariz's whereabouts unknown, their hopes rested on finding evidence that could prove his innocence and his nationality. Without it, their future together remained uncertain, and the weight of the situation pressed heavily on everyone involved. Kanval couldn't do much to save them. Establishing Aariz's identity was crucial, not through changed faces, but with proper documents.

The next morning, Kanval saw Kalsoom standing by the Jhelum River, observing its free flow as it originated in Kashmir and made its way into Pakistan. Sarfaraz joined them, looking at the historic bridge. 'One man cut the dam and a thousand people fell into the river,' he said, contemplating the significance of that act.

The stage was set for a heart-wrenching legal battle, with Kanval feeling utterly hopeless. However, fate intervened in a surprising way. As her house was being renovated, she watched as the old wooden almirah, a cherished family heirloom, was being moved out by the carpenters over a cart. The inclined drawer threw up a small plastic bag. Curiosity getting the better of her, Kanval picked up the bag and carefully opened it, discovering something that none of them had expected.

Meanwhile, in Mumbai, Iravati, was at her wit's end. Her only son was facing unjust charges and enduring immense suffering at the hands of the authorities. Just then, her phone rang, and Kanval was on the other end of the line. 'I should be able to save your son, Mummy. I got hold of Aariz Uncle's documents,' Kanval declared, her voice filled with determination and hope. Iravati couldn't believe what she was hearing. 'Where did you find them?' she asked. 'In Grandpa's almirah,' Kanval replied, instantly transporting Iravati back in time. She remembered how Tarannum had brought Aariz's passport to their house a day before they had to flee. Her father-in-law had asked Tarannum to bring the other documents so that he could apply for his visa the next day, and he had kept them in the drawers under his supervision.

Unfortunately, fate had other plans, and thirty years had passed without anyone knowing about those documents. They had turned a pale-yellow with time, but they still held the key to Kabir's freedom.

'I want Kabir home, Kanval,' Iravati said, her voice filled with a mix of desperation and determination.

The court proceedings began, and Kanval was partially prepared with the evidence. The judge appeared to be in his fifties, with a bleak nose—a no-nonsense person.

'Where is your client, Ms Raina?' he asked sternly.

'My client is not traceable, Your Honor. The police and agencies have looked for him everywhere,' Kanval replied, trying to keep her composure.

'Do you think he is dead or has been killed?'

'I cannot confirm that, your honour. But I do have his documents that confirm his Indian nationality,' Kanval said, presenting the papers to the judge. The judge examined the documents closely before handing them back to Kanval.

'And how does this help us?' he asked. Kanval hesitated for a moment before responding.

'Your Honor, my client's nationality is an important factor in determining his legal status in this case. If he is an Indian national, then he should be given the appropriate legal protections and his nationality be approved. He has anyway come under the militant rehabilitation policy that was devised.'

The judge looked at Kanval with a stern expression. 'Ms Raina, it is clear that your client has entered this state via an unauthorized route through Nepal. You must be aware that the recognized entry points under the government's policy for rehabilitation were Indira Gandhi New Delhi Airport, Wagah Attari in Punjab, Poonch, and Uri in Jammu and Kashmir State. Your client's actions are questionable. If he was settled across the border, why did he return here?' Kanval was out of words.

'Understand, Ms Raina, that your client has been charged with serious allegations. As per the chargesheet, your client was involved in active militant activities here in Kashmir. He not only crossed the LOC for arms training but also chose to return illegally,' the judge stated firmly. 'Your client's actions have put the security of this nation in jeopardy. It is not just about his nationality. It is about the illegal and dangerous activities he was involved in.' Kanval's heart sank. She knew she was losing the case.

Kanval remained silent, feeling the weight of the judge's words.

'Furthermore, if he arrived back here as most militants have done to be with their family, why did he not reunite with his family?' the judge continued. 'It seems that his actions were not those of a responsible citizen.'

Kalsoom, sitting in the back of the courtroom, was nervous beyond words. The judge turned back to Kanval.

'Ms Raina, it appears that your defence is weak. You cannot argue that your client was forced into militancy or anything of the sort. The charges against him are serious and his actions do not speak well of his character.'

'Your Honour, my client was not aware of the legal implications of his actions. He acted impulsively. He chose to return through Nepal because he was led to believe that it was the easiest way to enter India, as it would keep him away from the scrutiny of Pakistani authorities. As for not meeting his family, he was afraid that it would put them in danger.'

The judge looked at Kanval for a moment before nodding his head. 'Very well, Ms Raina. I will take your arguments into consideration. But I must remind you that your client's actions have grave consequences.'

'Ms Raina, you present these documents as proof of Aariz's nationality. However, I find it difficult to believe that he entered and left Pakistan undetected. Can you explain how such a significant act of illegal immigration went unnoticed?' the judge probed, his eyes fixed on Kanval.

'Your Honour, my client's journey was fraught with peril and danger. He was just a young child when he entered Pakistan, accompanied by militants. They used covert routes and took advantage of the chaotic circumstances at the time. Aariz's return from Pakistan was a testament to his resilience and honesty,' Kanval responded, her voice steady.

'Resilience or complicity? It is hard to ignore the fact that he travelled with militants, even if he claims innocence. Are we to overlook this association?' the judge retorted, his tone growing more accusatory.

'Your Honour, my client was not involved in any wrongdoings during his time in Pakistan. He was caught in a web of circumstances beyond his control. His actions since then demonstrate his commitment to a different path, his desire for a second chance,' Kanval asserted, her voice unwavering.

The judge's stern gaze bore down on Kanval. 'A second chance that he squandered by disappearing during his furlough. How can we trust him when he evades the law?'

Kanval stood tall, her eyes filled with conviction. 'Your Honour, Aariz's disappearance may be an act born out of fear and uncertainty.'

The judge's voice grew colder, his doubt evident. 'It seems to me that you're making excuses, Ms Raina. This case grows more complicated with every revelation.'

Kanval's voice quivered with determination. 'Your Honour, Aariz's absence is undoubtedly challenging, but it should not overshadow the truth we seek. His story is not one of evasion, but of a quest for self-discovery and a chance to rectify past mistakes. We must strive to unravel the enigma that surrounds him and provide him with the opportunity to present his side of the story.'

The judge's gaze hardened. 'Opportunity? Okay. Granted. Is he anyway planning to come here?'

Kanval knew that she had to act fast to turn the tide of the case in her favour. Kanval knew that she had to come up with something convincing.

'Ms Raina, I must say, you appear poorly prepared for such a significant case. The gravity of the charges against Aariz demands a stronger presentation.'

Kanval's voice regained its strength, determination etched on her face. 'Your Honour, I apologize if my preparation has fallen short. However, I assure you that my dedication to Aariz's defence is unwavering.'

The judge's voice became sharper, his doubts cutting through the air. 'Let us address another pressing concern. Aariz disappeared with the remaining funds after Armaan's treatment. Who's to say he didn't have ulterior motives? Could it be possible that he intended to use that money for nefarious purposes, to harm others?'

Kanval's eyes met the judge's unwavering gaze, her voice unwavering. 'Your Honour, I understand the weight of such suspicions. However, it is crucial to consider the context of my client's actions. His intentions were solely focused on securing the best possible care for Armaan.'

'Intentions alone are not sufficient to dismiss the possibility of dangerous motives, Ms Raina. We need concrete evidence to establish his innocence. Where is the proof that he did not plan to exploit those funds for malicious purposes?'

Kanval's voice quivered with determination, her eyes filled with unwavering faith. 'Your Honour, I admit that concrete evidence is lacking in this particular instance. However, Aariz's character, as demonstrated through his past actions, does not align with such sinister intentions. We must not jump to conclusions without substantial evidence.'

The judge's expression remained stoic. 'Ms Raina, your defence is fraught with uncertainties. As the presiding judge, it is my duty to ensure a fair trial based on sound evidence. You must provide a stronger foundation for your arguments and address these lingering doubts. The stakes are too high to proceed based on conjecture.

Kanval felt a knot form in her stomach. The evidence against her client was mounting and she had to come up with a convincing defence. Kanval's heart sank. She knew that there was no way to explain the missing money and the judge's tone made it clear that Aariz's disappearance was highly questionable. However, Kanval was determined.

'Your Honour, I understand the gravity of the situation. I will strive to strengthen my defence, gather more evidence and present a compelling case that upholds the principles of justice.

I am determined to unravel the truth and shed light on Aariz's story, no matter the challenges we face.'

The judge's eyes softened slightly. He leaned forward with cautious anticipation. 'Very well, Ms Raina. But remember, we cannot afford any missteps, especially on the question concerning the funds that Aariz has vanished with. What if those funds are invested in illegal activities, or worse, to harm or kill innocent people?'

'The only person I killed in my life was my own father, My Lord.'

All eyes turned to the source of the voice standing at the entrance of the courtroom.

Chapter 10

21 January 1990
Gawkadal, Srinagar

The once tranquil paradise of Kashmir was now a place of unrest. The skies seemed to reflect the turmoil below, as dark clouds loomed overhead, casting a gloomy shadow on the land. The birds had flown away, seeking refuge elsewhere. The deserted streets were a haunting sight, with abandoned homes and buildings, a reminder of the chaos that had consumed the city.

Amidst all the chaos, after performing the last rites of Iravati's father-in-law and Noman, Tarannum and Sarfaraz had left the city to ensure Iravati's safety. The couple had heard that the winter capital of Jammu City was the safest haven for the Pandits.

Meanwhile, Aariz was grappling with the aftermath of the tragedy that had befallen him. The accidental killing of his father had left him deeply disturbed and he had to be sedated to get some rest. The city was under curfew and the paramilitary forces patrolled the streets, making any movement impossible.

As Tarannum and Sarfaraz made their way to Jammu, the skies above Kashmir turned an ominous red. The turbulence was severe, mirroring the unrest that had taken over the city. The situation was dire and no one knew what lay ahead. The only thing that was certain was that the events of the past few days had left a deep scar on the city, and it would take a long time for it to heal. The military conducted door-to-door search operations to look out for militants and any weapons stored in the homes. Hundreds of men and young boys were picked up.

A large group of protestors hit the streets. Chaos, chants and sloganeering filled the skies.

Aariz could barely get up. He was guilt-ridden. Wain gach be jahannum manz, he thought, considering himself destined for hell after killing his father. He sobbed as he lay on the bed, uttering in a shaky voice, 'Baba, maafi deitav, Babaaa, please forgive me, Baba.'

The guilt and regret were eating him alive. He kept repeating the same line, 'Mye ha kor gunaahe Kabira, khudaya mye kar ta maaf.' He knew that he had committed a grave sin and that there was no way to undo it. It was too much for him to bear. Little did he know that he would end up with a role in ending his father's life. He was traumatized, looking at his own hands. With whatever little strength he had, he quickly made his way to the bathroom, washing his hands incessantly. He kept weeping in the bathroom for hours, wondering if he was fated to be in hell. There was no one around. Every two minutes, he washed his hands to wash his sins. There was no one to sympathize with him, no one to comfort him; everybody had vanished. 'Wain gach be jahannum manz. Wain gach be jahannum manz,' he kept repeating, convinced that he was destined for hell for killing his father.

The sounds of protest had intensified outside, interrupting his remorse. He walked towards the balcony only to witness a horrible sight. Protesters at one end of the bridge and military men at the other side of the bridge. The protesters were extremely agitated. The military men opened fire. Aariz collapsed on the floor looking at the sight. He quickly got up and hid himself in the upper attic of the house as the sound of mechanical gunshots echoed in his ears. People lay piled up on each other while their blood dripped into Jhelum, turning its colour red. Things had turned ugly and the area was cordoned off and Kashmir, once endowed with nature's implausible beauty, looked as if it had been struck with some evil eye. Twelve hours had passed, and the area remained completely silent, with closed windows and doors, everything almost shut. 'Mya karnei khuda saebvziheen maaf, ven gaxchi bi jehanamas.' Aariz trembled as his palpitations rose, thinking of burning in hell for the heinous crime he'd committed.

There was a sudden forceful pounding on the door that shook Aariz to his core. 'Mye yee ven police rathne.' Aariz thought the police had come to pick him up. His heart sank. He knew what this meant—he was in danger and he instantly fainted.

When he finally regained consciousness, Aariz found himself surrounded by strangers in a remote forest cabin. He couldn't help but wonder where he was and how he had ended up in this isolated forest home. The bitter cold had turned everything outside into a white, icy wonderland. 'Bea kati chus? Where am I?' Aariz looked around, trying to make sense of the situation, asking where he was. The other men ignored him, and he felt like a lost soul in a foreign land. It was Shabbir who approached him and tried to calm him down. Aariz learned that he had been brought to a militant hideout for his safety as the military was on the lookout for suspected militants in the area. The place was full of arms and ammunition, and Aariz couldn't help but feel out of place. He despised the food and spoke very little, consumed by his own guilt and fear.

One day, Aariz walked out of the hideout to a nearby stream. He hadn't offered a prayer in days and he felt like he was losing touch with his faith. The water was chilled, and as soon as Aariz wiped his face, a layer of ice formed on the surface. But it wasn't just the cold that was freezing Aariz's soul. It was the guilt of his sins, for which he knew Allah would punish him. Shabbir observed him from a distance, noticing the pain and turmoil in Aariz's eyes. He understood that Aariz needed someone to talk to and confide in.

Aariz prayed in the open, enduring the bone-chilling cold. At the end of prayer, tears streamed down his face as he begged for forgiveness and salvation with his forehead on the ground. It was during one of these moments that Shabbir approached him and overheard him repeatedly muttering 'Astagfirullah'. Shabbir tried comforting him, but Aariz collapsed. Shabbir called the others over, and they swiftly brought Aariz inside to warm him up. Aariz was freezing, not only from the cold weather but also from the weight of his own guilt. For days, he barely spoke, ate very little and remained consumed by remorse.

The hideout was located deep in the forests near Kupwara. The winter had been exceptionally harsh. Long icicles hung from the rooftops of the homes and pine trees, and chinar trees, creating a hauntingly beautiful landscape. But Aariz was too engulfed in his own pain to notice. Shabbir, on the other hand, had joined the militants willingly, driven by his belief in Kashmir's liberation.

Aariz couldn't shake off the guilt that burdened his soul. He continued to isolate himself, immersed in the remorse of his wrongdoing, anticipating punishment in hell from Allah. One day, both Shabbir and Aariz were sent to the nearby market to buy groceries. As they walked together, they passed a pond that housed a Sufi shrine, a mosque and a temple. It was surprising to see both a temple and a mosque within the same premises.

After some days, Aariz found himself returning to the place all by himself. Standing in a corner, he witnessed the lost essence of Kashmiriyat in those turbulent times. Aariz felt a pull and entered the courtyard. It was a 400-year-old Shiva temple, untouched and undisturbed. Aariz walked out into the courtyard and stopped in front of the pond. Upon seeing his reflection in the water, Aariz was instantly agitated. To him, he was the most disgusting person on earth.

Pouncing on a nearby rock, Aariz threw it in the water,

distorting his reflection, and ran away from the courtyard. However, as he ran, the skies filled with the sound of the afternoon Azaan, compelling him to perform his prayers.

When everyone left the mosque, it was silent and quiet like a cave. Aariz stayed back, bowing down in severe remorse. The Qari Sahab watched as Aariz bowed down in prolonged prostration and approached him, speaking softly, 'If your remorse is true, you will be forgiven.'

Aariz raised his head, eyes filled with tears of regret and despair. 'Even if you committed a grave sin like murder?' he asked in a trembling voice. The Qari paused, gazing deeply at him. 'I killed my father accidentally while trying to shoot someone else,' Aariz confessed, seeking solace from a stranger, desperately looking for a comforting response.

'And who was that someone else?' the Qari asked. Aariz hesitated, feeling the weight of shame and guilt on his shoulders. 'They were our neighbours, helping my family send me away from my beloved to a different country,' he finally revealed.

'So, you killed your father intending to kill your innocent neighbours?' the Qari observed. Aariz nodded, tears streaming down his face. 'I didn't mean to kill my father. I feared if our neighbours returned, they would help my uncle send me away from my father.'

The Qari placed a gentle hand on his shoulder and said, 'You cannot undo the past, but you can seek forgiveness and make amends. Allah is merciful to those who seek His forgiveness sincerely.'

Aariz looked up at the Qari, seeking solace. 'But how can I make amends for such a heinous crime?' he asked. The Qari replied, 'Your sin is great, but the opportunity for redemption is greater.'

As Aariz wiped away his tears, he asked, 'Will I be forgiven,

Qari Sahab?' The Qari looked at him and replied, 'That is for God to decide. But know that the guilt you carry will serve as a constant reminder to refrain from transgression. Soft hearts feel remorse and seek forgiveness. But do not be mistaken, forgiveness is not a get-out-of-jail-free card. You cannot simply ask for forgiveness and expect absolution. Forgiveness is a two-part process: first, sincerely repent and seek forgiveness with humility and contrition in your heart. Second, work to make amends for the wrong you have done. Only then can you hope to be truly forgiven by Allah.'

Aariz looked up at the Qari with wide eyes. 'But how can I ever make up for what I have done? My father is already dead.' The Qari put a hand on Aariz's shoulder. 'Allah is the most merciful and forgiving. He forgives those who seek forgiveness with sincerity in their hearts. If you truly regret what you have done, then you must take steps to make it right.' Aariz looked at him, seeking a way out of his torment through the Qari's wisdom.

Aariz listened carefully to the Qari's words and understood the gravity of his actions. He realized that seeking forgiveness was not just a way to escape the consequences of his actions but an obligation he had to fulfil. The Qari looked at Aariz with a calm expression and was about to leave, but in a moment, he turned back and asked him a question, 'Which remorse weighs heavier on your heart? Is it the remorse of killing your father or the remorse of trying to kill the neighbours who raised you?'

Aariz remained silent, unsure of how to respond. The Qari continued, 'The remorse of killing your father is understandable, but the remorse of trying to kill your neighbours should weigh heavier on your heart. As the Quran says, "Whoever kills a soul, it is as if he has killed all of humanity, and whoever saves a soul, it is as if he has saved all of humanity."'

Aariz sat alone, pondering over the Qari's words. He couldn't help but question himself, how could he have been so blind to his own actions? How could he have been so consumed by his anger that he didn't think about the consequences? Was he really capable of taking someone's life? These questions swirled in his mind, and the more he thought about it, the more he realized how much he had strayed from the right path. He knew he had to make things right, but he didn't know where to begin.

Confused, he made his way back to the hideout but the scene there was chaotic. Barely a few metres away, he saw the hideout exploding into a big ball of fire. It had come under attack from military personnel who had located it. A gun battle between the militants and the military ensued. Aariz collapsed on the ground with the loud explosion.

Shabbir and three other militants who were out gathering woods for the evening meal quickly rushed to the hideout upon hearing the explosion. Aariz had collapsed in front of the military, just a few metres away. Shabbir swiftly dragged him away, but they caught the eye of a soldier who began firing indiscriminately in their direction. A bullet pierced Aariz's arm and he screamed in pain.

The other militants acted swiftly, lifting him and making their way deeper into the woods. Aariz was in excruciating pain.

Upon reaching a nearby village, the militants barged into a small, single-storey house where a poor farmer resided with his family. The farmer, fearing for his life, tried to persuade them to seek shelter elsewhere due to the limited space, but his pleas fell on deaf ears. The militants, with their Kalashnikovs in hand, took over the upper floor of the house.

The farmer, filled with anxiety, dreaded the consequences of harbouring militants. He knew that if they were discovered, he would face severe punishment from the police. Meanwhile, Aariz, weak and in pain, was treated locally by the militants. They crudely removed the bullet, applied a local antiseptic and tied a cloth around his arm. Aariz's health deteriorated further as he struggled to keep down any food. Days later, as Aariz began to regain his strength, he noticed the farmer's forced smile and sensed his uneasiness. The farmer never wanted to shelter them, but he had no choice. Aariz realized the trouble they had caused him.

Aariz wanted to leave, but his desires were futile. The other militants were planning to cross the Line of Control into Pakistan, but Aariz resisted. He vehemently expressed his desire to go home, despite the others' explanations that returning would mean certain death as he would be picked up by the authorities, like hundreds of others had been. They had rescued him for this very reason—to save him from that fate. Aariz felt that death was a better option than this wretched life, but he also knew that his decision would endanger others.

His heart heavy with despair, Aariz couldn't bear the thought of leaving his home, his family and his beloved Kashmir. However, he understood the grim reality that going back would bring not only his own demise but also the arrest and suffering of his loved ones.

Aariz felt caught between the devil and the deep-blue sea. Death or fleeing from home? He had a choice: stay and face certain death, endangering relatives in Srinagar, or leave for a new life. It was a decision for survival.

All five quietly sneaked from the farmer's house, making their way into the woods seeking a nearest hideout. They knew travelling at night was best to avoid detection. Sustained by apples and stream water, they ascended the hill, resting every ten minutes. Finally, they stumbled upon a hidden location where other militants were present.

They discussed the possibility of crossing the LOC into Pakistan and a leader among them asked for verbal consent from those willing to take the dangerous journey. The young boys and men agreed without hesitation, recognizing the risks but feeling that they had no other choice. Each person was free to make their own decision. Aariz felt lost and helpless, hesitant to join them. But the militants presented the stark truth before him.

'We understand your attachment to this place,' one of the militants said, his voice tinged with understanding. 'But staying here will only lead to suffering and danger. The authorities won't differentiate between us and you. Perhaps you are already under their scrutiny.' 'I can't do it,' he finally spoke, his voice barely above a whisper. 'I can't leave everything behind. My family, my friends, they're here. How can I abandon them?'

The militants exchanged knowing glances, their expressions filled with a sense of understanding.

'Aariz,' one of them began gently, 'Staying here means exposing yourself to unimaginable danger. You'll be risking your life, and your loved ones will suffer the consequences. You have anyway killed your father; intentionally or unintentionally, the blood is on your hands and soon that will be reason enough for you to be dealt with strictly.'

Aariz's eyes welled up with tears. 'I just can't bear the thought of leaving forever,' he murmured, his voice choked with emotion.

The first militant knelt down, his gaze filled with compassion. 'Sometimes the hardest choices are the ones we must make to protect those we love. It's like being caught in a raging river. If you don't let go of the rocks, you'll be dragged down. You must swim to shore and find safety.'

Aariz's tears fell freely now as he grappled with the heaviness of his decision. 'I'm scared,' he admitted, his voice barely audible.

The second militant placed a hand on Aariz's shoulder, offering reassurance. 'Fear is natural, Aariz. We all feel it. We'll be with you every step of the way, supporting and protecting you.' Aariz took a deep breath, a mix of resignation and determination settling within him. He knew that deep down he couldn't ignore the truth they had presented.

We're not here to force you, Aariz,' one of them spoke softly. 'It's your choice, and we respect that. We simply want you to consider the consequences of staying behind.'

Aariz's eyes flickered with uncertainty as he looked into their eyes, searching for guidance.

'We've seen the destruction and suffering firsthand,' the other militant added, his voice tinged with sorrow. Aariz's heart wavered, torn between the familiarity of his home and the looming danger that awaited him. 'We can't guarantee an easy journey or a safe passage,' the first militant continued. 'But we can promise to face the unknown together.' Aariz's gaze shifted from one militant to the other, their words sinking deep into his soul. The weight of their conviction began to sway his decision.

'In the end, it's your choice, Aariz,' the second militant declared gently.'

Aariz, feeling lost and helpless, was reluctant to join them. Shabbir was filled with enthusiasm and conviction, and convinced him that there was nothing left for him in their current situation. Aariz didn't say yes, but he agreed to come along. Aariz's life had been disrupted by the conflict, causing his life's path to be diverted in a direction he'd never anticipated.

The next day, they set out with an experienced guide disguised as a shepherd, embarking on a treacherous journey into the unknown. All of them were draped in olive military uniforms and black boots to resemble security forces' attire, and were loaded with a bag full of explosives, a Kalashnikov and snacks. The guide took them on the hilly terrain away from the watch of security bunkers, along a steep mountain with a small ridge. It literally meant crawling on one's chest.

The movement was mostly limited to night, making the

journey far from easy. Death loomed, claiming some militants as they slipped in the valley gorges, while others were gunned down when lighting a cigarette, revealing their presence to the unknown figures in the dark. Snacks consisted mainly of dry fruits to keep them fuelled. During the day, the militants concealed themselves in thick forests and bushes. They were instructed to bury biscuit wrappers deep in the soil, ensuring no trace of their route was left behind. Silence was paramount during the journey, as any conversation would release vapours from their mouths, potentially attracting unwanted attention.

Some of them succumbed to the extreme cold, resembling hypothermia, and were laid to rest deep within the forest. The human convoy trekked for ten days and nights, slowly navigating the mountains with great caution. Aariz beheld the breathtaking heights of the Himalayan terrain, a sight he had never encountered despite residing in Kashmir. The route proved arduous, leaving the majority with scratchy red patches and bruises on their hands, chest and feet from constant crawling. Swollen and punctured feet plagued them, and some even battled lice infesting their wounds. Even the bravest among them harboured regret, shedding inconsolable tears at the chosen path.

To Aariz, this journey held no dread or hardening, as he had resigned himself to burning in hell upon death. He simply followed where life led him, mindful not to endanger others with his presence. They stealthily bypassed numerous Indian checkpoints under the cover of night, until the last, most perilous one came into view, sealing their fate forever. Despite the challenges and the loss of their companions, Aariz remained resolute. He perceived the journey as a metaphor for life, unpredictable, treacherous and unforgiving.

The rivers that meandered through the valley mirrored life itself, tranquil and serene one moment, tumultuous and menacing the next. Aariz felt a connection to these rivers. Continuing was his sole option, to confront whatever awaited him. And so, he trailed the guide, crawling over the mountain's rugged terrain, embracing the uncertainty that lay ahead.

One by one, slowly and steadily, they crawled beneath the last checkpoint, successfully entering Pakistani territory.

The sun began to rise, ushering in a new morning for them all. Aariz had finally arrived in Muzaffarabad. Amidst the jubilant crowd, Aariz stood feeling numb. The celebration of their arrival surrounded him, but he couldn't escape the sense of being lost and alone. Everything dear to him had been left behind and now he found himself in a foreign land, surrounded by similar landscapes but an uncertain future.

As he observed others laughing and embracing one another, Aariz couldn't shake the feeling of being an outsider, a stranger in a strange land. Shabbir embraced him tightly, attempting to offer comfort and encouragement, but even that couldn't alleviate the overwhelming sadness that engulfed him. Aariz gazed up at the sky, the same sky that had watched over him in his homeland, and pondered how he had ended up so far away from all that he cherished. Watching an eagle soaring high above, Aariz couldn't help but envy its freedom, its ability to fly away and leave it all behind. The stringent visa norms between Pakistan and India meant that ordinary people couldn't visit each other's countries, especially as a Kashmiri, considering the bitter history and the wars fought over Kashmir. These militants had defied those norms, sneaking into Pakistan illegally without passports. 'That was your past, forget it,' Shabbir reasoned with him as they gazed at the border fences that separated the two Kashmirs.

Hundreds of Kashmiris were already there. Each carrying their own stories and reasons for being in that place. Although Muzaffarabad shared similarities with Kashmir in its landscapes, there was an intangible difference. Despite being amidst people of the same background and culture, something was amiss. Aariz deeply missed his family, longing for Iravati's presence, knowing she would reprimand him for every petty annoyance. He yearned for her scolding. 'What if I hadn't tried to harm her? How did I develop such deep-seated anger?' After spending some time at the camp, it became evident that Aariz had little interest in whatever was happening there.

Daarji, the head of the Tanzeem, was visiting Muzaffarabad to oversee the new arrivals. As the new enrolments were introduced to him, he noticed the despondency in Aariz's face. Daarji belonged to a Punjabi Kashmiri ancestry. He felt a deep sense of empathy for the young boy who had already endured much pain and hardship in his short life. For reasons he kept to himself, Daarji knew that Aariz wasn't ready for the training enrolment. He motioned for Shabbir and Aariz to approach him. Standing before Daarji, the contrast between the two boys was stark. Shabbir appeared eager and enthusiastic, while Aariz seemed lost and alone. In a stern tone, he commanded, 'Naal Lahore chalo, we are going to Lahore.'

Shabbir's face fell, disappointment evident on his features. He had been looking forward to the training and returning to Kashmir. Aariz, on the other hand, didn't react at all. He simply stood there, his eyes downcast, lost in his own thoughts. Daarji could see the pain reflected in Aariz's eyes, and it stirred a sense of responsibility within him. Aariz felt his life slipping out of his control, governed by the relentless passage of time. As he crossed a bridge known as Domail, he observed the water flowing beneath it. Two streams confluence there, one of them was Jhelum that touched the footsteps of his home and flowed exactly at the point he stood. In a moment of despair, Aariz contemplated jumping into the river, seeking an end to his pain. He believed that the river, flowing from his homeland, carried the promise of peace in its waters. Just as he was about to make a move, his soul whispered to him. *This is haram,* it murmured. *A Muslim does not end his own life.* Aariz hesitated, his foot frozen in midair. However, another voice taunted him. *Since when did you care about haram and halal? You didn't care when you planned to kill Kaki. Why care now?* The conflicting voices battled within Aariz, tearing him apart. With a heavy swallow, he prepared to plunge into the river. However, a strong hand suddenly grabbed him from behind, pulling him back from the edge. 'Ae paaglaa, ruk,' Shabbir said firmly.

Aariz's mind was consumed by conflicting thoughts. The sight of the river evoked memories of home, but his desire to end his life clashed with his faith. 'Che traav mya kunizon.' Aariz resisted, asking Shabbir to leave him, but Shabbir's overpowering strength prevailed. He was dragged towards the waiting jeep that would take them to Lahore. Daarji was seated in the front. In absolute silence, both Shabbir and Aariz sat in the jeep as it made its way towards Punjab. Not a word was spoken. Daarji's presence naturally instilled silence. It served as a reminder that there was a guiding force that demanded obedience and discipline. It felt as though a guardian had been watching over him from the very beginning.

Soon, they reached Islamabad, and Shabbir's excitement knew no bounds. Daarji alighted to offer prayers at the Faisal Masjid, a magnificent architectural marvel. Inspired by Greek architecture, it featured a hexagonal grid layout and four exquisite minarets. Daarji walked a few paces ahead and stopped; the two boys remained seated. The driver understood the command and quickly instructed them to disembark for prayers. Aariz and Shabbir followed Daarji's lead. After a six-hour drive, they arrived in Lahore, the capital city of the Punjab province and the cultural heart of Pakistan. The journey had been a shock to Aariz, having taken him far away from their homeland. The scorching sun beat down mercilessly upon them, and the bustling old walled city was brimming with life and activity.

As Aariz continued his journey in Lahore, he was captivated by the bustling streets, narrow alleyways and brick homes. The bazaars were alive with the vibrant colours and aromas of spice vendors, tempting his senses with the mouth-watering local cuisine. Upon entering a large palatial mansion with an open courtyard, Aariz noticed armed men quickly approaching the jeep to receive Daarji. He watched in awe as Daarji instructed the men to take them to the upper portion of the haveli. The courtyard featured a spring and a baithak, while the haveli itself was divided into a Zanaan khana for females and a Mardan khana for men. A portion of the haveli served as the headquarters for social and political activities, where all significant decisions were made with Daarji's consultation. The multi-storeyed haveli showcased influences of Mughal, Sikh and Gothic architecture.

Days passed, and Aariz struggled to accept his fate. He found himself gradually immersed in Lahore's political world, with manual tasks of cleaning, washing and cooking within the haveli. Daarji held authority over every important decision in Lahore, ranging from construction to education, bureaucracy to social work. However, amidst all the activity, strict instructions of no bullying or making fun of the two boys were given to all men in the haveli.

While Shabbir eagerly took on all the work, striving to impress his immediate superiors and gain closer proximity to Daarji, Aariz showed little interest. The stern and disciplined presence of Daarji constantly reminded them of being under his watchful gaze. Aariz understood that he had to be cautious and obedient, avoiding any missteps. Regular prayers and recitation of the Quran were to be strictly observed by Shabbir and himself.

Aariz hardly spoke to anyone and moved through the haveli

like a ghost, following orders without question. His once-confident demeanour had been replaced by one of submission and obedience. He spent long hours in solitude, shedding tears as he reminisced about his home and the people he had left behind.

Lahore, with its hot and crowded streets and scarce shade from the scorching sun, felt suffocating to Aariz. Despite the grandeur of the haveli, he yearned for the simple joys of life back home. He longed for the cool air and the familiarity of his own people. Daarji, ever perceptive, noticed the sadness in Aariz's eyes. He understood that the boy was struggling to adapt to his new reality. Aariz missed going to the radio with Purushottam to watch musical programmes and longed for the days when he could bully and play with little Kabir. He even missed the commotion caused by Iravati leaving little Kanval at his home every morning when she went to the mandir, her cries waking him up daily. But Aariz knew he was being punished for his transgressions and that he had to accept his fate.

Years flew by, and as Aariz matured, he remained the same, except for his physical appearance. He had grown into a composed and handsome young man. Despite his minimalistic nature and silence, he caught the attention of Kalsoom, who had been enamoured with him since his arrival at the haveli. However, the austere environment did not permit any interaction. When Kalsoom proposed to Daarji that she take Aariz's hand in marriage, it surprised him. Finding a match for his beloved daughter was no easy feat, especially with the wealth and reputation at stake. Every proposal they received was filled with greed and selfishness, aiming to overthrow Daarji's dynasty. Choosing Kalsoom's spouse was crucial as they would become a part of Daarji's running hierarchy.

After much contemplation, Daarji called Aariz into his chamber. The young man was clueless about his fate, but Daarji's demeanour was different from his usual strictness. He appeared more composed and concerned. Daarji leaned back in his chair, fixing his eyes on Aariz.

'Generally, people cross the LOC for various reasons,' he said, his voice soft and contemplative. 'Some are fed up with the ongoing situation in Kashmir and choose to escape here. Others are lured by the promise of facilities if they join the Tanzeem, while some fight for an independent Kashmir. Around 1947 and 1948, when the Partition of India happened, the whole subcontinent was shaken. While there was violence all across Punjab and other parts during Partition, the valley stayed quiet. People were nervous, yes, but there was no real sign of what was happening elsewhere. It was in this atmosphere of cautious peace that Shaukat Dar, a respected trader of carpets and shawls, set out with his extended family for Lahore. With a growing market for Kashmiri craftsmanship, he hoped to turn fortune in his favour. Like many others, he believed that the worst had passed.

'But as their caravan crossed into Jammu, they stepped into a different reality. Waves of refugees fleeing West Punjab had poured into the region, bringing with them harrowing tales of massacres and displacement. The political stakes in Jammu were high, and tensions, once whispered, had begun to harden. In Udhampur, Shaukat's caravan was attacked. There was screaming, shooting, people running in every direction. In a matter of minutes, his entire family was gone. His wife, his three children, his parents, his siblings—every one of them was killed. Shaukat was shot too and left for dead. When he woke up, everything was silent. Smoke hung in the air. The Chenab River flowed nearby, heavy and red. He dragged himself to the riverbank. His legs moved, but his heart had stopped. There was nothing left to live for. The air smelled of blood and smoke. Bodies were lying everywhere. He walked towards it, not knowing why, or maybe knowing too well. He was ready to jump. There was nothing left. But then he heard a cry. A baby's cry. He turned and saw an infant lying in the arms of a dead woman. Her husband's body lay close by. The baby was still alive. Shaukat picked him up. He didn't know what gave him the strength, but something told him to walk, so he did that with the baby in his arms. He crossed from Jammu into Sialkot and kept going until he reached Lahore. Started life all over again in Lahore. Years passed. He remarried. Set up a home again. But that child never left his arms. He raised him like his own. Gave him his name. His love. His world. That child was me. Bakhtawar Shaukat Dar. But most just call me…Daarji.'

Aariz sat in silence, his mind swirling with emotions. He never expected Daarji to reveal his own story, to open up and share his vulnerabilities. The image Aariz held of Daarji shattered before his eyes. Today, Daarji spoke from his heart, urging Aariz to do the same. But how could he? Aariz had always been a man of few words, bottling up his pain, unable to find the courage to speak his truth.

'Maybe I'm not the right person to discuss your ordeal,' Aariz murmured, his voice tinged with resignation and longing. 'Although I know what you feel, it's time the right person be introduced in your life.' Aariz's eyes shot up, his curiosity piqued by Daarji's unexpected proposition. 'Daarji?' he uttered, surprise and hope lacing his voice.

Daarji's response carried love and compassion. 'Let the legacy pass across. Shaukat Sahab adopted me and gave me his name. To me, you are no less than an obedient son. I've never force-fed you anything, but I want a favour, my dear.' Aariz listened intently, his heart pounding. 'A favour? I'm a poor man, Daarji. I have nothing to offer except my submission, which I've already given.'

Daarji's eyes gleamed with fatherly warmth as he unveiled his request. 'So let me return the favour. As your guardian, let me arrange your marriage. I want Kalsoom to be married to you. I believe both of you can have a great future together, the best match.' Aariz's mind reeled, struggling to comprehend Daarji's proposal. Yet, Aariz felt no elation. 'You need healing, my dear,' Daarji insisted, his voice filled with assurance. 'Let the girl do her work. I guarantee you a lifetime of peace.'

Daarji left, leaving Aariz in disarray. His life had been shaped by the control of others, and now Daarji sought to seize authority over a crucial decision. Aariz's weakness consumed him, unable to deny Daarji's request. It was yet another choice he couldn't make for himself, trapped in submission and uncertainty.

He had allowed others to dictate his life for too long, burying his own desires beneath guilt and self-doubt. He couldn't resist Daarji's request, feeling the weight of his own weakness and Daarji's subtle desire. Again, he faced a choice he couldn't make, trapped in indecision and surrender.

The grand wedding ceremony unfolded with pomp and splendour, capturing the city's attention. But their union stirred resentment among those who sought to claim Daarji's throne. Aariz was perceived as weak, unsuitable for the legacy. Shabbir observed closely, loyal to Daarji, supporting and guiding Aariz through his weaknesses. Shabbir became a pillar of strength, believing in their potential more than in his own associates.

Recognizing Shabbir's dedication, Daarji arranged his marriage to his sister's daughter. With Shabbir by his side, Daarji felt relief, knowing he had two dependable individuals supporting him in his advancing age. Some years later, Kalsoom gave birth to a baby boy. Daarji named him Armaan, which means desire, as he desired to play with his grandson. Armaan inherited his father's tranquil Kashmiri features, with deep-blue eyes. However, it was later discovered that Armaan suffered from night blindness, which gradually deteriorated into blurry vision. Despite undergoing surgery, his eyesight was further diminished. No treatment seemed to help little Armaan. Aariz couldn't help but feel that it was another punishment for his sins.

The fate of his blind grandson weighed heavily on Daarji's heart. On one of their weekly visits to the Data Ganj Baksh Shrine, Aariz sat alone in a corner, contemplating his son's future. Observing him from a distance, a Sufi named Malang Jan approached Aariz and called out to him. 'Your eyes are filled with despair,' the Sufi remarked, his gaze penetrating. Aariz looked at him, his expression reflecting his inner turmoil. 'How do you know?' Aariz asked, surprised by the Sufi's perceptiveness.

'I have witnessed many hearts burdened with such pain,' he replied. Aariz, unable to contain his emotions, came straight to the point. 'All treatments have failed for my son. We have tried everything.'

'You have put your trust in doctors instead of the Creator who created the doctors,' he said gently. 'Do you believe you can achieve His mercy this way?'

Aariz was taken aback by the Sufi's words. 'Then what am I supposed to do? Wait for an invention?' he asked with a mix of surprise and frustration.

'That's precisely the problem with most of us. We may see a lot, but our understanding is limited. Allah is more merciful to His servants than a mother is to her child. Do you think your prayers fall on deaf ears?'

Aariz was intrigued. 'Please, enlighten me, Peer Sahab,' he requested.

'When Allah created the earth, He divided mercy into one hundred parts, keeping only one part on earth and reserving the remaining ninety-nine with Himself. It is because of that one part that His creations show mercy and compassion to one another. And on the Day of Judgement, He will complete it with the remaining ninety-nine mercies,' the Sufi explained.

Aariz couldn't help but question, 'So, where is this mercy now? I haven't felt any mercy in my life, Peer Sahab.'

The Sufi replied calmly, 'Because of that one mercy, a mother has compassion for her child and animals and birds show compassion towards one another. On the Day of Judgement, He will manifest the complete mercy, filling the distance between heaven and earth.'

Aariz, growing impatient, urged the Sufi to get to the point.

'When Allah can bestow that one mercy upon a man whose foundation is built on error, sins and anguish, and yet they remain joyful on earth, don't you think you will be left to taste the same?' the Sufi responded. 'I am still waiting for His mercy, Peer Sahab. Since the day I killed my father, I have not found any peace of mind. Why isn't He being merciful to my soul? He can simply grant me peace if He wants,' Aariz lamented.

The Sufi looked at him intently and said, 'Well, this is called arrogance. You are being thankless for the bounties He has blessed you with. People live miserable lives, dying from hunger, diseases and poverty. Yet, you tend to ignore their suffering and complain about something for which you are responsible.'

A deep silence enveloped them as Aariz contemplated the Sufi's words. Finally, he mustered the courage to ask, 'How do I attain His mercy, Peer Sahab?'

The Sufi replied, 'What is the greatest blessing in your life?'

'My son,' Aariz replied without hesitation.

'Then treat that blessing as the most valuable gift from Allah by taking good care of him,' the Sufi advised.

Aariz felt a sense of accusation and protested, 'Do you mean to say I am ignorant? I am not taking care of my child?

Am I not seeking treatment for him, Peer Sahab?'

The Sufi responded calmly, 'Certainly, you haven't sought Allah's mercy yet and that is a sin you are committing.'

'I give up, Peer Sahab. I give up. Please guide me,' Aariz surrendered, feeling a mix of frustration and hopelessness.

The Sufi rose to his feet and looked at him fiercely. 'Go back to your watan, your homeland. Your son will regain his eyesight where he actually belongs.'

Aariz was puzzled by the Sufi's response. But as Aariz blinked and opened his eyes, he found himself back in the reality of the dargah. He realized that it was all just a vivid dream, a creation of his own imagination. The Sufi, however, was still there. Aariz's heart skipped a beat. The Sufi's penetrating gaze met his own, as if he could see deep into Aariz's thoughts and struggles.

Aariz shook his head, trying to make sense of the experience. Was it a message from a higher power? Or simply a figment of his own subconscious? The dream had felt so real, as if the Sufi's words held a profound truth within them.

The Sufi, observing Aariz's confusion, offered a knowing smile. While Aariz couldn't fully comprehend the significance of the dream, he knew deep down that his son's healing and his own peace of mind lay on a path he had yet to uncover.

Aariz carried with him the memory of the Sufi's presence and the unspoken guidance he felt.

Aariz's life, like a chinar leaf, falls upon the flowing Jhelum. He encountered unpredictable twists, facing trials that shaped his path. The leaf surrendered to fate, trusting unseen forces. Inspired, Aariz understood true surrender meant letting go of desires and trusting Allah's wisdom.

When he broke the news to Kalsoom, it sent a wave of fury through her. She vehemently disagreed. Her reasons for disagreement were more inclined towards Daarji's wrath at the thought of returning to Kashmir, rather than Armaan's treatment. She feared the day when Daarji would discover Aariz's treachery and the ensuing destruction it would bring. Above all, would it really be that easy to go back to Kashmir? But one fateful incident etched itself deeply into Kalsoom's memory: the day Armaan slipped down the staircase, from a severe headache, and getting a grave, life-threatening injury to his delicate skull. Witnessing her son's suffering firsthand, Kalsoom realized the true gravity of his need for sight. The doctors had exhausted their expertise, unable to restore his vision. In the depths of despair, Kalsoom found herself at a crossroads, with only one option remaining. Reluctantly, she surrendered to Aariz's proposal, recognizing it as the sole path available for her son's well-being.

Amidst her grief and worries, Kalsoom's love for Armaan shone bright. Her motherly love surpassed all obstacles, propelling her to make the difficult choice and embark on a journey into the unknown.

'Sahab ji, Peer Sahab di sifarish di peeche zaroor koi hikmat hogi, there must be some wisdom behind his recommendation,' Kalsoom said. Aariz's heart felt contentment at Kalsoom's agreement. However, travelling to Kashmir would not be a simple task. It needed to be done carefully, without anyone knowing their intentions.

During those days, the State Government of Kashmir announced a militant rehabilitation policy for those militants who had gone to Pakistan but wanted to return after having a change of heart and giving up arms and ammunition. 'This policy favours us, Kalsoom. It's as if Kashmir is calling me back. Panun Kashmir! Our Kashmir!' Aariz exclaimed.

Aariz had researched and planned extensively. He learned about ex-militants who had settled in different cities of Pakistan but were now returning to their homeland. Many of them quietly left Pakistan with their wives and children, avoiding designated legal routes that would bring them under scrutiny from Pakistani authorities at immigration.

One late night, Aariz, Kalsoom and Armaan discreetly left Lahore for Karachi. From there, they boarded a flight to Kathmandu, Nepal. Upon arrival, they met border-crossing agents who demanded hefty sums to assist them in entering India. The agent handling their case asked for their passports and, to their shock, promptly tore them up and discarded them.

'Why did you do this?' Aariz protested.

'Your passports would identify you as Pakistani nationals, which would cause serious trouble at the Indian border. You must quietly sneak in as Indians on a family trip to Nepal, as Indians do not require a visa or passport to travel there,' the agent explained, handing them fake identity cards. Aariz was anyway determined to go to Kashmir, he felt he was an Indian national and it was his homecoming, so he cared less about what happened to his passport.

With the agent's help, they crossed the border. After three days of arduous travel on many buses and trains, Aariz finally set foot in Kashmir, returning after twenty years. It had been one of the scariest journeys of their lives.

Coming back home was like a reminiscence for Aariz. Witnessing the same old pine and chinar trees with the green mountains and meadows—nothing had changed in the landscape of Kashmir.

Aariz wanted to follow the law, so the moment they arrived in Srinagar, he surrendered to the police, admitting that they had crossed the border and returned under the policy. However, everything didn't go as smoothly as expected; there was an issue. Aariz had not taken the legal routes of compliance as determined under the rehabilitation policy. He had entered India illegally with his wife and son, without a passport and visa, through Nepal, which was not a recognized entry point under the militant rehabilitation policy.

As a result, he was slapped with various charges for being part of an anti-Indian insurgent group and was jailed, along with Kalsoom and Armaan, for six months. Later, on the insistence of a rights group and following the judge's verdict, Kalsoom was released along with Armaan, but Aariz remained in jail. The Hafiz Foundation assisted in sheltering Armaan and Kalsoom, helping them rent a house in Awantipora, away from the city and under strict surveillance.

After some years, Aariz was granted furlough. However, Aariz didn't want to jeopardize Sarfaraz's safety due to his presence, as things didn't go as planned. Any link or communication with Sarfaraz and Tarannum would put them in trouble, which Aariz wanted to avoid. Thus, Sarfaraz and Tarannum remained clueless about his return.

Kalsoom started working as a caretaker in the village and managed to accumulate some money for their survival. People were scared to talk to them, considering they had come from Pakistan, and avoided them, fearing police interrogation.

Aariz found it difficult to find employment during his furlough, as potential employers were concerned that his history would get them into trouble. They faced isolation. Aariz and his family were stateless and helpless until Kabir's return to the valley.

Chapter 11

The courtroom fell into a hushed silence. Aariz's narrative unfolded. His words resonated with vulnerability, his weary frame bearing the weight of an arduous journey through the darkest corridors of time. Aariz, once perceived as a menace, now appeared before them as a wounded soul in need of understanding and redemption.

'My esteemed lawyer, Kanval Raina, daughter of Iravati Raina, the very woman whom I had once fired upon,' he began, his voice laden with irony. 'She sits here by my side today, a symbol of redemption and the unyielding power of forgiveness.' Aariz paused for a moment, gathering his thoughts as the eyes of the courtroom remained fixed upon him.

'It took me a decade, a long and arduous journey through the labyrinth of my own soul, to comprehend the wisdom behind the Sufi's persuasion and the Qari's second state of approach. I realized that seeking forgiveness from Ira Kaki was not just an act of moral obligation; it was a spiritual compulsion that had haunted me, tormenting my very existence.'

The courtroom seemed to hold its breath as Aariz painted a vivid picture of the burdens he had carried, the shackles of guilt, the stifling of his own progress and the walls that confined his potential. 'Ira Kaki's son, in a selfless act of compassion, bestowed sight upon my once-blind child. It was a gift, a tangible manifestation of the boundless mercy that flows from the Divine. And in that moment, as Armaan's eyes were opened to the world, I felt a profound sense of humility and gratitude. It was as if Allah

Himself had extended his guidance, whispering his forgiveness and mercy upon my wounded soul.'

The irony was palpable, the man who had once caused harm and pain now stood before them, transformed and humbled, a living testament to the intricate workings of fate and the power of repentance.

'My Lord,' Aariz's voice resonated with a deep sense of reverence and realization, 'as I stand before you today, I am reminded of one of the Divine names of Allah, Al Wahhab, the Giver of gifts. For thirty years, I sought repentance, yearning for the ultimate gift of forgiveness and mercy.

'It was a journey of transformation, a path filled with trials and tribulations, but one that led me to the greatest gift I could have ever received. That gift, bestowed upon me by the grace of Al Wahhab, manifested itself in the form of Armaan's restored eyesight. It was a miraculous sign of Allah's benevolence and compassion, a testament to the power of sincere repentance and the fulfilment of my obligations.'

Aariz's eyes glimmered with a mix of humility and gratitude. 'Now, as I stand here, ready to face any verdict this honourable court deems fit, I carry within me the true liberation. The shackles that bound my pained soul for thirty years have been released and there is no greater freedom than that.'

In that moment, the courtroom fell into a profound silence, as the weight of Aariz's words echoed through the chamber. But the judge's stern gaze soon turned to the pressing question at hand.

'Why did you choose to go underground, evading arrest despite being on furlough? What happened to you? You appear injured and where is the remaining money?'

Aariz drew a deep breath, his eyes reflecting the turmoil of his recent past. 'Daarji passed away just days ago, and Shabbir, along with his men, were relentlessly tracking me. His intention was to persuade me, Kalsoom and Armaan to come back under his control. When news of my predicament here reached Shabbir, his anger knew no bounds.'

Aariz voice was steady but filled with sincerity. 'On that fateful day, I was on my way to the bank to deposit the funds back into Kabir's account. Armaan's treatment was completed. It was my moral obligation to return the rest of the money. Even though I had received it for Armaan's treatment, I felt it was only right to give back what was no longer required. One fateful day as I prepared to leave for the bank, Kalsoom carefully tucked the money into a thick envelope that I kept in the pocket of my pathani and wore the pheran to keep myself warm as it was cold outside. On a deserted bylane, I was seized and transported to an undisclosed location.'

Aariz's voice quivered with a mix of defiance and resilience. 'Shabbir confronted me over the phone, insisting I return and promising a safe passage, showing their extensive planning. I had jeopardized Kalsoom and Armaan, the people very dear to Daarji, and he was adamant that I leave. But I refused. I refused to allow anyone to dictate the course of my life any longer. Armaan had left for Mumbai with Kaki and Kalsoom had moved to our house in Srinagar. It would be a hurdle for them to get the three of us altogether. I resolved not to yield. I quietly slipped away, determined to break free from the chains that bound me. However, fate had other plans. In my desperate escape, I lost my footing and tumbled down the treacherous mountainside, fracturing my arm and injuring my forehead. Through sheer will and determination, I managed to reach a local hospital, where I sought treatment and then made my way here. As a gesture of my sincerity, Your Honour, I would like to present this envelope containing the remaining funds in my possession to the court.'

The courtroom held its breath, caught between awe and

empathy, as Aariz's harrowing tale unravelled before their eyes. His resolute spirit, tempered by the pain etched on his face, left an indelible impression. The judge released a deep breath and swiftly penned the verdict. Aariz held his breath, his hopes and fears mingling in a delicate dance, awaiting the outcome that would shape his future.

Mumbai

'Get the fuck out of my house!!!! You son of a traitor, fuck off right now!' Kabir stormed into the house, his face contorted with anger and pain, his words piercing through the air like shards of broken glass. His voice carried a venomous rage that sent shivers down Armaan's spine, leaving him in a state of sudden dismay. The room seemed to tremble under the rage of Kabir's words. Iravati was caught off guard by her son's outburst. 'Kabir? I don't believe this,' she pleaded.

Armaan stood frozen, his heart breaking with each syllable that fell from Kabir's lips. The man he once knew, the one who had fought for him and their family, now stood before him, transformed into a vessel of hatred and resentment. 'Mummy, I am sorry,' Kabir said, his voice laden with regret and anguish. 'Sorry for not believing in you, for disregarding your warnings, your concerns and your unwavering love. This is a painful lesson, a lesson that will forever remind me of the consequences of disrespecting one's own mother.'

The room fell into a heavy silence, the weight of Kabir's changed psyche hanging in the air like a suffocating cloud. His journey through the dark corridors of guilt and remorse had left scars on his soul, transforming him into a man consumed by bitterness and resentment. Iravati, her heart aching, was pushed aside, her pleas for understanding falling on deaf ears. Inside the confines of his room, Kabir unleashed his pain, his cries echoing with a haunting melancholy.

Armaan stood outside, his own heart in pieces, unable to comprehend the depth of Kabir's transformation. The impact of Kabir's change was concrete, his words cutting through the air like a dagger to the heart. The once-cherished love and affection had been replaced by a darkness that seemed to devour everything in its path.

Kabir's footsteps thundered through the house as he stormed into his room, the door slamming shut behind him. Iravati, her eyes filled with tears, followed him. 'Kabir, please, let's talk. I know you're angry, but we can't let this rage consume us,' Iravati pleaded, her voice laced with desperation.

'Talk? What is there left to say, Mummy? That man, Aariz, he tried to shoot you! How could you expect me to forgive that? How could you ask me to forget the pain and fear he caused?'

'Kabir, his past was filled with mistakes and regrets, but he's paid for them. He's changed, he's remorseful. Can't you find it in your heart to understand?'

A bitter laugh escaped Kabir's lips, tinged with a mix of anger and pain. 'Understand? How can I understand, Mummy? That man tore our family apart, and you expect me to nurture his son?'

Iravati's voice trembled as tears streamed down her face. 'Kabir, I know your heart is wounded, but holding on to this anger won't heal it. And above all, what has Armaan got to do with all this?'

'Mummy, I am sorry for not having believed you and your warnings, your concern, your worries and everything else that both I and Kanval did not respect. But for now, I have learned my lesson. This is a lesson for life, a lesson for disrespecting one's own mother,' Kabir whispered with anger and regret.

Armaan felt as if the ground had been pulled out from beneath him. He trembled with fear as he looked at the changed version of Kabir. 'Relax, Kabir, let's just talk,' Iravati insisted.

His reputation had gone for a toss. His arrest was the talk of the town and had caused him severe mental trauma. His affection for Armaan had landed him in jail, despite his mother's severe warning. There was a history to her mother's repeated protests to children, but his emotional ignorance had put him behind bars. He cried as if something had died within him. His sobbing inside the room made Iravati tremble. Armaan was in a state of shock. The rage in Kabir's eyes and his hurtful words broke Armaan's heart into pieces. He quickly walked out of the house, unable to contain Kabir's wrath.

Iravati quickly ran behind him and brought him back to the house. 'Armaan Jani, would you please trust me and keep calm? I promise your Bhaiyya will become normal in some time,' she assured a visibly shaken Armaan. Her repeated requests to open the door failed.

Kabir spent an entire night weeping and regretting his actions. Armaan mustered every ounce of courage within him as he approached Kabir's door. With trembling hands, he knocked, his voice laced with desperation, 'Kabir Bhaiyya, please...please open the door.'

A long, agonizing silence hung in the air before Kabir's voice boomed from the other side, filled with a potent mix of anger and betrayal. 'You think a few pathetic apologies can erase everything? You and your fuckin' father have ruined our lives!'

Iravati's eyes widened in shock and anger as she rushed to the scene. 'Is this the language I have taught you? This child has done nothing to deserve this hatred!'

The door swung open violently, revealing Kabir's haggard face, his eyes bloodshot and brimming with a toxic combination of rage and pain. He towered over Armaan, his voice dripping with bitterness, 'You don't understand, do you? You have no idea what it feels like to be cheated, to have your father try to take my mother's life!'

Tears streamed down Armaan's face as he desperately tried to hide behind Iravati upon seeing a raging Kabir.

Kanval walked in with Aariz, Sarfaraz and Kalsoom from Kashmir, their arrival further fuelling Kabir's fury. 'Stop right there, I said,' Kabir warned the Zargars. Kanval was embarrassed by the magnitude of hate visible in Kabir's eyes. 'Bhaiyya, what's wrong with you?'

'Shut up, Kanval, just shut up!' Kabir lashed out at Kanval. Kanval couldn't fathom that such brutal words would be directed at her by her own brother.

Unable to bear the weight of the tension, Kanval stepped forward, her voice filled with both sadness and defiance, 'Bhaiyya, they've come here seeking forgiveness, seeking reconciliation. Perhaps we have all endured so much pain, and what we truly need now is collective healing, a chance to mend the broken pieces of our lives.'

Kabir's eyes burned with an intensity that seemed to pierce through their souls. 'Healing? You think a few words can mend what's been shattered? You have no idea, none of you do. Leave before I do something we'll all regret.'

Aariz, his voice trembling with regret and pain, spoke up, his words weighed down by the burden of his past actions, 'Kabir, I know my mistakes are unforgivable and for that, I will carry the guilt forever. But I came here seeking redemption, seeking to make amends. Please, Kabir, find it in your heart to forgive.'

'Hey, all of you! Take this as my final warning. Leave this house immediately, or I'll expose you in front of the entire world!' Kabir's voice thundered, his anger escalating to a dangerous level. The tense atmosphere hung heavy with the weight of their fractured relationships. Aariz, devastated by Kabir's rejection, collapsed to the floor. He had come with the expectation of reconciliation and understanding, but instead, he faced Kabir's wall of resentment.

Despite the relatively lenient verdict and Kabir's acquittal, their relationship remained strained. The court recognized the circumstances and factors that had led Aariz to Pakistan, resulting in a relatively shorter prison term with a two-year extension. On the other hand, Kabir was cleared of all charges, as the court found no evidence of his direct involvement in any criminal activities.

Kabir's heart turned cold towards Armaan and everyone associated with him. He spoke with venomous disdain, 'My mother never taught us Kashmiri and I'm grateful she didn't. Otherwise I would have asked you to get the hell out of this house in a language you understand.'

Iravati, a mix of anger and disbelief in her voice, stood her ground. 'Kabir, is this how you speak to your elders? Regardless of your feelings towards Aariz, you cannot disrespect them in this manner.'

'Whoever they may be, Mummy, ask them to leave immediately,' Kabir retorted with contempt. 'I want no connection with these people. And if they refuse to go, I'll call the police to remove them forcefully.'

Kabir's rage and words were beyond what anyone had anticipated. He slammed the door shut, retreating into his room, leaving behind a shattered family struggling to comprehend the depth of his anger. Iravati's heart trembled with sorrow and regret as she confronted the humiliation and helplessness of the moment. Kanval, holding Armaan tightly, sought solace in his presence, their shared pain expressed through silent tears. With trembling hands and tear-filled eyes, Iravati turned to Sarfaraz with hopelessness.

'Bhailal,' she whispered, her voice quivering, 'I am lost.

…ave exhausted all my efforts to reach Kabir's tormented soul. …His mind is clouded and my words are falling upon deaf ears.'

Sarfaraz, filled with empathy, embraced Iravati, understanding the weight of her words and the depth of her despair. 'My dear sister,' he gently spoke, 'sometimes, the battles we fight within ourselves are the most formidable. Kabir's journey is his own, and only he can navigate its treacherous path. We can only offer our apologies.'

Sarfaraz, Aariz, Kalsoom and Armaan made their way out, consumed by a profound sense of loss. Armaan glanced back one final time, his gaze filled with bittersweet longing. But behind that closed door, only silence prevailed, an absence of the cherished brother in his heart. Kanval and Iravati stood intertwined, souls bound in tragedy.

Kabir's restless soul, burdened by grief, anxiety, panic attacks and stress, manifested in his actions. In desperation, he clung to Iravati. 'Mummy, please get me married. You were right. I need someone to share my pain.' Iravàti, prepared for this confrontation, responded cautiously, 'Marriage isn't the solution now, Kabir.' Kabir's frustration surfaced, bitterness in his words. 'You insisted before, I defied. Now my life lies in ruins. Get me married, Mummy. Perhaps that will salvage what remains.' A moment of silence settled before Iravati spoke measuredly, 'I was wrong, Kabir. Kanval was right.' Kabir's curiosity was sparked. 'Kanval was right? Enlighten me, Mummy.' Iravati took a deep breath, her voice laden with the guilt of past mistakes. 'Marriage wasn't what I wanted. It was a diversion to shield you from choices I believed were wrong.' 'You were never wrong, Mummy,' Kabir lamented, regret heavy in his voice. 'If anyone erred, it was me, for not heeding your advice. I've been deceived, my reputation shattered.' Iravati's voice softened, attempting to assuage his pain, 'Your reputation remains intact, Kabir. In the eyes of the law, you've emerged unscathed, as has Aariz.' 'I've been deceived, Mummy,' Kabir protested, anger simmering.

'They concealed the truth about Aariz, using me in their hidden agendas with their child,' Kabir lamented.

'In the eyes of the law, Kabir, Aariz has paid his dues. He endured imprisonment of the mind, soul and heart since the day he journeyed out of Kashmir,' Iravati calmly responded.

'No matter what the law says, anyone who harms my mother is forever a criminal in my eyes. I won't put on a display of forgiveness just because I voiced affirmations to that child who had now perished within me.'

Iravati bridged the divide with compassion, 'I have forgiven him, Kabir, with all my heart. He deserves that forgiveness. Perhaps you were too young to witness the full extent of those times and the complexities surrounding them. But as a community, we have healed and progressed, fuelled by education, prosperity and resilience.'

Kabir's voice cracked with emotions. 'Umika's father, did he die from a snake bite? Did Dad drown by accident? No, it was Aariz and others like him who snuffed out their lives. The onus of their deaths lies with those who forced them out. They are nothing short of murderers.'

Iravati countered passionately, 'If there were people like him, there were also people like Bhailal! You and I wouldn't be here if it weren't for him.'

Kabir questioned his mother's change of heart, astonished by her shift in perspective. Iravati responded firmly, 'I have every right to evolve, Kabir. I have every right to question and change if what I believed was wrong.'

Iravati explained, 'I was frozen, locked in that cold January night. It prevented me from truly living my life for myself and my children. Until I opened my eyes to the walls I had built, preventing me from embracing the connections fate had bestowed upon me.'

Kabir's frustration grew, his words laced with bitterness. 'Connections? What connections, Mummy? All I see is pain and betrayal from those connections and you expect me to find solace in these so-called connections?'

'Kabir, I understand your pain, and I acknowledge the wounds that have yet to heal. But sometimes, it is through facing our deepest wounds that we find the strength to heal and grow. Our lives are intertwined not just by the past, but also by the choices we make in the present.'

'You speak of choices as if they are a remedy for the injustice I have endured. Do you forget the agony I felt when Aariz tried to take your life? The betrayal I experienced when I discovered the truth about his family? Forgiveness may come easily to you, but I cannot erase the scars of the past.'

Iravati reached out, gently placing her hand on Kabir's trembling shoulder. 'Kabir, forgiveness is not about erasing the scars or condoning the wrongs that were done. It is about finding inner peace and breaking free from the chains of anger and resentment. By holding on to your anger, you are allowing those who hurt you to have power over your life.'

Iravati embraced her son, her voice filled with love and understanding. 'Letting go does not mean denying your pain, Kabir. It means reclaiming your power and choosing to live a life free from the burden of anger. It means acknowledging the past but not allowing it to define your present or future.'

'Which is exactly what needs to be corrected, and I will never make such a mistake. The agony I carry within me far surpasses anything anybody has experienced,' Kabir declared, his voice filled with a mixture of determination and pain.

Iravati's response cut through the air, leaving Kabir stunned.

'Ok then, be prepared, Kabir. Be prepared for the day when Armaan may come here, armed, aiming with a Kalashnikov, not just at you but at all of us, me, Kanval and you.'

The gravity of her words struck Kabir like a thunderbolt. 'What are you saying, Mummy?'

Iravati's eyes held a deep sadness as she looked into her son's eyes. 'Kabir, we must be his guiding light in this newfound world of sight. Just as a blind man regains his vision and must learn to navigate the dazzling array of colours, shapes and shadows, Armaan too needs our guidance. We cannot let him be consumed by his father's past. Instead, we must offer him a different perspective, showing him beauty and compassion, giving him better education and showing him the hope that exists beyond the darkness. Otherwise the regret will haunt him, echoing the pain of his father's tumultuous journey, circling his entire upbringing. By pushing Armaan away, by casting his family out of our home, you have inadvertently confined him to a narrow space of regret.'

'Let them go to hell,' Kabir retorted, his voice filled with defiance. 'If Armaan chooses that path, let him suffer the consequences. The law will teach him a lesson, just like it did his father. I don't give a damn and it's not my headache or yours.'

Her voice carried a mix of sorrow and urgency as she continued, 'Kabir, if Armaan continues to live in the shadow of Aariz's past, it will be an environment of constant pain, shame and regret for him. It might even influence his future in ways we can't predict. But if you open the door for him, it will provide opportunities for him to see the world, receive a good education and have the guidance and support he needs to thrive.'

Consumed by anger and pain, Kabir refused to listen. He abruptly rose from his seat, unable to bear the weight of the conversation any longer. 'I can't do this, Mummy. I won't be a part of their lives. Let them face the consequences of their actions.'

In the dimly lit room, Kanval sat beside Iravati, their faces reflecting their shared burdens. A sombre atmosphere enveloped them as they contemplated their roles, their struggles with Kabir and the desperate need to reach him.

'Mummy, we must persuade Bhaiyya to make the right decision for Armaan. You can motivate him, just as I pushed you.' Iravati gently shook her head. 'Kanval, it's not about motivation for Kabir. What he needs is an awakening.' Kanval looked puzzled. 'An awakening? What do you mean, Mummy?'

Iravati smiled and said, 'Before I got married to Purushottam, I lived in Handwara. Tarannum was my next-door neighbour. When we went to school, we often saw a very charismatic fakeer roaming in the village with his daffli, singing religious songs.

'Children used to line up, looking at the fakeer with fascination. During Ramazans, he would wander around, calling out to households to wake up for Sehri, the pre-dawn meal. He was treated respectfully by everyone in town. One day, as the fakeer slept under a tree, a mad dog bit him. In those days, dog bites, especially from mad dogs, were untreatable. The fakeer's health deteriorated, and he began behaving erratically. He would laugh out loud, make strange faces and walk in a peculiar manner. Children started making fun of him and tied a rope of tin cans around him, further irritating and infuriating him. He would crawl on the streets and maintain little hygiene.

'The villagers became worried and searched for the dog that had bit him. They found the dog dead and they assumed that the fakeer would die a miserable death. To make it easier for him, they tied him with a rope. No children were allowed to witness what was about to happen, but Tarannum and I quietly sneaked out to the nearby woods to witness the scene in secret. A white long dupatta was dipped in the ice-cold water of the nearby stream and spread over his body, covering him from head to toe.

Within minutes, Fakeer Gul's troubled soul found tranquillity.'

A tear slipped down Iravati's cheek as she recounted the story. Kanval's breath caught, her mind grasping the significance of the villagers' act. 'But what they didn't know was that the dog that bit him carried a dreadful disease.' 'Rabies,' Kanval interjected, her voice filled with sombre realization. 'People with rabies develop a fear of water due to the painful condition known as hydrophobia. Water, which is supposed to bring comfort and relief, becomes their source of torment.'

'Kanval, that story mirrors my own journey,' Iravati revealed, her voice filled with vulnerability. 'For so long, I was trapped in an escapist mentality, avoiding my fears and denying myself true liberation. It took time for that awakening, to confront my past and embrace my fears.'

Kanval's eyes widened, her heart stirred by her mother's confession. 'We have the power to break the chains that bind us, to find liberation by embracing our fears,' Iravati concluded, her voice infused with determination. 'Just as the fakeer found solace in the water that defied his disease, we too can find our own salvation by facing our demons and allowing ourselves to be free.'

Kanval's eyes sparkled with excitement as she grasped the wisdom behind her mother's words. 'If at all you are thinking that I can motivate Kabir for his awakening, Kanval, I must tell you that it won't happen that way,' Iravati gently expressed. 'Awakening is something that comes from within, a profound realization that takes time and introspection.'

Kanval's enthusiasm slightly waned as she absorbed her mother's words. 'So, it's not about external motivation, but a personal journey of self-discovery?'

Iravati nodded with a tender smile. 'Exactly, my dear. Each person's awakening is unique and deeply personal. We can provide guidance and support, but ultimately, Kabir must embark on his own path and find his inner awakening.'

ꟷ

As the days unfolded, Kabir found solace in his music, pouring his emotions into each melody. Yet, a deep inner conflict brewed within him, casting a shadow over his passion. The excitement that fuelled his connection to Kashmir, its people and Armaan slowly faded, suffocated by the weight of his past.

One day, an urge to redefine his musical journey gripped Kabir's heart. 'Mummy, I need to let go of this name,' Kabir declared. 'It no longer resonates with who I am and what I want to create.'

Confusion etched across Iravati's face. 'But how does changing the name help, Kabir?'

'It may or may not help,' Kabir replied earnestly. 'But I need this change'

Before Kabir could discuss further, Iravati redirected the conversation, focusing on Armaan's upcoming birthday.

'So?' Kabir responded coldly when his mother requested him to reach out to Armaan. 'I've already told you, Mummy, it's not happening. I won't subject myself to this drama anymore and that chapter is over for me.'

Leaving both Kanval and Iravati disheartened, Kabir walked away. His focus waned, and he struggled to find his creative flow. Each passing day reminded him of the turbulence that had shattered his world when Umika departed. Kabir sought solace in her presence, gazing at her portrait for guidance.

'Umika,' he whispered, 'if only you were here to guide me. Any signs? Indications of what I should do?'

Amidst solitude, Kabir grappled with his inner turmoil, questioning his choices and the chosen path. *I'd be the most shameless son if I sympathized with him and his damn family.* Kabir's inner conflict tormented him, his emotions simmering, ready to explode. Another opportunity from the tourism department of Jammu and Kashmir added complexity to his already troubled state.

'They want me to work on a documentary drama about the music of Kashmir, but I...' Kabir's voice trailed off, unable to articulate his turmoil. Iravati, perceptive as ever, suggested, 'Start with the poetry of Habba Khatoon.' Kanval, curious, asked, 'Who's she, Mummy?' 'She was a remarkable 16th-century poet, the Nightingale of Kashmir,' Iravati explained. 'She penned mystic poems, and the bridge in Srinagar was named after her.'

Kabir hesitated, his emotions running deep. 'This project is not happening, Mummy. Never, ever.'

Iravati's concern-filled voice chimed in, 'Kabir, this emotional hardening is the worst kind of trauma you can inflict upon yourself.'

Struggling to find words, Kabir expressed, 'This hardening has come as a result of being jailed, which was one of the worst things to happen to me. People look at me differently now, with suspicion and curiosity in their eyes.'

Iravati reassured him, 'You are not guilty, my dear. It's just the chaos in your mind playing tricks. Everyone knows you haven't done anything wrong. If that had been the case, the Tourism Department wouldn't have connected to you.'

Kabir's voice trembled as he shared his deepest scars. 'The most scarring thing about jail is not the loss of privacy or possessions, it's the way people look at you afterwards, as if you're diseased. It chips away at your self-esteem, no matter your position.'

Overwhelmed, Kabir blamed himself. 'All because of that foolish family I once craved for. I played with fire, thinking it wouldn't burn me.'

Iravati comforted him, urging him to relax and not dwell on the past. 'Ok, Kabir, let's set aside the legal matters for a moment. Aariz may have been involved in troubling incidents, but he wasn't a deliberate criminal. Now, think about that young boy whose future hangs in the balance.'

'Why should I even care about him, Mummy? He is not my responsibility. He is his parents' responsibility, particularly his father's, who put everyone's safety at risk, even that of his own wife and blind son.'

'You are right, Kabir. Aariz's return has caused turmoil, but as a father, he did what any responsible parent would do. Sacrificed his own comfort, security and peace for the sake of his child. And it yielded a positive outcome, something that can't be disregarded.'

'No matter how much you try to reason, Mummy, he will always be in the wrong in my eyes.'

'Since you long for fatherhood, let me present you with a question. If you were in his position, what would you have done? Take a moment to reflect on it.' Iravati's words sparked a deep stare from Kabir. He was taken aback by the question, feeling a mixture of confusion and introspection. He turned away, silently contemplating the role he would have played had he been in Aariz's shoes.

Iravati spoke, standing up and motioning for Kanval to leave the room. 'All those claims you made about yearning for love and experiencing parenthood emotions for Armaan were not genuine, Kabir. Love, if it truly exists, is unconditional. Just like every parent who loves their child unconditionally, you have overlooked the fundamental essence of parenting.'

'What? What are you saying?' Kabir rose from his seat, his confusion growing deeper.

'It wasn't love, Kabir. Love wouldn't lead you to despise him in spite of his lack of culpability in the crime. True parents never despise their children, even in the face of grave faults. That's the choice you made.'

'That can't be true, Mummy. I longed to see him with his eyesight restored. I genuinely wanted to help him,' Kabir insisted, his voice filled with confusion and desperation.

'Kabir, any charitable organization could have extended help to them if it weren't for you. It's not a remarkable deed and it doesn't necessarily signify love.'

'If it wasn't love, then what was it, Mummy?' Kabir asked, his voice tinged with a mix of frustration and a search for truth.

'I hate to break it to you, Kabir, but it was an attachment born out of sympathy, that's it. Love transcends all boundaries and conditions. It doesn't judge or abandon. It embraces unconditionally, even in the face of imperfections. True love, especially from a parent, is unwavering. I'm sorry to say this, but what you felt for Armaan was more like empathy for him for being handicapped. You chose to abandon him even though he had no connection to the crimes committed,' Iravati explained, her words resonating with firmness.

'I have something to confess, Kabir,' Iravati's voice carried a mix of vulnerability and awe. 'When you brought Armaan home, I couldn't bring myself to look at him.'

She paused, her eyes reflecting a mixture of pain and regret. 'But one day, as Armaan slipped and cried out in pain, I couldn't ignore him any longer. It was as if time stood still, and I found myself captivated by his features resembling a younger Aariz, his vulnerability and the depth of his sorrow.'

Iravati's voice grew softer. 'In that moment, as I gazed at him with attention, a wave of recognition washed over me. His eyes, his innocent face, they held a striking resemblance to someone I once knew. It was as if I was seeing another young Aariz. It took me back to that fateful night on the boat when Aariz, in a moment of desperation, accidentally shot Noman. As I watched in horror, I focused on his eyes, and what I saw etched into my memory forever; it was a glimpse of rage, anguish and a profound sense of loss.'

Iravati's gaze turned inward, lost in the memory. 'But Armaan's eyes tell a different tale. They carry a glimmer of something else, yearning, innocence and the desire for love and compassion. It is as if he has inherited the essence of Aariz's existence, yet rewritten his destiny.'

A contemplative silence hung in the air before Iravati continued. 'He carries within him the potential to break free from the chains of our past and forge a new path, one rooted in love, understanding, and resilience.'

Iravati looked at Kabir with a sense of truth and conviction. 'Kabir, let me ask you something. Did my father-in-law despise Aariz when he learned about his involvement in illicit activities? Did he create distance or abandon him?'

Kabir shook his head, unable to deny the truth in her words. 'No, he didn't. In fact, he guided his family on how to best support Aariz, even in the face of adversity.'

Iravati's voice grew stronger, her words carrying a weight of wisdom. 'You see, Kabir that is what true responsibility is all about. It's about standing by your loved ones when they stumble, even if their path is riddled with mistakes. It's about being there, offering guidance and helping them find their way back to the right path.'

She paused for a moment, allowing her words to sink in. 'Responsibility isn't just about providing for the physical needs of someone; it's about nurturing their emotional and moral well-being. It's about showing unwavering support, even when they make choices that disappoint us. Your grandfather understood this. He stood beside his family, guiding them towards a better future, even when it seemed challenging.'

'Well, isn't it fascinating how Grandpa's responsibility has brought us so much joy and prosperity? However I won't repeat the same mistake,' Kabir declared, determination shining in his eyes.

~

Days later, Kabir tried to focus on making music, but thoughts haunted him. Memories and questions swirled in his mind. He found himself staring at Umika's picture, searching for guidance. Suddenly, he received a message on his phone. Intrigued, he opened the message—a video featuring Armaan sitting across Jhelum with a guitar just above Chinar Kuth, bearing a message for Kabir.

Curious, Kabir played the video, his eyes fixed on the screen, waiting to discover what Armaan had to say.

'Although you forgot my birthday, I couldn't resist paying tribute to Umika Didi today. Hopefully, I'll do justice to the woman who brought me into your life. Let me present something I've learned from you,'

hukus bukus telli wann che kus
onum batta lodum deag
shaal kich kich waangano
Brahmi charas puane chhokum
Brahmish batanye tekhis tyakha.
Itkayne ne Itkayne
Tse Kus Be Kus Teli Wan su Kus
Moh Batuk Logum Deg
Shwas Khich Khich Wang-mayam
Bhruman daras Poyun chokum
Tekis Takya bane Tyuk
Tekis Takya bane Tyuk

'I couldn't resist giving a tribute to Umika Didi today. She means a lot to both of us, doesn't she? So, I thought I'd do something special for her and for you.

'Before I start, let me tell you about a new Urdu teacher we have at school. She loves Faiz Ahmed Faiz, just like Kanval Didi. She often shares his beautiful couplets that capture the essence of different situations. One day, she recited a couplet that spoke to me in a way nothing else ever has. It goes like this:

Aaye to yun ki jaise hamesha thhe meherbaan,
bhule to yun ki goya kabhi aashna na thhe.

When you came in my life, it was as if I had been the special one,
But when you left, it was as if we had never been acquainted.

'Those words hit me deep in my heart. They made me realize how much you meant to me, how you've always been there for me, even when things got tough. I may be young, but I can feel the weight of our connection, the affection that binds us together.

'I wish I were blind again, blind to the reality that surrounds me now. Because now, with my sight restored, I see everything, but I can't find the connection that once bound us. So, I yearn to be blind once more, just to feel the warmth of our bond again. When I couldn't see, every touch, every word, every moment with you was like a symphony playing in my heart. But now that I can see, it's as if the colours have faded and the music has gone silent. I long to go back to that time when your love enveloped me, even if it meant forever living in darkness, in that dark tunnel, amidst the shadows, I always found courage. But emerging into the blinding brightness of reality, I realized that it held nothing for me. Being blind was better for me, I hope to be blind again, hopefully it would fetch me your affection again or if not, the least I'll earn is your sympathy.'

The video ended. Kabir held his breath and then loosened it. He lacked the audacity to play the video again. Armaan's last words were too heavy to be heard again.

The torrential rains of July engulfed Mumbai, creating a watery labyrinth that kept people confined to their homes. Within the walls of his home studio, Kabir struggled to make progress, his mind weighed down by a whirlwind of thoughts. Armaan's words, the elusive tunnel in his dreams, his latest desire to be blind again, and Umika's profound words about roots and wings all came to a head within him.

Feeling overwhelmed, Kabir abandoned his attempts at music and left the studio, clutching a cup of coffee. It was noon and the sky had transformed into a canvas of relentless grey, unleashing a downpour. Kabir ventured into the rain-soaked garden, embracing the rain.

As the rain drenched him, Iravati and Kanval watched him from a distance. Amidst lush greenery, the Himalayan indigo, the hyacinth and the narcissus bloomed in vibrant hues, evoking a sense of miniaturized Kashmir. The sight puzzled Kanval. 'How is this possible?' She mused, captivated by the unexpected beauty that graced her garden. The flowers were believed to struggle in a different soil, but they flourished against all odds. They had been a parting gift from Tarannum.

'I was doubtful too, but with love, support and understanding, anything is possible,' Iravati said, hopeful as she watched Kabir soaking in the water. The rain intensified, reflected the storm within him. Concerned, Kanval voiced her worry about Kabir falling sick. But Iravati understood the significance of his immersion in the rain. 'Let him be there, Kanval,' she gently insisted. 'Sometimes, storms are necessary for growth and healing.'

As Iravati stepped into Kabir's room, her gaze fell upon him engrossed in a conversation with Rishab. 'So, it's going to be... Chinar Productions?' Iravati's eyebrows furrowed slightly, curiosity sparked within her. 'Let's keep it if Mummy agrees.' There was something about Kabir's tone that made her wonder if he had come to a realization, if he had embraced the legacy of Chinar Productions beyond mere acceptance.

~

At the footsteps of Chinar Kuth, Armaan sat numb, strumming the guitar, trying to compose a tune around one of Kabir's verses that he had read and learnt in the Mumbai studio while deeply looking at the running Jhelum. 'Ab us phool me mahak nahi, mahak nahi...,' he softly sang, 'the flower has lost its fragrance,' searching for the right tune to match his vocals. As he played, a shadow crept closer, casting a sense of anticipation over the ghat. Armaan felt a flicker of curiosity but ignored it, thinking that it was a passerby. 'Ab us phool me mahak nahi, rangat hai par chahak nahi, the flower has now lost its fragrance, its hues remain but not its joy,' sounds correct. He continued developing the opening verse.

Just as Armaan struggled with the pronunciation, a gentle voice broke the silence, correcting him, 'It's not "FOOL", Armaan. It's "PHOOL".' Armaan turned around, his eyes widening in surprise, trying to locate the source of the voice. He scanned the surroundings, unable to see anyone at first.

And then, gradually emerging from the shadows, Iravati stepped forward, a proud smile on her face. 'Armaan, this song will be recorded at Chinar Productions,' she said, her voice carrying a sense of pride and anticipation. Her words resonated in the air, adding an air of excitement to the moment.

Armaan's gaze shifted from Iravati to another figure stepping forward. Her eyes sparkled with warmth and encouragement. 'But remember, Armaan, only if you get the pronunciation correct. The details matter, let the words flow like the petals of a flower in your voice,' Kanval said

Armaan's heart filled with gratitude as he absorbed the support and guidance from Iravati and Kanval. The ghat of Jhelum seemed to hold its breath, a tangible energy building in the air.

And then, as the anticipation reached its peak, Kabir emerged into the scene, his presence commanding and magnetic. Armaan's eyes widened, a mixture of surprise and awe filling his gaze. The ghat of Jhelum transformed into a stage and the moment became an interplay of emotions and destiny.

'Only if you come to Mumbai,' Kabir's voice resounded, carrying with it a sense of acceptance and hope. His words hung in the air, leaving a lingering promise of a new beginning, an invitation to step into a world of dreams. Armaan's heart swelled with gratitude and determination. The ghat of Jhelum became a witness to their connection, a testament to the power of support and belief, while Sarfaraz and Kalsoom watched them from the Zoon Dub balcony.

In the timeless land of Kashmir, a new chapter began; the ghat of Jhelum stood witness, as if nature itself was celebrating the harmony that was once lost but was now found.

Zindagi
Chinar si,
Khizah bhi
Bahaar bhi

Life
is like the chinar,
it endures the fall,
and blooms again in spring.

—Umair Ahmed Khan

Verses from the Valley

(in translation)

I have included this well-known Kashmiri lullaby to enrich and reinforce the thematic essence of the manuscript. The translation and interpretation have been prepared by me, in consultation with several experts in the Kashmiri language.

Literal Translation (Line by Line)	**Symbolic Meaning**
Hokus bokus teli wan che kus Who is he? Who am I? *Teli wan che kus* Then tell me, who are you? *Onum Batukh Ladum Deigi* I caught a duck and placed it in the vessel. *Shwaas Kich Kich wamano* When my breath becomes pure, *Brahman zaran poieenn chokum* My mind bathes in the waters of divine love. *Teykis Teyka* I am like the sacred sandalwood. *Bani kyohoo* What more is there to do?	Who are you, who am I? Beyond appearances, who are we truly? We must look within ourselves. Who is the creator? We have been so deeply immersed in worldly pleasures and attachments that we have forgotten He resides within us. The Truth, the Divine, is found within, not in the external world. When the soul becomes pure and burns like fire, when ego and desire are consumed, you realize that God is both within and beyond.

I wrote this poem around the symbols of Kashmir. We all absorb the environment we grow up in, and these symbols reflect how the Valley has shaped its people—with beauty, harmony and resilience.

Ye fiza ye gulshan ye bahaar	This breeze, these gardens, this spring,
Ye Jhelum ye Nishaat ye Chinaar	The Jhelum, Nishat, and Chinar,
Ye darakht ye darya ye aabshaar	These trees, these rivers, these waterfalls,
Ye Jannat ye Firdaus ye Shehjaar	This paradise, this heaven, this shade,
Ye adab ye Nagar ye bazaar	This culture, this city, this marketplace,
Ye Kehwa ye Kesar ye miqdaar	This kehwa, this saffron, this abundance,
Ye Rubab ye Chenab ye ashaar	This rubab, this Chenab, these verses,
Ye Zoon ye Dub ye diyaar	This moon, this balcony, this homeland,
Ye tera hai ye mera hai	It is yours, it is mine,
Ye hamara hai	It is ours.
Aao milkar—	Come, let us—

Acknowledgements

This book came to me like a slow exhale, after a long pause in life that needed release. Writing it gave me strength, purpose and the quiet joy of finding myself again.

There are people without whom this book would never have found its voice. My colleague and senior RJ friend, Kanchan Chaudhary, stood by me through the most uncertain phases, with warmth and belief that steadied me.

I carry deep gratitude for my late grandfathers, one full of knowledge, the other full of wisdom, whose blessings still feel like an umbrella of maturity and protection over me.

The seed of this story lies in Kashmir, in a small ritual I never missed, visiting Raju Bhai's century-old dry fruit shop in downtown Habba Kadal. He resembled the late actor Rishi Kapoor, always greeting me with a wide smile, calling out 'RJ aa gaya!' and offering me a handful of berries and nuts to eat while my order was being packed. It became a tradition every time I visited Srinagar before returning to Mumbai.

After leaving the shop, I would take a left toward the bridge that connected the two ends of the old city. Beneath it flowed the Jhelum, carrying the reflections of time. On either side stood rows of old wooden houses, many still proud, others weary, broken and silent. One house in particular always caught my attention, what used to be a home once for someone, now standing in ruins yet breathing with its lost glory. Every time I passed by, it felt as if the house was calling me, wanting its story to be told.

My grandmother often watched me typing for hours, amused

and a little anxious, wondering what new project had taken over my life this time. I had recently left my corporate job, certain that staying there any longer would cost me my peace, perhaps even my health. I left for Kashmir without a plan, only a feeling that life would show me what to do next.

At a small resort, I came across a group of orphans on a picnic. They sang, laughed and played with a freedom that city children often lose. Watching them, listening to their stories, I felt something shift inside me. Each story deserved to be told. Together, these stories became the foundation, and that home in Habba Kadal, the trigger.

When I returned to Mumbai, my heart was full of gratitude. Radio became my space of expression. Every sound, every silence from Kashmir began to turn into words.

My heartfelt thanks to Mita Kapur, who is much more than a literary agent to me. She has been my first anchor, my sounding board, and my Siyahi family. To Rupa Publications, for believing in this story and giving it a home. To my editor, Dibakar Ghosh, for his insight and understanding, and Shatarupa Dhar, for her warmth and steady guidance during every stage of this book's making.

To my father, Akhlaque Ahmed, and my sister, Humera, for their enthusiasm and faith. To my aunt, Aasiyah, to whom I wrote letters as a child, unknowingly laying the foundation of my love for writing.

To my friends Asrar, Younis, Gulshan, Saqib, Basit and Anas in Kashmir, for their friendship and warmth. To Nysha, for being the foundation of calm in chaos. To Jahangir and Prof. Rubina, for cheering from afar.

I extend my gratitude to Dr Niha Qureshi for her invaluable assistance with both the linguistic and aesthetic aspect of this work.

To Nadia Jamil, for her courage, grace and wisdom that inspire me every day.

I also thank my radio listeners and my students, who have unknowingly kept my voice alive.

And lastly, to Kashmir itself, its air, its rivers, its trees, its people, for teaching me that wisdom often comes quietly, through observation and love.

To myself, for holding on when it was easier to let go and for the faith that never left, I thank the Almighty.